CASSIOPEIA

FLIGHT FROM SAVANNAH

Don Bozeman

iUniverse, Inc.
New York   Bloomington

Cassiopeia
Flight from Savannah

iUniverse books may be ordered through booksellers or by contacting:

iUniverse
1663 Liberty Drive
Bloomington, IN 47403
www.iuniverse.com
1-800-Authors (1-800-288-4677)

ISBN: 978-1-4401-6399-9 (pbk)
ISBN: 978-1-4401-6401-9 (cloth)
ISBN: 978-1-4401-6400-2 (ebook)

Printed in the United States of America

iUniverse rev. date: 08/07/2009

To my wife, Sydney, for her unfailing support and encouragement, and to all my friends in Savannah who were there for the conception, gestation and birth of Cassiopeia.

CHAPTER ONE

ENOCH STARED AT THE young slave girl from the smokehouse shadows, through a small gap between the logs where the chinking had fallen away. He stood motionless, vapor rising from his breath. It was early January at Roselawn Plantation and the temperature was near freezing. Hog killing always took place when January temperatures fell.

Despite the cold, Enoch's face glistened with sweat. He was filled with self-loathing. His sickness had returned. The sickness he thought John Penrose had beaten out of him fifteen years earlier. He could still feel the welts from the razor strop, pus filled and seeping for days. Enoch thought his demons had been banished. Now he knew better. He struggled to pull his eyes away, but they were drawn back to that slit between the logs.

"The fieldhands are gonna eat good tonight," Cassie thought as she pulled the colorless, homespun coat tighter against the cold. "Fresh cracklin' bread and chitlins."

She scooped the last scraps of rendered fat into a large tub then pulled the fire back from the blackened pot. She poured in a bucket of water and a measure of potash, stirring the mixture with a wooden paddle. She ladled the viscous, gray liquid into soap molds. Later, when it hardened, she would cut it into squares and store it in the wash shed, a process she would repeat many times over the next several days, until all the hogs had been slaughtered and she had made enough soap to wash Roselawn's clothes for a year.

She moved with the grace of a jungle cat, her supple fourteen-year old body mature beyond its years. Her angular features set her apart from the other house slaves. They were a legacy from her Bedouin forebears who came down from the north to rule over Dahomey and Sierra Leone. The aquiline nose and green-brown eyes were in sharp contrast to the broad noses, dark eyes, and ebony skin common to the tribes from Congo and Gambia. Her olive complexion was a shade lighter than that of her mother, Queen Omoru. Visible on the nape of her neck, just above the rough edging of her faded blue dress, were five tiny marks in the shape of an elongated 'w'. They were the color of the wild blackberries that sprang up along the edge of the marsh in springtime.

****

That night, fourteen years ago, when she was born, John Penrose took the bawling baby in his arms. When he turned her small form in the dim light of the oil lamp for a better look, he saw the small birthmark, low on her neck.

"We must name her Cassiopeia," he declared to the exhausted mother.

Queen Omoru stared back in blank incomprehension. Penrose attempted to explain the meaning of the name. Still she did not understand.

"Wait, I'll show you."

He scurried from the room, crossed the breezeway to the main house and entered his library. He positioned the rolling ladder so that he could reach the large, red-leather bound volume on the top shelf. He thumbed through the heavy book as he made his way back to the kitchen

It was unusual for him to take such a personal interest in the birth of a slave child, but this one was different. He leaned down near the bed and had the old midwife hold the lamp close.

"Look," he said to Queen, pointing to an illustration of the northern sky in the celestial atlas. "That mark on your baby is almost identical to the chair in the constellation of Cassiopeia. She was the Queen of

Ethiopia and legend has it that she boasted so of her beauty that it angered the Gods. Their punishment for such vanity was to make her sit in this chair, revolving for eternity in the night sky.

"Your Ma, Aba, claims you are descended from Arab royalty so I think naming her Cassiopeia is very fitting, don't you, Queen?" he said with a hint of irony.

Queen lay on her bed, covered in sweat, the tattered sheets under her sodden and bloody with afterbirth. The room, redolent of odors from years of cooking, was now wreathed in the smells of a new life. Janey, the toothless midwife from Wormslow busied herself cleaning up. She came over to wipe Queen's face.

"You gone be all right, chile. Da fust one's always da hardest. I done give you some laudanum fo da pain. I'll be goin' on home atter ya goes tuh sleep. Yo mama, Aba, she be able tuh tend tuh ya now."

They were in the small room off the kitchen that Queen shared with her Mother, Aba. The kitchen was set far back, a common practice to prevent kitchen fires from spreading to the main house. She looked up at the tall, gray-haired man holding her baby.

"Awright, Massa. If you think dat's a good name fo her, I reckon it's all right wit me. But if you don' mind I's gone call her Cassie. Dat udda name, it too long."

Even if she had wanted to protest she was too weak. And in the end it would have proved futile. John Penrose owned her, and she would do what he said.

****

"Cassie, if ya done wit da soap come on ovah heah an' hep us clean dese chitlins," her mother called. "We gots a whole big tub full an' it gone git dark soon."

Queen Omoru spoke in the Geechee dialect, a blend of Krio from Sierra Leone, Pidgin English from the slave traders and fragments of other East African tribal languages. The dialect she spoke had developed and flourished among the black slaves in the isolation of the barrier islands of coastal Georgia.

She threaded a long section of pig intestine onto a marsh reed, turning it inside out then dipping it into the water several times to wash the lining clean before stripping the muscle from the outer membrane. She put the membranes aside to be used later as sausage casings.

Enoch leaned against the logs with both hands, watching as Cassie moved toward the other women. He shook, visibly. He could feel the hot blood coursing through his veins. He had suppressed it for fourteen long years. Now it raged within him. His ears rang from the pounding of his heart. He reached down and passed his hand over the swelling in his breeches. He shuddered as he felt the spasm of nervefire explode in his loins and felt the gush of warmth spill down his leg. He cursed himself and stumbled out the back of the smokehouse, circling past the root cellar, salty sweat stinging his eyes. He clung to the shadows as he skirted the cane mill. He moved under the scuppernong arbor, its tangled cover of gnarled vines shielding him from the women's view. He emerged from the shadows at the far end, blinded by sweat and the brilliant sunlight. Reflexively, he raised his hand to shield his eyes. The blinding light accentuated a massive birthmark covering the entire right side of his face. The disfiguring crimson half-mask cascaded from above his right eye and flowed along his nose, down to the jaw, then swept back into the hairline behind his right ear.

****

Enoch Penrose was born at his father's home in Savannah, on the trustee lot assigned to John Penrose by General James Oglethorpe, founder of the trust colony of Georgia. Oglethorpe chose Penrose to come with him to Georgia for his carpentry and blacksmithing skills. They arrived in Savannah in February 1733 aboard the *Ann* along with one hundred and twenty wretched, seasick souls who had survived the voyage from Gravesend on the Thames.

Enoch's disfigurement made his life in the village of Savannah a living hell. Constant taunting drove him away from contact with the other children. He withdrew into the sanctuary of his home and into his mother's arms. Slowly, the taunts and jeers seeped into his very soul, turning his heart to stone. When forced to attend church by his father he would flee and hide among the gravestones, happier with the silence of the dead than the mocking of the living. On the rare occasions when the young boy spoke, it was with a pronounced stammer. The combination of afflictions made life so intolerable for Enoch that for days on end he would not leave the house, his only solace coming from his mother, Elizabeth Penrose. All she could offer the tormented boy was her love and the shelter of her home. His agony was reflected in her sorrowful eyes, his anguish almost as unbearable for her as it was for him. Her only response was to love him as she tried to shield him from the cruelty of the world outside his door.

****

That evening, after the last pig of the day had been butchered, the entire Penrose family gathered around the great table in the Roselawn dining room. It was a family tradition that sprang up around the first day of hog killing. There was John and his wife Elizabeth, Enoch, his younger brother Hiram, Hiram's wife Amanda and their daughter Sarah and Rebecca, sister to Hiram and Enoch.

"Lizzie, you and the girls in the kitchen have outdone yourselves," the master of the house said. "If we ate like this everyday we'd be so fat they'd have to roll us around in a wheelbarrow. That fresh pork with the cracklin' bread and the peas and greens was as good as I've ever had. Hiram, your notion to let those hogs run loose in the woods and fatten up on acorns for a month was a good'un. I don't think I've ever tasted sweeter meat. Those hams and sausages out in the smokehouse are gonna make fine eatin' this winter."

Enoch grimaced at the compliment paid his brother. He was jealous because his father favored Hiram. Nothing Enoch ever did warranted so much as a mention. He had tried so hard to win his father's favor, but John had long ago abandoned Enoch to his mother's care. He loved his son, but the hardness he saw in Enoch's eyes and his cruelty to the slaves and the animals convinced him that the affection he bore him as a child would never return. The scars were too deep, redemption too far beyond reach.

"Lizzie, I'd sure like some of your famous sweet potato pie tomorrow, with some of those fresh pork chops. You think you'll be able to do that?" John asked.

"I think we can, John," she said with a smile.

She was proud of what her man had created out of this wilderness. She loved to please him. The only place she felt she had failed him was with Enoch but she knew his relationship with the boy was never going to change.

"I'll make some fresh applesauce too. You always like that with the fresh pork."

She turned her attention to her daughter, Rebecca.

"Now, I can't think of a better end to the evening than having Rebecca play some of her new pieces on the piano. Let's go into the parlor for our coffee. Amanda got some new sheet music from the pastor over at Bethesda when she and Hiram were there last Sunday. George Whitfield had it sent over from London. I understand that the captain of a slave ship wrote one of the pieces. What's his name Amanda?"

"John Newton," Amanda said. "It's a very stirring hymn. I hear it's very popular at funerals. Rebecca, do you remember what it's called?"

"Amazing Grace," she said. "I'm not sure I can do it justice but I'll try."

Enoch stood to excuse himself.

"Goodnight Mama. I'm tired. I think I'll go on up to bed."

"Good night, son. I'll see you in the morning."

Only he caught the slight tremor in her voice. He knew she had heard John's comment to Hiram and that only she understood its effect on him. It was added weight for the cross she had to bear.

He crossed the hallway and started up the stairs, catching a glimpse of Aba, Queen, and Cassie sitting in the darkened dining room. Mama always allowed them to listen when the piano was played. She thought it was civilizing for them. The sight of Cassie brought back images from the smokehouse. He climbed the stairs slowly, silently cursing himself for his weakness.

Queen had cleared the last of the breakfast dishes when Elizabeth remembered her promise to John from the night before.

"Queen, I told Mr. Penrose last night that I'd make some sweet potato pies for supper tonight. Will you send Cassie down to the root cellar and bring me a peck of the best potatoes she can find? Oh! And a few apples. I want to make some fresh applesauce. Mr. Penrose has gone into town for the day but he'll be back by suppertime."

"Yes, ma'am. She's abuildin' the pot fires rat now. I's gonna send her soon's she gits back."

Nether woman noticed Enoch as he slipped out the back door. Queen called to Cassie as she came in.

"Miss Elizabeth wants some sweet taters. She gone make some pies for Massa. Go down an' git a peck o' da best'uns fo'er. She wants a half-peck o' apples, too. Ya better hurry on now. Ka'le an' Kimba is fixin' to start killin' da hogs an' ya gonna be needed fo da soap real soon."

"Yes, Mama," Cassie said.

She picked up two pails from the kitchen pantry and left by the back door. She started down the path to the smoke house, stopping along the way to add a few pieces of wood to the wash pot fires. Off to the right she could see the twins down by the pigpens. They struggled to lift a squealing, two hundred pound pig over the fence. Kimba held the squirming animal in the sand pit while Ka'le stunned it with a poll axe. He pierced its heart to let the blood drain out onto the sand, then slit its throat They dragged the lifeless form over to a large barrel set into the ground at an angle. Young boys scampered to keep it filled with scalding water. The two men grasped the pig by its hind legs and lowered it into the barrel for a few seconds before hauling it out and heaving it, steaming, onto a wooden platform. Before it could cool they furiously scraped the loosened hair from the carcass with broad, flat knives. The boys gathered up the coarse hair to be used later as binder for chinking.

Cassie stopped to watch as Ka'le slid his knife behind each of the pig's ankle tendons and then insert a stick tapered at each end, spreading its hind legs. He and Kimba lifted the carcass and hung it over a bar protruding from the smokehouse. Kimba placed a large tub beneath the pig's half-severed head. With his left hand holding the pig's diaphragm in place, Ka'le sliced its stomach open from just below the tail to the rib cage. When he removed his hand the entrails tumbled into the tub. He severed the steaming mass from the stomach cavity, then split the rib cage with a hatchet and removed the heart and lungs. They then placed the carcass back on the platform for butchering.

Cassie had witnessed this process many times. It held a morbid fascination for her. She would cover her ears to shut out the screams when they stuck the pigs. It always upset her when the animals were killed, although she understood the reason for it. Other things that happened at Roselawn also upset her. Things for which there was no reason.

It was seven-thirty. Cassie was surprised that none of the other house servants were outside. The tubs near the washhouse, scrubbed clean and filled with fresh water, sat unattended, awaiting a fresh supply of organs and intestines. Heavy white smoke escaped from under the eaves of the smokehouse. The hams, pork bellies and sausages, pulled from the salt barrels the night before, hung over the fire pit. Green pine boughs covered the hickory coals, preventing flare-ups and giving off clouds of aromatic smoke.

Cassie was on her knees, digging into the mound of sweet potatoes. The alternating layers of dirt and pine straw protected them from rot and freezing. She pulled a large smooth potato from the pile and turned to put it in the bucket when she saw him. At first she couldn't make out the figure. He stood silhouetted in the door of the cellar, shafts of morning sunlight streaming past. He stepped down into the pit of the cellar. Then she recognized him.

"Massa Enoch. What you doing here? Does Miss Elizabeth need something else?" she asked.

He pushed the door shut and stepped toward her. In the gloom of the cellar she could now make out his eyes. They burned with a strange fire. The vivid crimson birthmark seemed to glow. His silence sent chills through her.

"Massa Enoch! What you want?" she asked, panic rising..

The frightened girl jumped to her feet, knocking over the bucket. He moved toward her. She stepped back until she felt the rough texture of the wall through the thin fabric of her clothes. He clutched the front of her dress, ripping the garment from her, exposing the white camisole underneath. She clawed at her attacker, wild-eyed and bewildered.

"Why you doin' this Massa Enoch? What'd I do?" she screamed.

She struggled to get free but he grabbed her and pushed her down, pressing her against the scattered pine straw on the dirt floor. He grasped the front of her slip and yanked it down, exposing her breasts. He pulled it high, over her waist. She wore no undergarments. In his urgency, Enoch ripped the buttons from his britches and dropped them around his ankles. He knelt over the struggling girl.

CHAPTER TWO

THE CELLAR DOOR BURST open as he prepared to enter her. Hiram was repairing the cane mill nearby when he heard the commotion. With Cassie's first scream he dropped his tools and bolted toward the sound.

"Enoch, what the hell are you doing? Cassie, put your clothes on and go back to the house," Hiram said.

"Enoch, get your pants back on. For God's sake man, I thought we were through with all this."

"What are you doing here?" Enoch asked, an eternity passing before the words escaped his throat. "Mama said you went into Savannah with Papa."

"It's a good thing I didn't." Hiram glared at his brother, the anger in his voice prompting Enoch to back away.

"Why, Enoch, why? After all this time. After all these years. What made you do it?"

He placed both hands on the man's chest and slammed him against the wall.

"You're going to break your mother's heart. I don't want to be around when Papa gets home. You remember the last time. I don't know what he'll do."

"You don't have to tell him Hiram," Enoch said, pleadingly. "You can tell him one of the young nigger bucks did it. He'll believe you.

Cassie won't say anything if you tell her not to. It won't happen again, I promise. Please don't tell Mama."

Hiram was not as tall as his older brother, but he was much stockier. He outweighed Enoch by fifty pounds. Heavy black brows shaded his slate gray eyes, a birthright from his Welsh mother. His wavy black hair was pulled back severely and tied with a cord. He wore black homespun trousers stuffed into the tops of long hose. The heavy deerskin apron tied around his waist was stained with axle grease. The rage on his face cautioned Enoch to stop his pleading.

"I'm through covering up for you. I've protected you for the last time. Papa knows about some of the things you've done, both to the slaves and to the animals. He doesn't know the worst. I didn't tell him everything about the time Mose's son died. Big Boy would still be alive if you hadn't left him out in the field to die. Of all people, I would think you'd have more pity on someone like him. He couldn't help being a cripple any more than you could help that mark on your face or your stammer. You're evil Enoch, and if you're not stopped your evilness will consume this family. I'm going to have a long talk with Papa when he gets home. In the meantime you're going to stay out of trouble."

Hiram slammed the cellar door behind him. He took down the old, rusty lock from its peg above the door and hooked it through the hasp. Dejectedly, he walked toward the main house. It was not going to be a pleasant evening.

"Hiram, what happened? Why is Cassie locked in her room, crying?"

His mother was waiting for him on the porch, her apron pressed to her mouth. Fear filled her eyes.

"Where is Enoch? What has he done? Tell me, Hiram. What has he done?"

"Calm down, Mama. Everything's going to be all right."

In his heart he knew he was lying. With Enoch around nothing was ever again going to be all right. But, he couldn't tell her that. She had been so fragile since the fever took Emily and Adam. That had been over ten years ago. She took to her bed for weeks on end. She wouldn't eat. She wouldn't entertain visitors. She just locked herself in her room with their possessions and grieved. The only person she would allow in was Enoch. He was the only one she felt who truly understood her grief. She had been his rock for all those years when he closed out the world and lived in his own private agony, now he was her only comfort.

"He's locked in the root cellar, Ma. He tried to rape Cassie. He thought I was in town with Pa and I guess he thought he could get away with it. He's going to stay there until Pa gets back, then we'll decide what has to be done."

Elizabeth Penrose crumpled to the floor, grabbing at the bannister as she fell. She leaned against the white pickets and sobbed.

"Enoch. Oh, Enoch. Why, after all this time? I don't think I can stand it, Hiram. First the Lord takes my two precious babies and now the evil spirits have returned to haunt Enoch. What are we going to do, Hiram? You know how John feels about the way we treat the blacks. He won't stand for the kinds of things that go on at some of the other plantations. I respect him for that. God never gave us the right to abuse these poor creatures. Life is hard enough for them as it is. I wish there was no need for them. I wish we could turn them all loose tomorrow, but we can't. We're caught up in a vicious cycle of needing them to produce the crops and them needing us to provide for them. If we freed them I don't know how they'd survive."

"Don't worry, Ma. Pa and I will work something out. We're not going to let any harm come to Enoch but he can't be around Cassie anymore. You go on inside and get some rest. Pa will be home soon."

He helped the grieving woman to her feet and led her back into the house.

The setting sun turned the river to fire as John Penrose returned to Roselawn. He climbed down from the carriage and handed the reins to the waiting groom. Hiram waited on the porch. John knew something was wrong.

"Hiram, what are you doing out here so late? Shouldn't you be over at your place with Amanda and Sarah?

"Papa, we've got to talk."

He was taken aback at the alarm in Hiram's voice. He braced himself for the worst. His first thought was that someone had been killed. Accidents were not uncommon on a plantation with so much machinery and so many animals around.

"Pa, it's Enoch. I caught him in the root cellar. He was trying to rape Cassie. He tore her clothes off but nothing happened before I could get there. I don't know what came over him. He thought I had gone into Savannah with you. I guess he figured he could get away with it if we weren't here. He thought he could scare her into silence. I locked him in the cellar until you could get home. Mama is distraught. She's taken to her room again. You know how she dotes on that boy. He is her first born. If she knew all the things he has done it would kill her. But I can't tell her. Her heart's so broken already. I don't think she can take much more. What do you think we should do?"

Exasperation and sorrow fought for control of the old man's features. His shoulders slumped. He sat heavily on the rocking chair by the front door. He was bone tired from his trip into Savannah and the meetings with Governor Wright and the Loyalist council.

Things were not going well. There was news of more clashes up north and open rebellion here at home. The Liberty Boys continued to flout the law. They talked of insurrection nightly at Tondee's Tavern on Broughton Street. New edicts and provocations from London continued to inflame local passions. The colony seethed with discontent. The city was a Tory island in a Whig sea. Even Hiram had Whig sympathies. He kept them to himself in deference to his father's feelings.

John stared off into the distance. Dusk was drawing a curtain on the day. An osprey dived into the river, emerging with a flash of silver in its talons. Herons and egrets walked stiff legged through the marsh shallows, halting to stare fixedly into the water. A quick dart of the head and the small prey slid down their gullet. An emboldened raccoon dipped his paw into the water and slapped a fat mussel onto the bank. Iridescent shells lay scattered around him. There was not a more beautiful or peaceful place on earth than Roselawn at sunset. Today that beauty was suffused with pain and dread for the morrow.

"Come with me, Hiram. We must attend to Enoch."

They walked slowly up the path from the cellar, Enoch leading the way, shame and disgrace evidenced in his drooping shoulders. His father did not speak. He had just motioned with his head for Enoch to come out. The glint of the old man's steel-gray eyes told all. Enoch would rather take a beating. The silence was like a knife through his heart.

"Go into the parlor, Enoch. Hiram, bring him a glass of water. I'll be in directly. First, I'm going up to see your mother."

He stood on the first tread and composed himself before slowly ascending the stairs. "Poor woman," he thought. "Forty years we've been here. And the good Lord's been kind to us. But she's sure known her share of pain. Two stillborn, two taken by the fever, and now Enoch again. The boy has been a trial since he was born. He never accepted his mark as God's will. I thought after all this time he had straightened himself out but I guess I was wrong."

A muffled sob answered his tap. He pushed the door open to reveal a room engulfed in total darkness. No trace of sunlight penetrated the tightly drawn drapes. It was a room overflowing with grief. John walked over to the bedside table. He lit the candle.

"Elizabeth, I'm not going to do anything to hurt the boy but I can't let this go unpunished. Hiram and I will talk to Enoch tonight and decide what to do. You try to get some rest. I'll come up later and let you know what I've decided."

He sat on the edge of the bed and touched her tenderly. He wanted to reassure her that this too would pass. He kissed her on the forehead. After a second he rose and silently left the room.

Hiram sat across the room from his brother, arms folded across his chest staring into space. Enoch held his head in his hands and stared at the floor. He did not look up when his father entered the room.

"Enoch, what do you have to say for yourself? Have you lost your mind? I thought you had put this all behind you years ago."

Still staring at the floor, Enoch stammered, "I don't know Papa. I saw Cassie tending the pots and something just came over me. She reminded me so much of Queen at her age. I tried to walk away but I just couldn't. I went in the smokehouse thinking that it would go away and it didn't. It just got worse. When she left to join the others it sort of passed. Then this morning when I heard Queen tell her to fetch some potatoes from the root cellar something just snapped in my head. Anyways, Pa, I don't understand why you and Hiram are so mad. After all, she's just a nigger. It's not like she's a real person. Half the children running around most other plantations are *mulattoes*. Why should we be ashamed if we want to fuck 'em."

"Shut up, Enoch!" Hiram said in disgust as he jumped to his feet.

"She's a human being just like you are and she deserves to be treated as such. You have no right to abuse her. And you have no right to abuse any of the other slaves. If you had gotten help for Big Boy when he had that epileptic fit he'd still be alive. You let him lie there in the midddle of the field and choke on his own tongue while you stood there laughing and did nothing. You wouldn't even let the other men help him. You thought it was funny the way he flopped around. You've allowed your own self-pity to turn you into a monster. You think that if you can't get any joy out of life, then nobody else should."

Fire blazed from John Penrose's eyes.

"Is that true Enoch? Did you let Big Boy die?" John demanded.

"I thought he was just playing Pa. I didn't mean for him to die."

"You've done some despicable things in your life but that has to be the worst. It's probably a good thing I didn't know about it at the time. I don't know what I would have done.

"And now, this. Enoch, it's been fourteen years. I beat you within an inch of your life the last time. Are you telling me now that you only have this problem with Cassie because of the fact that she looks so much like Queen did? That you don't have these same feelings for any of the other slave girls?"

"No, Pa, it's just Cassie. Something comes over me when I see her. It's like some other person takes over my body and I'm looking at everything from the outside. I can't explain it. It just happens."

"Boy, I'm giving you fair warning. If you ever do anything like this again I'll put you on a boat back to London so fast you won't have time to button your pants. And you'll have to make your own way. I won't support you. You act up like this over there and you'll land in jail. I don't think you'll like the inside of the British prisons.

"As for now, I'm going to send you over to Ossabaw Island for a spell. I've leased two hundred acres from John Morel and hired an overseer for the property. His name is James Pelham. He'll be taking about twenty men over with him. There won't be any women for a while. So we'll remove that temptation from you. He's going to build rice fields and you're going to help him. I hope to have them producing by next year.

"I've sectioned off a hundred acres on the southwest side of the island, on the river. It's covered with the finest growth of long leaf pine in the colony. I'm sending Ka'le and Kimba with you to start tapping those trees for turpentine. I've ordered plans and material for a distillery near the sound. And a dock. So the boats will be able to sail right up to load their cargo. With all the shipbuilding going on, there's a strong market for turpentine and pitch in Europe right now. You do a good job and keep out of trouble and you can come back later in the year. Now, get out of here. I want to talk to Hiram."

Enoch glared at his brother. He left the room sullenly, stinging from his father's rebuke and angry at his looming exile.

"What was Pa going to talk to Hiram about that was so all-fired important that he couldn't hear it?" he wondered.

He hurried off toward the barns where he saddled his horse. He vaulted into the saddle and tore across the paddies behind the main house, toward the Thunderbolt River. The gray stallion's nostrils flared and its eyes rolled with fear as the whip came down on its flanks. The sharp bit cut into the corners of its mouth. Blood flecked foam dripped from its muzzle. The terrified animal stumbled, nearly falling, as Enoch urged him over a large oak that was left from the clearing of the rice fields.

"They treat me like a child," he shouted, as he reined in the bolting horse.

He sat, brooding, balanced on the skeletal remains of an abandoned dock, his legs dangling over the out-rushing tide. The horse stood nearby tethered to a gnarled cedar, winded and lathered from the furious run.

"They think they'll break me by sending me away. They think I'll forget about her. Well, I've got news for them. It may take me months or even years but in due time I WILL have her. She's mine."

Frenzied eyes stared up from the black water, dark and cold, reflecting the fragile image of a man descending into madness.

Hiram looked at his father. The years wore on the man. His hair had gone completely gray. He wore it pulled back and tied with a ribbon like his son. Those eyes that had witnessed a civilization being torn from the wilderness were now rheumy and sunken. The tropical sun had turned his skin to leather and carved deep crevices into his face. His shirt collar chafed at a large wen that had developed on the side of his neck. And now, after forty years of sacrifice to build a family and a community, he stood in peril of losing both.

"What are you going to do, Pa?"

"I don't know yet. Let's sleep on it and maybe we'll have clearer heads in the morning. I need to see to your mother now. She's not handling this very well. I'm going to grab a quick supper and then go up to her. I'll see you in the morning."

"Good night, Pa. I'm sorry that Enoch's brought all this trouble on you. I know you've got a lot of things on your mind these days. I'm sure we'll be able to work something out."

The father looked at the son.

"Hiram, I don't know what I'd do without you. You are the rock upon which all our troubles crash and you always stand up to the pressures. God bless you my son. Good night."

Hiram walked down the lane toward his house, beyond the slave quarters. His father was not a demonstrative man. What he had just said was more praise than Hiram had received in his lifetime. Despite the turmoil of the day it left him with an inner glow he had not experienced in a long time.

The next morning the two men were seated alone in the dining room. The sun had barely cleared the river. Neither had slept well knowing the decision that faced them in the morning.

"Hiram, you and I both know that sooner or later Enoch will go after Cassie again. As bad as I hate to say it, I'm convinced the boy is not right, mentally. In some way his brain doesn't function like yours or mine. It goes beyond just meanness. I don't know if he was born that way or it grew out of his condition, but in any case he's always goin' to be trouble. I've tried to beat it out of him and I've tried to scare it out of him and neither has worked. And, there's no way I'll be able to send him away, no matter what I say. That would kill his mother.

"This thing's been gnawing at me all night. I couldn't sleep. I went up to the roof about midnight. There was a full moon rising in the east and I could make out smoke from the monastery on Skidaway. I got to thinking about something Governor Wright said yesterday. He told us that a group of nuns had arrived at the monastery a few weeks ago. They came over from England. I understand they are refugees from a

Huguenot order that settled near Canterbury after fleeing the Catholic persecution in France.

"Several months ago Father Titus met with the headmaster at Bethesda. He asked the reverend to contact George Whitefield and ask him to intercede with the archbishop. It seems a large number of runaway or abandoned slave children has taken sanctuary at the monastery. Father Titus and the other brothers didn't feel like it was seemly for them to raise the girls. If the good reverend could convince the archbishop to send him some nuns, then St. Benedict's would agree to take Bethesda's girls as well and send their boys over to Bethesda. And so that's what they did.

"That set me to thinking. Maybe we can convince Father Titus to take Cassie at St. Benedict's. It would put her out of Enoch's reach and it would allow him to come back here after Ossabaw. I want you to go over there tomorrow. Take old Mose with you. Tell Father Titus that I'll pay for Cassie's keep and also tell him I'll help build a convent for the nuns. I won't say anything to Queen and Cassie until you get back."

CHAPTER THREE

JOHN PENROSE WAS GRANTED a small island just off the Isle of Hope, eight miles south of Savannah, as reward for his years of service to Oglethorpe and the community of Savannah. Broad expanses of tidal marsh rimmed the property on all sides. Three rivers surrounded the island, their ebb and flow dictated by the tides of the Atlantic. The Herb, The Skidaway and The Thunderbolt deposited their rich nutrients into its teeming marshes. Hundreds of species of sea creatures thrived in their rich layers of sediment. The lushness of those marshes and estuaries was ideal for producing rice and indigo. He built a small house and moved his family there.

Life on Roselawn in those early years was unrelenting drudgery and backbreaking labor. Together with his family, indentured servants and a few freedmen, Penrose began to clear the virgin forests of pine and oak. For the first few years he barely eked out a living. Extracting riches from rice and indigo was rendered impossible by the Trustees Charter. Its strictures banned three types of people from immigrating to the colony: Catholics, lawyers and slaves. It was the prohibition against slaves that proved the most controversial, because of the severe hardship it placed on the white farmers

By the 1740's, many planters routinely ignored the rule against slaves. They found it impossible to reclaim the swamps and forests with the limited labor available and the white workers couldn't survive the miasma of the marshes. They were decimated by the heat and malaria. Meanwhile, the rice and indigo farmers in South Carolina were amassing great fortunes. They were doing it on the backs of the Africans that flowed through the Charlestown slave market in ever increasing numbers. These black men from Africa were less susceptible to the sicknesses of the white man. In Africa they had developed immunities to tropical diseases and their dark skins better withstood the relentless heat. If Georgia wanted to share in that wealth she must have slaves.

John Penrose and Noble Jones ultimately decided to follow the lead of the other planters, and ignore the charter. Noble Jones, master of Wormslow Plantation on the Isle of Hope, lived just across the Herb River from Roselawn. He had held many important positions in the colony, among them sheriff, surveyor and doctor. The five hundred acres on the Isle of Hope that he called Wormslow were his reward

"John, I find it most disagreeable that we have to sneak off like thieves in the dark in order to make a go of it out here," Noble Jones said. "I've told the General repeatedly that we can't compete with South Carolina as long as we're denied slaves. His answer is always the same.

'It's out of my hands, Noble. That's the Trustee Charter signed by King George, and until it's changed I can't allow slavery in Georgia'.

"He says that, knowing full well there are farms all up and down these rivers that have brought slaves here from Charlestown."

John Penrose gripped the side of the wagon and placed his foot on the wheel's hub. He looked up at his neighbor.

"I understand, Noble. What I don't understand is what kind of a notion of a utopian society the trustees had in their heads when they drew up that damn fool charter. They sure didn't know anything about what life would be like here. If you read those pamphlets they put out to entice folks to sign up you'd think this was Eden we were coming to. Not one of them, save the General, has ever stepped foot on this land. Just let them try to scrape a living out of these swamps and they'll soon be hotfooting it back to London with their powdered wigs and starched collars. Well, I think it's just a matter of time until they have to change it. If nothing else, the charter itself expires in 1750. Then they'll have to rewrite the laws. As a royal colony, we'll have a say in how we are governed, and there's no way we're going to pretend that slavery doesn't exist here and that the survival of the colony doesn't depend on it."

He heaved himself up onto the wagon seat beside Jones and the caravan headed toward Savannah and the road toward Charlestown.

The two men had corresponded with Charles Carlton for several months. Carlton Hall was one of the largest and most successful plantations along the Ashley River, just outside Charlestown. It had several hundred acres under cultivation. Carlton was well aware of the experiment going on south of the Savannah River. He had visited the area many times and established friendships with several prominent planters and political leaders. Now all that groundwork was going to pay off. In exchange for the slaves he would lease to Jones and Penrose, Carlton would receive a percentage of their crops, and more importantly, their support after land ownership in Georgia was opened to South Carolinians. And, by leasing the slaves, Jones and Penrose remained within the letter of the law. Since they belonged to Carlton there was no legal Georgia ownership.

Ten days after his departure for South Carolina, John Penrose drove the covered wagon with its team of gray warm bloods back up the lane to Roselawn. Enoch was on the front veranda with his mother, helping her to shell peas, when he heard the jangle of the trace chains. He tore down the steps and bounded up to the seat by his father. He turned to peer into the darkness of the wagon, shielding his eyes from the sun. Seated on the bed of the wagon were five men and a woman. They were the first Negroes Enoch had ever seen.

Three of the men were very dark, of medium height and stocky build. The other two were taller, of medium build, with light brown skin and thin features. The woman too, was slim and thin-featured. She had an olive complexion and green eyes, flecked with brown.

****

Safi, Nobu, and Aba Omoru were kidnapped from their native village in Sierra Leone in 1740. The native slave traders took them to Bance Island on the coast and sold them to a Portuguese captain who held them in the island's fortress while he gathered enough slaves to fill his ship. Finally, on April 15, 1740, three hundred and fifty frightened, abused, and malnourished Africans, from across Sierra Leone and Dahomey, were herded aboard the *Aristides Espinola,* in chains. The next morning at ebb tide, the vessel drifted from its moorings. The crew could be seen scurrying through the rigging, setting her sails for a northwesterly tack, toward the West Indies. The captain stood on the bridge barking orders to the crew. He crossed himself and prayed for favorable spring trade winds.

"Batten down those deck hatches well, men. We don't want any seawater flooding the hold and drowning the cargo. And we don't want any of those heathens getting above decks if they should break loose."

The "Middle Passage" to Charlestown could take as long as three months. Eighty-five members of that wretched cargo would never see this new land, this America they had been told about. Starvation, dysentery, scurvy, and infections took their toll. The crew, long inured to the specter of death at sea, callously dumped their emaciated bodies overboard. No ceremony. No sympathy. The only fleeting evidence of their worldly existence was the crimson stain left by the sharks that trailed the ship. Each splash set off an unearthly wail from below the heaving decks.

Each day the sailors would go below to unshackle a few slaves at a time. They were lashed together and brought up on deck where they were doused with seawater to wash off the excrement and vomit covering their naked bodies. They were fed a small amount of mealy gruel with yams and a biscuit, and given enough water to sustain them until their next visit topside. Thus, the entire population was rotated. Some captives became morose and would not eat. They would be dragged on deck and force fed to keep them alive. Others, so enraged by their captivity and loss of freedom, attempted to throw themselves into the sea, choosing to die rather than live like animals.

Women and children were treated more leniently. The small children were given the run of the ship during the day and were penned up with their mothers at night. Night was a time of dread. It was in the dark that the more comely of the mothers were likely to suffer from the baser instincts of the sailors. Those who did not submit were held and forcibly raped.

July 1, 1740, the *Aristides Espinola* slid into its berth across the harbor from Charlestown. Its cargo was offloaded and penned in stockades on Sullivan's Island. They were quarantined there for several weeks. Infectious diseases were rampant. Those who survived the quarantine were judged to be free of disease.

Thaddeus Stevens was waiting on the wharf as the ship docked. He stood with his bookkeeper and tallied the adult slaves as they were marched off the ship.

"I contracted for 350 able bodied Africans, experienced in the growing of rice and indigo, and you bring me 265," the auction owner shouted at the Portuguese captain, after seeing the tally. "Do you know what this is going to cost me? I've already got customers lined up for them. This is coming out of your hide, not mine. You're going to ruin my business," he wailed.

The irate slave trader spent the next four weeks feeding and tending the survivors. To fetch top dollar they needed to be in excellent condition. The day before the auction his workers busily oiled and buffed the males, producing a glistening sheen on their ebony bodies. Tomorrow his investment would pay off.

Safi, Kofi and Aba Omoru were among the first to go on the block. Carlton Hall's overseer, Tom Patterson, needed rice workers. He also needed house slaves. Safi was seventeen, Kofi fifteen and Aba thirteen. When the three siblings were placed on the trading block Patterson determined to buy them as a lot.

Now, after many years of faithful service on the Carlton plantation, the three were once again being uprooted. They, together with another three field hands, were being torn from the slave society at Carlton Hall to be shipped off to Georgia. Their experience in rice plantation culture was urgently needed to help develop Roselawn's rice fields and Charles Carlton wanted to insure that his southern strategy would pay off. He was sending his best to Roselawn. He was also avoiding the scandal that would arise if the pregnant Aba delivered his son's child at Carlton Hall.

Enoch recoiled at the startling sight. "Who are they Papa, and why is their skin so black, and why are they chained up?"

"Whoa there, boy. One question at a time," the older man said. "These are Negroes. They come from Africa, on the other side of the ocean. They've been working on the Carlton plantation up near Charlestown. They are slaves. They are chained to keep them from running away. They're going to be working here on Roselawn now. They're going to help us prepare the rice fields down by the river. You stay away from them and don't be causing any trouble. We're going to be busy building them a house for the next few days. I don't want you gettin' in the way."

Elizabeth Penrose came down the steps, wiping her hands on her apron, smiling. She was a gaunt woman. The tendons in her neck formed a deep cavity beneath her chin. Savannah's harsh climate had not been kind to her. Straggly wisps of dirty gray hair escaped from beneath her blue bonnet. Her hands were red and calloused. She walked up to the wagon and peered over the rear gate.

"Is she the one?"

"Yes, Lizzie, this is Aba. Aba Omoru. She's expecting a child in about three months or so, but Mr. Carlton assures me she's a good house servant. I promised you some help. Here she is."

Mr. Penrose lowered the rear gate of the wagon. He took a key from his vest pocket and unlocked the shackles. Aba gave him a fierce look. She threw her legs over and stepped down onto the sandy soil of Roselawn for the first time.

"Aba, this is Mrs. Penrose. You'll be working for her in the house. Go on with her now. She's got a nice place ready for you to stay, off the kitchen."

The woman looked around warily then lifted up her skirts. She had a look of royalty. With head held high, she followed Elizabeth Penrose up the steps to her new home.

CHAPTER FOUR

MOSE AKALA WAS ONE of the oldest and most trusted of the slaves at Roselawn. He came from Angola and was delivered with over two hundred other slaves to the Lazaretto Creek quarantine station on the western tip of Tybee Island eighteen years ago. They were kept there for three months to guard against the spread of diseases brought from Africa. Mose was already in his thirties when he arrived in Savannah. He was captured with his entire family: wife, Sulu, fifteen-year old daughter Ora, and fourteen-year old twins Ka'le and Kimba. Through guile, bluster and sheer will he managed somehow to keep them all together. Now he stood alone on the block. John Penrose stared at the proud, burnished ebony figure.

"Tom. What's the story with this one?" John Penrose asked the auctioneer.

"His name is Mosu Akala," the auctioneer said. "He was taken in Angola with his whole family. He was a chief of their tribe. I hear he fought like a tiger to protect them. He was nearly dead from the beatings when the *pombeiros* got him to Luanda. The Portagee cap'n who bought him was so taken with the man's grit that he let the family stay together on the ship."

"Tom, I want you to put them on the block together. If he brought 'em through that hell, he deserves a chance to keep them with him."

"All right, Mr. Penrose, but if they don't fetch as much as I need to clear, I'll have to break 'em up."

Tom Pendergast needn't have worried. The amount bid by the master of Roselawn Plantation was not challenged by anyone there that day. Mosu Akala and his family would stay together thanks to John Penrose.

This proud chief from a small village in Angola did not ask to be a slave, but if Allah declared it, he would be this man's slave. This man whose eyes showed mercy and compassion.

Hiram and Mose pushed off from the Grimball Creek landing as the first rays of yellow sunlight pierced the tall pines across the river. The retreating tide carried them silently toward the Skidaway River. Mists rose in the cool morning air. The two men rowed in silence, waves lapping at the bow of the small, flat-bottomed boat. They eased silently into the stronger current of the Skidaway, bucking the flow, on a northerly heading. A school of bottlenose dolphins playfully circled the boat, their sleek black bodies arcing through the water. A bald eagle with twigs in its talons landed gracefully in the top of a tall pine tree. He and his mate were preparing their aerie for the nesting season. Hiram looked back at his companion.

"How you holding up, Mose? The current is pretty strong along here."

"I's awright Massa Hiram. We gonna be tuh da Modena cut direckly. I be's awright 'til den."

A short while later they slid the small craft into the narrow waterway separating Modena Island from Skidaway. After several twists and turns they emerged into the Thunderbolt River, resuming their southerly course. On its journey to the Atlantic, the river would carry them down the northeastern edge of Skidaway Island. Riding the strong currents, they made Priest's Landing before noon. Hiram tied up to the small dock and told Mose to stay with the boat.

"I'll have someone bring you something to eat, Mose. I shouldn't be more than an hour or so."

"Yassuh. I's gonna stay here and look atter da boat," Mose said. "Take yo time Massa Hiram. I reckon I might cotch myself a nap whilst ya's gone."

The Priory of Saint Benedict sat on a bluff overlooking Romerly Marsh with the barrier island of Wassaw visible in the distance. A watchtower on the northeast corner of the structure commanded an unobstructed view of the ocean where it divided Wassaw and theTybee marshes. Ships navigating those straits were a common sight. St. Benedicts's formed the southernmost outpost of the Anglican Church's *Society for the Propagation of the Gospel to Foreign Parts.* Father Titus and his friars were charged with bringing Christian enlightenment to both the settlers and the savages in the Georgia colony.

"Come in my son," the bearded ascetic said to Hiram.

The monk was clad in a dark brown cassock with a draping cowl. It was tied at the waist with a common rope. The man wore no adornments save the crucifix around his neck. He reached out a bony hand to welcome his visitor.

"It is so good to see you. How are your mother and father? I haven't seen them since I was last at Bethesda."

"They're fine, Father. Papa sends his best wishes to you and his praise for the work you are doing."

"May I offer you some tea and something to eat? You've got to be hungry from all that rowing."

"Thank you, Father. You're most kind. I must admit I worked up an appetite on the river. And if I may impose on your hospitality, I left my man Mose at the landing. I'm sure he would appreciate some food as well."

"By all means. I'll see to it right away," the gentle man said. "Come, walk with me to the refectory."

Hiram hungrily scooped up the last of the rabbit stew and sopped the gravy with a piece of bread fresh from the oven.

"That was really good, Father Titus. I suppose you have plenty of marsh rabbits out in the Romerly. We don't have quite so many on our side of the river. A lot of rails though. They make a tasty stew too."

"What brings you to Skidaway, Hiram? Don't get me wrong. We always welcome your company here, but it is a long boat ride from Roselawn."

"Father, you must be aware of the troubles we've had with Enoch in the past. He never got over the way he was marked as a baby. It seems to boil up in him sometimes. Pa has reached the end of his rope about what to do with him. He can't just send him away. That would be the death of Ma. You know how she's doted on him. Especially after Emily and Adam died."

Hiram paused.

"He tried to take our house servant Cassie yesterday. I caught him in the root cellar tearing off her clothes. He hadn't done anything like that for a long time. We all thought he was over those things. We were wrong. So Pa came up with an idea to keep Enoch away from Cassie.

"Pa heard in town that some nuns had come to St. Benedict's to help you with the runaways. He was wondering if he could impose on you to take the girl for a spell. Get her away from Enoch. He says he'll pay for her keep. He also said he'll help you build a convent for the nuns. It would sure make life easier for the family. And she's a good house worker. She'd be a big help to the sisters." Hiram let his words sink in.

Father Titus put his finger to his pursed lips as he gave thought to the request.

"She can come as far as I am concerned. But I must first ask the Mother Superior. The task of raising the child and looking after her will fall to the sisters. It will be her decision to make. Make yourself at home. I'll be back directly."

Hiram wandered around the grounds. Like all monasteries, St. Benedict's was laid out within a walled quadrangle. The main chapel was built against the north wall with the cloisters on either side. The kitchen, refectory, infirmary and workshops were arrayed to the south. Hastily erected dormitories for the nuns occupied a portion of the garden area behind the refectory.

"Hiram Penrose, I'd like you to meet Sister Marie Michel."

Hiram looked up to see a slender, middle-aged woman, clothed from neck to toe in black. A white wimple covered her head. It was fastened under her chin and flowed over her shoulders. A white silken sash girded her waist. Her mien was severe in the manner of a religious leader.

"Sister Marie, it is a pleasure to meet you. Welcome to St. Benedict's and welcome to Savannah."

"Thank you, Mr. Penrose. I am happy to be here. It's my sincere wish to serve God here in the wilderness and to win souls for his kingdom."

An unmistakable French accent shaded her perfect English. Hiram was always struck by how much prettier his language sounded when spoken by a Frenchman. He could sit in the tavern listening to Peter Tondee for hours on end.

"May I assume that Father Titus spoke to you of my father's request?"

"Yes he did Mr. Penrose, and while we had not planned to take in any but runaways and orphans, we certainly can make an exception in this case. Sister Bernadette had much experience with abused young novitiates in Canterbury. I'm certain she'll be able to give the proper guidance and influence to this young girl. Father told me of the generous offer you've made to support the girl and to help with our convent. Tell your father how much we appreciate his support of the church and particularly our humble efforts here at St. Benedict's."

"Thank you, Reverend Mother. I can't tell you how pleased Papa will be. It's truly an answer to his prayer. We would like to bring her over on Friday, if that's all right with you. The faster we can get her away from the situation the better. Enoch is going over to Ossabaw Island soon, but it will be at least a few weeks. It's best that Cassie leave as soon as possible.

"Father, when do you think you'll want to begin work on the convent? There are several weeks before planting season starts. We can send some boys over to help clear the land and cut some logs for you. And, if you'll make out a list of supplies I'll pick it up when I come back on Friday."

The sun was poised to drop behind the Herb River marshes when Hiram and Mose returned to Grimball's Landing.

"I reckon I'll see you in da mawnin Massa Hiram," Mose said, as he set off down the sandy path toward the slave cabins. "We gotta finish up wit da hogs befo we gits a hot spell."

"Good night, Mose. Tell Sulu I surely do miss her hoecakes since she got sick. Old Doc Minis is coming out to check on Ma tomorrow. I'll ask him to look in on Sulu while he's here."

"I's mighty obliged Massa Hiram. She ain't been doing too good.

I sho hopes he can help her. The root doctor from over to Wormslow says somebody done put a spell on her. He left her a potion and some kinda greens to put in a glass of water. I don't spect it's done no good." His voice trailed off in anguished resignation.

"That's great news, Hiram," his father said in response to the report from St. Benedict's.

He put his arms around his son and hugged him. It was an unusual show of affection. John Penrose was a stoic man, rarely given to displays of emotion. He stood more erect now, as if a great weight had been lifted. Elizabeth would be happy that she didn't have to worry about Enoch anymore.

"I'm going up now, to tell Miss Elizabeth what we're going to do. It's only two days til Friday so we better tell Queen and Cassie. Queen's going take it pretty hard, but she'll know it's for the best, and she'll be able to go over and visit with the girl some. Maybe someday Cassie will be able to come back home."

****

Cassie sat on a damask covered stool, at her mother's feet. She clung to Queen's hand, wide eyed with fear. Queen sat on a ladder back chair Hiram had brought from the dining room. She didn't know why she had been called to the parlor but she knew it must have something to do with Massa Enoch and Cassie, and she didn't think it could be anything good. For the past two days she was dreading this moment. She knew about the trip to Skidaway. Old Mose had told everyone. Not that he knew the reason but he 'reckoned' it was about Massa Enoch. Word of his attack on Cassie had spread like wildfire through the cabins.

John looked ill at ease. He twisted in his seat and reached for his small briar pipe. He filled it from the tin on the table beside him and lit it from the candle there. He watched the smoke curl toward the ceiling, all the time avoiding the women's eyes.

"Queen, I don't know what I can say about Enoch. That boy has been trouble since the day he was born. But you know all about that. Lord knows he had a right to be angry, being marked the way he was, but a normal person would've gotten over that a long time ago.

"I've decided to send him to our new property on Ossabaw for a while, but it'll be some time before we're ready for that. I don't think we can wait. In his current state he's obsessed with Cassie. Truthfully, I think the boy's lost his mind. There's no place to send him for help. I told him if he acts up again I'm going to send him back to England. But I can't really do that, because of Miss Elizabeth. She's not very stable as it is and that would drive her over the edge."

With compassion he looked at the frightened girl.

"Cassie, you haven't done anything wrong. You're a good girl. But, I've got to do something and I've tried to think what's best for everybody concerned. I've prayed about it long and hard.

"I don't want to do it, but for your own good I'm gonna send you to St. Benedict's on Skidaway. At least for a while. If things get straightened out with Enoch then you can come on back. Hiram says he'll take Queen and Aba over to see you every so often. There are already several young Negro girls over there. They're either runaways or they've been orphaned and there was nobody to take them in. The prior over there, Father Titus, is a good man, and he'll see that you are taken good care of. He's got six nuns who just came over from England and they're gonna help in raising you and the other girls. You'll be expected to work and earn your keep but I'll help out with that."

The soft mewl that rose in Cassie's throat turned slowly into a haunting wail.

"Mama, Mama. Do I hafta go? I don' wanna leave you and Mama Aba. Why, Mama, Why?"

"Hush, chile. Massa John ain't gone make ya do sumpin' if it ain't fo yo own good. He done said so."

Queen looked deep into Cassie's eyes, strong emotions welling up.

"Me and yo grandma, Aba, we gone miss ya sumpin awful round here but dis be fo da best. Ya go on over dere and ya do whut dem church folks tells ya. Dis whole mess, it gone be straightened out one o' dese days and den ya kin come on back home."

She released Cassie and looked at the two men.

"Massa John, when she gotta go?"

Cassie sat back down on the chair, bewildered, in disbelief.

"Friday, Queen. Hiram and Mose will take her over. I'll speak to Miss Elizabeth. I don't think she'll mind if you go along. I'd like you to meet the nuns who'll be looking after Cassie. It'll make you feel better about all this. She'll be in good hands."

"I thanks ya, Massa John. I'd lak to see whuh my chile's goin'. Come on Cas, we's gotta go tell Ma. She gone be mighty grieved 'bout dis."

CHAPTER FIVE

QUEEN PLACED CASSIE'S FEW possessions in an old blanket. She pulled the four corners together and tied them in a knot. Cassie waved a tearful good-bye to the slaves that had gathered outside the kitchen. Sulu got up from her sickbed. The parade to the dock was a somber one.

The light mist that fell on the small party as it left Grimball's Creek turned into a cold, skin-soaking drizzle before they arrived at Priest's Landing. Hiram brought two large squares of oilcloth from the sewing room. Queen and Cassie lay huddled under one piece in the middle of the boat. Hiram cut the other in two. He made holes for head and arms. He handed one to Mose while he donned the other. Together with their broad-brimmed leather hats, the makeshift ponchos managed to keep them reasonably dry.

"Halloo," came the cry from the lookout tower.

The youngest friar, Brother Anthony, had been posted to watch for the party. He rang the alarm bell to alert the others of their imminent arrival. A few minutes later Mose tossed a line to the smiling young man. Father Titus, Mother Superior Marie Michel and another nun hurried out the gates to welcome their visitors. Cassie peered from beneath the oilcloth. She had never been off Roselawn. She was entering a new life, in a new world, and she was wide-eyed with wonder.

"Come child, don't be afraid," Sister Marie said soothingly.

She reached down and took the frightened girl's hand and led her from the boat. Queen scampered onto the dock behind her as Mose threw the blanket up. They secured the boat and hurried to shelter. Once inside the common meeting room, across from the main chapel, and out of the rain, Hiram made formal introductions.

"Father Titus, Sister Marie, this is Cassie Omoru and her mother, Queen. And this is Mose," he said.

"Welcome to St. Benedict's. We look forward to Cassie joining our growing group of young girls. Queen, you can be sure that she will be well taken care of here. Sister Marie and her nuns have much experience in overseeing and teaching young girls back in England and France. Now I'd like you to meet Sister Bernadette."

A pudgy redheaded young woman in a nun's habit stepped from the shadows.

"She has been assigned as Cassie's mentor and teacher. She will see to the welfare and education of your daughter as long as she is here. It is our fervent prayer that this unfortunate situation will be resolved soon and that she can return to her family at Roselawn."

The young nun stepped forward to take Cassie's trembling hand. She appeared to be in her late twenties. Her habit, like that of the Mother Superior, was all black. She tied hers with a sash of blue, marking the level of her progression in the order. Her penetrating green eyes were set wide in a cherubic face. A wayward strand of copper-colored hair crept from beneath the rim of her wimple. Her full lips perched above a strong, dimpled chin. Her nose sat at a perceptible angle to her face, the result of an unfortunate fall from a horse when she was ten. Her radiant smile lit up the gloomy room.

"Don't be frightened Cassie. No one at Saint Benedict's will harm you. I promise to look after you. We have nine girls here. You'll make ten. Each of the other sisters already has two girls assigned to them. You'll be joining Esther, another young girl in my care. If you and your mother will come with me I'll introduce you to her and show you where you'll be living."

The rain had slackened as Sister Bernadette led them down a path of crushed oyster shells. The crunching sounds of six unsynchronized feet reverberated off the tabby walls of the workshop and the blacksmith shed. Off to the west was a small barn where two mules chewed contentedly on their daily ration of corn. In a sty next door several pigs vied noisily for the slops that had been poured into a hollow log trough. The young nun turned east, toward the marsh, passing under centuries old water oaks. She stopped before a square of six small buildings surrounding a slightly larger one.

"With the generous help of Mr. Penrose we hope to have more permanent houses ready in a few months," Bernadette said.

Bernadette led her to the single cabin at the far end of the compound. She stepped over the log threshold. There seated in the dim light beyond the fireplace was a young Negro girl, no more than twelve. She rhythmically lifted the dasher then plunged it down into the butter churn between her legs. The heavy splash told Cassie that the cream was nearly separated from the milk.

"Cassie, this is Esther. Her parents were runaways from a plantation in South Carolina, trying to reach sanctuary in Florida. Their boat was swamped in the Skidaway Narrows during last year's hurricane. Father McIlvane found her clinging to an uprooted tree in the river. She was half-dead when they got to her. Esther, go over to the kitchen and get the butter molds. Cassie and I'll help you finish up."

The young girl did not speak. She rose silently and disappeared out the front door.

"Cassie, I've told Esther that you came here from Roselawn Plantation because of some household problems there. I think she's too young to hear anything more than that. If you choose to tell her more in the future that's up to you. None of the other girls have been told anything. What you tell them is also up to you. None of the sisters will discuss it. It's your own private matter to be handled as you see fit. Now, do you or your mother have any questions for me before we go back to the boat?"

Queen was first to speak.

"Miss Bernadette, I don' know much bout yo religion but I's always tried tuh speak da bible tuh Cassie. I'd be much obliged if you'd larn her da bible. I'd also lak it if ya could larn her tuh read an' write. God, he works in 'sterious ways sometimes and maybe dis be one o' dem times. Dis may be Cassie's chance tuh git outten da slave life.

"Cassie, ya mind Miss Bernadette an' do whut she say. Iffen ya gits nuff book larnin' they ain't no telling whut ya kin do. I don' want'cha tuh go back tuh da boat wit me. I's gonna 'member ya rat here in yo new home. Me and Mama, we'll come tuh see ya when Massa Hiram can bring us. Take care o yoself chile."

Queen embraced the trembling girl, tears flowing freely down her cheeks. She kissed her on the forehead and left the cabin, nearly bowling over the returning Esther with her arms full of wooden molds. Cassie sat with her head in her hands, weeping silently. It had all happened so fast. One day she's in the kitchen laughing at Granny Aba and her stories of Africa. The next, she's caught up in this whirlwind and dropped into a land of black and brown robed strangers. Bernadette stood quietly for a moment, watching her. She placed a hand on Cassie's shoulder.

"It's all right to be scared and lonely and homesick for your family. I was when we were forced to leave our home in France. But then, after a while, I came to love my new home in England. I made new friends and learned a new language and I realized that life goes on. No matter what happens God is still there by your side, in your heart. His love and compassion will sustain you through all your troubles. He teaches you that happiness depends more on what is inside of you than what is outside of you.

" I hope that someday you will be reunited with your family and friends. However, until that day comes you must honor your mother's wishes and make the best of the situation. You have a great opportunity here that you would not have at Roselawn. You will be free to explore God's plan for you in this world. You'll be free to learn of his saving grace in a community of people who will love you and cherish you and teach you. Now come. Let's help Esther with the butter."

Esther was dipping yellow lumps from the churn and pressing them into a mold. Once filled, she turned the mold over and pressed down on the plunger, depositing a perfectly formed mound of butter. She looked up from her work at Cassie, giving her a small smile of reassurance. Cassie dabbed at the tears with her skirt.

"Maybe being in this place, in this house, won't be so bad after all," she thought.

For the first week she simply followed Bernadette and Esther around, helping them and learning the routine of the convent. The priory worship was based on a liturgical structure from the teachings of St. Benedict. It was a liturgy of rhythm, measure and discretion, not given to the austere practices of many orders but sufficient to the practical monastic requirements on the American frontier. It was as apt in the eighteenth century as in the sixth, when the revered saint wrote it. Benedict prescribed times for common prayer, meditative reading and manual labor. He also gave general guidelines for the structure and mission of the monastic movement, leaving the daily details to the prior or abbot.

The pealing of a bell woke everyone at five in the morning. Sleepy charges followed their nuns to the chapel for "lauds", or morning prayer, presided over by the prior or one of the brothers. Following a song, the reading of psalms and prayers of intercession, everyone scattered to their daily chores. Cassie and Esther would follow Bernadette back to their small cabin for a quick breakfast of porridge or biscuits and molasses with fried pork, then off to their work; collecting eggs, working in the garden, milking, cleaning, washing and tending the animals.

Throughout the day everyone paused in their labor at regular intervals to offer up prayers and praise to God. Cassie watched as Bernadette, kneeling among the tender shoots of early spring, prayed for her and Esther and all the souls at St. Benedict's. After supper everyone gathered again in the chapel for "vespers", with hymns, psalms and readings. Finally, when all light failed and all work was put away, there came the night prayer, the last prayer of the day, a time for reflecting on the day and examining one's conscience before retiring.

Cassie found the routine calming. The structure and formality of the services were a radical departure from the shouting and singing she was used to on Sundays in the slave cabins. This worship was hushed and reverent and reassuring. She began to think of herself as a special being created by God for a higher purpose. She marveled at the sacrifice of these holy people. They had given up their lives of relative comfort in England to come here and bring their God to this wilderness.

She had never been in a real church before. The beauty of the rustic chapel, its ornamentation and the colorful vestments had a calming effect each time she entered. Her workload, while tiring, was lighter than at Roselawn, and with the church services to look forward to she thrived. Each passing day her step became livelier and her smile broader. Bernadette observed as Cassie blossomed into a happy, confident young woman, a radiant butterfly emerging from its cocoon to take wing among the splendors of the island. She was a joy to teach and an apt pupil. Within a few months her grasp of English and simple arithmetic was amazing. She was able to read and write better than the girls who had been there for a much longer time.

The seasons passed fleetingly. Queen and Aba came occasionally to fill her with tales from Roselawn. Sulu had died and Uncle Mose was fading away from loneliness for her. Ka'le and Kimba spent more and more of the year on Ossabaw with Master Enoch. There were ten new cabins down by the water and Master John had rented another five hundred acres on Ossabaw. The demand for rice and indigo continued to grow and the plantation prospered along with it, but Master John's health was failing. He and Miss Elizabeth spent long periods at the Savannah house. The running of Roselawn fell to Hiram and Amanda. With each visit Cassie felt more secure at St. Benedict's and less homesick for her birthplace.

Bernadette sat in the corner of the new convent workshop, a mound of cotton at her feet. Afternoon showers had driven them inside where she and the girls carded cotton, separating the fiber from the seeds. Later she would spin it into yarn. Now the fading sun filtered through the windows. Lint drifted upwards on the shafts of light. She was startled by the question.

"Sister, can I become a nun?"

Bernadette continued to stare at the cotton, trying to conceal her startled look. She closed her eyes and prayed silently to God for guidance. Slowly she raised her head and looked at the girl.

"I don't know Cassie. It's a question that never arose before. Someone much higher in authority must answer your question. I will have to talk to the Mother Superior and Father Titus. They understand the ways of the church much better than I do."

CHAPTER SIX

ALMOST A YEAR HAD passed since father Titus sent Cassie's appeal to Charlestown. The bishop there had forwarded it to Canterbury. Dispatches between the colonies and England were frequently lost as packet ships fell prey to privateers and other fortunes of war.

In April 1775, Colonial partisans in Concord and Lexington, Massachusetts routed the British army as it tried to seize their stores of munitions. The colonial rabble then laid siege to Boston. New York was isolated and under martial law. The second Continental Congress, meeting in Philadelphia, chose George Washington to lead the revolutionary army.

On July 4th, 1775 a Provisional Congress met at Tondee's Tavern in Savannah to elect representatives to the Continental Congress. A Council of Safety was formed to govern the colony and Governor Wright was placed under house arrest. He escaped during a British naval bombardment and fled back to England. Most of the Tory plantation owners sought sanctuary in the city. Noble Jones and John Penrose retreated to their town houses where both were ill with yellow fever that torrid summer. Their sons, Wimberley Jones and Hiram Penrose would be swept up in the colony's epic struggle to throw off the yoke of King George.

In the midst of this turmoil and its conflicting loyalties, St. Benedict's went about the Lord's business. In late 1775, a letter from the office of the archbishop made its way down the coast from Charlestown.

Father Titus,

The Church in general and the Order of St. Benedict in particular have made no determinations on the advisability of allowing the ordination of Negro nuns. In the absence of such a ruling you are advised to follow the dictates of your conscience and the exigencies of your environment in such matters. The Church shall hold you blameless should future canon law conflict with your decision.

The Church of England
Ecclesiatical Council
Canterbury

On January 1ˢᵗ, 1777, Cassie Omoru began her novitiate training to become a Sister of the Order of St. Benedict.

****

Enoch stared out across the cresting whitecaps on Ossabaw Sound. He could barely make out the inlet at Hell's Gate, where the currents of the Ogeechee and Vernon rivers swirled around Racoon Key before running headlong into the surging Atlantic tide. Those battling currents and shifting sands had created a watery grave for many sailors attempting to negotiate the treacherous passage. But Enoch's gaze was fixed beyond Racoon Key. He saw the strip of land beyond, where Delegal and Adams Creeks merged to join the turbulence. She was there, somewhere on that island. What was she doing? He could see her with the nuns and the priests, singing, praying. Did she ever think of him? Were her only memories of him there in the root cellar, standing over her, threatening? For months he prayed to God for release from her. He tried to purge all thoughts of her from his mind. It was futile. The harder he tried the more obsessed he became. He threw himself into his work on the plantation, driving himself, the overseers and the slaves to the brink of exhaustion. Still she was there. In his dreams, in every waking moment, her image seared into his brain, taunting him, refusing to give him peace.

A small boat appeared on the horizon, breaking his concentration and pulling him back to the present. It was Ka'le returning from an errand to Roselawn. The sweating and exhausted man climbed wearily onto the dock. He was trembling.

" Massa Enoch, Massa Hiram say ya gots tuh come home rat now. Ya Pa, he daid from da fever. Da undertaker, he jes brung him back from Savannah. Miss Elizabeth say she gone bury him tomorrow in the cemetery hind da house, nex' tuh Miss Emily and Massa Adam. Dey ain't much light left but we mights git tuh da Wormslow landing by dark. Somebody dere'll fetch us over to Roselawn."

The flaming pitch pot on the dock sputtered as the same steady rain that had pelted the boat and its two soaked passengers in their passage from Ossabaw continued. The men sat back, their arms aching, their paddles across their knees, allowing the small vessel to drift the last few feet to the dock. Enoch turned to look across the narrows to Skidaway. He didn't expect to see her but he knew she was there, somewhere beyond the tree line. Knowing that somehow gave him comfort. Wearily, he hoisted himself onto the pier and followed Ka'le as they plodded up the path to Wormslow.

It was past ten by the time they made out the torches lighting the front porch at Roselawn. Several shiny black carriages were aligned under the large oaks beside the house, their staves drooping in the tall grass. Their teams were picketed nearby where they noisily chomped on the corn in their feedbags. The ornate hearse that brought John Penrose back to Roselawn for the last time, stood near the front walk, just off the veranda. It was palled in black. Tomorrow it would carry him down the lane behind the house to his final resting place; beneath the crepe myrtles he had planted to shade the graves of his young children.

Through the parlor windows black clad figures milled about as if choreographed for some macabre dance. Small groups clustered together in muted conversation. One by one they would break away to pause at the open casket, solitary, head bowed. Some were saying good-bye to an old friend. Others were paying tribute to a kind benefactor.

Each had his own story to tell about the man lying there in the peace of death.

Across the hallway the wives huddled around the widow, offering comfort, knowing it would do little to diminish her grief but needing to make the effort. Awkward phrases, offered to heal, sounded empty and inadequate.

Conversations hushed as Enoch entered the room. Hiram, standing nearest the casket and facing the door, saw his brother enter. He went to him and embraced him, dismissing for the moment their differences. This was a time to bind up and heal, not to break open old wounds. There were tears in Hiram's eyes. Enoch's were dry. Only one brother bridged the chasm between them. Hiram took no notice, concerned only that Enoch was safely home and that their mother's grief would be the less for it.

The last rig disappeared down the long drive, the horse's hooves echoing off the bridge as they headed back to Savannah. A few friends and relatives lingered behind. They trickled back into the house, joining the family in the parlor and dining room.

As was the custom at all southern funerals the neighbors responded with heaping dishes of fried chicken, vegetables, pies and cakes. No one found it strange that, at such a time when food was far from the mind, it should be provided in such abundance. It was tradition. It was expected. Enoch poked absentmindedly at the drumstick on his plate, watching Hiram and Rebecca as they received condolences from the stragglers. When the last guest had departed and only the family and servants remained, Enoch spoke.

"Hiram, what will happen to Roselawn and Ossabaw now that Pa is gone?"

Hiram raised his gaze to meet Enoch's. He saw no grief there, no remorse, no hint that the man had just buried his father. They had spoken only briefly since his arrival last night. Enoch had made the obligatory responses to the mourners then excused himself to bathe and get some rest. He said he was exhausted from the long row over from Ossabaw.

When he arose the next morning he spent most of the time with his mother, in her room. For the first time since his return Hiram began to take stock of his brother. What he saw was jarring. The man he saw was cold and unfeeling. He had grown hard on Ossabaw. His father had just been lowered into his grave and he only wanted to discuss what would happen to the estate. Hiram realized for the first time since Enoch went to Ossabaw that he no longer knew him. The troubled man who had been sent away to straighten out his life had been transformed into someone he didn't know. The steel-gray eyes that met his were those of a stranger.

"Mr. Sheftall will be here on Monday to read father's will," he answered, icily. "Out of respect for Mama and for Pa's memory there'll be no discussion of the estate until then. It's not appropriate. Now is the time to grieve and to comfort, the rest will wait."

---------------------------------- CHAPTER SEVEN ----------------------------------

THE LATE SEPTEMBER HURRICANE of 1778 destroyed more than half of Saint-Domingue's sugar cane crop. Phillipe Charpentier and his fellow planters could no longer afford the upkeep for their large numbers of slaves. The planter's reserves would be exhausted long before the next crop could be harvested. The *petite blancs* and mulattoes in Port au Prince and Cap Haitien were already feeling the pinch from shrinking plantation budgets.

"Phillipe, what will you do?"

Jacques Patin asked the question of his host as he dipped the tip of his Cuban cigar into the glass of vintage cognac. He and three other neighboring planters were relaxing after dinner on the veranda of Chateau Papillon. The imposing mansion rose from a promontory overlooking the *Bahia de Manzanilla*, outside Cap Haitien. The towering waves crashing onto the rocks below fractured the pale yellow reflections of the rising moon.

"It's no secret that I can't sustain 1,000 slaves. And there's no market for them on the island after the hurricane."

He paused for a brief moment, contemplating the watery scene below.

"I have learned from my brother in Paris that the fleet is preparing a new campaign in the Caribbean. They are working furiously to expand the army. King Louis must be running low on rum and cigars." he chuckled. "I have contacted the commander of the Legion de Saint-Domingue in Port au Prince. He has received orders to increase the Legion by 2,000 men in preparation for the campaign and has been authorized to pay up to fifty francs for each qualified recruit. I have promised him two hundred men. Those ten thousand francs will tide me over until the new crop is in. I suggest you contact him also if you are in similar circumstances."

"That's great news, Phillipe," said Pierre Aumont, the largest planter in northern Saint-Domingue. His fields, located in a lush river valley to the south, were still under water, his cane destroyed by the tornadic winds.

"I will drive down to Port au Prince tomorrow. Do any of you men want to accompany me?"

All three eagerly agreed to go.

The next day Phillipe Charpentier summoned his eight overseers to review their crop reports and to tell them of his decision to sell the slaves. Each was to select twenty-five men between the ages of fifteen and twenty-five and to bring them to the plantation headquarters by noon on Friday. The slaves were to be told only that they were needed for cleanup work at the main house. Charpentier wanted to avoid any trouble with their families. They would be told, after the men were safely off the plantation property, that their sons and husbands were going to serve in the king's army and that they would return as free men after their period of service was completed.

Denis Bernard smiled broadly as he drove his carriage the five miles back to his house. This was his chance to get rid of that troublemaking slave that was making his life miserable.

Andre Dupre was born on the island of Grenada. He arrived in Cap Haitien two years previously aboard a French merchant ship. He was sixteen. The captain had paid the spice merchant for the remaining years of his servitude. He bought him to replace the cabin boy that had been killed in the port of St.George. He was unaware Andre had been put up for sale because of his disruptive behavior. Repeated beatings by the merchant had failed to blunt the young man's rebelliousness. The captain too, soon discovered his mistake and off-loaded his problem to a slave trader in Cap Haitien. He soon became Denis Bernard's problem.

Years earlier, Andre's father, Etienne Dupre, with several other men from the small fishing village of Marigot, Saint-Domingue, was driven out to sea during a hurricane. The starving sailors were rescued by a passing Spanish warship and impressed into service for the Royal Navy. He would never see his beloved homeland again. He won his freedom after serving in the Spanish navy for six long years. He was put ashore in St. George, Grenada. With his meager savings he settled down in St. George and opened a small grocery in the black ghetto section. With hard work and perseverance Etienne Dupre eked out a modest living.

France took Grenada from the Spanish in 1672 and Etienne's abilities in both languages allowed him to bridge between the two cultures. He married Marie, a Spanish girl, who bore him six children. He sent his oldest son, Andre, to a small Catholic school run by French nuns on the island. He was preparing him to take over the business one day. It was not to be.

Constant conflicts with the British laid waste to the economy of Grenada and devastated most of the small, struggling shopkeepers. Etienne eventually was forced to sell his sons into indentured servitude to the more prosperous merchants just to keep his business afloat. Andre, the most highly educated, was placed with a French exporter of spices. Andre's native intelligence and six years of schooling made him an apt apprentice for the aging merchant. Nevertheless his seething resentment at the loss of his freedom made Andre rebellious and difficult to manage.

Now a French man-o-war lay at anchor in the bay, unable to dock at the quay because of its draft. The commander of the legion in Port-au-Prince had decided he couldn't risk marching this sullen group one hundred miles overland to the garrison. Andre and four others from Papillon were on the last longboat ferry to the ship, still unaware of their destination. One rampant rumor had them being transported back to Africa, although no reasonable explanation for that was offered. Another was that they were being sold to a plantation on the island of Martinique to clear hurricane damage there. No one was sure where they were going until they were marched into the fort at Port au Prince. There they found several hundred others already bivouacked on the sprawling parade ground.

"You have been selected to serve His Majesty, King Louis. He is giving you your freedom in exchange for six years of military service. If you perform well and cause no trouble you will be discharged as free men. You will train here for the next few weeks. Following that you will be deployed with the army as determined by orders from the French Admiralty. Your unit will be known as *Chasseurs Volontaires de Saint-Domingue*. Those of you who don't want to "volunteer" to serve His Majesty or commit acts of rebellion will be sold to slave traders."

The garrison commander spoke from atop a reviewing platform some fifteen feet above the compound. French soldiers strolled the parapets, rifles at the ready, poised to quell any disturbance from the milling slaves.

"Andre, what does this mean? " asked Louis Dufour. "What will they do with us?"

"Don't worry, Louis. I heard the army is sending most of the white French soldiers on an expedition. They will probably keep us here to protect Saint-Domingue."

The following morning the new conscripts were organized into hundred man units and assigned a French drill commander. They were issued private's uniforms and each given a replica rifle. Discipline and order were drilled into them for the next several weeks. Those determined to be loyal and reliable moved on to advanced training with real guns. They learned to load and fire the long rifles. They also were taught how to fix a bayonet and to use it in hand-to-hand combat. Each day the rifles were collected, carefully counted, and returned to the armory. There was no need to tempt fate.

On August twelfth, ten weeks to the day following Andre Dupre's arrival in Port au Prince, he was back aboard a warship heading out of the harbor. The French frigate *Fendant* had boarded the five hundred and fifty soldiers of the *Volontaires de Saint-Domingue* brigade and was rejoining the rest of the fleet at Saint Nicholas, a harbor on the most northwesterly point of the country.

"Well, Andre. This seems a strange way for us to protect Saint-

Domingue," Louis said with a chuckle. "What's your latest information on where we're going?"

"Captain de Vaudreuil hasn't confided in me yet. I'm sure I'll be called to his stateroom any minute now."

Andre smiled in mock annoyance as he cuffed his young friend on the ear.

CHAPTER EIGHT

A year passed. Cassie struggled to fulfill her vows. She despaired of making it through the five years of training required to become a nun. She attended daily classes under the supervision of Sister Bernadette and the Mother Superior. Some of the nuns with training in other subjects offered their support. In between her classes and her chores she stole every free moment to study the written guides describing the role of the nuns in the Order of St. Benedict. Most of the documents she was given had survived the journey from France to England and on to Georgia. They were written in French. Sister Bernadette determined that the path of least resistance was to teach Cassie to speak and read French. That seemed much easier than trying to translate all the documents into English. Every evening, following vespers, the sounds of French conjugations floated on the night air above the convent. Cassie's transition from the Geechee dialect to formal French was arduous, but she was determined to master this strange but beautiful language. Her mouth ached from trying to form the French words, but she soldiered on. She vowed to complete her training for the sisterhood of St. Benedict, no matter the cost.

*****

Hiram recognized the graying, stooped Negro man dressed in black and white livery. Old Thomas was Wimberley Jones' footman and his father Noble's before him. He was treated as one of the family. Crippled with arthritis, he walked with a pronounced shuffle. Despite his infirmities he insisted on continuing to serve the Jones family. Hiram walked down the steps to meet the carriage as it pulled into the driveway.

"How are you, Thomas? I hope nothing's wrong at Wormslow?"

"Nawsuh, Massa Hiram. Everbody's jes fine. Massa Wimberley, he sent me over here wit dis letter fo ya. He axed me to wait fo yo answer."

"Step around to the kitchen and Aba will give you something to drink. I'll be back out in a minute."

Hiram opened the envelope and began to read:

"My esteemed friend Hiram Penrose,

I take pen in hand to inform you that the recent unpleasantness between Mr. Lachlan McIntosh and Mr. Button Gwinnet has spiraled out of control. As you are aware, General Washington named Lachlan McIntosh to be Colonel of Georgia's Continental Battalion. Now, Mr. Gwinnett, as Commander-in-Chief of the Committee of Safety, is disputing Lachlan's authority over the Georgia militia and has openly condemned him. He blames him for the failure of the recent military expedition that Mr. Gwinnett ordered against the Spanish in Florida and has brought trumped up charges of treason against his brother, George McIntosh.

Well, you know Lachlan and his Scottish temper. He rose before the assembly and denounced Mr. Gwinnett in the strongest of terms. Now Mr. Gwinnett has demanded an apology or satisfaction. On May 16, instant, at sunrise in Sir James Wright's pasture, the two will duel with pistols. Lachlan has asked you and me to stand for him.

Please respond this instant whether you will honor his request.

Your obedient servant,

Wimberley Jones

Button Gwinnett was revered in the colonies. His was one of the three signatures from Georgia on the Declaration of Independence. His death in a duel would stir the passions of the community.

On the other hand, Lachlan McIntosh was a hero of the revolution, serving in the Georgia militia and with the continental army. His father had died a short time after being captured in a battle at New Inverness and spent two years in the Spanish prison at St. Augustine. Lachlan was sent to Bethesda to live with George Whitefield. There was no outcome to this argument that would not cause trouble in Savannah. Hiram handed the envelope to Thomas and helped the old man climb back into the buggy.

"Bad business this dueling, Thomas. These are both good men and both loyal to the cause of the revolution. I don't know why they can't just put aside their personal grievances and concentrate on fighting old King George instead. It seems when honor is at stake men lose sight of what's really worth fighting for. God help them both, but I must support Lachlan. He was one of my father's oldest friends. He came over with him on the "*Ann*".

"Take this note to Mr. Jones and tell him I will be by Wormslow the afternoon of the fifteenth. We'll need to spend the night in town since the duel is at sunrise."

Hiram and Wimberley rose well before dawn. They nibbled at their breakfasts downstairs in Mrs. Wilkes's boarding house. The black coffee jolted them awake but they had no appetite for the food. Mists still encircled the towering pines when they arrived at Sir James's pasture. Other members of the parties drifted in. They milled about anxiously, filled with anticipation and dread.

"Gentlemen, step forward," barked the judge selected to referee the event. He opened an ornately decorated, velvet-lined, wooden case.

"I have here a pair of single-shot dueling pistols. As the challenged party, Mr. McIntosh will select the first pistol."

The adversaries stepped forward. Lachlan McIntosh hefted both pistols. He held them at arms length, looking down the barrel of each, before selecting one. He handed the other to Button Gwinnett. The two men glared at each other. The judge explained the rules.

"Gentlemen, you will line up, back-to-back at the ribbon I have placed on the ground. I will give the order for you to cock your pistols. I will say ready and then count to twelve. You will pace twelve steps to the count. At the count of twelve you will turn and fire. As agreed, satisfaction will be had with first blood. If no blood is drawn each man shall withdraw from the field with honor intact. Seconds, leave the field. Sirs, are you ready?"

The two shots rang out simultaneously. The reports reverberated through the trees. Both men crumpled to the ground. Their seconds rushed to their aid. McIntosh's ball struck Gwinnett in the hip shattering the underlying bones. He was bleeding profusely. Gwinnett's shot struck McIntosh in the leg, the ball barely missing the bone and major arteries. Dr. Minis treated both men in the field then rushed them into town for further medical treatment.

"The news is not good Hiram," Wimberley Jones cautioned his friend. He had just returned from town. It was four days since the duel.

"Button Gwinnett is dead. Thankfully, Lachlan will recover from his wound. However, there are those among Gwinnett's friends who seek vengeance. They have brought charges of murder against Lachlan. This is not good for the cause. The duel itself has divided the community and now the trial will further polarize the two camps. I can't imagine a jury convicting Lachlan of murder since Mr. Gwinnett was the challenger. But, just holding a trial will serve to further inflame the partisans on each side."

"What can we do, Wimberley?" Hiram asked. "I agree with you that an impartial jury will acquit Lachlan but if he stays here the wounds will just continue to fester. And, his going back down the coast to Darien won't solve anything. That's too close."

"I agree with you. I met with some of the other men at Tondee's last night. We're going to send a letter to Henry Laurens in Philadelphia. We want him, as good friend and mentor to Lachlan, and as President of the Continental Congress, to intercede with General Washington. We're asking that Lachlan be reassigned to the General's staff until this all blows over."

Six months later, with the "not guilty" verdict still echoing through the streets of Savannah, Lieutenant General Lachlan McIntosh saddled his horse and set out for Valley Forge, Pennsylvania. He would spend that cruel winter of 1778 with Washington's troops.

 CHAPTER NINE

Bernadette had been summoned to the prior's office and was alarmed to find Mother Superior Marie Michel there as well. She mentally sorted through her activities of the last few days trying to figure out what she might have done to provoke a summons. Sister Marie saw the concern etched on Bernadette's face.

"Don't worry my dear, you're not in any trouble. Father Titus and I just need to talk to you about a matter of church doctrine. Take a seat, dear, and Father will explain."

Bernadette settled slowly into the chair next to Sister Marie, casting her eyes from one to the other.

"Sister Bernadette," the prior began, "we've received a letter from the bishop's office in Charlestown. He recently heard from the Council of Bishops at Canterbury where several matters of urgent concern were discussed. One of these, I regret to say, was occasioned by our petition concerning the ordination of Negro nuns. Unfortunately the majority of the conclave felt that there was too much controversy attached to the matter at this time. The two main concerns expressed were the current unpleasantness between the colonies and England and its effect on the Church. The other has to do with the ongoing slave trade and its divisive nature. Both concerns have led the council to decide that any ordination of Negro nuns must be denied for the present."

Bernadette's shock was apparent. The blood drained from her face.

She felt the room begin to spin. She reached for the chair beside her. She felt her grasp slipping.

Sister Marie was holding a cloth to her head. She tried to rise but was gently forced back.

"It's all right Bernadette. Just stay still for a minute. Here, take a sip of water."

The Mother Superior was on her knees cradling the head of her charge. Bernadette struggled to understand what was happening. Why was she on the floor? Why was the Mother Superior here? Why was she in the prior's office? Slowly, the shock bore through to her consciousness. It was true then. It was no dream. Father Titus really did say that Cassie could not become a nun. What can I tell her? How can I explain to her that all the work we have done is for nothing? It will break her heart. This is not fair. How can a bunch of old men in robes, sitting around a table three thousand miles away know what's in the heart of this girl? Why can't they see that she would be the best witness to these thousands of poor souls with no hope. One of their own? When she was seated again and had regained her composure she faced the prior.

"Father, does this mean that Cassie can never become a nun?"

"I don't know. The council hinted that they might reopen the discussion once this unpleasantness is concluded. The question is, will that be too late for Cassie. This decision took several years. Who knows how many more years it will take to reconsider it, and whether it will be favorable if they do. I'm afraid we can't raise unreasonable expectations in the child. Its better that we tell her the truth and then help her to understand it as best we can. Perhaps we can find a way for her and others like her to serve in some religious capacity without being fully ordained. Let me ponder it for a while."

Bernadette walked slowly back to her cabin, dreading the conversation that would follow.

****

"Cassie I need to talk with you. Please come and walk with me."

Sister Bernadette seemed extremely agitated. They walked quietly along the bluff above the river, Bernadette gathering her thoughts, trying to determine how best to approach the subject with Cassie. How could she break the news in a way that would not destroy the girl's spirit?

Below them several marsh birds scampered over the shell midden built long ago by some forgotten tribe. How ironic that this circular mound of seashells, a religious relic of an ancient culture, lay side-by-side with the priory. In the mists of history did some reluctant tribal chieftain stand here to explain a difficult decision to a temple maiden? Had things really changed that much over the centuries? Had our civilization advanced beyond the simplicity of those savages or did the dictates of some shaman far removed from this place change the course of their lives as well? She led the way down a sandy path into the midden, motioning for Cassie to sit.

"Cassie, I was called to see Father Titus today. He and Mother Marie have heard from the church leaders in England concerning the ordination of Negro nuns. I'm afraid, for the present time anyway, that it is not good news. The elders have said that it will not be allowed. They didn't close the door altogether, saying the subject may be raised again in the future, but we don't think it wise to place our faith in that. Instead, Father Titus is seeking to find another way that you can serve God and the church. I'm not sure what that will be but in the meantime I'd like for you to carry on with your studies so that whatever it is, you will be prepared for it. I know this is extremely disappointing to you, as it is to me. But as I've tried to teach you, and as you have seen in your own life, God does not always act in ways we would wish. His ways are not our ways. However, his ways are always the best."

Cassie sat very still for a long moment in the fading light, staring out across the spartina grass as the wind whipped it back and forth in great waves. When she was ready she faced her mentor and friend. She spoke in a voice choked with emotion.

"Sister, I always knew there was a chance that it wouldn't happen. But I told myself that I would prepare to be a nun and if it didn't work out I would find another way to serve God. I knew that what I was learning would make me a better person and would prepare me to help my people. That hasn't changed, and if you'll continue to teach me I will find a way to do that."

Bernadette sat down on the shell mound beside Cassie and put her arm around her. They sat there in silence as the first stars began to populate the eastern night sky. A crescent moon was rising over Wassaw. Off to the north, Cassieopeia kept watch over her heavenly family while she looked down on her young namesake.

"Cassie, you are one of the strongest and bravest people I have ever known, and whatever God has in store for you, I know you will find it. You will do great things in his name. Whether it be as a nun or in some other way, your spirit will prevail. Now let's go in before the bell rings for vespers. We have much to pray about tonight."

****

In the distance, across the salt marshes extending from Tybee Island to the Wassaw narrows, a fleet of warships lay at anchor. The loss of Savannah to the militia rabble in Georgia rankled the English. Now, General Henry Clinton, commander of the English forces in America, was sending Lt. Col. Archibald Campbell with a force of 3,500 men from New York to retake the city. The stalemate in the north could be overcome if the southern colonies were brought back into the fold. Thousands of loyal Tories would welcome the King back with open arms. Opening a southern front would occupy much of the American army, giving Clinton time to reinforce his northern garrisons and take the fight to Washington.

The British fleet arrived at the mouth of the Savannah River on December 23, 1778. It was soon joined by additional troops brought up from the south, under General Augustine Prevost. As the senior officer, Prevost took command of the expedition.

By New Year's Day, 1779, the union jack flew once more over Yamacraw Bluff, high above the Savannah waterfront. General Robert Howe's garrison of less than a thousand troops was no match for the overwhelming English force. With eighty-five of his men dead and 450 captured, Howe fled to Charlestown and the protection of General Benjamin Lincoln.

When news of the fall of Savannah reached Washington he was devastated. All his gains in the north were being undercut by English successes in the south. It appeared that the British "southern strategy" was working. Not one to wallow in pity, Washington quickly devised a plan to counterattack. He sent for General Lachlan McIntosh, pulling him from his command at Fort Pitt on the Indian frontier and ordering him back to Georgia to join forces with General Benjamin Lincoln. On March 5, 1779 McIntosh bid goodbye to his troops on the western frontier and began retracing his steps to Augusta, Georgia where he would once again take command of the Georgia Continentals.

Washington also called on Count Casamir Pulaski, another of his favorites, to support the campaign to retake Savannah. He was deeply indebted to General Pulaski for his work at Valley Forge during the brutal winter of 1778. Pulaski, a Polish citizen, brought all the experience gained from his European campaigns to bear and created a magnificent cavalry troop from the ragtag horse soldiers he inherited. His graduates proved decisive in many later battles. Now, Washington needed Pulaski to help stem the tide in the South. The count led his legion toward Savannah. An ornate red and gold banner fluttered atop the guidon's staff. It bore a circle of 13 gold stars surrounding a Masonic eye. It was sewn by the Moravian Sisters of Valley Forge, in gratitude for his service to America.

On May 4, 1778 Benjamin Franklin's diplomatic perseverance as commissioner to France finally paid dividends. Deteriorating relations between France and England convinced the government of King Louis XVI to sign a Treaty of Alliance with the United States of North America. On July 10, 1778 France declared war on England, bringing the French into the American Revolution on the side of America.

The entry of France into the war gave Washington options not previously available. He immediately contacted Henry Laurens and General Lincoln and the French legation in Charlestown, South Carolina. They were instructed to send an urgent appeal to the French Admiral, Count Charles-Henri Theodat d'Estaing to return and join in an effort to wrest Savannah from the British. Admiral d'Estaing was concluding a wildly successful campaign in the Caribbean where he took the islands of Grenada and St. Vincent from the English. His flagship lay at anchor in the harbor of St. George, Grenada when the dispatch from General Lincoln arrived.

d'Estaing's campaign to drive the British from the Caribbean followed on the heels of his embarrassing failure to destroy their fleet at Newport, Rhode Island earlier that summer. When he took his ships out to engage the British under Admiral Howe, both fleets were scattered by a raging tropical storm. The flagship *Languedoc* lost its mainmast and d'Estaing retreated to Boston harbor for repairs. He was accused of treason for abandoning the American force that was marching on the British garrison at Newport. General Sullivan, the American commander, leveled charges of cowardice against him. Ironically, the commander of one of Sullivan's regiments was d'Estaing's young countryman the Marquise de Lafayette. Open clashes erupted between the French and the Americans in Boston, resulting in the death of one French sailor. On November 1, 1778, in an effort to defuse the situation, d'Estaing left for the Caribbean.

Following his victories there he saw this invitation to rescue Savannah as a golden opportunity to redeem his honor with the Americans, and with the French court. The fleet weighed anchor on August 16, 1779, setting sail for Georgia.

****

Two soldiers lazed on the fantail of their ship as the fleet departed St. George. They were saying good-bye to their birthplace for the last time. Both had been sold to ship's captains in Grenada, and later wound up on the slave market in Saint-Domingue. Both were conscripted into the French army following the great hurricane.

"Henri, do you think you'll ever return to Grenada?" Andre Dupre asked the young boy.

"I don't think so, Andre. Last night, I was standing near an open hatch, having a smoke. I overheard two of the officers talking down below. They said we're going to a place called Savannah, in America, to fight against the English. Some day I will return to Saint-Domingue to fight for the freedom of my people. No man should be the property of another man. The English, French, Spanish and Portuguese all own Black slaves. My people were free in Africa. I want to see them free again." Young Henri Christophe picked up the small drum lying on the deck beside him and went below.

*****

Elizabeth Penrose took to her deathbed on July 22, 1779. She was sixty-six years old. She had returned to Roselawn to bury her husband four years earlier and had remained there. She didn't share John Penrose's Tory sympathies but she remained obedient and kept her opinions to herself. Now she just wanted to be near her family and to see her grandchildren grow up.

Hiram sent for Dr. Minis. His mother was dying. As much as he hated the idea, he could not deny her seeing Enoch one last time. Through all the years he had shielded her from as much of Enoch's troubling behavior as possible. The resentment he felt toward his brother had grown in the years since his father's funeral. On the few occasions when Enoch came back to Roselawn following their father's death, the gulf between them had widened. The animal wildness in his brother's eyes was still there. Reports of his cruelty continued. Fatefully, that day presented the final episode that would drive Hiram to action.

Ka'le had sent his youngest son, Isaac, to tell Hiram of Enoch's latest atrocity, thereby risking his own and his son's life in the process. If Enoch found out what Ka'le had done he would have killed him --- and Isaac.

Isaac told Hiram of Enoch's fit of rage. They were in the pine forest catfacing trees to draw out the resin. Uncle Kimba's son Toby didn't move fast enough to please Enoch, so he picked up one of the curved knives used to scar the trees and threw it at him. The tool struck the boy in the right leg, opening a deep wound in his thigh. He lay on the ground writhing in pain, blood gushing from the cut.

"Massa Hiram he was gonna bleed ta death iffen we didn't stop it. Massa Enoch snatched da rope outen my hand and hit me wit it. Den my daddy say, 'Massa Enoch, we gotta stop dat bleedin' or he gone die.' Well, Massa Enoch, he took a turpentine cup off a tree and set fire to it. He say, 'I'll show you how to stop the bleeding.' Massa, he took dat cup full of burning turpentine and he poured it on dat boy's leg. I ain't never seen no human bein' in sech misry in my life. He done passed out wit de pain. I could smell his flesh aburnin'. Then, Massa Enoch, he say, 'Well, I guess that ought to stop it. Now, get this sorry nigger back to the house and get Dr. Buzzard to look at him. I expect to see him back out in the woods in two days. I can't have nobody around here that don't earn his keep.' Wit dat he got on his horse and rode away. Toby, he got gangrene in dat leg and he died in three days. He won't hurtin' nobody Massa. Uncle Kimba done gone crazy. Daddy had to tie him down to keep him from going up to da main house and killing Massa Enoch. Daddy say if you don' do sumpin' all hell's gone break loose on Ossabaw."

Hiram turned away from Isaac, anger rising like a great gorge in his throat.

"Why, Enoch? Oh why?" he muttered. "What drives you to such evil?"

"Isaac, you stay here at Roselawn tonight. I'll go back with you to Ossabaw tomorrow."

****

Hiram's unannounced arrival stunned Enoch. Unaware of Ka'le's betrayal, he'd spent the evening deep in rum with the overseer, Jim Pelham, and Caleb Hawkins. He lay abed until noon. Haggard, bleary eyed and unshaven he stumbled onto the porch and slouched into a chair. His bullmastiff, Nero, crawled from under the porch emitting a low growl as Hiram approached.

Wild pigs were a scourge on Ossabaw. The feral hogs were descendants of domestic animals brought by the Spanish. When the Spaniards left or were wiped out by the natives, the pigs were left behind. Over the years they evolved into 300 pound predators with eight-inch tusks. They laid waste to the gardens and field crops and were a danger to the workers. Nero was Enoch's answer to the problem. The bullmastiff breed was developed in England to bring down bulls by clamping onto their noses and hanging on until the animal could no longer hold it's head up. The dogs could weigh as much as 150 pounds. Death usually resulted from loss of blood or suffocation.

Nero was a brindle colored brute with a black face and cold blue eyes. He was a one master animal and obeyed only Enoch's commands. Hiram suspected that Enoch found other, more sadistic ways to use Nero on the plantation. The big dog curled up at his master's feet, warily observing Hiram.

"Well, brother, to what do I owe the great pleasure of your visit?" Enoch greeted him, his voice dripping with sarcasm. "I thought you'd be too busy counting the money from Roselawn and Ossabaw to waste any time on your poor relations out here."

Hiram ignored Enoch's boozy mockery. He was shocked at how

dissipated his brother had become in the six months since his last visit. His eyes were sunken and the birthmark had intensified in color. His slight frame was more emaciated than ever. His clothes draped as if on a scarecrow.

"Enoch, I can't ignore your behavior any longer. The death of Kimba's boy is the last straw. In the name of all that's holy, how could you do that to a fellow human being? Just because he is a slave doesn't give you the right to abuse him. First there was Big Boy. Then Cassie. And who knows how many others I don't know about. Now it's Toby. You've gone too far this time. I've tried to protect Ma from all this, especially since Pa died. You know how frail she's been. But I can't do that anymore. You'll have to face her with all your warts exposed."

Enoch just stared back in sullen insolence.

"Why don't you go fuck yourself, Hiram. Ossabaw is mine and I'll treat these stinkin' niggers any way I want."

Hiram lunged up the steps to grab his brother by the throat. Nero rose to a menacing position, the throaty growl rising from deep within the trained killer's gut. Hiram stepped back. He composed himself and leveled a stare at Enoch.

"I'm going to ignore that for now, brother," as he spat out the last word with all the scorn he could muster. After today it won't matter. That's not the only reason I'm here.

"She's dying, Enoch. Your mother is dying. I don't want her to know what a monster you have become but she wants to see you and I can't deny her a dying wish. I haven't told her what you've done. How you make peace with that is up to you. All I know is that when she's gone you have to leave Roselawn. Pelham has to go too. And that piece of white trash that Pa ran off, Caleb Hawkins. I knew you'd hired him but I let it ride. I shouldn't have. He and Pelham both knew what you were doing and did nothing. Pack your belongings and get Pelham and Hawkins. We're leaving in fifteen minutes."

"You can't kick me off Ossabaw." Enoch stumbled, almost falling off the porch in his drunken haze. "Pa said in his will that I was to run things over here."

"Pa left both Roselawn and Ossabaw to me. He gave me the final say on what happens on both islands. I'm responsible for them and that makes me responsible for you and all the people here. You're my brother but you make me sick. I want you out of my sight. You and your cronies here can join the Tories in Savannah for all I care. You'll fit right in with Governor Wright's murderous crew. They've mistreated the good folk in town just as you have mistreated the folk on Ossabaw. There's blood on all your hands." Hiram rested his hand on the butt of his pistol to emphasize his command.

Elizabeth Penrose died on August 10, 1779. She was laid to rest in the small family plot, between her husband and her children. As soon as the mourners left, Enoch Penrose, James Pelham, and Caleb Hawkins walked across the causeway and through the gates of Roselawn, across the wooden bridge to the Isle of Hope. They were headed toward Savannah. Hiram gave Enoch ten pounds sterling.

"I never want to see the three of you on Roselawn again. Now that Ma's gone there's no reason for you to ever come back. I pray to God you'll come to terms with what you've done and repent of your sins. May He have mercy on your souls."

CHAPTER TEN

Major Anthony Phillips, adjutant to General Prevost, welcomed the three new recruits to His Majesty's Royal Army. The ranks of the regular army and the loyalist militia had been decimated by death and desertion. He welcomed any who would join to defend Savannah from the impending attack. It was only a matter of time until the Continentals tried to retake the city. Rumors of troop movements in South Carolina and upstate Georgia filtered in daily from their Tory spies. Prevost had asked General Clinton for permission to move the Highland Regiment under Colonel John Maitland down from Beaufort. Clinton denied the request saying they were needed to guard against a southern attack.

"Mr. Penrose, your father was a faithful subject to his King. I am glad to see you are upholding the family's honor. And what of your brother Hiram? Will he be joining us as well?" Phillips asked, knowing that Hiram was a Whig sympathizer.

"I'm afraid his loyalties lie elsewhere, Major. Only Mr. Pelham, Mr. Hawkins and I will be joining you," Enoch answered.

"Very well. The three of you report to the quartermaster on Broughton Street. He will supply you with uniforms and weapons, and he'll assign you to a billet. Come back here tomorrow morning and I'll have your military assignment. I understand that all of you honed your marksmanship skills on the game out on Ossabaw. I'll ask General Prevost about assigning you to the Delancey Regiment. He's lost several of his best shooters to desertion and the fever. He's been hounding me for weeks about replacements."

"Thank you, major. That sounds like a good spot for us. I've got a few scores to settle with some of those folks out there," Enoch said, with a sweep of his arm in the general direction of Roselawn. "Just put me where I can see them coming and I'll pick'em off. We'll see you in the morning," Enoch replied, with a tip of his hat.

The three outcasts crossed over from Bay Street to Broughton where they received their uniforms and rifles. The quartermaster assigned them to a makeshift log barracks on Bull Street, south of Johnson Square.

"Well Jim, I've come full circle," Enoch said as they walked past the square. "You see that house in through the trees back there? That was Pa's home before Roselawn. That's where he died. That's where I was born. I aim to get that property back, as well as the Ossabaw and the Roselawn properties. And, there's another thing that was taken away from me that I aim to get back. If Hiram thinks he's seen the last of me he's got another thought coming. We're gonna beat these Whigs and their sympathizers and when we do there'll be a day of reckoning in Georgia." His demonic eyes blazed with hatred.

****

The skies were threatening on that late August day. Charlestown had suffered through a particularly hot and rainy summer. The mood of the city was dark. Its citizens were anxious and irritable. Savannah and Augusta had fallen to the British just months before. A large contingent of Scottish Highlanders lurked just down the coast at Beaufort. The threat of an attack from the British fleet was an ever-present fear. The demands of an intractable and interminable war had stretched thin the civil fabric of the citizenry. Tempers were frayed.

Alarm bells rang in the distance from the fort on Sullivan's Island, across the harbor. Citizens of Charlestown rushed to Battery Point with their telescopes to determine the cause of the uproar. A line of ships, their sails half-rigged for entering the harbor, were crossing the bar, entering Charlestown Harbor. They were warships. Atop the palm log and sand barricades sleepy cannoneers could be seen scaling the ramparts to man their guns. Fear gripped the town.

Five ships emerged from the ocean mists, yet the fort's cannons remained silent. What were they waiting for? Then it became apparent. The pennants flying from the masts were not the Union Jack but the French Tricolor. Cheers rang out from the gathering crowd. One aging man dropped to his knees and bowed his head.

"Thank you, Lord. Our prayers have been answered."

Months before, General Benjamin Lincoln had dispatched a blockade-runner to find the French navy in the Caribbean. He urgently requested Admiral Count Henri d'Estaing to come to America's aid. The revolution in the South was not going well.

d'Estaing had fled Newport, Rhode Island late in 1778, licking his wounds from a failed encounter with the British fleet. He was roundly criticized for abandoning the American forces then attacking the British. Despite that, he went on to spectacular successes in his Caribbean campaign. He was reinvigorated by the triumphs and was anxious to redeem himself with the Americans; but more importantly, with his King.

The ships anchored in the narrows of the Cooper River, between Shutes Folly Island and Battery Point. Long boats were lowered to carry the French emissaries to meet with General Lincoln and to ferry supplies back to the ships.

"General Lincoln, it gives me great pleasure to report that Admiral d'Estaing has received your communication and will be awaiting your arrival in Savannah. He looks forward to a quick and complete victory over the British and to restoring Savannah and Georgia to its proper role as an American province."

Viscount Fontanges, Adjutant-General of d'Estaing's army, handed the formal response to General Lincoln.

"General, I welcome you on behalf of General Washington and all the American people. Your aid in our time of great need is deeply appreciated. Now, what can we do for you while you are here in Charlestown?"

"If you will be so kind, there are a few provisions I need before I sail to rejoin Admiral d'Estaing. Also, if you can provide a few small boats to help us ferry our men and armaments up the rivers to Savannah, it will greatly aid in our preparation for battle. If these can be arranged I plan to set sail with the ebb tide tomorrow. I look forward to rejoining you in Savannah where I am sure our combined forces will be more than a match for the English."

"We will be more than happy to supply what we can. The British blockade along the coast has prevented us from receiving many of the supplies we need. But whatever we have we will share with you. Now, I'd like for you and your officers to join the town fathers and me for supper this evening. In the meantime I will read the admirals letter and we can discuss plans for joining our forces in Savannah. Once more, let me say that we all owe you and your government our undying gratitude. With the fall of Savannah I believe the tide will turn in America's quest for freedom and her independence from Great Britain."

Over dinner that evening the two generals agreed that their two armies would meet on September 17th at de Estaing's headquarters. They would prepare a joint declaration to present to General Prevost demanding his surrender of the city.

CHAPTER ELEVEN

The plump, deep red tomatoes hung near the bottoms of the vines, where the intense summer sun had not scalded them. Cassie stooped to pick an especially large specimen. The summer growing season had been ideal, producing bumper crops in the gardens and fields of the abbey. The vegetable garden commanded a clear view of the Thunderbolt River. As she stood to place the prize tomato in the sweet grass basket she glanced toward the river. She froze, the basket suspended above the cart. She stared out across the water, transfixed. There, a column of war ships, their flanks bristling with cannon, sailed up the river. Red, white and blue pennants snapped in the wind atop the mainmasts. Flags of the same colors streamed from poles on the stern of each ship.

"Sister, sister, look, look!" she shouted.

There, under full sail, were more ships than she knew existed in all the world. They were enormous. They were making their way up the river toward Savannah

"Who are they sister? What are they doing here?"

Bernadette recognized the banners of her homeland.

"That is the French flag. Those are French warships. I can only imagine they are here to attack the English in Savannah. Come child, we must tell the prior."

On September 12, these same men-o-war had sailed up the Vernon

River past the southern tip of Skidaway Island. Its shallow depths had forced them to anchor near Racoon Key, well short of their destination, the small settlement at Beaulieu Plantation on a bluff overlooking Burnside Island. Philip Minis, leader of one of the prominent Jewish families in Savannah, had suggested Beaulieu as the best spot for the landing. It could accommodate the staging of a large number of troops and had ready access to Savannah. Colonel John Habersham went out to meet the flotilla and to assist in transferring the troops from the ships to the plantation. d'Estaing loaded fifteen hundred men of the expeditionary force into longboats and ferried them across the sound. Strong tides and squalls slowed their advance. They arrived at Beaulieu after darkness. The men in the first boats struggled up and down the shoreline. Their progress was marked by the sucking sound their boots made as they sank into the inky mud. They sought in vain for an easier path up the bluff. Finally, they resigned themselves to clambering up the fifteen-foot embankment with all their supplies and artillery. Soaked to the skin and shivering in the early evening chill, they hastily established their bivouac in the shadows of the plantation house. They improvised shelters from their coats and from canvas scavenged from the stores. The quartermaster had failed to load tents onto the boats. It would be morning before they could be brought over. At dawn, they emerged from their makeshift shelters. There, just a few hundred feet further upriver, was a dock and loading ramp.

Adding insult to the injury felt by having to sleep in the rain, the cooks arose to find that all their utensils were still on the ships. Large wash pots from the main house and the slave quarters were pressed into service to prepare the gruel they would have for breakfast. Each man had to fend for himself to find a cup, glass or other utensil to dip into the pot.

Andre Dupre cursed under his breath. Henri Christophe lay asleep at his feet, curled up around his blanket-draped drum, his greatcoat pulled over his head.

"Typical," he said, to no one in particular. "No one knows what's going on. All that slogging through the mud last night to drag those damned cannon up the bank when there was a loading ramp right there. Where is this God-forsaken place anyway?"

He slapped at the hordes of mosquitoes descending on the camp.

It was first light, their feeding time. His arms were covered with welts. Andre's platoon leader stood nearby, leaning against a longleaf pine.

"Some place called Buley," he said. "It's a rice plantation. I haven't seen any papers spelling it out but I'm told its about a dozen miles south of Savannah with a good road leading into town. We're supposed to meet up here with some of the Americans before moving on."

It was bitter irony that the plantation, established by French settlers, was named "*Beaulieu*," in honor of their home in France. The locals, unable to master the correct French pronunciation simply called it "Buley." The soldiers went off to battle, many of them to die, unaware that they had encamped on a faraway bit of home.

The weather turned bad. The remainder of the troops stayed on the ships in Ossabaw sound. They would not be able to come ashore for several days. By that time the first detachment would have moved north to meet the headquarters encampment.

Now Henri Comte d'Estaing stood on the bridge of *Languedoc*, leading the rest of his armada up the Thunderbolt River. He sailed past the mouths of the Skidaway and the Herb Rivers, the rice fields of Roselawn Plantation sliding by to port. The ship negotiated two sharp bends in the river as the small village of Thunderbolt came into view. Captain Boulainvillere signaled for the other ships to drop anchor under the bluff at Bonaventure Plantation. Levi Sheftall, another Jewish leader of the Savannah community, had arranged for d'Estaing to headquarter there. Tomorrow d'Estaing would offload his headquarters staff, soldiers with entrenching tools, armaments and other supplies.

Thunderbolt plantation belonged to Colonel John Mulryne. He had been instrumental in Governor Wright's escape to England during the 1776 capture of Savannah by the colonials. Mulryne and his family fled to Nassau in the Bahamas.

Andre, Louis and Henri along with others of the 1500 French soldiers camped at Beaulieu, spent almost every day scouring the area for provisions. Most of the locals spoke no French. These strange Negroes in unfamiliar uniforms were welcomed with pitchforks and muskets.

Twenty-four year old Vicomte Admiral Louis-Marie de Noailles, brother-in-law to the Marquis de Lafayette and son of Marie Antoinette's lady in waiting, Madame Etiquette, was in charge of the encampment. He knew that if he was to survive in this position he had to convince the farmers and plantation owners to provide him with livestock, grain and other foodstuffs for his troops. In desperation he turned to the headmaster at Bethesda, the nearby boy's home.

"Welcome to our home," Reverend Barkley said to the imposing military figure as he dismounted from his horse.

"I am Reverend Horace Barkley, headmaster of Bethesda. Won't you please come in?" He led the Admiral and his men into the home's modest parlor.

"Thank you, Reverend," Admiral de Noailles said.

"It is kind of you to receive me on such short notice. I understand the delicacy of your situation vis-à-vis the conflict between England and the colonies. I realize you must still turn to your benefactors in England for support. However, I also know you sympathize with the ideals of the revolution. It is in that vein that I come to seek your help."

"Go on, Admiral," Reverend Barkley said. "What is it that you think I can do for you?"

"Reverend, we have over 1500 men encamped at Buley. More will be coming ashore if this miserable weather ever lets up. We are running desperately low on provisions and our reception among the locals has been less than friendly. The troops we send out to secure provisions do not speak English, which makes it doubly difficult to communicate our needs to them. I was hoping that you might have someone here at the school who speaks French and might consider acting as our interpreter."

The Reverend Barkley stroked his beard. He tilted his head back in thought.

"It's too bad that Peter Tondee is not around. He was an orphan here at the school for several years after he came over from France. He owns a tavern in downtown Savannah. It is infamous as the gathering place for the Sons of Liberty. He had to flee when the English came back last year. We do have one young language instructor who has some familiarity with French, but I'm reluctant to assign him to you for the reasons you just described. Since I can't predict the outcome of this war I must maintain the neutrality of Bethesda. Whichever side wins, they must see us as servants of God and not involved in worldly matters.

"Having said that, however, there is a way I might be able to help you without compromising our position. Just a few miles from here on the north end of Skidaway Island is a small Anglican monastery of the Benedictine Order. For the past few years they have been sending us their orphaned and runaway boys in exchange for any girls who might show up here at Bethesda. Father Titus, who is the prior there, convinced the Church of England to dispatch a group of nuns to care for the girls. They established a convent under his supervision. It seems these sisters were part of a Huguenot order in France that fled to England during the Catholic persecution. You may be able to convince one of them to help you. It will depend on their attitude toward you. As a religious order they may be more prone to forgive you for persecuting them.

"Come Admiral, let me show you around our humble home. We always welcome the opportunity to create new ambassadors for our cause. Maybe when you return to court you can influence King Louis to contribute. One of our truest friends and benefactors is Benjamin Franklin. He is a close friend to George Whitefield, our founder. Did you have the opportunity to meet Mr. Franklin in Paris?"

"Indeed I did! I found him to be a most remarkable man. We spent many evenings, over wine, discussing philosophy and politics. It was through his untiring efforts that the King finally decided to enter the war on the side of America. I think he may be more popular in France than the King himself. Certainly he is among the women."

de Noailles rode under the brick arch over the entrance to Bethesda, toward Wormslow, with his two aides. He was intent on going to Skidaway to seek the help of Father Titus. Heavy thunderstorms pelted the road. The winds were fierce. de Noailles pulled his rain slicker tighter, trying to keep the water from seeping under his collar. Reverend Barkley had told him that Wimberley Jones, a staunch supporter of the revolution, and master of Wormslow, would help him to get to Skidaway. The same dock on Wormslow that Enoch and Ka'le had used when Enoch's father died was only a few hundred feet across the river from Skidaway Island.

A canopy of oaks extended nearly a mile from the gate to Wormslow's main house, a fortress looking, tabby structure of two floors was at the end of that passage. The three horsemen dismounted, handing the reins to the stable hands that came running up. They hurried toward the light coming from an open door. Wimberley Jones greeted them warmly.

"Come in gentlemen. I can see by your uniforms that you are with the French army at Buley. Step into the pantry area. We'll get some towels for you to dry off."

The visitors shed their slickers and apologized for the mess they were making.

"Do not be concerned, gentlemen. This is nothing compared to the black Georgia mud we track in from the fields."

There, on the large oval table where the family took informal meals, the servants prepared hot tea and biscuits with butter and fig preserves.

"Now, sirs," the host began, "You look like you've had a hard ride today. I think some tea and biscuits are in order. These preserves come from our own trees that were brought over from Spain."

"Thank you, sir," de Noailles said as he wiped the crumbs of biscuit from his mustache. "That was mighty delicious. We don't often enjoy sweets such as these aboard ship or in the field. It certainly beats the hard tack and moldy bread we've had recently."

"Admiral, while I am honored by your visit to our humble home, I'm sure there are far more pressing reasons for your soggy ride than the enjoyment of fig preserves," Wimberley said.

"My hosts at Buley suggested there might be someone at Bethesda who could help us with the locals. Reverend Barkley was very sympathetic to our problem but convinced me that his relationships with the church and his donors were too delicate for him to become involved. You see, we need someone fluent in both French and English to interpret for us. He was kind enough to suggest there may be someone on Skidaway Island who can help us. He further suggested that you might be willing to give us transport to the monastery."

"Yes Admiral, I'll be most pleased to have one of my men row you over to Skidaway. I'll do anything I can to help you run the British out of Savannah. As a matter of fact I've just received word that General McIntosh is on his way back to Savannah to join forces with you. As an officer in the Georgia militia I've been ordered to report to him with my men when he arrives.

"I will send a letter urging Father Titus to help you. He depends on us for much of his support. If he can help you I'm sure he will. If you leave immediately you should be able to get there and back before dark."

The rising tide covered the marsh grass, allowing the small flat-bottomed boat to negotiate the last few hundred yards up Runaway Negro Creek. The landing, on the western edge of Skidaway Island, was about a mile from the monastery. The path ran along the creek through a forest of majestic live oaks and towering pines. A mile or so across the island it opened onto the fields of the monastery. The delegation arrived at the gate before two in the afternoon. A brown robed monk answered the bell. He took them immediately to the prior. de Noailles related his request to Father Titus. He told him of his visit to Bethesda then handed him the letter from Wimberley Jones.

The prior took the letter. He moved across the room to let the light from a high window fall on it. He read the letter, then stood silently for a few moments. It was obvious the priest was weighing the consequences of any action he took in response to this request.

"Admiral de Noailles. The Benedictine Order was founded on principles of peace and monastic reflection. We are here in the wilderness to project those beliefs and to spread the gospel. You may not be aware that our ordination as priests requires an oath of allegiance to the Crown. I cannot in good conscience ask any of the brethren to violate this vow. I must remain loyal and obedient to the King. That does not nullify the fact that I have many sympathies for the cause of the Americans. This monastery would not have survived without their continued generous support.

"Individual abbeys, priories and monasteries of the Order of St. Benedict are given wide latitude in deciding local rules and practices. That is particularly true when they are at the edges of the empire, as we are here. Therefore I will allow you to speak with the sisters in our convent. They are not bound by the same strict vows as the priests. I will abide by whatever decision they reach as long as no one from this order is involved in any hostile activities. I must warn you that even though the Mother Superior is French by birth, she harbors strong feelings concerning the treatment of the Huguenots in France. If you'll wait here I'll summon her.

"In the meantime please enjoy our humble hospitality. Brother Howard will get you some tea and cakes if you'd like. I'll return shortly."

Sister Marie Michel, her shoes hidden beneath the flowing black robe, seemed to glide across the ground as she approached the prior's office. Father Titus opened the door and ushered her through into the room. Two oil lamps hung from a rafter, illuminating the office's spartan furnishings. There was a rough-hewn desk cut from the bole of a large cypress tree. Two benches, made from the twin halves of a small oak, each supported by four rounded staves, were placed against opposite walls. The only piece not created on the island was a tall bookcase on the wall facing the desk. It had belonged to Father Titus's family and was lovingly brought from England to house his bibles, hymnals and the writings of St. Benedict.

"Admiral de Noailles, this is Sister Marie Michel. She is the Mother Superior of our convent."

The Admiral responded in French, the slender nun smiling upon hearing her native tongue. She had encouraged the nuns and their charges to speak only English in the convent, but occasionally, when she was alone with the nuns, they would reminisce of the old days. They often lapsed into that sweet language, which best described their memories. Sister Marie spoke for a few minutes to the admiral in French before returning the conversation to English.

"Father Titus says that you are here to aid the colonists in retaking Savannah from the English and that you need someone who speaks French to interpret for you."

"Yes. France has joined forces with the American patriots in their bid to establish their independence. King Louis sees this as a just cause and has responded to General Washington's request for help.

"Before I discuss that, however, I think there is an unresolved question I should address. I know how painful the religious persecution in France has been for you and your people. It is a part of our history for which I am ashamed. Most of my fellow countrymen share my sentiments. In that sense I offer you my apologies and those of my government for the unkind measures that forced many of you from

France. I can assure you that this King and his government regret the suffering caused by those measures. In recognition of that change in our religious attitudes, he signed an edict restoring the rights of your people in France. He acknowledged the rights of the children of the reformation to worship God in their own fashion. I hope that you can find it in your heart to forgive us."

"Admiral, it has been a difficult road we have traveled for many years. Pain and sorrow were there each step of the way. But, in the spirit of Saint Benedict and his teachings we must continually seek enlightenment, forgiveness and reconciliation. Along the way, we who follow his teachings have prospered in the faith by our encounters with others, not necessarily those of our faith. In that process we have learned to thank God for the opportunities he opened to us. Like Christ, our suffering can make life better for others. We have been dispersed into the world to bring his message to the lost and the savage. Through our suffering we have grown stronger and been ennobled by the experiences God gave us.

"Neither you nor I are responsible for the beginning of those quarrels but both you and I can be a part of the solution to them. Now, with respect to your request."

"As you must know, we try to set ourselves apart from the world while we pursue God's work. I think it would be wrong if any of the sisters were placed in a position that might interfere with their mission or with their vows of peace. However, in the spirit of trying to support those who have helped us to establish this outpost, I may have a solution that will not upset our relationships with the church or the English.

"All of the sisters have taken vows which prevent them from becoming involved in worldly disputes such as this conflict. There are others here, however, who have not yet taken those vows that may be able to help you. We have a young novitiate who has studied with us for five years. She is an amazing young woman. Her capacity and enthusiasm to learn is boundless. She has studied French with Sister Bernadette for several years and has become quite fluent. Since she has not taken her vows you may speak with her. If she and Sister Bernadette are willing for her to help you then I will not stand in her way. My only requirements are that she not be placed in any danger and that she not take part in any conflict."

"Thank you, Sister. I assure you that if she agrees to help us I will see that she is not placed in any danger. We simply need someone to talk with the locals, primarily to negotiate the procurement of provisions for our troops. When that task is completed we will bring her back to you unharmed. And, His Majesty's government will be happy to participate in the furtherance of your work here."

Bernadette and Cassie had just come in from the garden. They needed a few minutes to make themselves presentable. While they busied themselves with bathing and changing their clothes, the Mother Superior explained what the Admiral was asking of Cassie.

"Mother, I've never been anywhere but here at the monastery and at Roselawn. If I go there to this Buley place, I'm afraid I may be forced back into slavery. I don't want that. I'm happy here. I don't understand what this is all about. Does it have something to do with those ships Sister Bernadette and I saw on the river?"

"Yes, my child, it does. This man who is asking you to help him is a French naval officer. He is a very powerful man. Mr. Wimberley Jones has asked us to help him. Much of the support for St. Benedict's comes from Mr. Jones and his friends on the other plantations, like Roselawn, where you came from. He has assured me that he will not allow any harm to come to you and that when the army moves into Savannah he'll make sure that you are brought safely back here. All we're asking is that you listen to him. If he can't convince you to go with him then he will not force you. It will be your decision alone."

Cassie had never seen anyone dressed in a military uniform. It frightened her. She clung to Bernadette's arm, her racing heart pounding. She looked at her mentor for reassurance.

"It's all right Cassie. Just be calm. The Admiral just wants to talk to you to see if you can help him."

de Noailles was surprised. He had expected to see a white girl as a novice in the convent. He waited a moment before speaking, letting the young girl regain her composure.

"Cassie, I am Admiral de Noailles of the French Navy." He addressed her in French. He wanted to assess her fluency in the language. "France has entered America's war for independence on the side of the colonials, against the British. I am here with 6,000 other French soldiers and sailors to help the Americans recapture the city of Savannah. 1,500 of those troops are under my command and are encamped at Buley Plantation. We need you to interpret for us so that we can obtain food for them."

de Noailles stopped. He could see the fear and hesitancy in the girl's eyes. He needed a way to convince her to help him. He thought of the black soldiers from Saint-Domingue.

"Cassie, among those soldiers at Buley are more than five hundred Negroes from the Caribbean island of Sainte-Domingue. Many of them are free men and the others will become free when they leave the army. They are fighting for their freedom as well as that of the Americans. I understand that you are a slave, sent here from Roselawn Plantation. If you will do this for me I will do my best to get your master at Roselawn to grant you your freedom in exchange."

She looked at the imposing figure and then back at Sister Bernadette.

"Sister, I'm scared. If I go with him I might be caught and forced back into slavery somewhere else. But if I do go there's a chance I might be truly free. As long as I'm a slave I'll never be able to leave Skidaway and I'll never be able to help my people. What should I do?"

"Oh, Cassie," Bernadette said. "I have come to love you like a sister in the years you have been here. You are the brightest and bravest person I have ever known. You have read every book we have and know more about St. Benedict's teachings than anyone here. For my own selfish reasons I don't want you to go. But, for your future and what you can mean to the church and your people I can't stand in your way.

" Admiral, are you sure you can protect her and that Mr. Penrose will give Cassie her freedom?"

"Sister, as to protecting her, I assure you she will be safe and I'll see that she is returned to you as soon as possible. As for Mr. Penrose, I can only say that with Mr. Jones persuasive help, I feel certain he will grant Cassie's freedom. After all Roselawn seems to have gotten along very well without her for five years. So, I don't think they really need her back."

Cassie again turned to Bernadette, her raw emotions rising to the surface.

"Sister, I don't want to leave here, but if I'm ever going to fulfill

God's plan for me to help my people I guess this is the opportunity that He is giving me. I must go with him."

She looked at de Noailles. With resignation she asked, "When do we have to leave?"

"I want to get back to Wormslow before dark and then head back to Buley at dawn. We need supplies badly and the sooner we get back the sooner we'll be able to get them."

"Sister, will you help me put a few clothes in a sack. I want to say goodbye to the other girls and the nuns. Admiral, I'll be ready in a few minutes."

Cassie and Bernadette walked off arm-in-arm toward the convent, crying every step of the way.

CHAPTER TWELVE

A cacophony of tree frogs drowned out the sounds of the boat as de Noaille's small band returned to Wormslow. The rain had stopped and the Isle of Good Hope was bathed in the afterglow of sunset. Wimberley Jones met them at the door.

"Mr. Jones, this is Cassie Omoru a novitiate from the monastery. She's been there about five years. The nuns all felt they would be breaking their vows if they took sides in this conflict but Cassie has not yet taken final vows. She was reluctant to come with me for fear of being sent back into slavery. I told her that if she would help us that I would ask her owner to set her free. She wants to become a nun and work among her people and she won't be able to do that as a slave. When this is all over will you go to Roselawn and ask Mr. Penrose to grant my request?"

"Casssie Omoru. That name's familiar. Is your mama a house servant at Roselawn?"

"Yes sir. Both my mama, Queen, and my grandma, Aba, worked in the house for Mr. Hiram. Grandma Aba passed away a while back."

"I remember some trouble a few years back when Hiram's daddy sent his brother Enoch off to Ossabaw. He'd been caught messing with a slave girl. Was that you Cassie?

She hung her head ashamedly, and said, "Yes sir, that was me."

"Admiral, I'll be happy to talk to Hiram. I'll be seeing him tomorrow.

Both of us have to leave to meet up with General McIntosh. As soon as we get back from running the Brits out of Savannah, I'm sure I can convince him to draw up the necessary papers to free Casssie."

Cassie breathed a sigh of relief. She now believed that it would really happen. Her dream of freedom was going to come true.

"Admiral, you and your men will dine with me tonight and we have rooms enough for all of you. Cassie, if you'll go into the kitchen, Aunt Maude will get you some supper and a place to sleep. It looks like your going to be very busy for the next few days."

Cassie scampered off to the kitchen, glad to be free of the presence of these intimidating white men. She would eat well that night and dream of freedom.

By noon of the following day the party had retraced its steps past Bethesda and was nearing Buley Plantation. The heat of the late summer sun vaporized the puddles of rainwater, sending shimmering waves into the air. Cassie trailed behind the huge warhorses. She was astride a small roan palfrey, on loan from Wimberley Jones. The white tabby plantation house sat on a bluff overlooking the Vernon River and Burnside Island. Wide verandas, draped with wisteria and fragrant jessamine, shaded three sides of the house. It was oriented to catch the easterly ocean breezes. Acrid wood smoke burned her nostrils. It rose from a hundred campfires, curled up through the lofty pines, and was carried across the road by the freshening breeze.

Once the tents had finally arrived at Beaulieu they were erected in a large field northeast of the main house. Cassie could hear the shouts and curses of the men as they battled the heat, the mosquitoes and the biting insects, the most fiendish of these being the nearly invisible sand gnat. The tiny creatures rose up in hovering swarms at every disturbance of the sandy soil. The locals called them "noseeums". The pain of their bite was excruciating.

Admiral de Noaille tethered his horse behind the house and beckoned for Cassie to follow him. He led her up the rear steps into the pantry serving room.

"Cassie, stay here. I'll be right back," he said.

Within minutes he returned, accompanied by a portly black

woman, her head bound with a white kerchief. The white man with her was in uniform.

"Cassie, this is Minnie. She is in charge of the house servants here at Buley. She will see to your quartering while you are here. Anything you need just ask Minnie."

"Now girl you don' worry 'bout nuthin. I gone see tuh it dat ya is taken care of. I's awready got a place fo ya tuh sleep in da room wit me. You gone take yo meals wit da rest o da house servants," Minnie said, as she shuffled off toward the kitchen behind the house. "Soon's dey is done wit ya, come on out tuh da kitchen."

The admiral continued his conversation.

"Cassie, I'd like you to meet Captain Rene Deschamps. He is my quartermaster, the officer in charge of our supplies. He will be meeting with you and the foraging party this afternoon to explain to you what provisions we most urgently need and where he thinks you will find them. You and the men will leave at first light tomorrow. I wish you luck and once again I thank you for your service."

Captain Deschamps addressed Cassie in impeccable French.

"I am most pleased to meet you Mlle. Omoru. As I'm sure the Admiral told you we are running desperately short of certain provisions. We have located most of what we need but have run into stiff and sometimes armed resistance from the farmers. They don't seem to understand that we will pay them well for their goods. They think we are trying to steal them or take them by force. We need their goodwill, therefore we hope that you will be able to translate our intentions to them and assure them that they are honorable."

Cassie listened as this dark haired man with deep blue eyes spoke to her in such perfect French. She was amazed at her ability to understand him. She thought her ease with the language when she spoke with the sisters was due to their close relationships. She was elated that her facility carried over to this handsome Frenchman's speech as well.

"Thank you., Monsieur Deschamps," she responded in French, almost as fluently as the dashing officer. "I hope that I can help you. I will do my best."

"That's all that I can ask of you. Go and get something to eat now, and I will call for you at three o'clock. We'll meet with the soldiers you'll be accompanying in the quartermaster's tent just west of the house."

Cassie didn't realize how hungry she was. She ate two plates of pork sausage with mustard greens and skillet cornbread.

"Chile, you gobbled dat down lak you ain't had nuthin to eat fo a week. I laks to see young fokes wit a big appetite. Reminds me of when I was a youngun like you an I wuz workin' in da fields. Trouble is, I kep on eatin lak dat when I moved into the Massa's house and now I's big as a barn," Minnie said as she came back from the pantry. "You look plumb tuckered out girl. Ya gots time to cotch a little nap fo ya hasta meet up wid dem sojers. I's gonna wake you befo den."

Casssie lay down on the cot in Minnie's room. It was almost identical to her old room back at Roselawn. Pangs of homesickness swept over her. Tears came to her eyes. It had been so long since she left. She was occasionally homesick, back at the monastery, but she was so busy the feelings were fleeting. Her only return to Roselawn in the intervening years came last year when her grandmother Aba died. Master Hiram sent a boat for her. So much had changed. There were several more slave cabins and lots of small black children running around that she didn't recognize. She worried that Enoch might be there but Hiram had made sure he stayed on Ossabaw.

As the widow of a tribal chief, Aba was buried with all the dignity and ceremony she would have received back in Dahomey. All the Penrose family, with the exception of Enoch, were at the funeral. The children she had cared for and nursed wept openly. Sarah was distraught. Following the last hymn she knelt by the fresh turned earth and placed a single red rose on the fresh mound.

Queen and Cassie were the last to leave the little graveyard behind the quarters. Cassie recognized many of the crudely carved names on the weathered wooden crosses. Both her great uncles, Kofi and Safi, were there, buried next to the grave of Aba. And dear old Mosu Akala, lying between his beloved Sulu and their tragic son "Big Boy." Memories of these courageous people brought tears to her eyes and a lump to her throat. She struggled to compose herself. She fought back the tears. She had to be strong if she was ever going to help these good and decent people who had been ripped from their native culture and forced to make a new life in bondage on foreign shores. Her memories of the childhood she spent with these wonderful people filled her with a renewed longing. She wanted to come back, free, and help those still living on Roselawn. When she won her freedom she would return to fight for theirs.

The brilliant sun broke through the wall of fog rolling in off the water, signaling a break in the oppressive September heat and a welcome respite from the monsoon rains of the past several days. Minnie was busily assembling supper for the Big House and had left a plate for Cassie on the kitchen table. She ate quickly and hurried over to the large mess tent for the meeting with the black soldiers from Saint-Domingue.

Most of the soldiers had finished their meager rations and were off about their various duties. There was water to fetch and firewood to be gathered as well as the relentless drilling required by the French officers. Louis Dufour remained in the mess tent. He was one of the soldiers selected to accompany Cassie on tomorrow's quest for food.

"Andre, we've already been trying to find food. All we got for our trouble was the chance to look down the muzzle of some mad farmer's rifle. If we're here to help these people I don't understand why they treat us this way. Why don't we just take what we need and to hell with them. We're sitting around in this God-forsaken place being eaten alive by mosquitoes and gnats and baking in the sun, and for what? If they don't want our help why don't we just get back on the boats and go back to Saint-Domingue."

"Louis, you and I are buried down here in the ranks with the other lowly foot soldiers," Andre said. "We don't know what's going on up at the Big House. I don't think the French care all that much for the Americans or their revolution. They just hate the English and this is another way to weaken their enemy. As soon as this is over we'll hightail it back to Saint-Domingue or Grenada or even France and this revolution will be forgotten. It's all about politics and alliances and how to hurt your enemies."

"If a few hundred soldiers get killed in the process its not a big problem for them. They'll just go back to the islands and force another thousand or two into service. You've got to admit though that this life sure beats working in the sugar cane fields. And besides, in a few more years we'll be free and we can decide for ourselves what we want to do. I'd like to go back to Grenada and find my brothers and see if I can get my father's old shop back."

"When we were there, after we drove the British out, I was able to go ashore for a few hours. I talked to some people who knew my family. They said my father had died but some of my brothers were still alive and had fled up into the mountains. I just hope they took my mother with them. I never forgave my father for selling me into bondage, but I now understand what great stress he was under. He did his best under very difficult circumstances. I'd just like to be able to put the family back together again."

His voice trailed off in reverie, his mind a thousand miles away on a mountaintop.

Andre sat with his back to the open tent flap, sipping from a metal cup of steaming coffee. He saw Louis' eyes flash as someone entered. He turned to see a lithe, olive skinned woman framed in the afternoon light. She reminded him of the beautiful mestizos he had known in Grenada. She had the same bone structure and carriage of his African ancestors and the dark, smoldering beauty of his Spanish mother. Her eyes were the color of green agate flecked with brown. She was the most beautiful woman he had ever seen. Captain Deschamps followed Cassie into the tent. He guided her to the table where Andre and Louis sat.

"Mlle. Omoru this is Corporal Andre Dupre and Private Louis Dufour. They will be driving the wagons on tomorrow's search. I am sending along three other men to help. Lieutenant Beaupre will be in charge of the detail. Here is a list of the provisions we need and a map of the area showing the farms and plantations where they are known to be. The lieutenant has a cashbox and a list of the prices he is authorized to pay.

"You soldiers are reminded to be on your best behavior. Mlle. Omoru will speak to the farmers in English and translate for you in French. You are to do as she says and treat her with the utmost respect. She is doing this as a favor to the Admiral. If you are successful today it will go a long way toward the success of our mission here in America. I wish you good luck and good hunting tomorrow.

The teams were already hitched to the wagons when Cassie arrived the next morning.

Andre hurried to the waiting wagons, ahead of the others. He wanted to make sure that Mlle. Cassie Omoru rode on the seat beside him. He was mesmerized by her beauty. He wanted to learn as much about her as he could.

"Mlle. Omoru. I would be honored if you would ride with me," Andre said.

He made an exaggerated bow to Cassie.

"Maybe you can tell me more about this revolution and about Savannah. Louis and I are from Saint-Domingue and don't know much about what's going on in the rest of the world," Andre said.

He stood by the front wheel and held out his hand to assist her.

"Why, thank you Mr. Dupre. I would be pleased to ride with you but I'm afraid I can't tell you much. You see, I've spent the last five years in a monastery on Skidaway Island. Before that I grew up as a house servant on Roselawn Plantation. Everything I know I learned from the sisters at St. Benedict's. I owe everything to them, especially to Sister Bernadette.

Andre flicked the horses with the reins. The traces tightened as they leaned into their collars. The wagon lurched forward down the rutted path. The three mounted soldiers cantered ahead while Louis followed in the second wagon.

"You mean you were a slave," Andre said. He was astonished.

"I still am," she said. "I belong to the family that owns Roselawn plantation. I was sent to St. Benedict's to get away from a bad situation. I will probably not go back there. But that doesn't change the fact that I am still a slave. The reason I agreed to work with the Admiral is that he promised to go to Hiram Penrose, my master, and ask him to set me free. He assured me that he and Mr. Wimberley Jones would personally speak to him."

"But, if you don't have to go back why does it matter whether he frees you or not? The folks at the monastery don't treat you as a slave, do they?"

"No. They've been wonderful to me. Sister Bernadette has taught me everything I know. She's the one who taught me to speak and read French. Thanks to her and the other sisters I now have this opportunity. I was studying to take my vows to become a nun but the church decided I couldn't. So, as long as I remain a slave I won't be able to leave St. Benedict's and go where I'm needed. I now know it's God's purpose for my life to go out into the world and help to improve the lives of my people. To help them find salvation and to minister to their physical and spiritual needs.

"What about you Andre? How did you wind up here in the French army fighting the British for the Americans?"

"I grew up free, on the island of Grenada. My father owned a small store and he was able to provide for me and my brothers. Until the French came. The island fell on hard times and my father lost his store. He was forced to sell his sons into bondage in order to pay his debts and stay out of jail. The shame and the guilt finally killed him.

"I was sold to a French ship's captain. I hated being a cabin boy. I made so much trouble for him that he finally sold me at a slave auction in Cap Haitien. When the hurricanes came and destroyed the sugar cane, our owner couldn't support all of us so he sold me to the French army. They said that after I serve for six years they'll take me back to Saint-Domingue and set me free. So you see we have a lot in common. We're both fighting for our freedom, you from a plantation owner in America and me from the French army and a plantation owner in Saint-Domingue."

Cassie and Andre rode on in silence for a while, unsure of where their conversation was taking them. Andre wanted desperately to know more about this beautiful and mysterious young woman but didn't want to appear too forward. He decided to bide his time.

Cassie was curious about Andre's world. She knew from her geography lessons that Saint-Domingue was on the island of Hispaniola in the Caribbean, inhabited mostly by slaves who were brought there by the French to grow sugar cane. The rest of the Island, called Domenica, was ruled by Spain. This was a new experience for her. All her past dealings with young black men had been as a slave at Roselawn. Her position as a house servant kept her away from any intimate contact with them. She was unsure how to behave in this situation. She was attracted to Andre but the vows she took as a novice precluded any relationship with men, beyond mere friendship. She realized she had to be very careful in this outside world to not offend God by breaking her vows. She must be very wary.

By the end of the day the foragers had called on eight farmers. All but two had been cooperative. After Cassie explained their mission and that they would pay them fairly for their animals and produce, they were happy to exchange them for hard currency. The economy in the colonies and especially in Georgia was in ruins. The British blockade had effectively stymied any foreign trade. Almost all trade now was by barter among the farmers and tradesmen. The occasional blockade-runner made it through with supplies but the prices were so outrageous as to be out of reach for most ordinary citizens.

The black slaves who loaded the wagons and herded the livestock stared in amazement at the sight of the uniformed black troops. They were equally astonished to hear the young black girl speaking to them and to the white soldiers in an unknown tongue.

Cassie saw for the first time the inhumane conditions existing on most of the plantations. She saw the cruel and malicious treatment by the overseers and owners. Many of the slaves she saw were scarred and crippled. They cowered in the presence of the whites like beaten dogs. She now understood that the relatively benign treatment of slaves at Roselawn was an exception. Aside from Enoch's cruelty she never saw any mistreatment there. All the more reason, she thought, to make the most of this opportunity so that she could be free to begin her mission to these wretched souls.

Darkness was enveloping the camp as the wagons trundled up to the quartermaster's tent with their precious cargo. Six steers and several sheep were pulled along unwillingly, their bleating and lowing sending the camp dogs into a frenzy of barking.

"Well, Mlle. Omoru, it appears that you had a very successful day," Captain Deschamps said. "Congratulations. I'll see to it that Minnie prepares a special dinner for you. I'd be honored if you would join me with some of the other officers."

Cassie was astonished at such an invitation. Nowhere in her world, except with the nuns at St. Benedict's, had she ever seen blacks intermingling socially with white people. She didn't think any good could come of it here either.

"Thank you, Captain Deschamps, but I'm very tired so I think I'll just have a quick supper with Miss Minnie and then turn in. It's been a long and tiring day and I'm sure tomorrow will bring more of the same."

"Very well, I understand. I will report your great success to the admiral. I'm certain he will be very pleased. I think your progress today will go a long way toward assuring the fulfillment of his promise to you. I will certainly add my voice in support. Have a good evening. I will see you first thing in the morning with tomorrow's assignment."

Cassie hungrily licked the last of the apple cobbler from her spoon. Minnie had made it especially for her at the urging of Deschamps. On top of the beef and potatoes she was completely full and ready for sleep. Within minutes of her head hitting the pillow the soft sounds of her breathing could be heard from the kitchen. Minnie smiled. She had done her part.

The next two days found the foraging caravan moving further and further afield as most of the nearby farms had supplied as much as they could afford. That meant that fewer farms could be reached during the daylight hours. Andre and Louis took to hanging lanterns from the tips of the wagon tongues to light the path for the horses as they returned in darkness. Cassie became wearier with each passing day. The soldiers and drivers were equally exhausted. Captain Deschamps recognized their need for rest.

"Tomorrow is Saturday. There will be no caravan. Nor will there be one on Sunday," he said to the returning troop. "We'll take the weekend off to rest the horses and the troops. We'll resume the mission on Monday morning."

Shouts of relief echoed up and down the line of soldiers. Andre and Louis jumped down from their seats, grins spreading from ear to ear.

"Thank you, Captain. We can certainly use the rest," Andre said "And Cassie is plumb tuckered out. We'll all be ready to go again after a couple of days rest."

He reached to help Cassie down, mindful that he didn't drag her dress across the dirty wagon wheel.

"Thank you, Andre," she said.

It was obvious after several days on the trail, sharing their stories, that a familiarity had settled over their relationship. She looked at him and smiled.

"I'll see you Monday."

"If you don't mind I'll see you back to the house. It's pretty dark out. You'll need a light to see the path."

He took the lantern that hung on the tongue of the wagon. He knew full well that she was more than capable of negotiating her way back. When they were out of earshot of the others Andre continued.

"Cassie, I'd like to take you down to that little beach on the river tomorrow. Maybe we can go for a swim. It's been mighty hot. You could even ask Miss Minnie to pack a lunch for us."

His heart was in his throat, afraid she would be offended and say no.

"Why, Andre, I think that would be very nice. I'll ask Miss Minnie if she can spare a few things for us and maybe even a little cider," she said, surprisingly. You realize of course, that I'm still bound by my vows and that nothing more than friendship with you is possible. Besides, as soon as we leave here you'll be going off to war and I'll be heading back to St. Benedict's. We'll probably never see each other again. You're obliged to serve the rest of your term with the army and I have to get back to my studies."

"I know, but it's a young man's right to dream."

She said goodnight at the door to the kitchen. He bent down, took her hand and pressed it to his lips.

"Good night, " he said.

As he straightened he looked into her eyes. It was a look that promised much more than this brief encounter on a remote Georgia plantation.

CHAPTER THIRTEEN

THE FIVE FRENCH WARSHIPS, escorted by American coastal frigates, had barely passed Sullivan's Island into the Atlantic when General Lincoln led his troops out of Charlestown. The march to Ebenezer would take several days. General McIntosh was already encamped at Millen's Plantation with 350 men. Lincoln had ordered General Pulaski's Polish Legion, fresh from their victory at Stono Ferry, to join him and McIntosh at Cherokee Hill.

"Colonel Marion, any word from your courier to Pulaski," Lincoln asked of Lt. Colonel Francis Marion.

Marion, whose guerilla exploits had long bedeviled the British and earned him the nickname, "The Swamp Fox," was riding alongside his commander.

"Yes sir. He arrived back this morning just before we left Charlestown. He reported that General Pulaski has secured the fort at Stono's Ferry and left a small garrison of militia to hold it. He left for Ebenezer two days ago and should arrive before we reach there."

"Good. We're going to need his cavalry if we have to storm the town. It'll be a lot easier than going in with just foot soldiers," he said. "With his legion, McIntosh's brigade, and the French we should have enough manpower to convince Prevost to surrender. He'll be a damn fool to take on our combined force. By my estimate he can't have more than twelve to fifteen hundred soldiers there, and if we can keep Maitland's garrison holed up in Port Royal there's no chance "Old Bullet Head" will risk the destruction of his command."

Prevost had been wounded in 1759 at the Battle of Quebec during the French and Indian Wars. He was left with a large depression in his temple where a spent ball had struck him.

Riding along with Lincoln and Marion was Colonel John Laurens in his regimental uniform and long plumed hat. The dashing twenty-seven year old was the son of Henry Laurens, former President of the Continental Congress, mentor to Lachlan McIntosh, and as rumors would have it, one of the richest men in America. John had been sent to England in 1772 to study law. He had returned in 1777 to join Washington's staff. He was considered impetuous and a daredevil by both Washington and General Greene. He was sent south to join Lincoln's army to defend his native state, South Carolina.

Other luminaries in Lincoln's entourage were Thomas Pinckney of Charleston aristocracy and Sergeant William Jasper, legendary scout across the southern Revolutionary frontier. Jasper's bravery in June of 1776 at the battle of Sullivan's Island was told and retold throughout the region. Facing withering fire from the British he leaped from the ramparts to rescue the fallen blue crescent flag of South Carolina and to remount it on a makeshift staff. Trunks of palmetto palms had been hurriedly thrown up as barricades facing the sea. British shells either bounced off the fibrous logs or buried themselves harmlessly into their mass. The fortifications proved so effective in saving Charlestown that the humble palmetto would be added, alongside the crescent, to the South Carolina flag.

Bringing up the rear of this strange blend of forces was the "Jew's Company" under Captain Richard Lushington, the only known Jewish military unit to serve during the entire revolution.

Lincoln's army arrived at Zubley's Ferry on the Savannah River on September 13, to discover the British had destroyed most of the boats and ferries. Colonel Laurens was dispatched to find any available watercraft to aid in getting the army across the river. He returned with two canoes, a rowboat and a damaged raft. With this makeshift flotilla about fifty men could be ferried across at a time. Two days later, on September 15, Lincoln reached Cherokee Hill, eight miles north of the city. He received word that Governor Rutledge had dispatched a small fleet of boats down the coast to help d'Estaing ferry his men, supplies and artillery ashore.

General Pulaski, who had crossed into Georgia ahead of McIntosh, sent a courier to d'Estaing that Lincoln was approaching the city with roughly a thousand infantry, two hundred and sixty mounted cavalry and eight cannon. He also informed d'Estaing that General McIntosh had crossed into the state with 350 men, mostly Georgia and Carolina militias, a motley crew that was battle weary and poorly equipped. Many wore hand made shoes and deerskin uniforms. There were no two outfits or headgear alike. They had moss packed in their musket kits for wadding, so sparse were their supplies.

Only the Pulaski Legion could hold a candle to the French when it came to fancy uniforms. The French were resplendent in royal blue coats with scarlet vests and high black boots. Each of the four regiments was identified with unique colors. They carried flags and banners of green, yellow, violet or black. Pulaski's lancers were arrayed in bright tunics with much gold braid and high collars. Their steel helmets were adorned with a sheaf of black feathers running from front to back.

CHAPTER FOURTEEN

SATURDAY MORNING BROKE BRIGHT and hot. Cassie arose early to help Minnie in the kitchen and to gather a few things for the picnic. She was interrupted by a bugle blast from the encampment outside. She ran to the door to see what the clamor was about. Soldiers were running in all directions, loading supplies onto wagons and collapsing the tents. Moments later Captain Deschamps ran into the kitchen.

"Cassie, we have received a dispatch from Admiral d'Estaing that he is getting ready to move on Savannah and we are to join him as soon as possible at the Greewich plantation, just east of the town. Since we were unable to gather all the supplies needed, Admiral de Noaille has asked that you move with us so that we can continue to gather provisions as we pass the planters between here and Savannah. He said it will take a couple of days for him to get to Greenwich where the rest of the Army will be waiting. He apologizes for this sudden change of plans but asked me to assure you that as soon as we are settled around the city that he will send you back to St. Benedict's with an escort. We are to set off immediately. Andre and Louis have the wagons ready out front. I'll see you at Greenwich tomorrow."

The young captain ran out of the kitchen before Cassie could offer any protest. This mission was spinning out of her control but she had no option but to comply. There was no way she could get back to Skidaway on her own without being taken as a runaway slave or worse.

She resigned herself to continuing down this God ordained path that she had been set upon.

****

General Prevost knew his army was no match for the combined forces of the Americans and the French. Once assured that the objective of the French was Savannah and not Charlestown he knew that he must call in all his outlying posts to aid in the city's defense.

"Major Phillips. Come in here at once," bellowed the general.

Major Phillips hurried into the general's office.

"My general, how may I be of service to you?" he asked.

"Major, it is imperative that we call in the forces at all the outposts if we're going to have any chance of defending Savannah. If our scouting reports are accurate General Lincoln is en route from Charlestown with at least fifteen hundred men. We also have received word that General McIntosh is moving down from Augusta with as many as five hundred regulars and militia. There are also rumors that General Pulaski's Polish Legion has crossed over the river into Georgia. Together with the French army we're looking at upwards of four thousand men. Even if we get all our outposts in we can't muster more than two thousand.

"Prepare urgent communications to Colonel Maitland at Beaufort and Colonel Cruger at Sunbury to proceed to Savannah with all due haste. And, make them aware that the French have taken Fort Tybee and have blockaded the river up to the Thunderbolt. It will be necessary for Maitland to find a route across the marshes to avoid the French.

"Also, Major, on your way out, alert the Sergeant of the Guard to summon all my staff for an emergency meeting."

A small fleet of British ships had been blockading the southern coast. They were completely surprised by the sudden arrival of the French. Several of their ships were captured. General Prevost ordered the abandonment of Fort Tybee. All munitions were to be brought into Savannah. All the guns were to be spiked and the remaining ships brought up channel to defend the city. The *Fowey*, the *Rose*, the *Keppel* and the *Germain*, all that remained of the command, sailed upriver and anchored off Yamacraw bluff with their guns trained down river.

"Gentlemen," Prevost began. "I don't need to tell you of the dire situation in which we find ourselves. We stand to face a combined French and American force of five thousand men. Currently we can muster no more than fifteen hundred able-bodied soldiers. In addition our fortifications are not sufficient to repel a concerted attack by such an overwhelming force. Therefore, I have called in all of our outlying posts. If Colonel Maitland at Beaufort and Colonel Cruger at Sunbury can make it safely into our city before the attack comes, we will have roughly twenty five hundred men. Even that will be insufficient under our present state of readiness.

"I am ordering all able bodied men under this command, together with the citizens of Savannah and their slaves, to urgently prepare the city for battle. Meanwhile, I have drawn up a plan of defensive assignments for your commands. You will assume these positions and then make all your men available to support Major Moncrief, my engineering officer, in defensive preparations. Here are your defensive assignments.

"The Wissenbach Regiment and General Delancey's Second Battalion will encamp behind the barracks. In case of an alarm, which will be announced by a beating to arms at both the barracks and the main guard, the troops are to repair to their several posts, without confusion or tumult.

"Captain Stuart, of the British Legion will take post with his men on the right, near the river.

"The main guard will be relieved by the convalescents from the Hessians.

"Major Wright's corps is to send their convalescents into the old fort. Twenty-four into the small redoubt and seventy into the left flank redoubt, on the road to Tattnall's.

"The militia will assemble in the rear of the barracks.

"The Light Infantry, The Dragoons and The Carolina Light Horse, as a reserve, two hundred yards behind the barracks.

"The King's Rangers, commanded by Lieutenant-Colonel Brown, in the small redoubt on the right, with fifty men, the remainder extending toward the large redoubt on the right.

"The Carolinians divided equally in the two large redoubts.

"The battalion men of the 60th Regiment in the right redoubt. The

Grenadiers on the left, extending along the *abatis* toward the barracks; the Hessians on their left so as to fill the space up to the barracks.

"On the left of the barracks, the Third Battalion of Skinner's, General Delancey's, and the New York Volunteers; and on their left the 71st Regiment, lining the *abatis* to the left flank redoubt, on the road to Tattnall's.

"Now, Major Moncrief will brief you on his plans for improving the fortifications and the work assignments for your men."

"Gentlemen," began the squat engineer, his face a permanent scowl behind his scraggly beard.

"I have ordered the cannon stripped from most of the ships of the line to be brought into the city. The *Rose* and the *Savannah* and four transports have been sunk at "Five Fathom Hole" to prevent the French fleet from coming upriver within cannon range of the city. Several smaller vessels have been sunk above the city with a boom across the river to prevent fire rafts or troops being moved in behind the lines.

"There will be a total of thirteen redoubts linked by trenches and *abatis*, with a total of fifteen batteries consisting of 76 guns ranging from six to eighteen pounds. I already have five hundred slaves at work in the trenches. Most of your men will be employed in cutting the trees to construct the *abatis*.

"The *Keppel* and the *Germain* will be anchored above the city with a clear view of the Musgrove marshes. Their cannon can be brought to bear down to the Spring Hill redoubt. I will meet separately with each commander to give more explicit directions for your men. Thank you for your kind attention."

"Very good, Major Moncrief," General Prevost said, dismissing his chief engineer.

" So you see, gentlemen, if God grants us the time, we can turn the city of Savannah into a near impregnable fortress. You have your orders. I wish you good luck and Godspeed."

****

Colonel John Maitland lay in his bed inside the fort at Beaufort, South Carolina. He had contracted a racking fever the week before, along with at least one hundred of his troops. His aide rapped lightly on his door.

"Colonel, pardon my interruption but I have an urgent communication from General Prevost in Savannah."

"Come in, Robert. Bring the candle over to my bed so that I can read the message," Maitland said as he gripped the bed rail and swung his feet over the side of the bunk. His bedclothes were soaked with his sweat. He reached for the communication with a trembling left hand. His right had been lost in 1759 at the battle of Lagos Bay. Maitland put on his reading glasses and read the letter aloud.

"My esteemed Colonel Maitland,

This instant we have espied a fleet of French warships off the coast at Tybee Island. I can only conclude that the French are joining forces with the colonial rabble to attack Savannah. I am, therefore, ordering you to proceed with all due haste to Savannah to join with me in her defense. The French have blockaded the mouth of the Savannah River and probably have ships as far upriver as the Thunderbolt. I have sunk several small ships below the city to prevent them from coming further upstream. Use great caution when you approach Savannah.

Respectfully yours,
General Augustin Prevost, Commanding

"Robert, assemble the regiment. Instruct them to prepare to move on Savannah." Maitland took a cloth from his washstand and dipped it into a basin of cool water. He squeezed out the water and washed his face. The coolness of the rag felt good on his fevered brow.

On September 12, Colonel John Maitland and his Scottish Highlanders, together with several companies of German Hessian mercenaries, boarded their ships and set sail for Savannah.

****

Enoch Penrose, James Pelham and Caleb Hawkins fell in with their company for the march with the Delancey Battalion to their encampment behind the barracks. Once there they began the tasks of erecting tents and preparing the bivouac. Toward mid-afternoon their company commander, Lieutenant Oswald Scott, assembled his troops and gave them their battle assignments.

"Men, when you hear the beat to arms you are to assemble here immediately. We will then proceed directly to our posts. We will deploy to the left of the barracks along the trenches behind the *abatis*. It will be our assignment to hold off any enemy surge that makes it through the *abatis* and the trenches. We'll be waiting on top of the ramparts.

"In the meantime we have beeen seconded to Chief Engineer Moncrief to reinforce the ramparts behind the trenches in front of our position. So, grab your picks, shovels and axes and follow me."

"Damn," Enoch swore. "I didn't join up with these Tories to dig ditches. I'm here to offer my services as a rifleman."

"Better watch what you say, Enoch," Pelham said. "One of these redcoats will put you on report for insubordination, or worse yet, treason. You don't want to find yourself dangling from a hangman's rope."

"Jim, I don't plan to be around long enough to get fitted for no rope necktie. As soon as this little skirmish is over and we've run the ragtag Whigs and their sympathizers off, I'm heading south. I've got a few scores to settle. I hope you and Caleb are planning on joining me. If I get back what's rightfully mine there'll be something in it for you too. I'm going to need an overseer for Roselawn. Besides, I suspect you've got a little burr under your saddle for the way Hiram treated you."

Enoch grudgingly picked up an axe and trudged off toward the forest beyond the Tattnall Road gates.

****

Hiram Penrose and Wimberley Jones rode down the long avenue of interlocking oaks, passing under the great brick and tabby arch at the entrance to Wormslow Plantation. Each wore the Georgia militia uniform of a captain. Each carried their flintlock rifles in fancy leather scabbards. Their sabers slapped against their legs with each canter of the horses.

"Hiram, I have a favor to ask of you. A few days ago, Admiral de Noailles called on me at Wormslow. He is a senior officer of the French force encamped at Buley. It seems that his soldiers were having trouble rustling up enough supplies from the local gentry to feed his army. None of his foragers speak English and the farmers certainly don't *parlez vous Francais*, so he needed someone to help pave the way for them. He first went to Bethesda but Reverend Barkley didn't have any one who speaks French. So he told the admiral there might be someone at St. Benedict's who could help him.

He sent de Noaillles over to Wormslow knowing that we'd be able to get him over to Skidaway. I agreed to have some of my boys row him over. He came back a few hours later and you'll never guess who was with him."

"Who? One of the nuns? I know they all speak French. As a matter of fact I met several of them when I took the daughter of one of our house servants over there a few years back. The mother superior is Sister Marie Michel, I believe. They are a pretty impressive group. They're doing a wonderful job with the young girls," Hiram said

"That's who came back with him. Cassie Omuru. The girl you took over there."

"No! You must be joking. She doesn't speak French. When she left Roselawn, she barely spoke decent English."

"When's the last time you saw her? She speaks French, Latin and who knows what else. It seems she is very intelligent and has absorbed every thing the sisters threw at her. Why, she was talking to de Noailles and his men like she was raised in Paris. Darnedest thing you've ever seen."

"Well, I'll be. But, you started out saying you needed a favor. What does Cassie have to do with that?" Hiram asked.

"None of the sisters could respond to de Noailles because of their vows, and the monastery has to be careful. They are, after all, an arm of the Church of England and their support comes from many places on both sides of our conflict. But, since Cassie is still a novice and indeed may never become a nun, it was felt that she could help the American cause and not endanger the church's position.

"She was very reluctant to do this. She's never been out in the world and she's afraid. If slave chasers catch her she could be sold back into slavery even though she still belongs to you. She and the sisters only agreed for her to do this if de Noailles would promise to petition you for her freedom after this is all over. He told them that he would and he asked me if I would try to help persuade you. I told him that I would. Seeing as how it's been five years since she left Roselawn and you seem to have gotten along very well without her.

"She wants to work among the Negroes to try to help better their lot in life. She can't ever do that as a slave. She finally decided this was the only opportunity she would ever have to gain her freedom. So, she agreed."

"I don't know Wimberley. We've never freed any of our slaves. I don't even know the legal process that's necessary to do that. I suppose if you tell them they're free they're still subject to the same treatment that Cassie is so fearful of if she's caught."

"My father, before he died, wanted to reward one of his oldest and most faithful house servants with his freedom," Wimberley said. "He set the man free along with his wife and their three children. He gave him enough money to start up a small gristmill. The old fellow was eternally grateful and has done well. Papa went to Mr. Sheftall and he drafted what's called a "Writ of Manumission". It's a legal paper that proves to the world the freedom of the person named in the document. The paper is registered at the courthouse. So, what do you say Hiram, will you do it?"

"I'll have to speak to Amanda, Cassie worked for her in the house, along with her mother Queen. If Amanda's willing to do it I guess I'd go along with it."

"Great. We'll be able to tell Admiral de Noailles when we meet him in Savannah. Thank you, Hiram."

The ride to join General Lincoln took them across the marshes and pine barrens lying south of the city. The well-worn trail finally crossed the Louisville Road before merging with the Augusta Road. It was late afternoon when they passed Musgrove Plantation, land given to Mary Musgrove, the half-breed Creek Indian princess who was instrumental in keeping the peace between Oglethorpe and the native tribes.

"Do you know General Lincoln, Wimberley?" Hiram asked.

"I met him once in Charlestown. That was nearly two years ago when Washington first sent him south to shore up the defenses in Carolina and Georgia. He's not a very imposing military figure. He's a little portly and he has an annoying habit of dozing off at odd times. Sometimes even in mid-sentence. He played a big role in the early conflicts with the British in Massachusetts and he is widely regarded as a very competent military strategist. He was wounded in the battle leading up to General Burgoyne's surrender. He nearly lost his leg and still walks with a decided limp. I just hope he brought a large enough force to take on the British in Savannah."

"Do you know how many soldiers the French have?" Hiram asked.

"Admiral de Noailles told me that he has 1500 in Buley. He said that d'Estaing has another 2500 aboard ship waiting for the storms to pass. I'm guessing that we'll have over 5000 men altogether. That should frighten the devil out of "Old Bullet Head" and Governor Wright. If they have any sense they'll pack up and get out of there before it comes to war. I don't see any way the British can hold out against these numbers. They can't have more than 1500 able bodied soldiers. We know that Maitland is still tied up in Beaufort and Cruger is still in Sunbury.

"This whole thing will be over as soon as we unite with the French. We'll be back at Wormslow and Roselawn in a few days. And Savannah will be back in the hands of our people, where it should be."

"Where is General McIntosh," Jones asked the sentry guarding the entrance to the sprawling encampment at Cherokee Hill.

"I'm sorry sir, but I understand he's not arrived. He's on his way down from the Millen Plantation and is expected here before dark."

"Thank you, corporal. Now, can you direct us to General Lincoln's tent?"

"Yes sir, he's down near the pond under that big grove of hickory trees. He's been meeting with all his officers for the past hour or so."

The two tired, dusty officers nudged their horses over toward the horse pens and dismounted. They unsaddled their mounts directing the guards to see that they got some feed and water. They walked over to the command tent. General Lincoln and his senior officers had moved outside under the trees to escape the stifling heat of the tent. They were sitting on campstools, huddled around a small table, focused intently on a map of Savannah and its environs that was unfurled on the table.

General Lincoln looked up from the map. He smiled at the tall officer approaching him.

"Captain Jones. How good to see you. I haven't seen you since we met in Charlestown. How are you?"

"I'm fine sir. How good of you to remember me. May I introduce Captain Hiram Penrose of the Georgia Militia."

Hiram saluted as the general arose to shake his hand.

"How do you do Captain Penrose. I'm happy to see the two of you joining our merry little band," he said. "I was hoping your General McIntosh would be here by now but I reckon he'll be along shortly. By the way, did you see or hear anything of Count Pulaski's Legion on your way out from Savannah?"

"Yes, sir. We stopped to eat at the tavern just west of the Musgrove place. There was a group of soldiers there just back from patrol. They told us that Admiral d'Estaing had invited the general to join him at his headquarters in Thunderbolt."

Lincoln was a pious man, not given to cursing, but he came close on this bit of news. Exasperation was evident in his tone and the set of his jaw.

"It was my desire that Pulaski wait here for me, so that we could join Count d'Estaing as a united American army!" He spat out the words. "But I see that is not to be. When General McIntosh arrives we will proceed to our rendezvous with the French."

CHAPTER FIFTEEN

ANDRE URGED THE TIRING, sweaty horses down the sandy lane toward a farmhouse, set well back into the woods, just north of the Montgomery community. They forded a small stream that emptied into the marsh fronting the house. Cassie, as had become her custom, sat beside him. It was the second day since leaving Beaulieu and the wagons were nearly filled with corn, wheat, potatoes and other farm products. Louis trailed along behind in the convoy, occasionally dozing off only to be rudely awakened by a poke in the ribs from one of the mounted soldiers. They hoped to finish their foraging before dark and move back onto the main road toward Greenwich. Captain Graham had given instructions for them to rejoin the army by noon of the seventeenth.

"Cassie, you've been mighty quiet for the last few miles. Is something bothering you?" Andre asked

"I've just been thinking that after we deliver the wagons to Captain Graham tomorrow, I'll be heading back to Skidaway Island while you and Louis and all the other soldiers head off to battle. I'm anxious to get back to see the sisters but at the same time these last few days have been really exciting. I've seen more of the world than I had seen in my whole life before. And I've met so many interesting people. Such as you and Louis and the captain and the admiral. Things I've only read about in the books have come to life in front of my eyes. It's all a bit frightening and yet somehow I don't want it to end.

"I've become very fond of you and Louis. I feel a kinship with you. Your stories of life on Saint-Domingue seem so different from my life and yet in ways they are the same. Your desires to escape the life of the plantations and to be free are just like mine. Your wish to be reunited with your mother and brothers are the same as my wish to rejoin my mother. Yet, your road to freedom is so different from mine. You're fighting an enemy you don't know for a cause that's not yours just so that at the end of it all you'll be free. I'm helping an army that I don't know, to fight an enemy I don't know, so that I too can be free. It seems that God sets us on strange paths sometimes to achieve his own purposes."

"I know. Who would have thought when I left Grenada on that ship so many years ago that I would wind up here in America with this beautiful princess of Africa sitting beside me on a wagon full of vegetables."

Cassie laughed.

"I've never had anyone tell me I'm beautiful, Andre. Do you really think so?"

"I wouldn't say it if I didn't mean it. You remind me so much of my mother. Her parents came to Grenada from Spain. You have the same flashing eyes and smooth, beautiful skin. And your hair is like hers. Dark and curly and shining in the moonlight."

Andre caught himself up short. He didn't want to get so familiar that he would frighten her away. But he did want her to know how he felt and to hope that there might be something more for them than these few days riding a wagon through the Georgia countryside.

"Oh, hush, Andre, you're embarrassing me. You know, I wish we'd had a chance to have that picnic. I've never been alone with a man before. I mean totally alone. I think it would have been fun to lie on the beach and run in the water and enjoy each other's company. It's too bad we'll never have that opportunity."

She looked at him wistfully as the iron wagon wheels jolted over the corduroy cattle guard in front of the farmhouse.

****

The cook fires were reduced to a few glowing embers when General

McIntosh brought his brigade into the Cherokee Hill encampment. He reported immediately to General Lincoln.

"Did you receive my dispatches, sir? The ones concerning our activities on the way down from Augusta?" McIntosh asked.

"Yes I did, General. Great work. I'm sure glad we don't have to worry about someone sneaking up on us from that direction. When we finish here in Savannah I'm going to send a few more men up there to reinforce those garrisons. I don't want Tarleton or some other of Cornwallis's men overrunning those posts. If we can hang on to Savannah, Charlestown, Augusta and the forts along the river I believe we can bring the British to their knees. They've already pretty much abandoned their northern campaign and are placing all their eggs in their "southern strategy" basket. It's our job to see that those eggs get broken before they can hatch.

"It's certainly good to see you. Later I want to hear all about your adventures on the frontier. Now, get your men fed and bedded down for the night. We're leaving at first light to join Count d'Estaing at Greenwich.

"Oh, by the way. Two captains from the Georgia militia reported to me this afternoon. They were looking for you. A Captain Wimberley Jones and a Captain Hiram Penrose. I told them I would let you know they are here. They've pitched a tent over beyond the horse pens. I'll have someone notify them of your arrival and ask them to report to you immediately."

"Thank you, General. I've been looking forward to their arrival. We lost several of our line officers during the campaign. I sure need them to take over a couple of our rifle companies

"They are both excellent men. Wimberley's father came over on the *Ann* with Oglethorpe. Noble Jones was the backbone of our community. He remained loyal to his king until the end. He died just a few years ago. Both Wimberley and Hiram were at my side during the unfortunate episode with Button Gwinnett. What a waste. The man just could not put the good of the cause ahead of his personal ambition. My God! How we could have used his wisdom during these terrible times." McIntosh paused to look around the sprawling encampment.

"General, I didn't see the colorful banners of my old friend, Count Pulaski, as we came in. Is he not joining us?"

Lincoln bristled.

"That's a very sore subject. I discovered upon my arrival that Count d'Estaing summoned Pulaski to his headquarters before I got here. That was a direct breach of my orders. I've never operated with the French before. I hope this is not what I can expect from them."

"I'm sorry General. I'm sure it's just a misunderstanding. Surely the admiral knows you have been given equal command of this expedition by General Washington."

"I hope you're right. This campaign depends upon the highest level of coordination and communication between our commands. With all the different languages being spoken we surely need to speak with one voice.

"You'd better get along now, General. We all need to be rested and sharp for the next few days. Good night."

Captains Jones and Penrose were walking up to McIntosh's tent when he arrived from his visit to General Lincoln.

"Good evening, sir," Captain Jones said, a broad smile lighting his face. He and Captain Penrose saluted. McIntosh returned the salute and ushered them into his tent.

"Good to see you, my dear friends. It's been a long, long time since I left here to join General Washington. It's pleasing to me to see you looking so well."

He hesitated, a slight catch in his throat.

"Tell me. Is there any word of my wife and family?"

"Lachlan, they are still in Savannah," Jones said. "Prevost was asked to allow the women and children to leave the city but he refused. There's been no direct word from them for three weeks.

"The British have pulled all their outposts in and I'm sure they've sent for Maitland and Cruger. I just hope the French left enough ships at Port Royal and Hilton Head to block Maitland so he can't try to relieve Prevost. Without those troops I don't think the British can hope to repel an attack by our combined forces. If Prevost is smart he'll surrender as soon as we show up. In the meantime reports are that he is furiously extending and improving the city's defenses. Fires are burning all night and they've clear-cut a half-mile wide field around the entire town. If we must attack, that open field will expose our men to an unimpeded line of fire from the ramparts.

"What of d'Estaing? I understand from General Lincoln that he has landed his force at Buley and sent the ships on to Thunderbolt, at the Mulryne plantation. He also told me that Pulaski proceeded to join the French there, notwithstanding the general's order that the count wait for him here at Cherokee Hill. What do you two make of this?"

"I'm not sure," Jones said. "I have met one of his senior officers, an Admiral de Noailles. He is in charge of the encampment at Buley. He came to me for help in getting someone to interpret for his troops on their foraging missions. I was very impressed with the man. If the others are as competent as he seems, I don't see a problem. I just think there was a miscommunication due to the language difference. We'll know soon enough. d'Estaing has asked General Lincoln to join him at Greenwich tomorrow."

Greenwich was a grand plantation a mile or two north of Thunderbolt, close to the river and on a small promontory near Causton Bluff. The night before, the Bowens, owners of Greenwich, had entertained D'Estaing and Pulaski there.

****

Count Pulaski handed the bottle of brandy back to Admiral d'Estaing. He sat across the fire from the admiral, Viscount de Noailles to his right. He and his men had arrived in camp just before sunset and pitched their tents alongside the contingent from Thunderbolt.

"Admiral, it has been a while since I enjoyed such a wonderful cognac. Probably not since I left Europe. Thank you for the fine dinner. I'm sure the local provisions are not quite up to the *haute cuisine* standards of Paris, but it is a far cry better than what I have had recently. I must say, as much as I do admire the zeal of the Americans in their quest for independence, I sometimes tire of their crudeness and backwoods manners. And their food is even worse than that of the Hessians.

"It was quite different with General Washington and his officers. Although they were at times quite deprived of food and drink, they always comported themselves as true gentlemen and with great dignity. I don't believe you've had the opportunity to meet Washington?"

"No," d'Estaing said. "I had hoped to meet him after Newport, but the unfortunate turn of events there forced me to withdraw from the field and I was unable to do so. I understand that his is a quite imposing presence. I have a full-length portrait of Washington, given to me by John Hancock. It hangs in my stateroom aboard the *Languedoc*. I have the greatest admiration for him."

"I don't think I've ever met, even among all the crowned heads of Europe, a more impressive figure than he," Pulaski said. "I served under the best field commanders in Europe. None of them inspired my confidence as Washington does. If anyone can lead this scruffy bunch of patriots to victory, it will be General Washington."

d'Estaing drained the last of his cognac.

"When this war is over, and America has won its freedom, I hope to return and personally congratulate him, as well as my dear friend, Mr. Franklin."

"Ah, yes," de Noailles interjected. He closed his eyes in reminiscence.

"I can see Mr. Franklin now, holding court in Paris, surrounded by the ladies and the international literati. It would be wonderful to sit with him again. What an intelligence he possesses. I've never known anyone his equal. With men such as these how can America fail?"

"Admiral, Count, with your permission I will beg my leave," de Noailles said. I must see to my men. They've had a tiring march from Buley and I must see to the preparations for tomorrow."

"By all means," d'Estaing said. "I'll not be far behind you."

The camp was two miles east of Thunderbolt. All the soldiers that were well enough to travel had made the move on the fifteenth. Several hundred remained at the camp on Mulryne Plantation, too ill to march. The daily death toll both in the camp and aboard the ships was staggering, lending even more urgency to confront Prevost and bring a conclusion to this engagement. The admiral rested a weary head in his hands as he gathered his thoughts. When he was ready he straightened, placed his hands on his knees and looked across the fire at his guest with a level and confident gaze.

"Tomorrow, I'm going to deliver an ultimatum to General Prevost and Governor Wright. I'm going to demand they lay down their arms and surrender the city. There are many reasons that I need to finish this and get my ships back to sea. We continue to lose men daily to the vaporous diseases that seem to rise up from these swamps. We're also vulnerable to those unpredictable tropical storms that seem to hit this part of the world each year at this time. I've been through one such storm in the islands and it's not something I wish to experience again. It was the remnant of one of those storms that demasted my ship at Newport, forcing me to abandon the battle."

Pulaski was startled at the pronouncement by d'Estaing.

"Sir, if I may?" he asked.

"By all means Count Pulaski. Say what you will," d'Estaing offered.

"It is my understanding that General Lincoln has been given equal command of this mission. Don't you think it appropriate that he be present for the demand to surrender?"

d'Estaing's eyes flashed, imperceptibly, and then a thin smile returned to his face.

"My dear Count. I have just related to you the necessity for expedience. What matters it if Lincoln or I present the paper. It's a foregone conclusion that he will make the same decision. In the interest of time I am simply expediting the obvious."

Pulaski did not respond. He sat silently with his thoughts. What d'Estaing was proposing was, if not outright insubordination, at the least highly irregular. One might argue the benefit of the doubt in his favor under the peculiar circumstances of this alliance. After all, France is a world power, while this ragtag bunch of rebels is fighting to establish their right to exist as a nation. He let it pass. "General Lincoln can defend his own position tomorrow; if he chooses," he thought.

"Count d'Estaing, once again, thank you for the superb hospitality you have shown me this evening. With your permission I will rejoin my men. We have much to do before the sun rises tomorrow. I bid you good evening sir."

"And a good evening to you Count Pulaski. Tomorrow's events should prove to be momentous."

CHAPTER SIXTEEN

THE WAGONS RUMBLED INTO camp a scant hour before the main body straggled in from Beaulieu. Cassie helped Andre, Louis and the other men unload and set up the mess tents. She was exhausted from the arduous two-day drive and was anxious to finish and get some rest. As soon as the last peg was driven into the ground she left for her own tent and flopped onto her cot. She was so bone-tired she didn't even bother to remove any of her clothes. Within minutes she was asleep. She slept so deeply that even the usual dreams of St. Benedict's and Roselawn could not penetrate her subconscious.

It was well past midnight when she awoke, suddenly aware that she was not alone. She threw off the covers and jumped to her feet, ready to scream. Then, in the thin shaft of moonlight spilling through the tent flap, she could make out a familiar face. She saw that it was Andre.

"Andre, you scared me to death. What is it? Do we have to leave already? What time is it? It seems like I just got to bed."

"No, Cassie. It's nothing like that. I couldn't sleep, and knowing that tomorrow will be our last day I just had to talk to you. I know that you have promised God and the sisters that you will devote your life to his work among your people, but I just felt that it may be possible for you to do that and still have a life beyond the church. I know missionary families who came to Grenada and Saint-Domingue who were committed to their cause, but still had time for their own needs and desires. I think God wants us all to be happy. I think He needs people like you and me who can do His work as well as set a godly example in our own personal lives. I wanted to ask you to think about the future and whether we may share that future together someday. I know that after this is over I have to go back to my ship. I don't know where I will go from there but I do know that when I am free, if you'll let me, I'm coming back here. I want you to be my wife. I want to spend the rest of my life with you. I will do whatever you ask me to do. I just want to be with you. What do you say, Cassie? Will you at least think about it?"

The torrent of words came so fast Cassie had difficulty comprehending what Andre was saying. She fell back on the bed, dazed. She looked up at him in the dim light, bewildered. After a time she spoke.

"Andre, I don't know what to say. I have never let myself think of anything beyond my vows. All that I have done, all the studying, all the hard work, have been with that one purpose in mind. I don't even know if I would be allowed to do what you are suggesting and still be considered a disciple of St. Benedict. This is such a shock to me. Of course I have learned to care for you too in these past few days. I find you kind and intelligent and caring, but I don't know if that's enough to say that I love you or that I want to spend the rest of my life with you. Such a huge decision as this requires a lot of prayer and thought. Please, let me think about it and we can talk more in the morning."

"Cassie, I know this is all so sudden, but there's not much time and I couldn't bear the thought of leaving you and not ever knowing if there was at least a small chance that you might love me as well. I'll go now, but please pray about this. I'll come by before reveille. I hope then that you will have the answer I seek. Good night."

Before leaving, he drew her up from the bed and held her tightly in his arms. He kissed her full on the lips and then let her slide back onto the bed. Before she could protest he was gone.

Cassie sat there, her head spinning in a thousand different directions. Until that moment, when he kissed her, the first kiss she had ever had, she knew that she could never agree to his request. Now, after the kiss, she began to have doubts. She had never experienced these feelings. She had known the love of her mother and grandmother, and she had been loved by the sisters of St. Benedict's, but this was different. The emotions coursing through her were strange and troubling. She knew that whatever happened tomorrow, her life would never be the same after tonight.

****

Cassie could hear the sentries in the distance, their challenges ringing across the marsh at the changing of the guard. She had slept fitfully since Andre left. A few rays of light were breaking through the dark clouds hanging above the eastern horizon when she arose. Andre would return shortly. What would she tell him? She clasped her hands in prayer and knelt, leaning against the cot.

"Dear God. Please tell me what to do? For the past five years I have dedicated my life to You. I have studied and prayed with the sisters. I have seen how devoted and strong they are. Their faith in You is unshakable. I felt that my faith and belief was as strong as theirs and yet I find myself wavering. Is my faith so shallow that it can be lost in an instant? Was I ever really as strong as I thought I was? Or, is there another way You can open to me that will let me serve You and still follow an earthly path as well? Please help me, Oh Lord. Please tell me what to say to Andre when he returns?"

She was startled by a great flurry of wings as she stepped outside her tent. A young red-tailed hawk swooped into a flock of mourning doves that was feeding on the trampled corn. She stared in horror as the hawk seized one of the doves and soared skyward with the poor bird clutched in its talons. Suddenly the hawk emitted an earsplitting shriek as it was swallowed up by a large shadow. A great horned owl, its wings spread in a giant arc, dropped down from its perch high in a tree. The hunter had become the hunted. Angered by the hawk's poaching of its intended prey and taking advantage of the opportunity, the owl snatched the small hawk in midair. The large bird's talons sank deep into the hawk's back as the smaller bird twisted furiously to defend itself. The attempt was futile. With a few strong beats of its five-foot wings the nocturnal raptor soared over the marsh toward its nest at the top of a cypress.

Cassie stood motionless, mouth agape, watching the drama unfold. The terrified dove flew in her direction, swerving tto avoid her, and crashing into a limb overhanging the tent. A feather, loosened in the attack, fell from its wing. It floated in the heavy morning air, suspended for an eternity, finally coming to rest in Cassie's outstretched hand. She held the feather toward the light and then brushed it against her cheek. It was so soft and so delicate. Her cheek was moist. Had she been crying? She felt it. Her fingertip was red. In the dim light she hadn't seen the blood. "God, are you telling me something?" she asked.

Her mind flashed back to Roselawn. To the many tales she had heard at Aba's knee, stories of signs and omens brought to her people by the spirits. She spoke of the *Vodun* rites in Africa where the blood of sacrificed animals was dripped onto fetishes to feed the spirits. She told how the priests would interpret the fetishes and translate the messages from those spirits. In the dark corners of most slave quarters in America, *Vodun* was still being practiced, its African animist rituals blending with the Christian missionary message. There remained a steadfast belief in the spirit world, and in its ability to guide the paths of the believers.

A strange calmness washed over her. Her worries lifted. They seemed to drift away like the mists hanging over the marsh. At that moment she was certain that God had answered her prayer. The sign was as bright and clear as any her ancestors had ever been given.

"God, is that dove my sign? Has its blood freed me as Christ's blood did?" She felt a surge of joy and relief as she realized her answer to Andre would be, yes.

****

Andre could barely make her out, standing there outside the tent when he returned. This early in the morning the light was still dim. She stood still, watching as he approached. She held a feather in her hand. There was smear of blood on her cheek.

"Are you hurt?" he asked, alarmed. "What happened?"

He rushed to take her in his arms. She stepped back, still not sure how to react to him. This strange new world didn't come with a set of rules. She would have to feel her way along. Guard against her impulses. Listen to the little voice of caution in her head. She placed her hand on his chest, holding him at a distance.

"I'm fine Andre," she said calmly. "Come and sit with me."

They sat on the fallen trunk of a tree.

She told him of how she had prayed and cried and asked God to help her. She told him of Aba and her stories of Africa and the *Vodun* priests with their fetishes and signs. She told him of the owl, the hawk and the dove. She told him of the feather and how it came to her.

"I believe God sent that dove to find that corn on the ground. I believe He sent the hawk to seize the dove, and I believe He sent the owl to free the dove from the hawk. And I believe He dropped this bloody feather in my hand as His sign to me. He set me free to serve Him. Free, in body and in spirit. Free, wherever I am. Free, to love and be loved. He's telling me that the two of us together can serve Him more powerfully than either of us could alone."

She hesitated, suddenly unsure of this revelation. Still afraid to let herself accept that God would do this for her.

"Andre, am I crazy?" she asked. "Can all this be mere chance? Do I want to be with you so much that I am reading my own wishes into something that has no meaning at all? Do you think God still speaks to us as He did to all those people in the bible?"

Andre put his finger to her lips.

"Shhhhh. Calm down. Of course I believe that God speaks to us. If He spoke to Noah and Moses and Joshua, why would He suddenly decide at some point in time to stop speaking to man? We don't know how He spoke to them or to the other people in the bible but I believe that however He did it, He's still doing it.

" Listen, there was this little, dried up, toothless old man in Cap Haitien. If you saw him on the street you wouldn't look twice. But at night, under the stars, around a fire, with drums beating, he became a beacon of hope for those who sought his help and believed in his powers. With his bag of bones, string of beads, and bloody sacrifices, he found the answers to life's questions for them. However, for those who scoffed at him, nothing ever seemed to work out. Now, you tell me, how much of that did the priest cause to happen and how much was a result of their trust in his powers?"

"Oh, Andre. I want to believe. But how will you ever get back here? When those ships sail away you'll be in another world. You'll be at the mercy of men who don't know or care about you and me. Five years is such a long time. Will you really come back when you are free? How will you get back from so far away?"

"Cassie, I'll come back from the ends of the earth for you if I have to. But for now, you must go back to St. Benedict's and wait for me. Stay with the sisters. Tell them about us. They'll understand. They'll take care of you. If we really believe what God told you today then we know it will all work out. Believe. We must believe."

His words soothed her jangled nerves. The calmness returned. She did believe.

"I spoke to the captain about your escort back to the monastery. He said that this should all be over in two or three days. He thinks the British will surrender soon. When they do he said he would let me and Louis take you back. In the meantime he said you can stay here with the quartermasters, out of harms way. He said we're going to be moving closer to the city today, so I won't see you again until this is over. Captain Deschamps will look after you until then. Listen to him. He's a good man."

" I pray that you're right, Andre. You take care of yourself and don't do anything foolish."

This time she didn't step back. He reached out and took her in his arms. He held her tightly. He kissed her gently on the lips. Her world went spinning again. She watched as he disappeared into the mists.

CHAPTER SEVENTEEN

Captain Padraig Moran of the Dillon regiment was summoned to d'Estaing's tent early on the morning of the sixteenth of September.

The admiral thought that he would be done with this disease-ridden pesthole by now. He counted on a swift surrender by Prevost and a speedy departure of his fleet, leaving Savannah in the hands of the Americans and returning to France to receive the accolades of the court. Now, more than two weeks later, he sat in the heat and the rain surrounded by pestilence and death, enduring the privations of this god-forsaken wilderness. He would wait no longer.

"Captain. I want you to deliver this summons to General Prevost at his headquarters in Savannah. As a gentleman, who fully understands the protocols of war, I'm certain he will honor your white flag of truce and grant you entry. You are to stay until the general has fashioned a reply and then bring it to me immediately."

He smiled wryly at the young officer who was resplendent in the uniform of the Dillon Regiment.

"I suggest that you exchange your Irish uniform for a French one. The general may not have such a well-honed sense of humor as to forgive a fellow Briton come seeking his surrender."

d'Estaing and his aides snickered at the irony. Moran was chosen for his ability to speak both French and English and to be able to judge Prevost's reaction to the summons. The Dillon regiment, with its distinctive red and black flag, enjoyed a long and storied history in the service of France. Its commander, Arthur Dillon, was great-grandson to the daughter of King Charles II. The regiment was comprised of Irish refugees, going back several generations.

Prevost adjusted his reading glasses before reading the communiqué from d'Estaing.

"Count d'Estaing summons His Excellency General Prevost to surrender to the arms of the King of France. He apprises him that he will be personally responsible for all the events and misfortunes that may arise from a defense, which, by the superiority of the force which attacks him, both by sea and land, is rendered manifestly vain and of no effect."

Thus began the ultimatum handed to General Prevost by Captain Padraig Moran on the morning of September 16, 1779.

d"Estaing's harangue went on for four more paragraphs in which he warned Prevost not to destroy anything of value in the city or he would be held personally responsible. He also recounted his great victories against Lord McCartney and the British garrisons in the Caribbean and how futile their defense had been.

Prevost read the document with a mix of concern and disdain. He knew that without Maitland's reinforcements and more time to prepare the city for attack, d'Estaing's legions could overwhelm his inferior numbers. He called his lieutenants together to prepare a response. He sent Captain Moran away to await his reply.

"Gentlemen," he addressed his staff, "the call for surrender we have expected for several days has arrived."

He passed the document around.

"Bit of a pompous ass I would say," one aide muttered. When the officers had finished reading Prevost began again.

"I think we all agree that under our present state of preparedness, and without Maitland's reinforcements, it is unlikely that we can repulse a concerted attack by the French and American forces. Yet I do not feel we should surrender without knowing whether Maitland will make it. Nor do I want to turn over the city to d'Estaing's *carte blanche* demands. Therefore, I propose that we ask for a clarification as to what terms and conditions we are to surrender and a twenty-four hour truce in which to consider them."

Captain Moran arrived back at camp late in the morning with the response from General Prevost.

"Sir-

I am just now honored with your Excellency's letter of this date containing a summons for me to surrender this town to the arms of his Majesty the King of France, which I had just delayed to answer, til I had shown it to the King's civil Governor.

"I hope your Excellency will have a better opinion of me, and of British troops, to think either will surrender on a general summons, without any specific terms.

"If you, sir, have anything specific to propose that may of honor be accepted by me, you can mention them, both with regard to civil and military, and I will then give my answer. In the meantime I will promise, upon my honor, that nothing, with my consent or knowledge, shall be destroyed, in this town or river."

d'Estaing's formal reply to Prevost was full of flowery phrases. He observed the unwritten code governing the conduct of war in the eighteenth century. Killing or maiming your adversary in the most gruesome manner possible was perfectly acceptable on the battlefield, but to disrespect him in formal correspondence was an unpardonable offense.

He agreed with Prevost that it was certainly the right of the besieged to propose terms under which he may surrender, and by all means to do so. However, it was ultimately the besieger's decision as to which of the terms offered would be acceptable.

He also informed him that he was aware that the British forces were continuing to entrench and fortify their positions in violation of the previously agreed demands. Therefore, he said, the French were justified in continuing to deploy their own forces around the city, even though they would not come so close as to endanger the truce. Then d'Estaing added a most peculiar postscript to his reply:

"I apprise your Excellency that I have not been able to refuse the army of the United States uniting itself with that of the King. The junction will probably be effected this day. If I have not an answer, therefore, immediately, you must confer in the future with General Lincoln and me."

Despite the fact that he had been invited to participate in this action by the the Americans and was asked to do so jointly with General Lincoln, d'Estaing considered himself to be in command, and that he held the ultimate authority. If his disdain for the American army was not evident prior to this, his note to Prevost removed all doubt. He would suffer this rabble to assist him in this undertaking, but let no one question who was in charge.

Prevost, for his part, needed to play a waiting game. He knew from his informants that Maitland was nearing Savannah. He was somewhere out there in the labyrinthine rivers and marshes to the north of the city. If he could just hold out for another twenty-four hours he was sure that Maitland, with his eight hundred Scottish Highland regulars, would arrive. With that number, and with the hourly improvement in the city's defenses, he could afford to reject the summons to surrender.

****

Maitland could see the masts of the French ships rising above the mists off Tybee. He was blocked from an approach across the open waters of the Atlantic. His maps showed no other waterway that would take him through the seemingly impenetrable wall of sea grass.

Disappointment showed on the fatigued faces of Maitland and his men. They were ready to surrender to the ache of their weary arms. They had transferred from the *Vigilante* and the galleys into smaller craft that could navigate the shallow waters. They left the larger ships at Buck Island near Hilton Head. They spent the next night on Daufuskie, feasting on shellfish, fresh from the sound, and catching as much rest as possible. A half-day of steady rowing had brought them to this point. Now, stymied by the green barrier, all seemed lost. Maitland knew time was running out. He feared that even if he got to Savannah by the next morning it would be too late. He was certain the French would pursue their advantage and attack before his arrival.

The flotilla of small boats continued to probe the numerous tributaries flowing out of the marsh. Their incursions proved fruitless, repeatedly petering out into dead ends. Maitland was distraught. He was weighing his options when the scout boat returned. It was escorting a small jon boat carrying several Negro fishermen. He could hear their conversation across the still water. They were speaking a Carolina low-country dialect: Gullah.

"Colonel," his chief scout addressed his commander. "These men are from Daufuskie Island. They live on one of the plantations there. They tell me they have been fishing these waters for years and are familiar with all the creeks and passages through the marsh. I asked this man if there is a way to get to Savannah without entering the river south of "Five Fathom Hole." He said there are two looping tidal creeks that almost meet between here and the Back River. They are separated by a small channel called Wall's Cut."

"Does he think we can get through there?" Maitland asked, a glimmer of hope in his voice.

"He says the cut is a few hundred feet long but is passable at high tide. He thinks we'll probably have to push the boats through but once we're on the other side we'll emerge into the Wright River. It runs behind Elba Island to the Savannah, west of "Five Fathom Hole." Once there it's only two or three miles upriver to the bluff."

"All right then!" Maitland exulted, thrusting his arms into the air. "Ask him if he'll take us through. Tell him it's for the King of England and that if he gets us there before the French attack, he'll be a great hero. Also, tell him he'll be handsomely rewarded."

Maitland gazed skyward. The sun was already at its zenith. They had no time to waste.

d'Estaing responded haughtily to the request for a twenty-four hour truce. He reminded Prevost once again how futile his position was and that by continuing to flaunt their previous agreements he left him no choice but to continue preparations for battle. He sent Dillon and de Noailles to encircle the city. He also posted troops at all four "entrances into the wood" so that none of the British troops could venture out to attack his men. He confirmed that, absent surrender by the British, he would lay siege to the city at sundown tomorrow.

Dawn broke on the sixteenth. The heat was less oppressive, but the rain continued. The ground around the camp and along the siege lines was churned into a sea of mud under the trampling hooves of the horses and the booted soldiers. Shortly after the colors were raised at eight a.m. the vanguard of General Lincoln's army rode into camp. By nine the entire contingent had arrived and was settling into their campsites. General Lincoln went immediately to Admiral d'Estaing's tent.

"Count d'Estaing, It is indeed a pleasure to meet you. America is truly grateful to the King of France. He has come to our aid at a most opportune time. I welcome you to Savannah."

"General Lincoln, it is an honor for me to represent my King and to lend support to your noble cause. I look forward to a rapid conclusion to this expedition and to returning the city of Savannah to its rightful owners."

"Thank you, Admiral," Lincoln said. "Now, if I may, I'd like a word with you in private, before we get down to the business of planning this expedition, as you call it."

"Certainly, General, come into my tent. We can have some breakfast while we talk."

Lincoln followed the admiral into his tent where there were tea and biscuits on the table.

"Count d'Estaing," Lincoln began, "I realize that you are in a hurry to finish your work here and put back to sea before the British or the storms come. However, I would have considered it a helpful gesture had you awaited my arrival before dispatching your summons to General Prevost." He continued standing, maintaining his stern expression.

"My dear General, I meant no discourtesy to you. I have the utmost respect for your gallant service to General Washington and the American cause. It was simply my zeal to get on with the task at hand and, as you say, put back to sea as hastily as possible. Please forgive me, sir. Now if I may serve you some tea and biscuits?"

Lincoln sat down, deciding, in the interest of maintaining civil relations with the French, to not pursue the subject further.

"Count, what is the present state of your relations with the British?"

d'Estaing took a sip of tea. He closed his eyes and savored the taste a moment before replying.

"They asked that we give them terms and conditions for their surrender and to afford them a twenty-four hour truce in which to study the demands. I acceded to this request knowing full well that they would continue their preparations for battle. However, as I told the general, it was of little consequence since we had such overwhelming force on our side. If they have not submitted by the sounding of retreat tomorrow we will resume hostilities."

At that moment, unknown to the French and American commanders, Lt. Col. John Maitland was moving upriver under cover of the two British vessels *Keppel* and *Comet* that had been sent downstream to defend against the French. By nightfall, reports came in confirming the arrival of Maitland's troops. Shouts of joy rang out from one end of town to the other as they began scaling Yamacraw Bluff.

d'Estaing and Lincoln, hearing the calamitous news, wanted to see for themselves. They moved to Brewton's Hill early the next morning, just in time to see the last few boatloads of the Highlanders pass in the distance. Lincoln sat dozing in his camp chair. The count turned to one of his aides, in obvious disgust.

"It's not bad enough that these reinforcements have arrived but General Lincoln has fallen asleep in his chair."

A major quarrel erupted among the various factions in the camp at Greenwich as to where the blame lay for allowing Maitland to reach Savannah. General Lincoln contended that Fontanges had agreed, at the council of war in Charlestown, that the French would seal off the Port Royal river passages to prevent just such an outcome. d"Estaing countered that he had ordered just that but that the Charlestown pilots aboard the French ships refused to cross the bars. They claimed that the deep draft of the warships made it entirely too risky. On whomever, or whatever, the ultimate blame lay, this single oversight doomed the entire expedition to failure.

****

Maitland's triumphant march into Savannah coincided with

deliberations by the Governor's Council concerning their response to d'Estaing's summons to surrender. Upon learning of this he hurried immediately to join the council. Exhausted and reeling from the debilitating fever, he entered the chamber as one member had risen to talk of surrender. Maitland fixed the man with his flinty eyes. The officer, intimidated by Maitland's glare, halted in mid-sentence and took his seat. Maitland's biting Scottish brogue rose above the din of the meeting.

"The man who utters a syllable recommending surrender makes me his decided enemy. It is necessary that either he or I should fail."

He turned to meet the gaze of every man in the room. They averted their eyes in shame.

"I abhor the word capitulation. If I survive to go home to Britain, I will report to the King the name of the first officer who dares to propose capitulation."

His towering rhetoric brought the council to its feet in ringing affirmation. His courage and determination carried the day. Prevost immediately penned his reply to d'Estaing.

"The unanimous determination has been made that we cannot look upon our post as absolutely impregnable, yet may be and ought to be defended. The King, my master, pays these men to fight, and fight they must, and we decline your terms. Therefore, with the firing of the evening gun, one hour before sundown, hostilities will recommence, in accordance with your terms."

The addition of Maitland's regiment, Cruger's battalion and others brought in from the ships and outlying posts raised the total complement of fighting men available to Prevost to 3200.

CHAPTER EIGHTEEN

THE FIERCE WINDS THAT had prevented the remaining troops from landing finally relented. The frigates *La Fortunee* and *La Blanche* returned to their anchorages off Ossabaw. For eight days a steady stream of longboats ferried the soldiers ashore. At Beaulieu they were fed, reassembled, formed up and marched north toward Greenwich.

A second squadron of ships screened the waters off the coast, guarding against a British surprise attack. On the twenty-fourth, *Sagittaire,* a 54-gun frigate, happened upon *Experiment,* a smaller British ship en-route from New York to Savannah. The *Experiment,* heavily damaged in the same storm that delayed the French, fell easy prey to the larger ship. Captain James Wallace, son-in-law of Governor Wright, surrendered his ship and its valuable cargo. She carried 700,000 pounds of provisions for the embattled garrison at Savannah. Of even more importance to Governor Wright and General Prevost, she carried the garrison's payroll, 30,000 pounds/silver --along with Major General George Garth, the officer assigned to relieve Prevost.

With fresh troops streaming into camp, d'Estaing began to redeploy his forces. From the marshes on the east to Musgrove Swamp on the west, the city's southern defenses extended almost two miles. The city proper covered the central one-third. Open fields ran in either direction down to the marshes. There were only about five hundred nondescript structures along the streets and around the six squares of Oglethorpe's planned city. The only landmark rising above them was the spire of Christ Church. With the river to its back, and the impenetrable marshes to either side, the town's only vulnerability lay to the south. Here Prevost focused his entire defense. The soldiers, slaves and citizens worked feverishly, day and night, to throw up breastworks, dig trenches, and construct a bristling barrier of pointed stakes, *abatis,* to impale both charging horses and men.

The French moved their main camp from Greenwich to within a mile and a half of the southeastern boundary of the town. Lincoln's command was further west, near Louisville Road. On the twenty-first both armies moved forward to within twelve hundred yards of the fort to begin preparations for the siege.

The twelve hundred American troops, along with Pulaski's legion, took up positions at the extreme eastern end of town, hard against Musgrove's swamp. de Noailles with nine hundred men filled in adjacent to the American lines. His command was a mix of French units and West Indians. d'Estaing occupied the center of the French army with a combined force of one thousand French regulars and the contingent from Saint-Domingue. Dillon's division of nine hundred men anchored the line east of d'Estaing. Beyond him, swinging to the north, were the powder magazine, cattle pens and the hospital. Between these support facilities and the eastern parapets were the dragoons and de Rouvraise's seven hundred and fifty Volunteer Chasseurs. The sun was setting as the drums beat retreat. On the evening of 21 September 1779, an army of five thousand men lay siege to Savannah.

During the evening of the twenty-second, de Noailles sent out a detachment of fifty soldiers from the regiment of Guadaloupe to capture a small British outpost that was pestering his line. Under the command of Major de Guillaume the sortie rushed headlong into the enemy, thereby losing the element of surprise. The British reacted furiously, sending the French retreating back toward their lines. de Noailles, who was following in close support, rushed in to rescue de Guiallume and, sensing their desperate plight, ordered a retreat. Four soldiers were killed and several men from Guadaloupe were wounded.

A second sortie was launched. de Noailles ordered a heavy barrage of artillery while sending forward a company of selected sharpshooters to suppress the enemy fire. Under this cover, Major Pierre L'Enfant with five men, attempted to burn the barrier of trees that would impede their advance when the attack began. L'Enfant was successful in torching the trees, however the greenness of the wood and the intermittent rain soon quenched the fires. He dejectedly returned to the lines with his squad intact..

Conventional siege tactics called for the digging of trenches in a zigzag pattern toward the enemy position and then expanding the trenches horizontally. Siege weapons such as cannon and mortars were then brought forward to bombard the fortress. The final trenches were designed to be within seventy-five yards of the fortress wall where point blank firing could penetrate the ramparts, creating openings through which the soldiers could enter. Typically at this point, under the arcane and unwritten rules of eighteenth century warfare, the besieged would surrender after negotiating favorable terms.

On the twenty-third, under the protection of six hand picked rifle companies, work parties completed the zigzag trenches to within 300 yards of the British, then extended them horizontally for several hundred feet.

On the twenty-fourth, the heavy fog blanketing the area lifted. The British, alarmed at the discovery of the trenches, launched a sortie of six hundred men. They advanced to within a few yards of the trenches before being repelled by the French riflemen. The French officer in charge, with a burst of enthusiasm, ordered his troops out of the trenches to pursue the British. His foolhardiness exposed his men to the artillery atop the redoubts. In the ensuing battle the French lost seventy men killed and wounded, including several officers.

On the command of their captain, Andre Dupre and Louis Dufour were among the first to scramble out of the trench. They raced forward, rifles at the ready, to engage the fleeing British soldiers. Too late, the impetuous officer realized his error. Withering fire from the parapets laced into the onrushing French. One of the redcoats Andre was chasing leaped over a small creek. He turned, dropped to one knee, and brought his rifle up on a line with Andre's chest. Andre froze in his tracks, certain that he was about to die. He heard the click of the hammer and saw the cascade of sparks as the flint scraped along the pan. Then, blessed silence. The rain-dampened powder did not ignite. The sparks briefly illuminated a malevolent face, twisted in hatred.

Andre recoiled at the hideous mask of red. The soldier shook his fist and cursed at Andre.

"You niggers are gonna die. You don't belong in those uniforms fighting alongside white folks. We're gonna catch you and string you up to the nearest tree," he sneered.

The man ran to join his retreating unit just as the moon broke through. To Andre his shouts were gibberish. He didn't understand English.

"Back, back," shouted the French commander. "We're too close. We're in range of their artillery. They'll chew us to bits."

They bolted for the trenches amid deafening shell bursts. The concussion of a falling mortar sent Andre catapulting through he air. He landed with a thud on the mound of dirt it threw up in front of their trench. He groped for his musket and looked around for Louis.

"Louis, Louis, where are you?" Andre screamed. He heard the familiar voice of his friend calling from inside the crater created by the explosion. Andre's ears ached from the concussive pressure. He put his hand to his ear. It came away bloody. Louis' voice came from deep in a well. Andre crawled toward the sound. He peered over the pile of dirt. Louis was lying on his back, a crimson stain spreading across the white shirt beneath his tunic.

"Louis, where are you hit?"

Louis pulled up his shirt to reveal a ragged wound in his right side. The piece of hot metal had struck a glancing blow across the ribcage. A quarter inch deep furrow exposed bone and flesh. Andre quickly assessed the wound as painful but not life threatening. If he could stop the bleeding. He grabbed Louis by his arms and dragged him back to the trench. The two cascaded over the side, landing in a tangle of limbs at the bottom. Louis screamed in pain and grabbed his side. Andre looked around for his sergeant or captain. He wanted to know what to do. There was no one else in the trench.

"Stay still, Louis."

He removed Louis' tunic, pulled the bloody shirt off and tore two long strips from it. He tied them together. He took the rest of the shirt in a wad and pressed it hard against the wound. Louis fainted from the pain. Andre held it there for a few minutes until the flow of blood subsided. He took the long strip of cloth and tied it around

Louis' chest to hold the compress firmly in place. By now several other soldiers had returned.

"Where is the captain?" Andre asked.

The man he spoke to stared ahead, blankly, his back stiff against the wall of the trench. He looked at Andre. His mouth opened, his lips moved, but no words escaped. He shook his head slowly, as if to clear some apparition too horrible to contemplate. He tried again and in a faint whisper said, "They're both dead. Him and the sergeant. They were cut down by the same shell. I've never seen anything like that in my life. The sergeant's head flew in one direction and his body in another. The captain was blown clean in two."

Clumps of bloody, matted hair and flesh clung to his uniform. Andre felt a rush of nausea. He worked hard to suppress the gorge in his throat.

"I've got to get Louis to the hospital. If he doesn't get this wound attended to right away he'll bleed to death. If anyone shows up to take muster tell him where we've gone. I'll be back as soon as I get Louis taken care of. Come on Louis, I'll get you to the hospital tent."

Andre walked and dragged the dazed soldier the half-mile back toward the eastern marsh. The hospital was located on a small knoll with trenches dug around it to carry off the water. The tent flaps were flung back over the ropes revealing several cots and tables inside. Outside, fires burned around several bulbous black pots of boiling water. Two doctors attended a sergeant brought in minutes before with a head wound. Andre helped Louis into the tent and onto one of the tables. Louis lay back, fatigued and disoriented. Blood had seeped through the compress and now stained his tunic and trousers.

"Doctor, my friend has been wounded. He's losing a lot of blood. Please do something?"

One of the doctors looked over.

"I'll be with you in a minute. This man will die if we don't close this wound in his head. Your friend's injury looks like it can wait. Grab a fresh bandage and hold it against the wound until we can get to him."

The doctor returned to swabbing the sergeant's head with a cotton rag soaked in water. His companion was busy threading a skein of catgut into a curved needle.

Twenty minutes passed. A steady stream of wounded found their way to the hospital. Three more doctors arrived and began to treat the most seriously injured. The blood from Louis' wound turned progressively darker as it clotted. He lapsed in and out of consciousness as the pain increased.

"Let's see what we have here," one of the newly arrived doctors said to Andre. What happened to this man?"

"He was hit by an exploding shell," Andre answered. "It bounced off his ribs. He's lucky it didn't hit him straight on or he'd be a goner for sure. It made a nasty gash."

The doctor lifted the bandage to examine the wound. Most of the bleeding had stopped.

"We'll get this cleaned up. May need to sew him up some. I think he'll be all right in a couple of days. We'll send him back to his unit when he's fit. You'd better get on back now. Looks like things are going to heat up a bit."

Andre leaned over and whispered into Louis' ear.

"I'll be back to check on you tomorrow. You take it easy and keep that wound clean. Don't want it getting infected. See you later."

He stepped into the sunlight and turned right, away from the battlefield. Two hundred yards away stood the quartermaster tents and the cattle pens. Andre hurried in that direction. Captain Deschamps sat at a small field desk, outside his tent, poring over his accounts. He looked up, startled by the sudden appearance of Andre.

"What are you doing here, Andre?" he asked. "I thought your unit was on the line with Admiral d'Estaing."

"Sir, we came under attack a short while ago. I'm sure you must have heard the bombs going off. We ran the redcoats off but when we came up out of the trenches they cut us down with their cannons. Louis was hurt pretty bad. We lost our company commander and our sergeant so I didn't know what to do. Louis needed help so I brought him to the hospital. He's going to be there a few days."

Andre stopped speaking as he groped for words to appease the captain before asking the question uppermost in is mind.

"I know I have to get back to my position sir, but I just had to know if she's all right."

"She's doing fine Andre. She's helping the cooks over there."

He pointed to the smoke rising on the other side of the mess compound.

"Can I see her, sir, just for a minute, please?" Andre pleaded with the captain.

"No, Andre. You must return to your unit. I'll tell her you were here."

****

Still smarting from the losses sustained on the two previous days, de Noailles began to construct mortar and cannon emplacements along the length of the trenches. Only two eighteen-pounders were ready by seven on the morning of the twenty-fifth. d'Estaing became impatient and commanded de Noailles to begin the bombardment of the city. Shells began to rain down on Savannah that day and would continue sporadically until October 8th.

The bombardment had little material effect on the town. de Noailles ordered his cannoneers to cease fire. He handed his engineers new orders to dismantle and remodel the emplacements to accommodate more and larger cannons. By Monday morning they had brought in more guns from the ships. They positioned twelve new guns into the expanded pits, capable of lobbing twelve and eighteen pound shells. Another two hundred yards further to left, toward the Americans, a second position was constructed to house nine mortars. Simultaneously the Americans erected their own emplacement of sixteen-pound guns.

The two-day cessation of shelling puzzled the British command. They needed to know what the French were up to. A reconnoitering force was sent out at one o'clock on the morning of the 27th. They were met with stiff resistance by the French and had to retire to the safety of the fort without discovering the new construction. The basic mission had failed, however the French troops guarding the work parties became spooked and started firing at ghosts. Twice during the remaining hours of darkness they fired on their own work parties, resulting in several casualties.

de Noailles himself, alarmed by the intelligence he was receiving, believed that his position was again under attack by a large contingent of the British. He ordered his entire regiment to position themselves between the trenches and the fort to intercept the imagined British advance. It didn't take long for him to realize his error. He ordered the recovery of the injured and dead, and then retreated to his previous positions.

The French frigate *La Truite,* together with several war galleys, positioned itself in the Back River and began to bombard the city from the northeast.

The new batteries were completed and the siege began again in earnest at midnight on October 3rd. Day and night, shells rained down on the defenseless citizens of Savannah. Most sought shelter in their cellars or under the bluff by the river, taking whatever provisions they could. The shrieks and cries of women and children filled the air. Many buildings were burned or destroyed by the rain of fire; among them the house of Chief Justice Anthony Stokes, together with all the legal papers of the colony.

In one of a mounting series of self-inflicted wounds, the French battery crews were mistakenly served a barrel of rum, instead of their normal ration of grog. The ensuing drunken chaos forced de Noailles to order a ceasefire at two o'clock. The drunken gunners were lobbing shells into their own trenches.

Morning drum call sounded at four a.m. from the fort. On that prearranged signal the newly positioned cannons and mortars to the right and left of the trenches commenced firing. The compounded fire, despite all its sound and fury, did little to damage the breastworks, which were constructed mostly of sand. The structures within the fort continued to bear the brunt of the fusillade. The larger bombs wreaked even more havoc on the civilian population of the city. A mulatto man and three Negroes were killed in the basement of the Lieutenant Governor's house. Seven Negroes were killed in a house near the church. Two women and two children were killed in the Laurie house on Broughton Street.

The days dragged on with the shelling becoming more intermittent. Young children, emboldened by the inability of the attackers to inflict mortal damage on the city, turned the event into a lucrative game. Between salvos they rushed out into the streets and covered the smoking balls with sand. When the bombs cooled they were collected and sold to the British soldiers for sixpence each. The French and Americans got their shells back in the return fire.

On September 29, under a flag of truce, General McIntosh again petitioned General Prevost to allow the women and children to leave the city. Prevost refused, wrongly thinking that their continued presence in the city would be cause for reduced shelling. The widespread death and destruction that followed changed his mind. He sent a messenger to d'Estaing on the eighth, proposing to place the non-combatants on ships and send them down river to safety. This time d'Estaing refused, even though General McIntosh and several other Americans had families in the city. Failing to gain the release of the families, Prevost had them all moved across the river to the relative safety of the plantations on Hutcheson Island.

When the French fleet first appeared off the coast of Georgia in early September the British had only twenty-three guns defending the city. Now, having moved the guns from the ships, they had positioned one hundred and twenty-three cannons and mortars around the perimeter, guarding every approach. Felled trees, their cropped branches joined to form an impenetrable barrier, fronted the row of breastworks. *Chevaux de frise,* sharpened logs set into the ground at an angle, protected the salients against both cavalry charges and onrushing infantry. d'Estaing's failure to immediately attack had allowed the British to throw up an almost impenetrable defense. His belief in the invincibility of his army led him to ignore the obvious. The British officers, in their journals, agreed that an immediate frontal assault on the city would have prevailed within ten minutes. Hubris and indecision were the ultimate undoing of the proud French commander.

October 8th dawned with feeble bursts of shelling from the two sides. Like two tired fighters stumbling around the ring, they each waited for the other to surrender and fall. It began to dawn on the besiegers that the city was not going to surrender. There were only two options remaining, retreat or attack. Major John Jones, aide to McIntosh, wrote in a letter to his wife.

"Any hour we expect them to capitulate. However, many agree with me they will not – not until we compel them by storm."

Jones, a devout Presbyterian who believed in predestination, prepared his wife for the worst by saying: "If it's in my fate to survive this action, I will. If otherwise, the Lord's will be done." She had already suffered the loss of their home, land, slaves and business to confiscation by the British. Now, Polly Jones was about to lose her husband.

Time was running out. Supplies were running low. The food rations, consisting mostly of rice, were universally detested by the French. Munitions were rapidly being depleted. The hurricane season was looming. The troops had been in the trenches for days. They were wet and miserable. Their light linen West Indian uniforms offered little protection from the nighttime cold or the daytime heat. Aboard the ships matters were even worse. Scurvy was rampant. The jaundiced sailors, reduced to eating salted fish and meat, were running out of fresh water. They were dying at the rate of thirty-five a day. Their ships were in ill repair. They cursed their commander for bringing them into this pesthole. In an attempt at humor, d'Estaing jested, "If they really need water there seems to be plenty seeping into their holds." There's little wonder that mutiny was in the air.

Meanwhile, the British larder was sufficiently stocked to carry them into the new-year. The moment of truth had arrived for d'Estaing and Lincoln.

"Gentlemen," d'Estaing began, "I am informed by my engineers that it will take another ten days to complete the final parallel siege entrenchments. Employing the normal siege tactics, it will take an additional ten days to reach the enemy lines. I have already kept my men and ships here for four weeks longer than I anticipated. All the problems that besieged us when we arrived are still with us and have been magnified by the interval. The British fleet lurks somewhere to the east. Storm clouds are gathering over the Caribbean. Supplies of food, water and armaments are shrinking. My ships lie at anchor, battered and broken and not fit for battle as their crews die of disease and starvation. The only avenues remaining open to us are to attack or withdraw from the field."

d'Estaing had already made up his mind. He couldn't bear to think of the condemnation he would receive, in France and in America, if once again he fled the field of battle as he had at Newport. The time had arrived for the *beau moment* as he was fond of saying. That moment that always came when he saw success imminent. But this beautiful moment would prove anything but. He described this strange siege as "Penelope's Web," ever doing but never done. French honor was at stake, and if he must he would choose the only option he could live with, that last alternative, "the forlorn hope" of victory.

"After all other resources have failed, one must take sword in hand," he declared to his assembled senior officers. "Our spies have told me that the British are most vulnerable on the western side of the town. That redoubt and its palisades are manned by poorly trained militia. That is also the position where the woods come closest to the town. That will give us cover to within five hundred yards of the wall. Also, there is a single trench fronting the fort there, and it has been dug with two overlapping arms. With surprise our lines can pass between the break. In addition, the *abatis* does not extend all the way to the river. I propose that we make the Spring Hill redoubt the center of our attack."

The reaction of his officers was immediate and harsh. de Noailles argued that the point of attack was not practical. General Kurt von Stedingk, a Swedish nobleman, felt that the perceived advantages of attacking the Spring Hill redoubt would be more than offset by the difficulties presented by the bogs and marshes fronting it. General Dillon and several other officers strongly opposed the plan and voted to abandon the field. The consensus of the entire officer corps was that a direct frontal assault was beyond the capability of their force. de Noailles pressed strongly his disagreement with the location of the attack.

"My general, there are those present, including myself, who do not agree that the point of attack you have chosen is the best. We feel that a thrust against the south quadrant, where the trenches have been opened, would be more advantageous."

d'Estaing would not be dissuaded.

"Viscount de Noailles, your opinions are those of an old man. Where is your blood for combat?"

His subordinate's hackles rose. But, sensing that further argument would be fruitless, he held his tongue. Flushed with anger at the humiliating rebuke, he bit off his words in response.

"Sir, I assure you that when the time comes for courage and valor you will not find them wanting in this young man."

d'Estaing ignored him and continued his harangue of the reluctant officers. He plowed ahead with his plan, ignoring the views of his staff. He had set his ship on a collision course with the British and he would not trim his sails.

"The French have an obligation to the American cause and the honor of our King demands that the siege not be raised without striking a vigorous blow. Thus, the decision has been made. Savannah will be captured and this business finished."

He dismissed the senior officers and summoned an aide. He sent him to bring General Lincoln to his tent. When Lincoln arrived he found de Estaing leaning over the battle maps arrayed across his field desk. He appeared deep in thought, as if mesmerized by some spectral vision staring up at him, some looming dread. After a few moments he looked up.

"General Lincoln. I am forced to conclude that the events of the past few days and the diminishing chances of taking the city by siege, leave us only two alternatives. We either abandon the field of battle or we attack. And I sir, for one, did not bring my forty-five ships and 4,000 men all the way from Grenada to desert your great cause. To skulk off, cowardly, into the night. I have a duty to my King and to General Washington to see this enterprise to conclusion. Therefore, I have instructed my commanders to prepare their troops for an assault on the city to commence at four o'clock in the morning, tomorrow."

Lincoln was shocked. Like the French officers before him he was reluctant to send his men against the fortress that had been thrown up by the British during d'Estaing's vacillation. But, what was he to do? After all, it was his government that had urged the French to come to his aid. And, d'Estaing was supplying three times more soldiers.

"If we abandon this battle," Lincoln thought, "then we will surely lose Georgia and probably the rest of the South. Cornwallis' strategy will have succeeded and the entire revolution will hang in the balance. All the struggles and sacrifices will have been for naught. d'Estaing is right, we have no other choice."

"Very well, Count d'Estaing, attack it is. Do you have a plan as to how we shall position our forces?"

"I do, General. Please call your staff to meet with mine. I will present my plan when all the officers are together."

Lincoln returned to his lines, anticipation and dread battling for control of his emotions. At last his men would see the action he had prepared them for. Sadly, he feared, many of them would die in the process. He called his officers together to tell them of d'Estaing's decision. Their response mirrored that of the French. The little gamecock, Francis Marion, erupted.

"My God! Whoever heard of such a thing before? First, allow your enemy time to entrench, and then fight him?" He was remembering the awful price paid by the British when they attacked Bunker Hill.

General Pulaski was adamantly opposed to a frontal attack against the newly erected barricades around Savannah. He hurriedly penned a counter-proposal to d'Estaing.

"My Esteemed Count d'Estaing,

Having studied the fortifications and deployment of the enemy, it is my considered opinion that three points of attack would be preferable to the single point you have proposed. I recommend one against the British right flank along the Augusta Road, another on the British left wing by the Americans under General McIntosh, and a third main attack near the right center of the British line, under your eminence's command.

I remain your humble servant,
Count Kazimierz Pulaski

d'Estaing was as dismissive of Pulaski's suggestions as he was those of his own staff. He was fixated on his own plan and nothing would change his mind. Pride and arrogance carried the day.

With both staffs assembled d'Estaing laid out his strategy for the attack. His command would be divided into three groups. He would lead General Dillon's Corps. Colonel Stedingk would command the main infantry. Viscount de Noailles and General Lincoln would hold a third force in reserve to seize opportunities or to cover a retreat, should that become necessary. The Americans would form the third column of attack. At d'Estaings signal, the *chasseurs* from Martinique and the troops in the trenches would feint toward the center of the British lines to draw their defenses away from the area of the Spring Hill redoubt. The commanders huddled for the next hour, making sure the right units were mobilized in the right positions for the attack.

CHAPTER NINETEEN

ENOCH PENROSE AND JAMES Pelham waited beside the gate leading out of the center of the city to the south. Flickers from the enemy campfires filtered through the few remaining pine saplings left from the burning and clearing. Enoch pulled his watch from his vest pocket. He pressed the catch that released the cover. The lid popped up. He felt a strange emotion. The watch evoked one of the few warm memories from his childhood. It was a gift from his father on his tenth birthday.

He held the watch at an angle so that he could make out its face in the pale moonlight. It was half past eight. At exactly nine he and Jim were to proceed to a point fifty yards past the *abatis*. There they would place a stake in the ground and tie a union jack pennant to it. They were instructed to then hide nearby. A man should approach the stake at ten o'clock, remove the cloth, and tie it to the barrel of his rifle. This would be their signal to approach the man and ask his name. If he gave the correct answer they were to identify themselves and escort him back into the city, taking him immediately to General Prevost's headquarters.

Enoch checked his watch again. It was twenty minutes past ten.

"Come on Jim. He ain't coming. I don't know who this fellow is but I think we've been sent on a wild goose chase. I'm getting cold out here. I need a couple of shots of whisky to warm me up."

"I don't know Enoch. We go back there without him we're gonna be in big trouble. I don't know who he is either, but he sure seems pretty important for them to go to all this trouble to get him in there. I think we ought to wait a few more minutes."

Enoch stood, dusting the dirt from the seat of his pants.

"That's your problem, Jim. You're a fraidy cat. You're too scared of those pretty red uniforms. Those officers are so full of horseshit it makes me sick. If I didn't think those idiots could help me get back what's mine I'da been gone a long time ago."

Enoch reached for his gun. It was propped against the fallen tree on which they had been sitting. He froze in mid-move. The cold steel of a knife was pressed against his neck.

"You boys sure do make fine sentries," said the disembodied voice from the darkness. "I could hear you from a mile away. You can't be regular army or you wouldn't be grousing and making noise like that. That'll get you in big trouble, like your friend here says. Now, what's your names?"

Enoch's stutter became even more pronounced as he tried to answer the stranger's question.

"M-m-m-my n-n-n-n-name's Enoch P-p-p-p-penrose. Th-th-this is J-j-jim P-p-p-pelham.

"You better be glad you got that right, boy," the voice said. "Otherwise, you would've found your head lying in the mud. I'm Sergeant James Curry. Now, I believe you're s'posed to take me to General Prevost."

"Yes sir," Jim Pelham said quickly, not waiting for Enoch's lazy tongue to form the words.

Fifteen minutes later, Sergeant Major James Curry of the Charlestown Grenadiers sat across the table from General Prevost and his senior staff. Ten minutes after that they knew every detail of the attack that was to come at four in the morning.

"Thank you, Sergeant Major. You've performed a valuable service for your King. Note will be made of this in my report. I think you'll find an extra ration of whisky waiting for you in the mess. Then you'd better report to my adjutant for assignment. I think you'll be needed in a few hours."

Prevost began to address his officers as the door closed behind Sergeant Curry.

"Colonel Maitland, I want you to place your regiment in reserve behind the Charlestown Grenadiers, who are manning the lines around the Spring Hill redoubt. d'Estaing expects you to be defending the center of our line when he makes the initial feint. He believes he can breach our defenses before you can move to head him off. I want you to be in a position to repel his surge at Spring Hill. We will shift the majority of the units toward the west to defend the Spring Hill redoubt and Ebenezer batteries. Leave only enough men in the eastern and southern positions to defend against the diversionary attacks.

****

Hiram sat with his back to the fire. General McIntosh stood across from him, facing the fire. Shadows from the flickering flames danced across his face. He addressed his officers.

"Men, I don't necessarily agree with the plan of battle devised by the French, but it has the concurrence of General Lincoln. I will obey his orders. Tomorrow morning at four o'clock Colonel Huger will take five hundred men from the Georgia and South Carolina militias and lead a feint at the eastern end of the British lines. If they bite then he'll draw their defenses eastward. Colonel Huger will move into a position as close as possible to the city before first light. At the signal he will attack Savannah. The French will attempt a similar diversion in the center of the lines.

"Colonel Laurens and I will lead the rest of our command across the Augusta road and, together with Count Pulaski's cavalry, we'll attack from the west. The French will form two columns to our right for a frontal assault on the Spring Hill redoubt and the Ebenezer batteries.

"General Lincoln has ordered that all of us wear a white cockade on our hats to identify ourselves in the early morning light. Each soldier will also be issued forty cartridges and a spare flint. These will be provided to all units by the quartermasters before midnight. Good luck and may God's blessings be upon us all.

****

Louis had returned to his unit just in time for the major bombardment to begin. His wound was well scabbed over and the oozing around the stitches had stopped. He bandaged it with a poultice of lard and meal. He moved gingerly, the excruciating pain radiating with each jarring step.

You don't look so good, Louis," Andre said. "I think they should have kept you in the hospital a while longer. You're in no condition to fight."

"The doctor said if we attacked he was going to need all those beds for the wounded. He said he didn't know if we would attack, but he had to be ready just in case. He sent some other soldiers back to the lines in worse shape than I am." He hesitated. Andre could tell he had something else on his mind.

"What is it Louis? Is there something you're not telling me?" Andre asked.

"Andre, I saw Cassie before I left."

Andre stiffened.

"Where did you see her Louis? Is she all right?"

"Don't worry Andre. She's fine. Captain Deschamps brought her down to the hospital with him when he delivered some supplies to the doctors. She's doing all right but she's awful worried about you. When we were alone she told me about you two. How you're planning to come back here when you leave the army. She said when we leave she's going back to the monastery and wait for you. That's gonna be an awful long wait, Andre. Do you really think you can get back here when you're released? And, if you can, do you think she'll still be waiting for you?"

"I'll get back here all right, or I'll die trying. And I know she'll be waiting for me. Her master, Mr. Penrose, is going to set her free. I just know he is. After what she's done for the Americans and all the petitions on her behalf I don't see how he can refuse. If she's free, she'll wait."

"I sure hope so. I sure do," Louis said. "Maybe I'll just come back here with you. Find myself a nice woman like you got and settle down here in Georgia. I don't see much of a future in Saint-Domingue as long as the French are there."

Andre smiled. It was good to have a friend like Louis. He reminded him of his brothers back in Grenada. He missed his family. Louis and Henri were his only family now.

For the next few days Andre covered for Louis, allowing his wound to heal. They remained in the trenches across from the city defenses. Occasional forays by both sides tested the alertness of the other. They resulted in little actual shooting. Mostly saber rattling.

The number of shells flying over their positions tapered off after the first two days. In the beginning the noise of the shells passing overhead had terrified the soldiers. These were the first battle conditions most of them had ever experienced. Some were there on that terrifying first night when their own bombs rained down on their trenches. They were fast becoming inured to the eerie whistling sound the bombs made in flight. So much so, that when they stopped, the silence itself became deafening. The steady stream of fire seemed to have little effect on the enemy's resolve to stay the course. Finally, late on the afternoon of the eighth, the firing ceased. Shortly after dark, when the prying eyes of the men on the parapets couldn't see them, the men were assembled behind their trenches. Their company commander, Lt. Gerard Aubrey, spoke.

"Men, the Admiral has decided that we will attack in the morning. His plan is to try and confuse the enemy with two diversionary feints. If we're successful we'll pull most of their defenses to the east of the city. Then our main force will concentrate on the two redoubts on the southwestern corner of their defenses. General Isaac Huger will take five hundred Americans and attack from the east. The men of Martinique will join with de Sabliere's men in these trenches, and attack the center of the British lines. We will move to the east with the other Chasseurs de Saint-Domingue to rejoin the de Noailles command. There we'll be held in reserve for support of the advancing army, or, God forbid, to cover their retreat."

"I guess that means we won't be in the fight," Louis whispered excitedly to Andre as he picked up his rifle and bedroll.

"I guess so," Andre said. "That's just as well seeing that you're in no condition to fight. I can't see you charging into battle with that big tear in your side. I'm sure when they break through into the city we'll have to follow to help clean up. Don't know what we're likely to find. Those townsfolk have got to be mighty upset at all those shells we threw at them. Hopefully they'll just lay down their guns and be glad to have it done with.

"I don't expect we'll hang around too long. Some of the officers were saying the admiral wants to turn Savannah over to the Americans and get us out of here. He's afraid a storm may set in or the British navy may show up. I hope he takes us back to Saint-Domingue. Maybe he'll leave us there in the fort at The Cap."

"You really think that could happen, Andre. It sure would be good to see my folks." Louis closed his eyes. Visions of the white beaches and green mountains they left behind a few short months ago filled his thoughts.

"I sure hope so. I don't want to get any further away from here than I can help. I know I won't be able to see her but I'll feel better knowing she's not so far away. Who knows? He could take us all the way to France or somewhere else in the world. No telling then how long it would take to get back."

They fell into line behind the other soldiers. The row of white cockaded hats wound its way eastward in the dark. A pale moon rising in front of them lent meager light to their path. Louis walked ahead of Andre, his musket slung casually over his shoulder. Andre carried both their rolls. Louis's ribcage was still very sore. The weight of the bouncing roll would be unbearable.

"Thank you my friend, I'll make it up to you when you get shot," he said, jokingly.

They walked on in silence, each lost to his private thoughts. Louis dreamed of home. Andre dreamed of Cassie. So near and yet so far away. There were rumors some of the soldiers from Martinique had deserted before the army broke camp at Beaulieu. He himself had wrestled with the idea of deserting. It would have been easier when they were alone in the camp. Now it would be perilous. He recalled the swift and harsh punishment of other deserters when they were caught. In Grenada, one member of his company ran off with a young girl. They were found two weeks later, hiding in a cave. The entire unit was forced to witness his execution by a firing squad. No! It's better to get back here in one piece a few years from now than to risk being strung up from one of these big oak trees.

****

The Jewish cemetery in Savannah sat on a small knoll southwest of the city. In everyday life the citizens of the town turned to the Jews for many of their services, such as medicine and law. In death they relegated them to this small plot of ground, outside the city. Here, de Noailles established his camp. The site gave him a clear view of the battlefield. He could gauge the progress of the battle and deploy his reserves where needed at a moment's notice.

The field flowing down from the cemetery, toward the city, was saturated from the early autumn storms. Small rivulets coursed through the sandy soil, merging to form streams into Musgrove swamp. de Noailles surveyed the field through his telescope. He stared at the sodden landscape and said, "Von Stedingk was right."

General Lincoln placed his chair near de Noailles' field desk. Simple headstones surrounded the site. The names Nunez, Sheftall and Minis were prominent. These were among the forty-one Jewish families who arrived in Savannah on the *William and Sarah,* four months after Oglethorpe. Most had come from England where they had fled from the Inquisition in Spain and Portugal. Life in England was more tolerable than on the Iberian Peninsula but bigotry and prejudice did not recognize national boundaries. The lure of a fresh start in a new land beckoned. They set out on their journey without the permission of the government. Upon that discovery, London demanded the unauthorized settlers be returned immediately. Oglethorpe ignored the order. He had lost his only physician to the fever. There was a doctor among the Jews.

CHAPTER NINETEEN

Cassie stayed busy around the quartermaster's commissary. She couldn't stand to be idle. When she was, she imagined all sorts of calamities befalling Andre. She helped the cooks prepare and distribute the food. Infrequently, they allowed her to go with the wagons as they distributed the food and supplies to the lines. She used these opportunities to look for the black troops. On one such trip she saw a large contingent of black soldiers digging a trench. She was sure she would find Andre among them.

"Pardon me," she said to a sergeant leaning on his musket, watching the soldiers at their work. "Are you with the men from Saint-Domingue?"

"No, ma'am," he said. "We're from Martinique. The group you're looking for is down thataway." He pointed toward the sound of the cannons in the distance.

"I don't think it's a good idea for you to get too close to those guns. They've misfired a few times and wound up hitting their own men."

Now Cassie was more alarmed than ever. She had seen what a piece of shrapnel did to Louis. She could only imagine the effects from the explosion of a large shell. She shook the thought from her mind and started back toward the wagon.

"Thank you," she said as she left the sergeant standing there, her mind filled with dread for Andre. It was hard to comprehend. Just a few weeks ago she was picking tomatoes in the convent garden, unaware of the military intrigue swirling around Savannah. Now she was in the midst of it, concerned for the safety of a man she had known for only a few weks. A man she had fallen in love with and with whom she had promised to share the rest of her life. If she closed her eyes would all this be gone when she opened them again? Would this all have been a dream? Would she awaken in her bed across from Esther to discover that none of this ever happened? Cassie was jarred from her reverie by the wagon driver's shout.

"Ma'am, we gotta get outa here. They're getting ready to move all these soldiers. They say there's going to be big battle tomorrow. We'd better get back and see what the captain wants us to do."

No, it's not a dream. It's all too real. The man I love is out there somewhere in those woods preparing for battle. And I don't know if I'll ever see him again.

****

Colonel Huger led his detachment through the rice fields east of town in darkness. He wanted to be in place just outside the walls when the signal came. He would move when he heard the drums from the French soldiers as they came out of their trenches to attack the center of the British line. His troops, cold and wet from their trek through the mire of the rice fields, moved into position just before four and readied themselves for battle.

At precisely six, the sound of drums drifted across the marsh and echoed off the fortress walls. Huger gave the command to attack. Both his divisions rose up as one and streamed toward the enemy. The British were ready. Colonel Cruger and Major Wright, forewarned by Sergeant Murray's intelligence, met the onrushing Americans with withering fire. Colonel Huger, realizing too late that the British were waiting for him, ordered an immediate retreat and left twenty-eight of his men dead and wounded on the field.

The French charge fared no better. The artillery and musket fire concentrated at the point of attack drove them back. Lt. Col Hamilton's North Carolina loyalist volunteers decimated the onrushing French while not suffering a single casualty. The two feints, intended to divert major elements of the British garrison, had no significant effect. Sergeant Murray had done his job well.

de Estaing also heard the distant drums. From his position in the pines, some one hundred and fifty yards from the marshy clearing, he ordered his troops to prepare for battle. From the parapets the defenders could discern the movement of men through the lifting fog. The bone-chilling skirl of bagpipes floated out on the crisp morning air. The message was crystal clear. Prevost was telling d'Estaing that not only was he ready for him but that his best troops, the Scottish Highlanders, were positioned behind the western redoubts. The Admiral knew instantly that his plan had been compromised. His head told him that now was the time to abort the mission. He knew he was sending his legions into the teeth of the enemy with no advantage, no element of surprise. Carnage was inevitable. Wisdom called for discretion. Honor cried out for redemption. Better to die in valorous combat than to face the French court at Versailles following yet another humiliating defeat.

The French formed into three divisions under Dillon, Von Stedingk and de Noailles. Dillon dispatched Betisy with a small group to silence the Ebenezer battery to the right of Spring Hill. Left unmolested the defenders in Ebenezer commanded a clear view of the right flank of the advancing French. They had to be silenced.

Von Stedingk veered left, toward the Augusta road, to attack Spring Hill from the east. de Noailles formed his division among the Jewish gravestones, as a reserve force. The Americans, under McIntosh also moved left, between Dillon and von Stedingk.

To the drumbeats of the *pas de charge* the columns advanced at double time. Cries of *Vive le Roi* rang out up and down the line. The British rose up above the parapets, also with white cockades in their hats to confuse the French. They laid down a deadly enfilade of musket and mortar fire as the French vanguard hacked through the *abatis*. Their comrades, hard on their heels, poured through the openings and surged up the slope toward the redoubt. The fire was devastating. Dillon, seeing the futility of the charge, ordered his column left, toward the Americans.

Von Stedingk's column, fighting through the mire of Musgrove's swamp, arrived late. Maitland was ready. As the invaders poured onto the Augusta road causeway and turned toward the fort they were met with a cannonade of grapeshot and chain. Maitland had positioned a battery at ground level outside the Augusta gate, pointed directly down the Augusta road. The carnage was indescribable. Men were cut in half. Limbs, heads and torsos littered the roadway. Dante's inferno was visited on the invaders.

Dillon reassembled further to the left. He offered rewards to any of his men who could bridge the marsh with bundles of sticks to build a footpath through the quagmire. Not one man stepped forward. When informed that his offer was insulting to these proud men, Dillon withdrew the offer. Immediately, nearly two hundred of his "Wild Geese" battalion surged forward to bridge the marsh. Only ninety survived the assault.

The main force charged forward, across their *fascine* bridge and over the entrenchments. Their commander, Major Thomas Brown was killed instantly. Dillon, with eighty soldiers, breached the line and advanced on the parapet. With reinforcements he could have carried the day. Sadly, none came. The line was still strung out down the road and through the swamp. Many were barefoot, having lost their shoes to the sucking mud. The British within the fort regrouped and forced the vanguard back into the trenches. Nearly all were killed. The action came so fast and furious that neither side had time to reload. Hand-to-hand combat broke out. A few intrepid French soldiers were able to plant their banners atop the parapet before being driven back.

Chaos reigned. Fresh troops advancing from the swamp were met by waves of wounded and retreating comrades. d'Estaing himself nearly made it into the redoubt before being cut down by a British bullet. He fell back, lying among the dead. Subordinates rushed forward to retrieve him and were cut down in turn. The retreat of Dillon's division began in earnest. The soldiers carried off as many of the wounded as possible. Those fleeing choked the Augusta road. The throngs could not escape back through the swamp. They could only flee down the causeway. More cannon were positioned at the head of the road. The amplified broadsides shredded the fleeing French forces, cutting them down like scythes through grain.

The British ships *Comet, Thunder* and *Germain,* anchored in the

Savannah River north of town, pounded the lines with their cannon. The slaughter on the causeway defied description.

d'Estaing rose from his litter, his injured arm in a sling, and ordered his men to regroup and charge again. Three times they charged, en masse, into the trenches and up the ramparts. Three times they were driven back with staggering casualties.

Meanwhile, von Stedingk scaled the Spring Hill redoubt and planted his flag. Now certain of victory he shouted.

"We are resolved to conquer the whole army with one accord. We crossed the marsh and sunk to our waists. The day must be ours."

Like Dillon before him, von Stedingk could not maintain his position. Looking back across the field he saw most of his line still mired in the swamp, unable to come to his assistance.

Maitland, sensing the peril represented by von Stedingk, threw his reserves into the breach. His marines and grenadiers launched a furious charge with sword and bayonet, driving the enemy from the ramparts and back into the ditch below, to be butchered. Von Stedingk's epitaph for the fallen, "The moment of retreat, with the cries of our dying comrades piercing my heart, was the bitterest of my life."

General Pulaski had waited patiently to enter the fray. His assignment was to pour through the openings created by the advancing Americans and to circle behind the British lines to attack from the rear. When he emerged from the woods east of the fort, Pulaski was appalled to discover that neither the French nor the Americans had breached the enemy's lines. His years of battlefield experience told him that if he did not strike now that the battle would be surely lost. He issued orders to Colonel Daniel Horry of South Carolina to form two columns with the South Carolina and the Georgia dragoons for an assault on the redoubts. Horry complied. The horses reared in anticipation of the charge with their riders struggling to restrain them. The men drew their sabers. Pulaski gazed heavenward. He uttered a short prayer for success and deliverance before issuing his final command.

"Forward," he shouted above the bugle's blare and the clatter of two hundred sets of horses' hooves, churning through the mud and sand toward the inferno that was Savannah. The Polish count spied a small opening through the wall of fallen trees. He led the charge. As he reached the breach, his scarlet and gold banner in his left hand and his saber in his right, withering bursts of grapeshot and canister tore through the charging ranks. Men and horses fell to the ground with sickening thuds. Yet the charge continued, only to be blocked by the barricades.

Pulaski forged ahead, skirting the northern end of the barricade, and charged up the ramparts toward the redoubt. Suddenly, his magnificent black stallion reared. A ball of grapeshot had opened a gaping wound in Pulaski's thigh, throwing him to the ground. The riders following him were incredulous. They could not believe that this legend, survivor of so many battles, had fallen in combat. His aides, Majors Rogowski and Bentalou, ran to his side. Blood poured from the thigh wound and from a second to the chest. What was initially believed to be a minor wound was discovered to be much more serious. Pulaski looked up at his aides and muttered, "Jesus, Mary and Joseph," the same names he had prayed to for help his entire religious life. Colonel Horry arrived to see his commander rendered *hors de combat.*

"What shall we do General?" he asked of the stricken Pulaski.

"Follow my lancers to whom I have given my order of attack," Pulaski commanded. Brave to the end, he committed his legion to continue the assault, even in the face of such devastation. Major Bentalou took the fallen banner from his beloved general. His left hand shattered by enemy fire, he grasped it in his right and remounted his horse. Pulaski's faithful aide renewed the charge into the gates of hell. Once more they were forced to fall back, leaving more wounded and dying in their wake.

Realizing the futility of sacrificing even more men, the commanders ordered retreat. Pulaski's horsemen mingled with the surge of French and American troops as they thronged the causeway. Captain Thomas Glascock of the Polish Legion returned to carry Pulaski from the field. The Count had fought his final battle. He was removed to the safety of the cemetery where Dr. Lynah removed the canister shot from his groin. He dropped the gory souvenir into his pocket. Pulaski suffered through the agony without complaint, with legendary stoicism.

To the left of Pulaski and closer to the river, Colonel John Laurens led his men from South Carolina out of the woods and swamp. His charge was to stay to the left of Pulaski and when Spring Hill fell, to attack the ramparts between the redoubt and the river. His soldiers advanced to the trenches where they came under heavy fire and could move no further. Most of the militia bolted and ran. Three hundred continental regulars returned again and again to the battle, only to be turned back with massive losses.

Lieutenant Alexander Hume surged to the top of the parapet where he planted two South Carolina regimental flags, only to fall back, mortally wounded. Around his neck he wore the scarf he had painted with the likeness of his fiancé. They were to be married the following week. The fierce resistance forced the Carolinians to retreat. They were able to take one banner with them. The other fell into the hands of the British. The rescued flag was handed down the line to Sergeant William Jasper, hero of Sullivan's Island. Moments later he too was cut down by enemy fire. Jasper was taken to the rear. Before drawing his last breath he asked the men around him to take the sword given to him by Governor Rutledge after Sullivan's Island, and give it to his father. His last words were, "Please tell him that I wore it with honor."

Meanwhile, General McIntosh moved his men further north toward the river, in an attempt to circumvent the barrier of trees and escape the confusion created by Dillon's swing to the left. In so doing, the retreating forces of General Dillon cut him off from Colonel Lauren's command. While Laurens hurried his men into place to enter the Spring Hill redoubt after the line was breached, McIntosh led his Carolina militia and Georgia continentals into the opening created by Pulaski's charge. The galling fire so disrupted the advance that fully two-thirds of his men fell back in disarray and left the field. The remaining soldiers continued to sweep northwards and became mired in the Yamacraw swamp. Major Glasier of the British Grenadiers seized this opportunity to counterattack. He led his troops over the wall and hit McIntosh's flank as they struggled to escape the mire.

Hiram Penrose had followed his leader into the battle. He kneeled to fire into the charging enemy just as McIntosh ordered his men to retreat. The musket recoiled against his shoulder and he saw his red-coated target stagger and fall. He fell back to the cover of the *abatis*, praying that the barrier would deter the onrushing enemy. He furiously reloaded his gun just as the British reached the barrier.

"Come on, Hiram, we've got to get out of here," Wimberley Jones shouted above the din of the battle. "We can't breach their lines. Pulaski and d'Estaing are both down. The situation is hopeless. Come on!"

"I'm going to get off one more shot," Hiram shouted.

Hiram rose. He steadied his rifle on a limb and took aim at an advancing English soldier. He eased the hammer back and began to squeeze the trigger. A tree branch knocked the soldier's hat from his head. Hiram froze. There was no mistaking that crimson half-mask. It was Enoch. Hiram released the hammer. He could not shoot his own brother. He ran to join the retreating army. As he reached the line he felt a searing pain in his back. He fell to the ground, hitting his head on a smooth rock and rolling over the embankment.

Major Glasier surveyed the field beyond the barrier, considering an advance. An onrushing line of black soldiers was taking up positions beyond the trenches. They began firing broadsides into his men. He ordered his troops back into the fort. Hiram Penrose had been spared a bayonet thrust. Enoch Penrose had been spared death at the hands of his brother.

Colonel Maitland, hearing the drumbeats and bugle calls of retreat, ordered all his men to the wall to deal a final blow. He became so certain that he could utterly annihilate the fleeing army that he sent his Highlanders over the wall in pursuit.

de Noailles had recognized early on that the battle was not going well. When his commander and Pulaski both went down and the charge on Spring Hill was repulsed, he alerted the Saint-Dominguean brigade to ready for action. When d'Estaing was brought to safety among the headstones, de Noailles knew it was time to act. He calmly marched his columns down the slope from the cemetery and formed lines behind the trenches to give cover to the retreating army. The fleeing troops were able to regroup behind de Noailles' lines. Maitland, staring into the barrels of five hundred muskets behind the mounds of dirt beyond the trenches, thought better of his counter attack and returned to the safety of the fortress walls. Further needless massacre was avoided. When de Noailles determined that no more attacks were coming he ordered his drummer to beat retreat. Henri Christophe drummed the order to fall back. The five hundred men of Saint-Domingue fired a retreating volley and orderly withdrew to the safety of the woods around the cemetery.

A lone Scottish sharpshooter, high in the palisade at Spring Hill, took careful aim at the last figure in the line crossing back over the Augusta road. He squeezed the trigger. Andre Dupre pitched forward off the road, his body falling across his rifle. His head fell awkwardly across the stock. Trickling water lapped at his cheek. Blackness overcame him.

CHAPTER TWENTY

CASSIE HAD BEEN UP all night. She knew the battle was imminent. She could not sleep knowing that Andre and Louis and the rest of the friends she had made in the last few weeks were facing battle. She sat on a flour barrel and leaned her head back against a tent pole. The first shots from Huger's assault on West Savannah startled her. She leaped off the barrel and ran toward the front of the tent. Deschamps, who only minutes earlier had received orders to move his wagons to the front, caught her as she emerged through the tent flap. He was to bring food, supplies and the medical teams with all their paraphernalia. It was already obvious to de Noailles, as he looked across at the imposing fortifications around Spring Hill and the formidable terrain between, that this would be a bloody day.

"Cassie, you'd better come with us," the quartermaster said. "There'll be no one here to look after you. Besides, I'm sure the doctor's will need all the help they can get before this day is through. We'll join Admiral deNoailles in the rear of the lines where his troops are being held in reserve." Cassie's heart leapt.

"Aren't Andre and Louis with him?" she asked.

"Yes," Deschamps replied. "All the men from Saint-Domingue are in his reserve corps.

Fighting was well underway when the first wagons rolled up behind the cemetery. Cassie stood on the wagon seat, holding on to the canvas supports, searching the sea of upturned faces, looking for Andre.

"There!" she shouted, pointing to a small cluster of men sitting on the gravestones. "There's Andre! Stop the wagon!"

She jumped down and ran to him. Andre looked around warily. He didn't want her to get into trouble with the officers. He saw no one nearby who would interfere and beckoned for her to follow him. He led her further into the graveyard and stepped behind a tree.

"Cassie, how did you get here?"

"Captain Deschamps had to bring all the wagons and doctors here. He said that I should come along because there would be no one left at the camp and besides he thought the doctors might need my help. Do you think you'll be in the battle, Andre? He said you were in some kind of reserve unit. Does that mean you won't have to fight?" she asked, her cracking voice betraying her fear. The booming echoes of cannon in the distance and the sounds of musket fire lent urgency to her pleas.

"I don't know Cassie. I guess if everything goes all right they won't need us. I sure hope so. I'll do my duty when the time comes, but I'd just as soon not have those folks shooting at me."

A few hundred feet further back in the pines there were several other tents arranged around campfires. Civilians, driven from their homes in Savannah by the Tories the year before, had learned of the impending battle. They believed, as the allied armies believed, that their city soon would be liberated from the English. They hovered on the fringes of the battle anxious to swoop in and reclaim their property. Several of the men had advanced to the far left end of the cemetery where they could get a better view of the battle. Small children, oblivious to the pending slaughter, ran gleefully through the camp pointing and firing stick guns at each other, mimicking the soldiers. The women tended the pots as their wash, hung on makeshift clotheslines, snapped briskly in the strong breeze.

"Who are those people Andre?" Cassie asked.

"I was told that they are refugees from Savannah and they're just waiting to go back in after it's liberated. They were forced to leave with little more than the clothes on their backs and what little they could carry. Most of them have been living from hand-to-mouth in the woods. The folks on the farms and plantations have helped them as much as they could but it's been really bad. Malnutrition and disease have killed a bunch of them. They're a sad sight. I hope we can get their homes back for them."

"Captain Deschamps said that he was called up to the front in a hurry by Admiral de Noailles because the Admiral thought there were going to be a lot of people hurt today and they would need all the doctors and supplies and food we could bring," Cassie said. "What have you heard?"

"It doesn't look good. Those poor devils have to cross five hundred yards of open swamp just to get to the trenches. Then a barrier of sharpened branches faces them, even before they try to scale the sides of the fort. There can't help but be a lot of casualties. It's not going to be a pretty sight out there."

"Cassie, I'd better get back to my unit now. If they find me missing there'll be hell to pay. You stick close to Captain Deschamps and you'll be all right. If things get really bad and we have to go in you'll know it. Remember the little drummer boy you met at Buley, Henri Christophe? Well, he's our lead drummer now. If you hear him tapping out an order to advance that means we're going in. But don't you worry. I'm going to be all right."

Andre embraced Cassie then kissed her before he stepped from behind the tree and ran back to his unit. She stood there for a few minutes, dazed. Events were cascading onto one another and she was having difficulty comprehending everything. Finally she shook herself to clear her head and walked back over to the wagons. Captain Deschamps was dispatching units closer to the front in readiness for action, should they be needed. He saw Cassie coming toward him from the woods.

"Did you find Andre?" he asked.

"Yes. He is waiting in the cemetery to find out if the reserves will be needed. He said he didn't think so, but not to worry. He said it's not likely they'll be sent to the front, just lend support. I sure hope he's right."

"You just stick close to me, Cassie. We won't we getting within range of their guns so you don't have to worry."

Half an hour passed as the clamor of battle grew. Cassie stood on the wagon and peered into the smoke and fog rolling off the battlefield.

She could see tiny men running like ants through the marsh, bogging down, and then struggling to free themselves, many of them falling and then disappearing into the murky water. Beyond them were other men, seemingly even smaller at such a distance, running up the embankments and toppling into the trenches. Beyond them yet others were trying to scale the walls of the fort and being brutally repelled by the soldiers on the parapets. Several blue and white clad figures were impaled on the sharp limbs of the *abatis*. They hung there like lambs on a spit. Doll-like figures tumbled down the sides of the palisade and into the trenches, falling on countless other mangled bodies from the initial assault. She was sickened by the spectacle and turned away.

"Please, dear God, don't send Andre into that hell."

Minutes later, a trickle of soldiers, some bleeding, others limping, straggled back into the camp. The doctors responded immediately. Those more seriously wounded were loaded into the covered wagons where the operating tables had been placed. Their assistants tended to the less severely injured, cleaning out their wounds and binding them with linen.

The trickle rapidly became a torrent. Cassie was pressed into service. She had received some medical training from the sisters at St. Benedict's but the gaping wounds she now encountered were beyond the worst she had ever seen. She did the best she could to make sure the wounds were cleaned and that pressure bandages were applied to stanch the bleeding. Despite her best efforts many of the men lapsed into unconsciousness from blood loss. Many died.

She had been exposed to death at Roselawn and at the monastery but she was not prepared for the magnitude of the calamity unfolding around her. The only saving grace, in the midst of this unspeakable bloodshed, was that it took her mind off Andre.

Then she heard it. The unmistakable tattoo of drums. She looked toward the cemetery. The *Chasseurs de Saint-Domingue* were lining up to go into battle. Her heart dropped. Her worst fears were being realized. Andre was going into harm's way.

Henri Christophe, his drum bouncing off his leg as he marched, followed de Noailles at the head of the first column of soldiers. Andre and Louis were in the second rank. Andre looked over at her as he passed. She tried desperately to not let him see her crying. She forced herself to smile, all the time wanting to cry out to him. He could not break rank or even wave. He turned his head slightly in her direction and winked at her. She held her composure until the column had passed then fell to her knees and broke down in sobs.

"Oh, Andre. I'll never see you again," she whispered to the wind.

The stream of troops from the battle rose to a climax by seven a.m. By eight the rout was complete and the reserve troops, sent in to cover the retreat of the defeated army, began to return to camp. Cassie resumed her perch atop the wagon anxiously surveying each group as it straggled in. Her alarm grew as she saw the numbers slow to a trickle, and still no Andre. She persuaded herself that she had simply missed him among the clumps of returning soldiers. She jumped down from the wagon and ran to the cemetery. She saw several familiar faces from the previous week. She asked each in turn if he'd seen Andre or knew what had happened to him. They all shook their head. She was preparing to go back to assist the doctors when she saw a familiar figure. The man was leaning against a tree, his face in shadow. He was holding his side in pain. Hesitantly, she approached him. As she got closer she recognized the man. It was Louis Dufour, Andre's closest friend among the Sainte-Domingueans. He had been wounded before the battle. She saw him back at the camp hospital.

"Louis! Louis! Thank God you are alive. Has your wound reopened? Can I help you?" she asked.

Cassie!" he exclaimed. "No. It's sore and bleeding a little. I'll be all right. What's happening?"

"Most of the army, those able to travel, have headed back toward the camps. Others are staying to help with the wounded and to look for survivors," Cassie said. "Louis, I haven't seen Andre. Do you know if he made it back? All the other members of your unit have been accounted for." Her voice rose as her panic increased.

Louis looked away and then stared down at the ground. When he raised his eyes to meet hers she could see on his face the answer that she had dreaded.

"Andre was the last one to leave the battle. He was right behind me as we crossed the causeway running toward the east. I was running through the marsh to get away from the guns. We were nearly out of range when I looked back to see where Andre was. He turned to fire his rifle one last time. As he lowered the gun I saw him grab his head. He dropped the gun and fell into the marsh. I wanted to go back for him but my commander told me not to. That it was too dangerous. I'm sorry, Cassie. I don't know if he is dead or not. It didn't look good. Head wounds are usually fatal. I'm sorry."

Cassie screamed in despair.

"Louis, will you show me where he fell?" she asked. "I have to know whether he is dead or just wounded. I cannot leave this place without knowing."

"I don't know, Cassie. It's mighty dangerous out there. You can still hear occasional shots. And, I don't know if I would be allowed to."

It was now nine in the morning. A lone rider rode past where Louis and Cassie were standing. He had just left de Noaille's tent where de Estaing was being attended. The officer carried his saber held high. Affixed to it was a white flag.

"What does that mean, Louis?" Cassie asked, as the officer urged his mount into a canter.

"I think they're going to ask for a ceasefire so the dead and wounded can be recovered. That probably means the fighting is over. I can't imagine the general will send us in again, seeing how the English are so dug in. There would just be hundreds more lying out there."

de Noailles emerged from the tent and trained his glass on the lone rider as he negotiated the trenches and the *abatis*. He saw him dismount and climb the ramp up to Spring Hill and then disappear behind the parapet. An interminable ten minutes later the emissary emerged and retraced his steps to the cemetery. He handed a note to de Noailles, who read it and then returned to his tent. He summoned all the officers within earshot for instructions.

"General Prevost has most graciously submitted to our request for a ceasefire so that the dead and wounded can be properly attended to," he began. "It is now fast approaching ten o'clock which is the appointed hour for the truce to begin. I want each of you to select your ablest men to be assigned to the lead surgeon and to the quartermaster, Captain Deschamps, for the recovery and burial teams. We have until three o'clock this afternoon to complete this sad and difficult task, so step lively and make every second count. As you can see, many hundreds of our brave comrades-in-arms lie fallen in the field. Accord them the utmost dignity possible under such trying circumstances." He painfully surveyed the killing field one last time before dismissing the officers.

Louis and Cassie watched as the various teams reported to the doctors and to Captain Deschamps.

"Louis!" Cassie exclaimed excitedly. "It looks like all those men are going to Captain Deschamps to be assigned wagons and tools to go out and help the wounded. Do you think we can convince him to let us have a wagon? He already knows us since we helped him get all that food and stuff for the soldiers. Besides, I've been helping out at the hospital tent next to his headquarters. He knows I can help with the wounded. Please, Louis, please," she pleaded. "It's the only way I can know for sure what happened to Andre."

Louis stared at her as if she had asked him for the moon.

"He won't do that. He's been told to look after you until this is over so we can get you back to Skidaway without you getting hurt. There's no way he's going to let you go out there on that field where you may get shot or some unexploded bomb may go off."

"Louis, if you don't ask him I will. Now, I'm not leaving here until I know. If you don't get us a wagon I'll just go out there on foot. And don't you try to stop me."

Faced with her fury, Louis decided that asking the captain was the easier path. Besides, he knew Deschamps would say no and then it would be over with. Ten minutes later Cassie was once again seated on the familiar wagon bench she had occupied for so many days in the previous few weeks. Only this time she was riding with Louis, not Andre.

"See, Louis, you don't ever know what you can do until you ask," she good-naturedly chided him. "The captain knows we make a good team and he knows from experience that you will take good care of me. And, there's no one else among the soldiers better prepared to tend to the wounded than I am. Come on, show me where you last saw Andre."

They picked their way through a landscape sprung fullblown from some apocalyptic painting. The horrific images were mind searing.. Corpses hung from splintered trees or were impaled on sharpened timbers, their mouths agape in the scream of death. Horses, their stomachs ripped open by canisters, emptied their entrails into the crimson water. Human and animal parts jumbled together in ghoulish pools forming the unspeakable cauldron of some evil beast.

Cassie pressed a cloth against her nose and mouth. She closed her eyes as she struggled to push back against the overwhelming urge to vomit. Nothing she had ever witnessed came close to equaling the human devastation laid out before her. She had heard the pigs die. She had seen them bled and butchered to provide for the plantation and even though it sickened her, she had participated because Queen and Aba told her she had to do it. Now, this horrifying scene would haunt her for the rest of her life. She could never face the screams again.

"Over there," Louis said, pointing past the outthrust of the redoubt. "That's where the road leaves the city towards Augusta. It's built up into a causeway that crosses through the swamp. That's where most of the killing came. So many men were trying to get away from the guns, and down that road lay the fastest way out. The British opened those gates and set cannons up to point straight down that road. Load after load of chains and blades and grapeshot tore through those poor bastards. Pretty soon the whole road was clogged with bodies. Men were shoving them out of the way and over the embankments into the marsh just to clear a path."

Louis stopped the wagon where the road began to narrow as it met the marsh. Other teams were searching through the tangled bodies, checking to see if any were alive. Behind them the British had come down from the ramparts and begun separating the injured from the dead. They carefully placed the dead into the trenches for burial. Random shouts rang out from the teams when they found someone alive. These were loaded onto the wagons for transport back to the field hospital. Those who were mortally wounded were left for the burial teams. Louis drove a little further down the causeway. The mid-morning October sun turned the field into a broiling stench. Crows and vultures vied with each other for clumps of scattered flesh. The rescuers tried in vain to drive them away. It was a losing battle. Finally they just ignored the birds and went about their grisly task.

"I think it was near here that I last saw Andre," Louis whispered. He felt as if he were on sacred ground. Reverence for those who had fallen seemed appropriate.

"Let's get down and look around."

Cassie stepped onto the wheel and jumped to the ground. She followed Louis as he searched the roadside for Andre. She was appalled as she stepped over the blue and white clad bodies of the French. Lying scattered among them were the Americans, robed in homespun and buckskin. Everywhere she turned she was confronted with relentless death. The moans of the living tore at her heart. She wanted to help them but was driven by desperation to find Andre. She stiffened her resolve and followed Louis, averting her eyes to relieve her guilt.

Louis slid down the blood slicked embankment. He landed awkwardly on his all fours astride a fallen soldier whose head was lying across his rifle. The man's face was only inches from the small stream running beneath him. The soldier was black and wore the uniform of the *Chasseurs*. He grasped the still figure by the shoulder and turned him over. It was Andre.

"Cassie, it's Andre!" he shouted.

The body was limp and didn't respond to being disturbed. His hair was matted with blood. A trickle still seeped from the vicious head wound and dripped into the water, to be quickly carried away in the current. Cassie dropped to her knees beside Andre. She cradled his head.

"Is he dead, Louis?" she asked through her tears. "Please tell me he's not dead."

Louis inspected the wound and examined the rest of his head.

"It doesn't appear that the bullet penetrated his skull," he said. "If it just grazed him he may still be alive."

Louis checked to see if Andre had any other wounds. He didn't see any. He opened the tunic and placed his ear to Andre's chest. After a few agonizing seconds he looked up at Cassie and began to smile.

"He has a heartbeat. It's weak but it's steady. Help me get him back to the wagon and we'll take him back to the hospital."

Cassie was overjoyed. Her beloved Andre was still alive. Now they had to get medical attention. If he hadn't lost too much blood there was a chance. She ripped off a piece of her skirt and fashioned a bandage that she wrapped around Andre's head to stop the bleeding. Then she stepped between Andre's legs while Louis grabbed him under the shoulders and they carried him back to the wagon. Louis winced with pain from his own wound.

Getting the limp form of Andre up the embankment took all the combined strength of the two. They laid him on the ground while Louis went to bring the wagon closer. Cassie continued to minister to Andre. She tore another square of cloth from her dress and ran back down the slope to dip it in the water. She wanted to cleanse the wound so she could judge how deep and serious it was. She dipped the cloth into the cleanest pool she could find and wrung it out before retracing her steps back to where Andre lay. She slipped as she reached the crest of the ditch and fell backwards, coming to rest against one of the Americans. The force of her fall caused the man to slide further down the bank and roll onto his back. Cassie looked at the man and screamed. Louis had moved the wagon as close as possible and arrived back just in time to see Cassie tumble. He heard her scream and ran to her side.

"What's the matter? Are you hurt?

She sat frozen, staring at the American officer. Her face was contorted in anguish and tears cascaded down her cheeks. She attempted to speak but no words would form.

"Cassie, snap out of it! Tell me what's wrong!" Louis demanded.

"Louis," she stammered. The words came out in halting bursts. "That man --- that's Master Hiram Penrose --- from Roselawn Plantation. He's my master. He owns me."

"My God, Cassie!"

Cassie crawled over to the prostrate form of Hiram Penrose. There was caked blood on his vest where the bullet had exited below his shoulder. She felt his head.

"He's still warm," she said. "See if you can feel a pulse."

Louis knelt next to Cassie and felt the man's wrist.

"I can't feel anything," he said as he moved Cassie away. "Let me see if I can hear his heart." Louis put his ear to Hiram's chest. He listened intently for several seconds.

"Cassie, I can hear a faint heartbeat. He's still alive. I think the others left him for dead but he's still alive. Come on. We've got to get him and Andre back to the hospital so the doctors can do something for them." He sprinted back to Andre, who was still unconscious on the roadway. He and Cassie lifted him into the wagon and then went back to retrieve Hiram Penrose. He was a stockier man in his middle years and weighed more than Andre. They struggled to get him up the slope but Cassie couldn't lift him. Louis laid Hiram back down.

"Cassie, you stay here. I'll be right back."

She watched him disappear beyond the wagon. She realized he was backing it toward the ditch. Louis held the bridle of the horse tightly to make sure he didn't let the wagon slip over the edge. He stopped just a few feet short and ran to the back. He reached inside the wagon bed and grabbed a long length of rope. He tied a loop in one end of the rope and tied the other to the back of the wagon. When he had secured it firmly he ran back down the bank.

"Here Cassie," he said, handing her the rope. "When I lift him up you slip the rope over his head and under his arms."

Louis grasped Hiram by the collars of his coat and raised him to a sitting position so that Cassie could drop the loop over his head. He let the rope slide below one arm and then the other until it was girdling Hiram's chest. He then laid him down on the slope.

"Cassie, I'm going to pull him up the slope. You guide the rope so that it doesn't get tangled up. I know this might hurt him more but if we don't get him to a doctor he will die."

Slowly the rope tensed and Hiram began to slide up the embankment. Within seconds he was clear of the ditch and Louis was back by their side.

"He's still too heavy for us to lift but I have an idea."

He ran down the road to a wagon that had been destroyed by cannon fire. He wrested two wide boards from its side and dragged them back.

"I'm going to make a ramp and maybe we can drag Mr. Penrose up into the wagon. I'll get inside and try to pull him up while you hold him on the boards."

Louis spread some wet clay on the board surface then leaped onto the wagon. He pulled Andre forward making room to maneuver Hiram into the wagon.

"All right, Cassie, throw me the rope."

Louis braced his feet firmly on the wagon's side struts and heaved on the rope. Slowly Hiram slid up the ramp. When he was fully inside Louis fastened the tailgate. He took Cassie's arm firmly and dragged her to the wagon seat.

"Come on girl, we've got work to do. Get back there and see what you can do for them while I get us back to camp."

Louis picked his way back through the littered field to the edge of the cemetery. As soon as he tied the horse to a tree he ran over to where some doctors were gathered with the wounded.

"Doctor, I've got a wounded American officer and a Saint-Dominguean soldier in my wagon. They're both alive but unconscious. Can you come and look at them?"

"Not now, soldier. Can't you see I'm busy? I'll get to them as soon as I can."

Louis was frantic. When the doctor turned his back he grabbed one of the medical kits.

"Cassie, we're not going to get any help from them. You and I have to do what we can. Here, I took these from their wagon." He thrust the bag and the bandages toward Cassie. "You've been watching the doctors at work back at the camp. You know more about this than I do. You tell me what to do and I'll help you."

"I'll start with Andre. While I clean out his wound and dress it, you get Master Penrose's coat and vest off and start cleaning his wounds."

The crusted blood in Andre's black curly hair covered a nasty gash in his scalp that ran from above his right eye to a point above his ear. She couldn't tell if his skull was cracked or not. She prayed that it wasn't. She began to clean the blood and debris from the bloody crease with swatches of cotton and a pan of water. It was a slow and tedious process. She wanted to avoid further injury. When she had finished and bandaged his head a mound of red cotton lay at her feet.

"It's a good thing he's unconscious," she said. "The pain would be unbearable. How are you doing with Master Hiram?"

Louis had taken a knife to cut the garments away from the wound. Fresh blood rimmed the hole in Hiram's shoulder. The projectile had entered below the right shoulder blade and exited from the small hollow below the clavicle. The entry wound was relatively small. Where the bullet exited there was a jagged hole nearly an inch in diameter. He had fallen in such a way that he came to rest with his right shoulder pressed against a rounded stone in the embankment. It looked like a ballast stone from a ship, used in the construction of the causeway. His shirt and vest were pushed into the wound by the stone, forming a natural compress against the flow of blood. That stone saved his life. Left to bleed freely Hiram Penrose would have died within minutes. As it was, he had lost a large amount of blood. Only time would tell if the loss was fatal.

"What are we going to do now Louis?" Cassie asked.

"I don't know," he said. "I guess we need to see if we can get them back to the main camp where there should be more doctors. Load some more of that straw into the wagon and we'll head back."

Cassie jumped down and hurriedly piled more straw into the bed of the wagon. She climbed back aboard and began to mound the straw to make the two men more comfortable. The wagon lurched forward as Louis turned east. He threaded his way through the tumult until he found the trail through the majestic oaks that had brought them to this scene of devastation.

Within minutes the forest engulfed them. Shafts of sunlight interspersed with shadows as the sun lowered in the west. Small bands of soldiers straggled toward the sanctuary of the camps. Many bore the scars of the battle. Others, unmarked, assisted them. Louis heard a strange sound and turned to see Cassie leaning her ear close to Hiram's mouth.

"He's coming to," she said. "He just tried to talk. I couldn't make out what he said."

They rode on. The wagon bumped over a large outcropping of roots, jostling the passengers. The large man lying on the straw screamed.

"He's awake, Louis. Master Hiram is awake. But he's in a lot of pain."

"Water. I want some water," her master said.

"Louis. His lips are parched. He's lost a lot of blood and hasn't had anything to drink for several hours. Do we have any water?"

Louis reached under the seat. He felt through the straw and pulled out a wooden flask he dropped there earlier. He held it next to his ear and shook it vigorously. A small splash of water bounced around inside.

"Here. There's a little in this flask. It won't go very far. We'll be able to get some more up ahead. There was a public well off to the side, about half way back to camp."

Cassie pulled the cork from the flask and held it to her master's mouth. He greedily inhaled the cool liquid, coughing as the water choked him. He again cried out in pain lapsing back into unconsciousness with the exertion. He fell back onto the straw.

"Louis, I don't think we ought to go any further. Both Master Hiram and Andre have lost a lot of blood and the bouncing is causing their wounds to re-open. Do you think we can pull off the road and rest?

"I guess it'll be all right. The trail's going to be clogged up as we get closer to camp. We won't be able to see the trails too much longer anyway. I'll pull off when we can find an opening in the woods."

Minutes later Louis reined the horses off the road and into a copse of oaks that shielded them from the main road. He gingerly stepped off the wagon. His side was still very painful. He unhitched the traces from the doubletree then loosened the hame strings and removed the collars. Freed of their yokes the horses shivered vigorously, relieving their tired muscles. He walked them further into the woods where a small stream flowed and let them take their fill of water. Louis tethered each with a length of rope that allowed them to forage among the patches of dried sedge.

When he returned to the wagon he found Cassie redressing the wound on Andre's head. He had begun to stir slightly and Cassie was whispering to him, encouraging him to open his eyes and speak. She thought she heard a slight murmur. His breathing seemed more normal and his pulse was stronger. She held the flask to his lips and poured a bit of water in. He coughed but swallowed and she gave him more.

She turned her attention to Master Hiram. She had earlier draped his coat over his chest and covered him with a blanket and straw. He began to shiver as the damp evening air began to roll in. She pulled back the blanket and removed the coat. It was caked with dried blood but there were no telltale signs of fresh bleeding. He too was breathing normally and seemed to be in less pain now that the jostling had stopped. She gave him the last of the water.

Cassie made them both as comfortable as possible under the warm straw and then sought to prepare herself for a night in the woods. She was terribly hungry, not having eaten since leaving the base camp that morning. In their haste to get their charges back to camp for help they had neglected to bring any food from the mess wagon by the cemetery. Foolishly they thought they could reach camp before dark descended

"Oh well," she thought. "I've been hungry before. At least we're safe out here in the woods."

In the fading light Louis took his knife and hacked several arms full of the broom sedge that grew rampantly in the sunny opening. He spread it under the wagon and covered it with the lone remaining blanket.

"I hope you don't mind sharing this pallet with me?" he said with a wry smile. "I assure you that you will be perfectly safe."

"I'm not worried, Louis. I know you are a perfect gentleman. I just wish you had some food to share with me. I'm really hungry after this trying day."

"Sorry," he said. "You'll just have to wait until the morning."

Both were asleep in minutes.

"There's the trail to the well," Louis shouted. "I'll turn off here so you can fill the flask."

The wagon entered the clearing around the well. Several civilians were gathered there, filling their containers with water. Cassie recognized some of them from the camp near the cemetery. She got down with the flask and walked over to the windlass that drew the water bucket. She loosened the rope allowing the bucket to fall into the water. When it had capsized and filled she began to turn the handle, winding the rope around the crude wooden cylinder. She had finished filling her flask when someone grabbed her by the arm.

"What are you doing, nigger? This here well's for white folks only. You and that buck up on the wagon better get outta here before sumpin' bad happens."

A red-faced backwoodsman, his breath heavy with liquor, was standing over Cassie. He scowled at her and raised his hand as if to strike her. At that moment a thick oak limb came crashing down on the man's skull, sending him to the ground. Cassie looked up to see Louis standing over the prostrate form.

"Come on Cassie. We better clear out of here. Grab the water and let's go."

They jumped back into the wagon and Louis turned it back

toward the main trail His path was blocked by several of the fallen man's followers. They were armed with sticks and pitchforks. The trail they had taken from the main road passed on beyond the well and continued southward. Louis jerked the reins and turned the horses around. One lash of his whip and they were hurtling down that trail. He didn't know where it led but he was certain it had to be better than facing that mob.

Cassie looked back at the unruly rabble in pursuit. One man stepped from the woods and ran around the well. She watched in horror as he poured powder into the barrel of his musket and followed it with a round metal ball. He forced the wadding and ball down into the barrel with his ramrod. He tipped his powder horn and poured a measure into the pan. In his anxious fury he dropped the horn, spilling the rest of the powder onto the ground. He dropped to one knee and hoisted the long rifle to his shoulder. He sighted down the barrel. The flash, as it responded to the striking flint, ignited the powder in the barrel sending a puff of gray-black smoke into the air. Fractions of a second later she heard the ball whiz by her head. It struck the back of the driver's seat sending splinters flying in all directions. Louis cried out in pain as one struck him in the face. Blood spurted from the wound and ran down his cheek, dripping from his jaw.

Cassie felt the spray of tiny projectiles. Dust from the splintering wood flew into her eyes. She grabbed the flask and poured water into her cupped hand to flush out the dust. It was only then that she could look back through blurry tears at the shooter. She watched as he ripped off his hat and slammed it to the ground. What she saw sent chills through her very being. The blood-red face that had haunted her dreams for five long years was leering at her just as it had that long ago day in the root cellar.

CHAPTER TWENTY-ONE

LOUIS KEPT THE HORSES at a gallop for what seemed an eternity. Cassie's two patients marked each pothole in the rugged trail with renewed cries of pain. Finally, after ten minutes, Louis pulled on the reins to slow the lathered steeds to a walk. Their sides heaved mightily with each gasping breath they took, their eyes wide with panic.

Cassie looked again down the road, half expecting to see a red face chasing her. She calmed herself. She had seen no horses near the well. There was no reason to believe he could have caught up to them. She breathed deeply and climbed up onto the seat by Louis.

"Louis, you've still got that splinter in your cheek. We've got to stop so I can get it out."

Louis reached his hand up to his face. He felt the piece of wood projecting from his cheek. He moved his tongue to the side and could feel the ragged edge protruding into his mouth. The adrenaline pumping through his body during the chase had numbed him to all but getting them to safety. Suddenly he tasted the blood and could feel the throbbing.

"Stop the wagon!" Cassie commanded. Louis pulled the horses to a stop.

Cassie reached back for the shirt Louis had cut off Hiram Penrose. She took the hem of the shirt in her teeth and made a small tear. She ripped two large strips from the shirt and wadded them into balls.

"Louis, I'm going to pull that splinter out of your face. I know it's going to hurt like all sin but I've got to do it. As soon as it's out you take this wad of cloth and put it in your mouth against the hole and hold it there with your tongue. I'll hold the other one against your face. We need to keep them there for several minutes to allow the blood to clot."

Cassie took the splinter between her fingers.

"You ready, Louis?" she asked. He nodded and braced himself on the seat.

Cassie turned the splinter slightly, to release its hold on his flesh as she began to pull. At first the piece of wood resisted, puffing out his cheek, then it slowly began to slide from the rough hole. Louis recoiled from the pain. The blood that had been oozing around the wood spurted when it came free.

"Put that rag in your mouth, Louis," she said. "I know it hurts but you've got to stop the blood."

She pressed the other rag tightly against his face then cast a wary glance over her shoulder. She had to be sure no one was coming.

"Hand me the reins. You're in no condition to drive this team. Hold those rags tight while I get us out of here?"

She urged the horses forward. They continued to heave and snort from the furious gallop but soon steadied into a brisk trot. The road wound through more oak groves before it emerged into a thinly forested stretch of pine barrens.

Cassie drove on in silence, casting an occasional glance at Louis to see if the bleeding had stopped. She debated whether to tell Louis about Enoch and what had gone on at Roselawn and why she was at St. Benedict's. He already knew about Master Hiram so she reasoned that she might as well tell Louis the whole story. He was bound to wonder why that man with the red face was chasing them. And she knew he *would* be chasing them.

"Louis, that man back there. The one who shot at us. I think he might be Master Enoch, Master Hiram's brother."

Louis' eyes flashed white. He struggled to talk. The pain and the rag rendered his words unintelligible.

"Hush, Louis. You don't have to say anything. It's a long story and I think you need to hear it. I haven't even told all of this to Andre.

"Five years ago, before I was sent to Skidaway, something bad happened at Roselawn. One morning Master Enoch followed me to the root cellar. He thought his daddy and brother had gone into Savannah. He ripped my clothes off and tried to rape me. Fortunately, Master Hiram had not gone with his daddy. He was working on the cane mill nearby. When I screamed he came running. He knocked Master Enoch off me. I could tell he was powerfully upset at his brother. He yelled at him. I thought he was going to hit him. Instead he locked Master Enoch in the root cellar and waited for his daddy to get back from town.

"Master John was furious. He wanted to send Enoch away. He said maybe to England. But he couldn't do that because of Miss Elizabeth, his wife. She was in poor health and she doted on Enoch even though she knew he did bad things. She loved him when nobody else in the world could. After a while, Master John decided he was going to send Master Enoch to their plantation on Ossabaw Island, to keep him out of trouble. But he couldn't do that right away so he came up with the idea of sending me over to St. Benedict's Monastery on Skidaway Island to keep me away from him. He knew the monastery was taking in orphans and runaways.

"Before I left, my mother, Queeen, sat me down to tell me why everyone was so upset and why I had to go away. She told me that on many plantations it wasn't unusual for white masters to take up with their slave women, but that Master John would not allow that on Roselawn.. He was very religious and believed it to be a sin in God's eyes. If he caught any of his overseers or workers messing around with the slaves he would horsewhip them and send them off the island.

"One man in particular I remember. Caleb Hawkins. He was a servant who owed money to Master John and was working off his debt. He started bothering Uncle Mose's girl, Hattie. Uncle Mose told Master John, who went down to the quarters and waited for Hawkins to show up. When Caleb Hawkins came into the cabin he hit Uncle Mose and knocked him to the ground. Then he grabbed Hattie. That was when Master John stepped out from behind the door. He hit Hawkins so hard that he knocked him unconscious. He dragged him outside and whipped him with a plowline. He nearly beat him to death. Then he hauled him down to the river and threw him off the dock. He told him,

'If you can swim you'd better head for the other side. If you can't swim you can drown for all I care. In either case I never want to see your face around here again. That's how strong he was against mistreating the slaves.

Cassie paused again. The story she was relating to Louis was very painful. It tore the scab off bitter memories that she didn't want to revisit. But she knew that Louis --- and Andre --- needed to understand the events that had brought the three of them to this point. Cassie began to cry.

"A few years later, after Master John died, Master Hiram took over Roselawn. He found out that his brother was still doing terrible things out there on Ossabaw. He'd finally had enough. The final straw came when he learned that Master Enoch cut one of the boys with a logging tool and he died of gangrene. Master Hiram went over to Ossabaw and confronted his brother. He verified everything he had been told. He told Enoch to take his two cronies and to leave. I understand they all went into Savannah where they joined the British army.

Anyway, I think that was Master Enoch back at the well. He's got a terrible birthmark that covers half his face. Before I left Roselawn one of the other house servants heard him swear that he wouldn't give up until he got me. If that was him, and he recognized me, I know he'll be coming after me. Granny Aba said he was crazy. She said that he was a fragile boy and that when Master John whipped him so bad it pushed him over the edge. He went mad. I know he's going to come after me Louis. What'll I do?"

Louis took the rag from his mouth and gently tested the wound with his tongue. The taste of blood was still there but the steady bleeding had stopped. Through clenched teeth he said, "Don't you worry about him, Cassie. I'm going to get you and Andre and Mr. Penrose out of here and to some place that's safe. We can't go back to the camp. Enoch knows from my uniform that I'm a French soldier. That's the first place he'll look. Being a native of these parts it won't be hard for him to blend in with the others milling about the camps. He'll say he lost a slave girl in all the confusion and he'll describe you. Someone who saw you will tell him and he'll know you've been there. I don't believe he could've seen Andre and Master Hiram in the wagon bed so he'll think it's just the two of us. He saw us leave the main road to get to the well.

He'll probably think I was headed back to my unit when we stopped for water. There's no reason for him to think I won't try to get back to the camp. I don't believe he knows you were working with us. He may think you ran away from St. Benedict's and somehow got caught up in the fighting. Do you have any idea where this road leads?"

"No, I'm as lost as you are. But, I think we're headed in the general direction of that last farm we stopped at. The one that had the cattle guard across the road."

"I remember. I was half asleep when we hit that gate. I nearly jumped off the wagon. It sounded like guns going off. If we are near there we're not too far from the road to Buley. If we can find Buley do you think you can get us to Roselawn?"

Cassie was confused.

"Louis, if you take me back to Roselawn it'll take you forever to get back to Thunderbolt. Won't you be accused of desertion?"

"Look, Cassie. You saw how they treated us when we tried to get help for Andre and Master Hiram. It won't be any different if we go back. They were trying to take care of hundreds of wounded men and bury hundreds more. In all that confusion they'll never miss Andre and me. They'll think we are both dead. None of our unit was there when we got back to the cemetery. They had already gone. I didn't see anyone I knew. Captain Deschamps knows we went out to find Andre but he has no way of knowing if we ever got back. For all he knows we could have been killed. They'll be so busy loading the ships to get out of here that one or two missing soldiers won't make any difference.

"Besides, Andre and I talked about how he was planning to come back here for you some day. I told him that I didn't hold much hope for a future in Saint-Domingue as long as the French were there and maybe I'd just come back with him. I'd find myself a good woman like you and settle down here in America. I was just kidding around, but why not? Why not now? I f we try to take Andre and Mr. Hiram back to the camp they'll die for certain. No one's going to have time to take care of them. Their best chance is to take them someplace they can be tended to. The only place I can think of is where you came from, Roselawn."

Cassie stared at Louis, astonished.

"You'd do that for me and Andre? Do you know what you are

saying? If we start down that road there'll be no turning back. You'll be a black man running away with another black man and a black woman in a place where there aren't any free blacks. You're a slave yourself, and Andre, until the French see fit to free you, and if you run that'll never happen. If we're caught there's no telling where we may wind up."

"Not as long as he's with us," Louis said, jerking a thumb over his shoulder. "Mr. Hiram is our key to getting back to Roselawn. As long as we're with him, no one is going to question who we are. We belong to him. He's still in the uniform of an American officer. We can say that we were assigned to him, and he brought us to Savannah from his plantation. Now. We need to find some other clothes for me and Andre. It'll be hard to explain why two plantation blacks are wearing French uniforms.

CHAPTER TWENTY-TWO

THAT NIGHT, AFTER THE battle, Enoch, Pelham and Hawkins changed out of their uniforms and into their old clothes. After dark they slipped out of the barracks and climbed over the palisade, east of the Tattnall gate. Each carried his musket, a bedroll and a rucksack. They passed through the trenches where the previous morning the French had mounted their feint against Savannah. In the darkness Enoch stumbled over bodies lying in the shallow water of a trench. They had begun to bloat and smell. Enoch paused to nudge one with the toe of his boot. In the faint light of the half-moon he could see the man was black, probably a slave or conscript from the West Indies. Murray had told them there were a lot of blacks with the French.

"Damn niggers. I wish we coulda killed them all. Dressed up like a bunch of dandies. Parading back and forth like they wuz white folks. Serves'em right for throwing in with those snotty French bastards. They all got what they deserved. I'll be glad when they take their stink out of here."

"Yeah." Hawkins responded. "If we'da had'em over to Ossabaw they wouldn't have been puttin' on airs like that. All these niggers are good for is workin. And the women for fuckin," he said through a toothy grin. "Yore pa sure didn't hold no truck with that. He near beat me to death and then nearly drownded me in the Herb River. That was after he caught me messin around with one of them black wenches down in the quarter. I never understood why he was so agin it. It was common at all the other places I worked. But he sure didn't like it." His voice trailed off in puzzlement.

Enoch frowned at Hawkins but said nothing. He didn't see any need to go into that. If Hawkins hadn't heard about him and Cassie there was no point in bringing the subject up now. He just put his head down and trudged ahead. He knew they were not far from the road to the French camp. He was intent on getting beyond there and onto the trail to Montgomery Crossroads. They had to be careful of stragglers from the battle. He didn't want to get bogged down in any explanation of who they were or why they were out here in the woods. He figured they were close to the road and decided they should bed down in the woods until first light.

Enoch was startled awake by a sharp flurry of quail wings. The birds had been flushed from their cover in the broom sedge by sounds on the road.

"Shhh," he said, as the others popped up.

Enoch propped himself on his elbows. He heard someone on the road ahead. He peered intently through the underbrush and cocked his head to pick up the voices.

"They're speaking English. But I can't make out if they're Tories or rebels."

He waited, then smiled and whispered.

"They're some of the folks who got run out of town by the British when Savannah fell last year. They were hoping to get back in if the British were beaten. They seem to be just wandering around now. No place to go, I guess. I don't recognize anybody. We can probably tag along with them without raising any suspicions. I'll tell them we were up river and got wind that the colonials were going to free Savannah. Now we're trying to get down to Sunbury to rejoin our militia unit."

When the strangers had passed Enoch led the others onto the roadway. He called to the man leading the party.

"Howdy, stranger. I'm Jess Wagner and these are two of my militia buddies, Jim and Caleb. We got separated from our unit after the fightin and we're trying to get back down to Sunbury."

The ragged man wheezed a boozy greeting through toothless gums.

"Howdy, yoreself, stranger. You're welcome to come along with us. We're going as far as Montgomery Crossroads. Hoping to get us some work there. Things has been mighty tough since last year. The Brits and Tories took all our belongings and then run us off. Been wandering around doing odd jobs since. Jest trying to hold skin and bones together. We wuz sure hoping to get back into town after you boys whupped them redcoats. Guess we'll just have to wait a spell longer."

Enoch and his companions fell in behind the small group of refugees. There were three men, two women and five children. The children delighted in darting in and out of the woods and scaring the grownups. They were too young to realize how desperate their lives really were.

A short time later the group turned off the main road onto a trail to the right. When Enoch reached their turnoff he could make out a clearing about two hundred yards further into the woods.

"I know that place," he said. "It's the old McCrary well. Used to be a small farm here. It's all grown over now since the McCrary's died of the smallpox. Pa used to stop here when we went into Savannah. He'd water the horses and refill our flasks. The trail beyond runs on down to Montgomery Crossroads. Must be about five or six more miles."

The three stragglers had nearly caught up to the group ahead when Enoch saw one of the men yelling at a black woman beside the well. She was just fastening the windlass rope after pulling up a bucket of water. He couldn't make out what the man said but he could tell he was really angry. Then the man grabbed the girl's arm and pushed her to the ground. Before he could hit her a big black buck in uniform slammed him in the head with a tree limb. The man collapsed like he'd been poleaxed. The black grabbed the girl up and threw her into a wagon that was tied by the well. He urged the team back toward the road but the other two men blocked his way. They were brandishing the pitchforks that had been slung over their shoulders. The driver jerked on the reins and turned the horses around the well, whipping them down the trail toward Montgomery.

By now Enoch had closed the distance to the well. He caught a glimpse of the young black girl as she rose up on her hands and knees to peer over the tailgate. He didn't believe his eyes. It was Cassie. She was older and more filled out, but there was no mistaking that it was her. How the hell did she get out here and in the company of a black French soldier?

Without stopping to think Enoch unslung his musket and loaded it with powder and shot. He rammed the ball and wad home then grabbed his powder horn to fill the flash pan. In his haste he dropped the horn. He fell to one knee and aimed the rifle at the buck on the wagon seat. Even with his long squirrel rifle the target was rapidly moving out of range. He judged the distance and the wind and aimed a foot above and to the right of Louis' head before squeezing the trigger. He saw the ball explode the backrest of the seat.

"God damn it," he mumbled, slamming his tricorn to the ground. "I must be losing my touch. When I'm in practice I'd make that shot nine times out of ten."

Enoch walked over to Jim Pelham.

"You know that girl I told you 'bout. The one from Roselawn that went over to Skidaway when I was sent to Ossabaw?"

"Yeah, the one your pa gave you such a hard time about?"

"That's the one. I'll be damned if that wasn't her in that wagon. You boys gather up your stuff. We're gonna find out what the hell she's doing out here with that nigger soldier."

He doffed his hat to the toothless man.

"Much obliged for your hospitality. I think we'll just go on out ahead of you. I think I know the way to Montgomery Cross from here. It'll be easy to get from there to the Ogeechee Ferry and on down to Sunbury. If you're ever down in that neck of the woods, give us a holler."

No reason to give the strangers any more information than that, he thought. Can't ever be too careful.

****

Cassie slowed the horses to a walk. She couldn't risk wearing them out. She must rely on the team to take them away from Enoch. She glanced over at Louis to see if the bleeding had stopped. He had removed the rag from his mouth but still held the one against his face. His elbows rested on his knees. The pain and fatigue had soaked into his bones. He began to doze off. Cassie smiled. Poor Louis. She had put him through a lot today. Sadly, she thought, it was probably only the beginning. She fought to push the red-faced image from her mind.

She gave the horses their lead and they plodded steadily ahead. She wrapped the reins loosely around the whip stand and stepped back over the seat. André's moans had subsided and now she could detect a slight snore. Good. He was sleeping peacefully. Master Hiram still shivered under the blanket. The chill in the air was giving way as the sun began to rise overhead. The day would get much warmer.

Cassie picked up the water flask. She cradled Hiram's head on her lap and pressed the rim to his mouth. He roused himself and drank greedily from the flask. He was dehydrated from the bleeding and twenty-four hours with no water. He opened his eyes. He could feel the throbbing lump on the side of his head. He looked down and saw the blood-encrusted bandage wrapped around his chest. He saw a face through the fog of his brain. It seemed familiar yet distant. It slowly came into focus.

"Cassie? Is that you, Cassie? Where am I? What happened to me?"

"Yes, Master Hiram, it's me. You were shot. I was there with the French. I was helping them. They had asked me to help interpret for them."

"Yes, I remember. Wimberley Jones told me. But how in the world did you get mixed up in the fight. Wimberley said they were supposed to send you back to St. Benedict's before they left Buley. That was weeks ago."

Yes sir, that's right. But things kinda got out of hand and one thing led to another and, well, there I was."

"The last thing I remember," Hiram continued, "we were pulling back, down the Augusta road. I had just passed the tree barricade when it felt like someone hit me in the back with a pickaxe. I remember falling toward the marsh. I must have hit my head on a rock or something. I don't remember anything after that. How did I get here?"

"I was sent in with the folks to look for the wounded," Cassie said. "I'd been working with the doctors at the camp hospital and they taught me how to tend to wounds. The man I was with, Louis, he's the one up on the wagon seat, he and I were looking for his friend André. I'd been working with them since I went to Buley. He said he last saw Andre near the marsh, by the causeway. Well, we found him and when we were trying to get him up the bank, I stumbled over another man and he rolled down the bank. When he turned over on his back I could see it was you. I couldn't believe it. Louis and I dragged you and Andre up to the wagon and finally got you into it and took you back up to where the doctors were, near the cemetery. We tried to get them to take care of you but they were so busy they couldn't look after you right away. So, Louis and I, we got some supplies and cleaned up your wounds as best we could and bandaged them. We then decided to take you back to the main camp where maybe the other doctors there could look after you. That's when all the trouble began."

"What trouble?" Hiram asked.

"We stopped at a well to water the horses and get some water for you when a crowd of people came up. They started shouting and hitting me. Louis hit one of them with a big stick and then we skedaddled out of there. You won't believe what happened next. One of the men picked up his rifle and shot at us. The bullet hit the seat by Louis. Just missed my head. Splinters flew everywhere. One struck Louis in the face. He's still trying to stop the bleeding. But the craziest thing is Master Hiram --- I think the man who shot at us was Master Enoch."

Hiram tried to sit up. The fresh burst of memory shocked him. He remembered that the last face he saw before he was shot was Enoch's. He remembered that he had a British soldier in his sights and when the man's hat fell off and he saw that flash of red he stopped. It was Enoch. He remembered thinking, "I can't shoot my own brother".

"It was Enoch, Cassie. I remember seeing him just before I was shot. He was wearing a British uniform. If his hat hadn't been knocked off so that I could see his face I would have shot him. Somehow he got out of Savannah. He must be headed south. He must know that I was here with the militia. I don't know what he's up to but I have to get home. Amanda is alone with Sarah and Rebecca. I've got to get to her before Enoch does. I don't know what he might do."

" Master Hiram, if he saw me and recognized me, won't he try to follow me?" she asked.

"Yes. You're right. He probably will. The fact that he left Savannah and was moving south, tells me he's either headed to Roselawn, or to Skidaway. He has some sort of plan. He probably thought you were still at St. Benedict's and he may have been trying to get there. He must still be possessed with getting to you."

Hiram tried to sit up. The pain of the effort was excruciating. He fell back to the straw. "Cassie, tell me about the young man lying there," he said through clenched teeth. "Is he seriously injured?"

"His name is Andre Dupre. He's a member of the unit from Saint-Domingue, part of the French army. Both Andre and Louis were slaves on a sugar cane plantation. They were forced into service with a promise of freedom if they would serve for six years. He has a head wound. It doesn't seem to have fractured the skull but he's been unconscious ever since we pulled him out of the marsh. He would have drowned if his musket hadn't held his head above water."

Through blurry eyes Hiram stared up at the striking face. He could see that she had the features of her mother, Queen, but he saw more now. She looked almost European even though the Bedouin influence still predominated. Her figure was lithe and athletic. Whatever had transpired at St. Benedict's over the past five years, both physically and intellectually, had produced a remarkable young woman.

He marveled at the transformation of the teenage house servant he took to St. Benedict's, into an intelligent, articulate young woman. He had never known blacks with much education. Most plantation owners wouldn't permit their slaves to be taught. Roselawn had allowed it, but didn't encourage it. Following the Stono Rebellion South Carolina went so far as to pass a law forbidding the teaching of slaves. Education became equated with insurrection. A few slaves, those who had been educated in Africa by the Spanish or Portuguese, tried to teach others. When caught, their punishment was swift and severe.

"Cassie, I have an idea. If Enoch is following you it won't be hard for him to track this wagon. When we get to Montgomery Crossroads I want you and Louis to take the road north toward Thunderbolt. We'll drive until we cross the main road between Savannah and Thunderbolt. That road will be covered with wagon tracks from the returning soldiers. If Enoch follows us, he'll lose our track among all the others. We'll drive a little further east and pick up the road down the Herb River to Isle of Hope and then over to Roselawn. Since he didn't see me in the wagon, I'm betting that he'll think your driver headed back to join his unit and took you with him. He'll have to be very careful if he starts nosing around the camp asking a lot of questions. If they find out he's a British soldier he'll be in big trouble. In any case it'll give us a big head start at getting back to Roselawn.

"Now, I have a question to ask you. What about Louis and Andre? Were they going to take you back to Skidaway and then return to Thunderbolt, or had they planned to stay there with you?"

Cassie was startled by the question. It took her a minute to decide how to respond. She finally decided that the truth would serve her best.

"Master Hiram, you know that I wanted to become a nun. When the church wouldn't allow it, I decided to continue my education and training in the hope that someday the church would change its mind. If not, I would still find a way to serve the Lord and my people. When the admiral asked me to help him he promised me that he would ask you to grant my freedom. I figured that helping him might be the only chance I would ever have to be free, so I did it. Now, with the French leaving, and him not having spoken to you, I don't know what will happen.

"Andre and I spent a lot of time together over the last few weeks. We talked about our hopes and dreams, where we both came from and what the future might hold for us. I know it might sound crazy to you but in that short period of time we fell in love. I had never even been alone with a man but I knew after that time with Andre that I loved him and I wanted to marry him. We agreed that I would go back to St. Benedict's and wait for him to finish his service and when he was free he would come back to me.

"Now, with all that's happening, Louis and I want to take him back to St. Benedict's where he can be taken care of. I heard all kinds of stories when I was at the hospital. About the sickness and disease aboard those ships and how so many people were dying every day. I know that if they go back, their wounds will get infected, and with no one to take care of them, they'll probably die. Louis and I had already decided that no one would miss two more soldiers. There were so many killed yesterday and thrown into graves that there's no way they can know who's dead and who's alive."

"I thought so," Hiram said. "I could see the way you looked at him. I haven't seen that look in a girl's eyes since I asked Amanda to marry me. I can't say that I disagree with your reasoning. The French are going to be a long time recovering from yesterday's disaster."

Hiram took Cassie's hand. Her first instinct was to pull it back. White men didn't hold hands with slaves. He held tight.

"Look. I owe you my life. If you had left me back there in that ditch I'd be in one of those graves myself. I've got a hole through my shoulder. It stands to get infected too, just like Louis and Andre." He winced and stopped talking as the pain radiated down his arm.

"Wimberley told me about the admiral's promise to you. He asked me if I would honor it. I told him that Miss Amanda would have to make that decision since you worked in the house for her. I don't think that will be a problem now that I owe my life to you. As soon as we get back to Roselawn I'll draw up the necessary papers. I don't know when we'll be able to get them legally recorded since our courts are all up in Augusta. But I'll get them notarized and give you a copy. That should suffice until I can get them recorded."

Tears welled in Cassie's eyes. They overflowed down her cheeks.

"Oh, Master Hiram. Will you really do that? I can't believe it. Will I really be free?"

"Yes you will, and you won't have to call me Master anymore. You'll be your own master."

CHAPTER TWENTY-THREE

A SCANT HOUR HAD passed since d'Estaing led his army across the marsh toward the ramparts surrounding Savannah. In that short period over eleven hundred French and American men were killed or wounded. In the entire Revolution only Bunker Hill was bloodier. Only there, the British had paid the higher price and suffered the brunt of the casualties. d'Estaing once again had tasted the bitter fruit of defeat as reward for his pride and arrogance. The British casualties were eighteen killed and thirty-nine wounded. For every lone casualty of the British, twenty French and American soldiers had fallen.

His command was in tatters. Many of his senior officers were dead or wounded. Pulaski was dying. General von Stedingk, who lost over four hundred men in that glorious charge up Spring Hill, was grievously wounded, as were Fontanges and Betisy. Nearly fifty officers in total were dead or injured. Not a single unit left the field unscathed. The dead and dying lay strewn about the bloody battlefield. The moaning and wailing from the conscious wounded drove daggers through the hearts of their colleagues.

The trenches were filled with the mangled bodies of French and Americans. The field beyond the trenches for one hundred yards was a sea of death. The landscape was painted crimson as torrents of blood drained from the wounded. John Laurens, picking his way through the bodies was so sickened by the carnage that he threw down his sword in disgust at the colossal waste of human life.

Shortly after eight o'clock a lone emissary held a white flag aloft as he crossed the marsh. It was fastened to the point of his saber. He made his way through the grisly killing field and climbed the slope up to Spring Hill. He carried a request from d'Estaing for a ceasefire to allow the wounded to be recovered and the dead to be buried. The request was granted, initially until three, but in light of the overwhelming number of dead and wounded, it was mercifully extended until dusk.

By ten o'clock the bulk of the army was back in the camps south of town. In the space of ten hours they had marched, assembled, attacked, retreated and reassembled, back at the point where they started. Those assigned to bury and recover labored all morning and afternoon to carry out their gruesome task. There were pitifully few doctors for the massive effort. They performed battlefield triage, deciding which of the injured had any chance of surviving their wounds. The rest were left to die. The shortage of linens to bind up the wounds meant that many went untreated. Flies and insects feasted on the gore. Vultures circled overhead, awaiting their chance to participate. The raucous call of fish crows filled the nearby trees. They flew down to warily peck at the bloody corpses only to be shooed away by the soldiers. Hundreds of the dead were laid like cordwood in the trenches and covered with the wet sand piled up around them. Many others were taken back to the camp at Springfield Plantation where their clothing and belongings were salvaged before mass burial in a long trench. French, American, Polish, Irish and Norwegian, lying side by side in death, stripped of their dignity as well as their clothes. It was an ignominious end for the fallen warriors. Their bravery and heroism were in vain. There was precious little time to mourn the dead.

d'Estaing, running a high fever from his two wounds, rode back to Thunderbolt under his own power. He summoned Dr. Lynah to tend his wounds. Touching his chest he said, "I have a deep wound here, which is not in your power to cure."

He then sent the doctor to the American ship *Wasp* to attend General Pulaski. There was little to be done for the Polish warrior. Lynah had removed a large grapeshot from his groin in the field. Now, Lynah re-dressed his wounds before leaving the ship.

On the quarterdeck, the ship's captain inquired about the general's condition. Lynah merely shook his head. The *Wasp* put to sea the next day. She had barely cleared Tybee before the infection killed Pulaski. The crew swathed the great man in the finest linen remaining aboard the ship and then consigned his body to the deep. The war hero of two continents, victorious in numerous battles, joined the other victims of d'Estaing's madness.

d'Estaing sent word to General Lincoln that he was lifting the siege and then turned over to de Noailles and Dillon the responsibility for determining how to best disengage from the debacle. Lincoln and the Americans tried to dissuade d'Estaing but he would have none of it. Even a letter from Governor Rutledge of South Carolina did not budge him. Rutledge urged the French to move over land to Charlestown for embarkation. He was hoping to persuade the Admiral to continue the battle. d'Estaing would not relent. He insisted they would board the ships at Thunderbolt and Causton Bluff and set sail from there. A detachment of three hundred men was sent to form a line between the camps and the town to prevent a surprise attack.

de Noailles and Dillon argued vehemently for the over-land withdrawal to Charlestown. d'Estaing was enraged. In a fit of pique, he informed them that if they persisted he would replace them with General Bougainville. He feared that a withdrawal over land would only encourage more desertions. Countless numbers had already fled. Sentinels were placed around the entire bivouac to prevent more from running off.

On Sunday, October 17th, d'Estaing allowed the most seriously wounded to be evacuated over land to Charlestown. Those with lesser wounds began boarding the ships for their journey home. They embarked from Kincaid's Landing on Causton Creek for the ships lying at anchor in the river. The next day all the tents and equipment were boarded.

Monday morning dawned with the sounds of the Americans breaking camp for their march back to Charlestown. The French began to move their forces toward Thunderbolt and Causton Bluff. By Sunday the first ship was ready for departure. The *Fier Rodrigue* with its merchant convoy in tow, weighed anchor and proceeded down the river toward the open sea and points north.

On Monday several more ships left for the Leeward Islands. Admiral de Grasse followed, then swung north, bound for the Chesapeake and an eventual engagement with General Cornwallis at Yorktown.

A strong storm blew through on Thursday. The *Languedoc* snapped one of its mooring cables and the other had to be to cut free to avoid grounding. d'Estaing signaled that he had to put to sea immediately. The violent winds, outer bands of the hurricane he had feared, forced several other ships to cut loose their moorings and follow the *Languedoc* downriver.

October 30th saw the last of the French armada slipping out to sea. The waters around Thunderbolt were empty and silent. Only a few fishing skiffs and coastal freighters remained where the French fleet had anchored for nearly two months.

CHAPTER TWENTY-FOUR

THE HOOF PRINTS OF the hurtling horses cut deeply into the soft Georgia sand, throwing up clay from the hardpan beneath. Enoch followed them at a steady pace. Pelham and Hawkins lagged behind.

"What's your all-fired hurry Enoch?" Pelham asked as they caught up to the kneeling man. "They'll be there when we get there. It don't matter where they're going. We can follow those prints 'til hell freezes over. Slow down so we can catch our breath."

Enoch was squatting, staring intently at the tracks.

"They stopped running here," he said. "Those horses must've been pretty tuckered out. I figure they came through here 'bout an hour ago. They're probably past the crossroad by now. One of those horses has a split shoe." He pointed to a print with a raised slit of earth where the clay had compacted. Enoch got to his feet and squinted up at the sun. He fished his watch from his pocket and flipped open the cover. Absently, he twirled the watch on its fob then replaced it in his pocket.

"Half past ten. Let's keep going. If they're headed to Roselawn I want to get there before Hiram gets back. If they're going to Skidaway I want to know that too. Then I'll avoid Hiram. He can wait. I reckon he'll be tied up back in Savannah while the colonials decide what to do. I don't think they'll be going after old "Bullet Head" again, seeing as how we whupped their ass already. So, as I see it, they'll either hunker down and wait us out, or Lincoln will take his men back to Charlestown. In either case Hiram and the other local militiamen will fold their tents and go home in a day or two."

"Why are you so hell bent on catching up to them two blacks, Enoch," Caleb asked. "If anybody oughta be mad at them it's that fella back there by the well with that big knot on his head."

"It has nothing to do with being mad Caleb. I recognized that girl. She was a slave at Roselawn. She worked in our kitchen with her ma, Queen, and her grandma, Aba. My pa sent her away to that monastery on Skidaway about five years ago. That was before you went to work for Pa." He stared intently at the roughhewn man, debating whether he should tell him the rest of the story. Deciding he would find out sooner or later, he began.

"You know back there when you was talking about him beating you for messing around with the blacks. Well, I got a couple of tastes of that same medicine from him. Once was almost twenty years ago. He took the hide clean off me with his strop. The second time was five years ago. And that girl in the wagon is the reason why. She's the one who caused Pa to send me to Ossabaw. She's the one that started all this trouble. If she'da kept her mouth shut none of that would have happened. She just didn't know her place. She started screaming when I touched her. Now it's my turn. When I catch up to her we'll see if she still wants to scream. Only this time it won't do her any good."

"Lawsy, me. Enoch. I didn't know you fancied them black bitches. I knew how yore pa felt and I figured you wuz the same way."

"There are lots of things you don't know about me, Caleb. Let's just leave it at that."

The sun was at its zenith when the trio reached the crossroads. There was no one in sight. Enoch again knelt to read the signs of the horses that had recently passed through. He found the print with a crack on the right side. He followed the trail with his eyes. He was surprised to see that the ruts bore left at the intersection.

"Well, I'll be damned. They're headed toward the French camp in Thunderbolt," he said. "You can see the wagon turning here. There's the broken shoe we've been following. That nigger soldier is going back to join the others. I reckon he decided to go back to the islands. I don't know what he'll do with Cassie. I wish to God I knew why she was here in the first place."

"What'll you do now Enoch?" Pelham asked.

"I'm going to follow them, of course. I have a debt to settle with that girl and I intend to settle it."

"But Enoch," Caleb chimed in, "Those Frenchies are not gonna take too kindly to three Tories parading through their camp."

"Don't you think I know that? I'm not stupid. I'll figure something out before we get there."

Thunderbolt was five miles northeast. At a steady pace they could be there in less than two hours. Enoch motioned for the other two to follow him as he set off. A half-hour later he stepped off the road and crossed through the woods for about a quarter mile. When they emerged they were in a small settlement with two stores and a blacksmith shop.

"One of those stores is a sutler for the Georgia militia. I overheard Hiram say he bought his uniform there," Enoch said. "We're gonna go in there and act like we're buying some supplies. Caleb, while me and Jim keep the merchant busy I want you to go into the back room. In the drawers on the back wall they keep pieces of the militia uniforms. I want you to get three shirts, three vests and three hats. The pants and shoes we're wearing will be all right. You bundle those clothes up and sneak out the back door. Meantime, I'll buy some more gunpowder and balls. We'll meet up with you back up the trail. You wait until I get the clerk's back turned to you before you take off. If he gets suspicious that you're gone I'll tell him you've got dysentery and you probably went out back to shit. You think you can handle that?"

"Sure, Enoch. Won't be the first time I stole something from a store. Say, while you're gettin that gunpowder do you think you can git me a piece of that horehound candy. I've got a sweet tooth for that stuff. I ain't had none in a long spell."

"I will Caleb, but you'd better not mess up on the uniforms. They'll be our ticket into the French camp."

"Afternoon, gentlemen. Can I help you?" the fawning clerk asked.

The rounded collar of his starched shirt was fastened with a fancy pin. His apron was stained with blood from the butcher shop. Fresh cuts of mutton hung among the cured hams and sausages. The owner was preparing for a surge of customers. Business had been dismal during the siege. Everyone was either up at the front gawking at the soldiers or they were keeping out of sight until things settled down. Now that the British were secure in Savannah he just prayed that they would stay there. Every time they came out and set up their outposts he was forced to hide all his militia supplies. He hoped that wouldn't happen this time.

"Yes sir, you sure can," Enoch answered. "I was taking a shot at a deer this morning and I dropped my powder horn. Spilt it all over the wet ground. I need a pound of gunpowder. And I might as well get some more balls. Let me have twenty-five of the .69 caliber balls and some wadding."

"Certainly sir. Might you be with the militia? I've seen several of them come through here in the last day or so."

"Yes sir, we belong to the Georgia militia. Our unit got split up during the fighting and we're trying to catch up to them. We're headed to Sunbury. That's where we used to train. Now that the Brits have left there we'll be taking over the fort again. Maybe we can keep them out this time.

"Oh, and could I get a piece of that horehound candy. My friend has a bad case of the runs. The candy kinda settles his stomach. I expect he's out back now relieving himself."

"Much obliged," Enoch said as he handed over one of the few remaining coins from the ten pounds Hiram gave him.

He scooped up the sack of powder and the box of balls and put them in his rucksack. He put the candy in his pocket.

"Once I get back what's rightfully mine I can buy anything I want and not have to worry about it," he thought.

"Thank you, gentlemen," the clerk said. "Godspeed on your journey to Sunbury and God bless you. At least you've got the English holed up in town for a spell. Too bad you didn't run them off, but at least they're penned up for a while. I don't think they'll be out here bothering me again."

Enoch picked up his long rifle. He left it leaning on the doorsill when he came in. He took a quick look toward the rear of the store. Caleb was nowhere in sight. Thank goodness. The last thing we need right now is a run in with a crazed store clerk. The poor fellow's just trying to scrape a living out of this godforsaken place. Enoch and Jim caught up with Caleb after about a half-mile. He was all grins and proud as a peacock.

"How'd I do Enoch?" he shouted, waving the clothes. "I think I even got the right sizes. Mine's a little bigger than yours and Jim's. Here. Try 'em on. See how they fit."

Enoch started to rebuke his coarse companion for the outburst but thought better of it. No harm done. It's not often he gets a chance to shine. Besides, he needed to keep both men on his side. He was going to need them to find Cassie and to face Hiram.

"You did good, Caleb," he smiled. "Couldn't have done better myself."

Caleb wore a tobacco stained grin from ear to ear.

The men slipped into the shirts and vests. They perched the tricorns atop their heads.

"Don't we look the dandies?" Caleb said. "I ain't been so dressed up since I got married."

Enoch could only imagine the poor wretch that wound up in bed with this slovenly creature. She probably ran off after a while, or died in childbirth. More's the blessing. The fewer young Calebs running around, the better.

"All right, boys. We better spread a little mud and dirt on these fancy duds. Gotta convince those snots that we were in the battle. If anybody asks you which militia unit we were with, tell 'em Colonel Twiggs's Georgia battalion. Won't raise any suspicions."

Minutes later the uniforms looked suitably battle worn, even a couple of bullet holes for effect. Enoch stuffed his old clothes into his bag. The others followed suit. They resumed their trek toward Thunderbolt. They reached the road leading into the camp by midafternoon. It was a quagmire from the hundreds of horses and men passing through. Any hope of finding a unique hoof print disappeared into the churned up mud.

"Damn," Enoch cursed. "We'll never follow their track in this mess. The only thing we know for sure is that they came this far. If they were going to Roselawn or Skidaway, they woulda kept on straight down the road. It stands to reason that the young buck is trying to find his way back to his outfit. Let's just mosey on down by the tents and try to find out where the black units are located."

*****

A large hospital had been set up at Thunderbolt. It was overwhelmed by the flood of wounded. A second was erected to handle the overflow, further upriver at Greenwich. Over three hundred were housed there. Chaos reigned throughout the camps. The deaths mounted, in camp and aboard ship. The regiments from Armagnac and Auxerrois together with a company of marines, were sent to form a line facing Savannah. Dillon and de Noailles were unsure of the British intentions. A few feeble tests of their lines were mounted in the first couple of days but were easily fended off. Out of fear and uncertainty on their part, the British began feverishly to erect additional defenses on the eastern edge of town. No attack came. After a day or two all was quiet on the eastern front. It became apparent that the allied forces of France and America had their fill of fighting and were preparing to evacuate.

d'Estaing continued to run a high fever from his wounds. That did not prevent him from exercising strict control over his lieutenants. Both colonels resisted their urges to countermand his orders. Sullenly, they began to prepare for an orderly withdrawal. Under such chaotic conditions, that was a tall order.

It took almost a week to complete the tasks of burying the dead, tending the wounded and preparing for debarkation. Cannon needed to be re-installed on the ships. The paraphernalia of war essential to support 4,000 men in the field, had to be dismantled, crated and moved to the docks, a task further bedeviled by a shortage of colonial wagons and teams. A constant stream of longboats moved back and forth, carrying the mountains of cartage to the various ships.

General Lincoln, resigned to the fact that d'Estaing would not change his mind, began the long trek back to Charlestown. The regular army, including McIntosh's battalion and the remnants of Pulaski's Legion broke camp on October 19th. Members of the Georgia militia melted back into the countryside, returning to their families and their farms, to wait.

The citizens of Savannah awoke to the slow, mournful pealing of bells on the twenty-fourth. They rang out across the marshes from the spire of Christ Church. The French found this curious since the raucous clamor of those same bells had joyfully proclaimed victory only a few days earlier. d'Estaing, lying wounded in his tent, was puzzled. Before his departure from Thunderbolt he would learn that the architect of his defeat, Colonel John Maitland, had died of the fever he brought with him to Savannah from his Beaufort sickbed. It was a final bitter reminder of how time and fate had conspired to defeat him. That same day the *Fier Rodrigue,* first French ship to leave Savannah, crossed the bar at Tybee and sailed north in convoy with several supply ships. Over the next four days other ships slipped their anchorages and stole out to sea.

On the fifth day, the strong hurricane winds d'Estaing had feared roared in. battering the few remaining ships still at anchor off Thunderbolt and Causton Bluff. The flagship *Languedoc,* with d'Estaing back aboard, was forced to put to sea when her mooring cables snapped. The others, seeing their flagship driven away, weighed anchor and followed. On the 28th of October, the last threat to Savannah and her British occupiers slipped out to sea.

CHAPTER TWENTY-FIVE

LOUIS' SWOLLEN FACE WAS swathed in a long strip of muslin from Hiram's shirt. His right eye was swollen shut but the bleeding had stopped. Cassie sat on the straw between Hiram and Andre, who continued to drift in and out of consciousness. She thought he recognized her but he couldn't focus long enough to speak. Hiram was now conscious for longer periods of time. His fever had abated somewhat, but his clothes were still wet with perspiration. They had completed the northward leg of their journey to Roselawn. Near the original French camp, the wagon merged with the main road to Thunderbolt.

"Look, there's the hospital tent and the cattle pens," Cassie said. "It was only two days ago that I left here. It seems like a lifetime."

"Yeah," Louis said. "I was there just a few days before that. I can't believe everything that's happened since."

A few soldiers were still flowing back from the battlefield. Most had already returned. Others continued to minister to the dead and wounded. Naval crews struggled to dismantle the batteries and haul the cannons back to the ships. The clamor became louder as they approached. The sounds awakened Hiram. Cassie helped him to a sitting position, carefully cradling his right arm. He surveyed his surroundings. The once familiar area was hardly recognizable. A sprawling tent city had sprung up among the pines and along the periphery of the marsh. Pens of cattle and horses spread across several acres. Soldiers milled about in bewildered confusion, scurrying to carry out their officer's orders. No one paid much attention to a single wagon driven by a black soldier.

"Cassie tell Louis to continue down this road toward Thunderbolt until we intersect a major trail to the south. I think it's a couple of miles. That will be Skidaway Road. It'll take us to the Isle of Hope. Roselawn is only seven or eight miles from that crossing."

The detour added almost twenty miles to their journey, but if it threw Enoch off track it would be worth it. Traffic on the road dwindled the further east they traveled.. They reached the Skidaway intersection a mile before Thunderbolt. It was a well-worn trail connecting the rice plantations to the city. Louis tugged on the right rein, urging the team into a slow turn. The bustle along the Thunderbolt road gave way to the occasional wagon or buggy whose occupants were absorbed with their own concerns. Word of the British victory had spread rapidly and most farmers and planters were sticking close to home. They feared that when the French and American armies left, the British might again begin venturing out from their sanctuary. The citizenry needed to be prepared. Militia groups had to be re-formed. Strategies must be developed to frustrate the enemy patrols. A continuation of the occupation of the last eighteen months seemed inevitable. Life would carry on under the constant threat of the English and their Tory allies. Spirits throughout the colony sank to their lowest ebb of the war. The very existence of the revolution hung in the balance.

The wagon rumbled across the long wooden bridge connecting the Isle of Hope to the mainland. It was just past four in the afternoon. Both patients were finally sleeping, if not peacefully, at least with less obvious pain. Cassie reached over to shake Hiram awake.

"Master Hiram, we're here. We just crossed the bridge."

She helped him to sit up. It was a painful effort. He cast about for landmarks and saw the great oak that marked the fork to Wormslow in one direction and Roselawn in the other.

"Tell Louis to take the left fork," Hiram wheezed. Each breath introduced more pain.

"*Louis, tourner a gauche ici, sil vous plait.*"

The words rolled effortlessly off Cassie's tongue. Hiram was still marveling at her fluency in a language that she hadn't known existed five years earlier. He always knew that Cassie was intelligent, as were Queen and Aba, the matriarch. He just had no idea how intelligent. Under the teaching and guidance of the nuns she had surpassed anyone he knew save a few scholars in Charlestown. He shook his head and smiled.

"How little we know of the talents of those we have enslaved".

The Grimball's Creek landing emerged at the end of a moss draped tunnel of oaks. This was an Indian trail, dating to a time, eons before the arrival of the Spanish. It snaked through the woods for more than a mile past the fork. John Penrose had painstakingly built the bridge and causeway across to the island that was Roselawn plantation. Hiram was never so happy to see the big house looming across the marsh. He was home. Unbelievably, he was home.

****

There were a few questioning glances, but most of the soldiers were too busy carrying out their own duties to worry about the three Americans wandering around camp. They assumed them to be local militia sent to help with the horses and wagons. The locals furnished the bulk of the transport. They rambled around for nearly an hour before Pelham touched Enoch on the arm.

"There they are," he said, pointing toward a clutch of tents near the marsh.

"All right. Here's what we're going to do," Enoch said. "We'll walk into that camp and tell their commander that we have been sent here to help them move their stuff to the ships. After we ease any concerns we'll wander around to see if we can spot Cassie or the black that was driving the wagon."

Once inside the circle of tents, Enoch saw a much larger tent in the middle of the compound. There was a flurry of activity around the area.

"There's their headquarters," he said. "You two just keep quiet. Leave the talking to me."

He walked over to a young major seated at a field desk. He was writing out orders.

"Pardon me, sir. We wuz sent up here by Colonel Twiggs to lend a hand with hauling yore stuff to the docks." Enoch said, adapting the backwoods demeanor least likely to raise suspicions. The officer looked up from his writing with a puzzled expression.

"*Je ne parle pas Anglais,*" the man said, with a gallic shrug of his shoulders.

"Whad he say?" Caleb piped up.

"I told you to shut up, Caleb. I'll handle this." He gave his companion a withering look.

"It's apparent that he doesn't speak English."

The officer rose from his seat and summoned a black sergeant standing nearby. He spoke a few words to him. The sergeant saluted and walked away toward the main camp. The major turned back to Enoch.

"*Juste un instant, je vais envoyer pour un traducteur.*"

Enoch's contorted face relaxed.

"Oh. I get it. He's sending for a translator."

Enoch summoned up all he could remember from the French lessons his mother had insisted he take.

"*Merci, Monsieur,*" he said in mangled French.

He smiled broadly and stepped away to await the messenger's return. Several minutes passed. The officer returned to his task at hand. Enoch, Jim and Caleb wandered around, checking out the soldiers near the tent.

The sergeant returned with a middle-aged white soldier in an unfamiliar uniform. He spoke briefly to the major who was pointing toward Enoch. The soldier walked over to him.

"Good evening," he said in heavily accented English. "I am Captain Nordsen. I serve under General von Stedingk. May I help you?"

"I believe you can, Captain," Enoch answered. "Me and my friends here are with the Georgia Militia. Twigg's battalion. We've been sent over to help with gettin yore stuff over to the ships. We were told to report to the officer in charge of the black units."

The Swede took a few seconds to sort out Enoch's local speech patterns, and then smiled.

" That's very kind of you sir. Major Vincent there is in charge of this group. Come with me and I'll tell him of your mission."

"Major Vincent," the soldier announced their presence.

The major looked up from his journal.

"These men are part of the Georgia militia. They've been sent by Colonel Twiggs to assist with transport to the ships. They are an advance party. He says more men and wagons will be here tomorrow."

"Good. Please convey my gratitude to these men. We can certainly use more help getting to the ships. We lost so many of our wagons and horses in the battle."

"Captain." Enoch said. "Will you ask the major if one of his men came in earlier today in one of our wagons. He was riding with a black woman. He brought some of our gear with him and me and the boys need that to camp tonight."

A jumble of French, English and Swedish followed. After several gestures and flourishes the soldier replied.

"I'm sorry but he has not seen anyone like that. He says you are welcome to bed down here with his men until tomorrow. Maybe then he can find your equipment. Meanwhile, enjoy our hospitality. The cook fires are still going. Help yourself."

"Thank the major for me," Enoch said. "We'll have a bit of supper and then bed down over by the creek. Gotta be ready for tomorrow. Lotta work to do."

The three men ambled off leaving the Swedish soldier to inform the major of their intentions. The two were still heavily engaged in conversation when he looked back.

"Come on," Enoch said. "Let's get some grub and then look around."

They found a group of men huddled around a boiling pot. It contained a stew of some sort.

"Yore major there," he said, pointing back toward Vincent. "He said we could have something to eat with you."

The upturned faces displayed no understanding. He again pointed toward the major and mimed a spoon and bowl. The nearest soldier nodded and smiled. He handed each a small metal bowl and spoon. He dipped into the cauldron and ladled a foul smelling liquid into their bowls. Strange looking pieces of meat floated to the top.

"That don't look like no meat I ever seen," Caleb said. "I've eaten about everything you can drag out of these swamps or catch out of these waters, and I don't recollect nothin' like that."

Pelham glared at Caleb.

"Just shut up and eat it Caleb. It's the best offer you're going to get tonight. If it hasn't killed these niggers it won't hurt you."

Enoch smiled. He was glad to see Pelham shouldering some of the burden of Caleb.

After supper the three wandered around the encampment. A few campfires remained ablaze. They stared at the soldiers gathered around each, looking for the driver and the woman. An hour of fruitless wandering left Enoch irritable.

"God damn it!" he said. "I know that nigger and the girl must be around here somewhere. They can't just disappear like that. Maybe there's more than one nigger unit. Let's bed down for the night and get a fresh start tomorrow, when we can see what we're doing."

He led the others to a secluded area beyond the tent village, near the creek. They pulled out their bedrolls and plopped to the ground.

"I shore am tuckered out," Caleb said. "It's been a dadblamed long day. I ain't walked so fur in years." He was snoring before the others could close their eyes.

****

Queen, from her elevated vantage point, could see the wagon speeding up the road. She was in Master John's observatory for its monthly cleaning. The space wasn't used often since Master John died but Master Hiram insisted that it be kept as his pa had left it. Despite the recent rains, plumes of dust rose from the wagon's wheels. At this distance she couldn't make out the driver or the occupants. "It couldn't be Master Hiram", she thought. "He'd be on his horse."

News had come the day before of the defeat. The reports of massive casualties were alarming. Everyone on the plantation was anxious. Besides Master Hiram there were several militiamen from Roselawn and neighboring plantations who had gone to fight. There were also a few slaves who went along to assist their masters.

She could see that the driver was a black man. He was wearing a military uniform that she didn't recognize. There was a woman sitting behind him on the floor of the wagon and as they came closer she could see two figures lying in the wagon bed. She picked up a small telescope left on the desk by Mr. Penrose and trained it on the approaching wagon. Queen gasped. "That's Cassie!" What was she doing in a wagon with a strange soldier, and who were the two men lying on the floor? She adjusted the focus and looked again. She nearly dropped the instrument. It was Master Hiram and he was covered in blood.

"Oh my Lawd," she shouted. "Dat's Massa Hiram an he been hurt. And, dat's my Cassie wit'im." She bolted down the stairs yelling at the top of her lungs.

"Miss Amanda! Miss Amanda! Deys a wagon coming. I think it's Massa. He look lak he been hurt. And Lawsy me, I believe it my Cassie wit'im. How in de worl she wind up in da wagon wit Massa."

Queen was out the door and down the steps before the horses reined to a stop. She ran to the wagon, placed her foot on the side step and vaulted over. She grabbed Cassie and squeezed her tightly.

"Lawsy, chile. How you git here?"

She had no time to wait for an answer. Amanda and Cleophas, the groomsman, were there, reaching into the wagon, trying to help Hiram.

"Cleophas, you get up in the wagon with Queen and help Master Penrose down. We'll take him into the small bedroom off the parlor. No need to take him upstairs. Be careful! Don't aggravate his wound. My goodness, he's so pale."

The four of them were able to get Hiram up the steps, across the veranda and into the house. Amanda removed his bloody clothes. Hiram roused and tried to speak.

"Mandy, it's good to be home. I'm sorry I got into such a mess."

"Shhhh," she said. "You're home and right now that's all that matters."

"Mandy," he rasped, "help Cassie take care of those two boys. They saved my life. I'd be lying dead in a ditch on the Augusta road if it wasn't for them."

His voice trailed off and his eyes closed. The exertion pushed him back into unconsciousness.

"Queen, we must get his fever down. Get a bucket of cold water from the deep well. And as many towels as you can find."

"Yes'm, Miss Amanda an iffen ya don mind I'll call old Thomas tuh bring some o his potions. His poultices draws out da pizens real good," Queen added.

"Yes. Anything to help. Master Hiram is very ill. That wound in his shoulder looks mighty bad. I just pray he doesn't develop an infection. We have to keep it open and draining, otherwise it will."

Queen hurried off to get the cold water and to fetch Thomas. When she returned Hiram was resting more quietly, his breathing less labored. Amanda took the towels, dipped them into the cool water and applied them generously to Hiram's torso and arms. He shivered with the initial shock of the cold compresses, and then settled back into a deeper sleep.

"Queen, have you ever seen a gunshot wound like this before?" Amanda asked.

"Yes'm. Bout eight, ten year ago. It wuz when ya wuz staying in town fo a while. One of da houseboys ovuh tuh Wormslow got shot. Him an his brother wuz lookin' fo deer. One jumped up outten a cane break tween da boys an' one of 'em shot witout seein' da udder one. Dat bullet tore through dat boy's leg an' it broke the big bone. He most bled tuh death fo they gots him back. Dey sent fo Thomas. Wormslow don't have no herb an potion man den. I went 'long tuh help.

"Thomas, he tied a cord 'round dat boy's leg tuh cut off da blood an he put some powder in da hole, den he bound it up wit a poultice. It had cornmeal an' herbs an bark in it. Dat boy wuz mighty sick fo a long spell. Thomas kept changin' dat poultice evuh day fo a week. Da boy done gots well atter a while."

Thomas was brought from a plantation near Summerville, South Carolina. Their master had died and his widow couldn't carry on. Thomas was now an old man in his seventies, stooped and with a scraggly white beard. His hair had receded, revealing a glistening black pate with a thin band of cotton running from ear to ear. Concern for his master was etched on his face.

"Thomas, Mr. Hiram is very sick. He's lost a lot of blood. I'm afraid infection has set in. We're trying to get his fever down but that won't help much if the infection worsens. Queen says you once helped save a boy over at Wormslow with a gunshot wound. Please do whatever you can for my husband."

Amanda broke down. She put her face in her hands and sobbed. Her pillar of strength was lying there, seriously injured, and there was precious little she could do. She must depend on the skills of this untrained slave to save his life. She could only pray.

"Don' ya worry, Missy. I's seen wuss dan dis befo. Ya jest gimmee a little while an Massa Hiram, he gone be good as new."

Thomas' words were braver than his heart. He knew it would take all his skills and a large measure of divine intervention to save his master. He lifted the bandage covering the wound. The overpowering stench of infection wafted up. The rim of the hole was red and suppurating pus oozed from within. Hiram's body was throwing everything it had into the fight. Was it enough? It remained to be seen which was stronger, his will and resistance, or the infection. Thomas hoped to shift the odds in Hiram's favor. He began to clean the wound.

Amanda said, "Cassie, you go and take care of those two boys. Take them into the kitchen. They can take Aba's old room. Nobody's used it since she died. I'll send Thomas in as soon as we have Master resting quietly. Then I want to hear all about how you wound up helping him get here from Savannah."

"Yes ma'am," Cassie said.

Cassie ran outside. She hadn't yet had time to catch her breath. Louis and one of the house servants had already carried Andre into the kitchen. He was still in a stupor and not able to sit in a chair.

"Miss Amanda said we can put him in Grandma's old room. It's just across the hall from the kitchen."

Darkness was settling over Roselawn when Thomas came to look at Andre. He entered the small room where Cassie was sitting on the edge of the bed.

"What happent tuh da boy, Cassie?" he asked as he unwrapped the cloth around Andre's head.

"He was hit by a bullet or shell fragment. Looks like it glanced off his skull. We can't tell if it crushed the bone underneath or anything. He's been awake a little, but he keeps falling back to sleep."

Thomas examined the gash running across Andre's temple. The hair was again matted with dried blood and mortared into the wound.

"Bring me a pan of hot water, Cassie. Cleophas git me a razor an some soap."

The groomsman had followed Thomas into the kitchen.

Thomas gingerly dabbed the cloth around the wound, softening the caked mass. Andre winced but didn't cry out. The old man soaped the area and shaved the intruding hair.

"Dere. Won't hafta worry bout dat hair gittin' in da cut no mo'," he said as he washed the razor, folded it and returned it to its case. He took a magnifying glass from his bag.

"Cleophas, hold dat lamp a little closer fo me."

Thomas leaned over Andre, running the glass across the wound. He brought it back to the middle of the gash, just above the eye.

"Looks lak dat bullet took out some bone here. Don' think it went all da way through. A lil bit closer an da boy woulda lost his eye."

He opened his bag and retrieved two small brown bottles that he sat on the bedside table. He asked Cassie for some clean linen. He pulled the corks from both bottles and poured a small amount of the powdered contents into a mortar cup. He added about a cup of heated cornmeal and mixed the ingredients thoroughly with the pestle. He took a pan of warmed turpentine from the stove and poured some into the mixture creating a thick paste. He layered the paste onto the cloth and folded the edges over before applying it to Andre's scalp.

"Dat oughta draw out da pizens. It don' look lak da cut's too deep. Let'im sleep. He oughta be a lots better in da mawnin."

"What's da matter wit dis 'un?" Thomas asked, looking at Louis.

Louis had been sitting quietly in the shadows, happy to be still and not in charge anymore. His side throbbed and he just wanted to lie down and go to sleep.

"Lemme look at'cha boy. Take off yo coat an lie down here," he said, pointing to the other bunk. Cassie interpreted and Louis dutifully followed the old man's instructions. He was too tired to protest.

"Ummm," Thomas mused. "What happent tuh him?"

"A shell exploded near him and a piece struck him in the side. It didn't break any ribs but it sure took a slice out of him."

Thomas probed the wound with his fingers.

"Looks lak it all scabbed over all right. Jes take summa dis salve I's gonna leave ya and rub it on dat scab twice a day. It ain't infected. Ya oughta be all healed up in a few days."

Thomas placed his potions back into the bag and snapped it shut. He rose to leave. Cassie walked to the door with him.

"Thomas, is Andre going to be all right?" she asked.

"I sholy do think so, chile. He a strong young man wit a strong constitution. He gon be fine." He stopped on the step. "It da Massa I worries 'bout. He pow'ful sick Missy. It mosly up tuh da Lawd now."

The shuffling shadow disappeared around the corner of the kitchen. Cassie sat on the steps listening to the frogs and crickets as they performed their evening concert. How could such a perfect moment of peace exist in the midst of such tragedy? She shook her head and wondered aloud, "What now?"

CHAPTER TWENTY-SIX

THE SOUNDS OF THE camp coming awake stirred Enoch from his dreams. He was back at Roselawn in a time long ago, when life was still bearable and his mother was still there. He was dreaming of Cassie and Queen. He was the master of Roselawn and free to do as he wished. His long suppressed fantasies were loosed from the moralistic bonds of a puritanical father. He could indulge his sexual desires without worrying about the rules. A bugle's blare pulled him up from the depths of his dream. The wet spot on the front of his trousers began to spread.

"God damn!" he exclaimed. "Now I gotta walk around all day smelling of cum."

He decided to walk down to the waters edge and strip off his clothes. He bathed, then washed out his underwear and pants and threw them across a nearby wax myrtle to dry. He took the other pair of pants from his rucksack.

"Shit. Now I've gotta wait around all day for these clothes to dry."

Jim and Caleb, roused by the bugle, had joined him.

"Why you doing a wash this early in the mawnin' Enoch?" Caleb asked. "I thought we wuz gonna look for that black girl and her nigger driver."

Enoch gave Caleb a look of utter disgust.

"What an idiot," he thought. "I don't know why I ever hired him back after Pa ran him off. Too late to worry about that now. I'm gonna need him to help find Cassie. Besides, that mean streak in him might come in handy if we run into trouble."

"Caleb, don't you ever think before you open that big mouth of yours?" Jim said. "Sometimes a man just needs to bathe and wash his clothes. Judging by the way you smell you might do well to follow Enoch's example. When's the last time you had a bath?"

Caleb seethed at the insult. He was slow witted but he could tell when folks were poking fun at him.

"Jim, you got no right talking to me that way. I had a bath just last month. It ain't like we've had a lot of free time lately, what with the drillin and diggin and fightin. You don't smell lak no rose yoself. When's the last time you had a bath?"

Without warning Jim grabbed Caleb by the shirtfront and pushed him backwards into the lagoon. He came up splashing and spewing water.

"Since we've gotta be here all day anyhow, just go ahead and clean yourself up," Jim taunted him. He turned to speak to Enoch but before he could say anything Caleb launched himself from the water, tackling Jim from behind. He dragged him toward the water and pulled him in. The two men began thrashing about in a vain attempt to drown each other.

"You idiots. Get outta there. You've probably washed most of the stink off you by now anyway. Besides, I don't think that old bull gator is taking too kindly to you disturbing his nest."

The knobby spine of a twelve-foot alligator cut through the water toward them. They fell over each other trying to scramble up the bank to safety. Enoch, bent double with laughter at the sight of the two men as they fell on the grass, panting, exhausted from their antics. Jim sat up and stared menacingly at Enoch. Finally, seeing how ludicrous the two must look, splayed out on the bank like beached whales, he too began to laugh. Soon Caleb couldn't restrain himself and joined in. It was several minutes before they regained their composure. The French soldiers nearby looked on, perplexed. Crazy Americans.

The clothes were dry by early afternoon when Enoch returned. He had borrowed a shirt from Jim and gone off on his own, looking for Cassie. It took two hours to cover the Saint-Domingue camp. With all the movement involved in preparing to de-camp he wasn't certain he had seen everyone. He backtracked several times until he was satisfied his quarry was not there. Jim and Caleb were dressed and lazing under the shade of a cabbage palm when he returned.

"You sure been gone a long time, Enoch. Did you find anything?" Jim asked.

"Naw. Just more niggers than I've ever seen in one place. You could set up a mighty big plantation with all these boys. I did find out there's another black unit here from the islands. I think they said Martinique, wherever that is. They're bedded down closer to Thunderbolt. We'll stay here for the night and head over there in the morning. Maybe they'll serve up some more of that muskrat stew for Caleb."

"You can fun me all you want, Enoch, but I've had muskrat stew before and that wadn't it," Caleb answered the jibe. "Maybe if you drop the musk part. Coulda been rats. Although I don't think even these black boys would eat rats. Maybe I'll see if I can spear us a couple of fish for supper."

Caleb wandered off to find an elder sapling he could sharpen for a spear. He came back fifteen minutes later with a long limb from which he had stripped all the branches. He sat on a stump and took out his knife to begin fashioning his spear. When he was finished it was an inch in diameter at the base and tapered to a sharp point at the other end. He reached in his rucksack and pulled out a tin containing two sharpened metal barbs. He drilled out two angled holes with his leather punch, three inches from the end of the taper. He inserted the barbs so they protruded a half-inch. He tapped slivers of wood into the holes, securing them in place.

"There," he exclaimed! "You show me a fish and he's good as mine. You boys start a fire. I'll be back directly with our supper." He disappeared behind a thicket of palmettos and cabbage palms.

"Jim, what do you know about Caleb?" Enoch asked. "If I remember right you first recommended him to Pa. Where does he come from?"

"First I ever saw him was down in Darien when I worked on the McKay plantation. He was only about eighteen or so then. Most of the Scots that came over were from two clans, the McKays and the McIntoshs. There were a few indentured servants and one of those families was Hawkins's. Caleb's father had worked off five years of his indebtedness when he died so when Caleb came of age he had to finish out the two years still owed. He stayed on for a while but the farming life didn't suit him so he set out for the Okefenokee to hunt and trap. Made a living for a while as a fur trader, but he got crosswise with the law and took off back to Darien. He went back to work for me on the McKay place and when your Pa hired me I recommended Caleb. He's a real hard worker. Strong as an ox. Just a little slow-witted and hot-headed."

"He scares me sometimes," Enoch said. "I'll look up and catch him staring at me. Like some dark cloud is moving behind his eyes. We need to keep an eye on him. He can be helpful but he can be dangerous too."

Enoch had taken out his tinder kit and placed some elderberry pith on dried moss and pinefat splinters. He hit the flint rock against the metal striker several times causing sparks to fall on the pith. Jim blew on the tiny embers they created. Within minutes the moss and kindling caught. The fire was well established when Caleb came crashing back through the underbrush, the gig over his shoulder. A fat bellied catfish flopped back and forth trying to free itself from the shaft through its gut. Caleb removed the barbs from the spear and slid the writhing fish onto the ground where it continued to flop around.

"Watch those fins boys. If he sticks one of those in ya, you'll get the pizen for sure. Had one fin me in the leg down in the swamp once. I was way out on one of the floating islands. Nobody within five miles. My leg swole up the size of a middling pine sapling. It turned a bilious yellow color with red streaks through it. Thought I was gonna die fo' sure. If I hadn't a had that fish to eat and water to drink, I would've. Took me near five days to get my sense back."

Caleb carefully slid his hand up behind the fins so the fish couldn't flex them. He drove the point of his knife through its head and impaled it on a stump. With another knife he girdled the fish just behind the head. Grasping the exposed skin with a pair of pliers he peeled it off the flesh in one quick pull. He severed the fish's head then gutted and filleted it. He impaled the fillets on the spear and placed it on two forked branches over the fire.

"Keep that turning for about ten or fifteen minutes and we'll be ready to eat," he said to Jim. "I'm gonna see if I can rustle up some grog." Caleb ambled off in the direction of the main camp, returning with a bottle of amber colored liquid.

Enoch roused his companions before first light. He wanted to get out of camp before anyone noticed and started asking questions. They were halfway to Thunderbolt before the first bugle sounded.

"The fellow I talked to back there said the Martinique detachment was camped near the Mulryne Plantation's slave quarters," Enoch said. "I was over to the place once with my pa when I was about ten or twelve years old. I hated the children there. They just stared at me and made funny faces. That's why I never wanted to leave Roselawn. All the children were hateful and mean. It's not like I wanted to be born this way."

Enoch had that distant look in his eyes. It was as if he were seeing and feeling the abuses and insults that dogged him everywhere he went. It took a conscious effort to bring himself back to the present.

"That looks like the turn off I remember."

The tree-lined avenue weaved in and out of the rice paddies along the creek that bisected the property. Early rays of sunlight filtered through the smoke and mist hovering over the camp.

"This must be it," Jim said. "I see a bunch of blacks walking back and forth to those latrines down by the creek."

The three men walked toward the center of the encampment. Soldiers on both sides of the trail were busy with their campfires, preparing breakfast. A few looked up to see who was passing by, then went back to their chores. Odd groups of Americans were a common sight since the battle. Three more raised little concern.

Several officers were gathered around a tent with the French tricolor waving from the center pole above. Enoch approached one of them.

"Pardon me, sir," he began. "Do you speak English?"

The officer looked up from the paper he was reading.

"Yes, I do. What can I do for you?"

"Sir, I was sent by one of our officers, Captain Penrose. He is with the Georgia militia. One of his servants was with him in camp at Savannah and after the battle she disappeared. He was told that she left the field in a wagon with one of the black French soldiers. He's concerned that she thought he wasn't coming back for her and asked for help to get back home. Have you seen anyone like that?"

The officer tweaked his mustache.

"I do recall a wagon with a soldier wearing a Saint- Domingue uniform coming by a couple of days ago. There was a girl sitting in the box of the wagon. They continued on toward the river." He pointed east, toward Thunderbolt.

"Thank you very much sir. That must have been the one. Can you tell me if that soldier's unit has any troops in Thunderbolt?"

"I don't believe so. Only headquarters are located there."

"You've been very helpful, sir. I'm sure Mr. Penrose will be extremely appreciative. Good day to you, sir."

Enoch started back down the serpentine path to the main road. A great blue heron, startled by their approach, lifted from the flooded paddy and with two mighty swoops of its wings glided silently to the other bank.

When they were out of earshot he said, "I don't know what that buck is up to. If there are no more black units ahead, why did he go toward the river? It don't make no sense."

They plodded on in silence, Enoch deep in thought. Jim and Caleb kept their counsel. They had seen this look before and suffered his wrath when they interrupted him.

"That's it!" Enoch exclaimed, stopping dead in his tracks. "It has to be."

The other two stood mute, hesitant to ask what revelation he had experienced.

"She musta recognized me back at the well. She knew I would follow her so she had that nigger driver detour through the camps to throw us off their track. She thought we'd lose them in the middle of all those soldiers. She thought we'd just give up. I gotta give her credit. She's pretty smart for a black bitch. I know exactly what she's up to. She's taken the road along the river back to Roselawn. Thought she'd fool me, throw me off her trail. Well, I ain't as dumb as she thinks I am. Come on, we're going to Roselawn."

"What about Hiram?" Jim asked. "He made it pretty clear that he didn't want to see us back there again."

"Don't you worry about him. He's probably still with the militia trying to figure out what to do. If he ain't, and he's back at Roselawn, that's just too bad. I'll cross that bridge when I get to it."

CHAPTER TWENTY-SEVEN

ANDRE WAS AWAKE AND more alert when Cassie looked in on him the next morning. She helped him into the kitchen where Louis was already sitting at the table trying to cool the steaming cup of coffee before him. He added more milk and tested it again.

"You just sit there with Louis while I make some breakfast for you," she said. "You two haven't had much to eat for the last few days."

Two young grandchildren of old Mose were charged with keeping the fire going all night in the massive black cook stove that filled the back wall of the kitchen. That stove was Elizabeth Penrose's pride and joy. John had ordered it for her from a company way up in New Hampshire. It was a Christmas surprise seven years ago. There was nothing like it on any plantation south of Charlestown. Every visitor to Roselawn received a personal tour of the kitchen.

Cassie lifted one of the eyes to check the flames. She opened the door to the firebox and threw in more wood. She crossed to the pantry which was set several steps below the kitchen to take advantage of the cooler temperatures below ground. She took the remains of a slab of bacon from its hook and gathered up eggs, grits, flour, and lard. She stepped out back to the springhouse for a pitcher of cold milk.

"Well, now I'm ready," she said as she measured flour into a wooden mixing bowl. She cut in a spoon of lard and made a depression in the middle of the mixture. She broke two eggs into the depression and poured in a little milk, pulling the flour into the middle little by little as the dough began to take shape. She threw in a pinch of yeast and continued to combine the ingredients, blending them into a spongy dough that she dropped in small clumps onto a baking sheet. When the biscuits were safely in the oven she sliced the bacon and placed it in the cast iron skillet, already heating on the stove. By the time the pot of grits began to pop and gurgle the biscuits, bacon and eggs were ready.

"You boys are in for a real treat. I bet you've never had grits before," she said as she ladled the creamy cereal onto their plates.

Andre poked at the white mass with his fork and took a small bite. The face he made confirmed his dislike of the foul concoction.

"Whew, I don't think I like your *greets*," he said, pushing them away from his eggs.

"Aw, you haven't given them a chance," Cassie said. "Let me put a little salt and pepper and a little butter on them, then try them again."

Andre tried the new mixture. His look was a little less disapproving. He vainly attempted to finish his serving. He dropped his fork in mock disgust.

"I tell you what, Cassie. If you don't make me eat *greets*, I won't make you eat snails."

Cassie laughed, recalling her experience with the slimy creatures in St. Benedict's gardens. She winked at Andre and replied, "*d'accord*."

"I must say that the bacon, eggs and biscuits are excellent," Louis chimed in. "But I also must agree with Andre about the *greets*."

The door from the breezeway to the main house swung open as Queen and Thomas entered. The look on their faces foretold bad news.

"Massa Hiram ain' doin' so good," she said in a sad whisper.

Thomas followed her to the table and sat down alongside Andre.

"His fever done come down some but he slips in and out. Miss Amanda, she up all night, sittin by his bed. She done plum wore out. I tried tuh git 'er to rest some an let Miss Becky or Miss Sarah stay wit 'im. She won' listen. She gone wear herself out, she not keerful. Lawd, I don know what we gone do if Massa dies."

Cassie looked at her mother with sympathy and admiration. The woman had lived her entire life on this plantation in bondage to this white family and yet she genuinely loved them. Despite the depredations of slavery, they had become her family, especially since Aba died and Cassie went away to St. Benedict's.

"Come on in here, Mama, and let me fix you some breakfast. I expect you and Thomas have been up most of the night yourselves."

"Ya mama ain't slept a hour all night," Thomas added. "She an Miss Amanda been puttin' dem cold towels on da Massa. Da pizen's got him good. Dat bullet hole, it ain't a drainin' lak I wants it to."

Thomas leaned over toward Andre, peering at his scalp.

"Ya seems a bit mo lively dis mawning, Andre. How ya feelin'?"

"I feel much better, thank you sir. My head doesn't hurt as much and the swelling seems to be going down but it throbs and I still get dizzy when I stand up," Andre said.

"I wants ya tuh keep warmin' dat poultice up an puttin' it agin da cut. Gotta keep it a drainin. Gotta keep dat cut from gittin infected."

"Yes sir, I'll do that," Andre said.

"An' how bout you young fella?" Thomas said to Louis. "Ya puttin' dat salve on lak I tol' ya?"

"Yes sir. It seems to be helping. There's less soreness and the swelling is going down. I'll be fine in a few days," Louis answered.

Thomas touched Louis' cheek.

"Better put summa dat salve on here too. Ya face be feelin' a little fevered."

Queen picked at her breakfast, visibly distraught over Master Hiram. She rose and picked up the dirty dishes. She raked the scraps into the slops bucket and put the dishes in a pan. Absentmindedly she dipped hot water from the reservoir of the stove and poured it over the dirty dishes. Cassie put her arms around her.

"It's all right Mama, I'll finish up here. You go get some rest. I'm sure Master Hiram will be better when you wake up."

Queen squeezed her daughter tightly.

"I sholy has missed ya, chile. 'Specially since Ma died. It's powful lonely sometimes in da middle o' da night. I's glad yo's here. I'll lie down a spell iffen you'll go over an' stay wif Miss Amanda. See ya kin git'er tuh rest some. We all gonna need all da strength we's got tuh git through dis."

Cassie wanted desperately to tell her mother about Andre. And about how she came to be in that wagon with him and Master Hiram. And about all the things that had happened to her over the past few days and weeks. Queen needed to know about Enoch and the fact that he may be prowling around out there somewhere, planning more of his evil. But she knew the time was not right. Her mother needed to rest and Cassie needed a time and a place of quiet and repose to tell her story to Queen. She would wait.

Hiram's eyes were open but unseeing. Amanda's back was to Cassie. She didn't hear her enter the room. She was wringing out yet another cloth to place on his forehead.

"Miss Amanda, Mama told me to come over and see if I could convince you to get some rest. Why don't you lie down for a spell? I'll stay here and take care of Master Hiram."

Amanda's face was a portrait of grief. The wear of time and the strain of seeing Hiram like this were reflected in the dark eyes and deep lines. Her attempt at a smile failed. She burst into tears.

"Oh, Cassie. I don't know what I'll do if he dies. We've been together now for over thirty years. We worked side by side with his folks to build this place. Now his father's gone. Miss Lizzy is gone. Enoch's gone, God knows where. It's just Becky, Sarah and me. I don't know if I can manage without Hiram."

"Shhhh," Cassie said. "Don't go talking like that. We're going to make it through this. All of us together are going to get through this trouble. Now you just go upstairs and lie down for a while. I'll call you if I need you."

Reluctantly, Amanda followed Cassie's instructions. She rose to leave.

"I'll have Sarah come down and sit with you," she said, leaning over to press her fingers to Hiram's brow before leaving.

Cassie took one of the towels from the water basin and wrung it out. She placed it on Hiram's chest. He shivered at the shock and his eyes opened again, this time with more clarity than she had seen before.

"Cassie? Is that you, Cassie?" He struggled to focus on her face. Amanda stopped at the sound of his voice.

"Yes, Master Hiram, it's me. Be quiet now and save your strength."

Ignoring her plea he continued.

"Cassie, if I don't make it through this you must take those boys and go back to Skidaway. We both know that Enoch will come here looking for you. Sooner or later he's going to figure out you didn't stay at the camps. When he does he's going to head this way. If I were well it wouldn't matter, I could handle him. But in this condition I won't be able to stop him. Especially if he's got Pelham and Hawkins with him. It's obvious that he'll stop at nothing to find you. I don't understand what's driving him but his is clearly a tormented soul. He'll kill those boys if he has to, to get at you. Neither of them is in any condition to protect you and I don't have enough help here to do it. I don't think he'll harm me or my family, but I can't be sure of that. I think you'd better take Queen with you too. If you're gone and she's here he may take out his anger on her. I don't think he'll follow you to St. Benedict's. I know he's done some terrible things in his life but I don't believe he'll violate the church. Not if he has any respect for the memory of his mother." His eyes closed again and he drifted off.

"Cassie, what is Hiram talking about?" Amanda asked.

"Miss Amanda, when Louis and I were trying to get back here with Master Hiram and Andre, we stopped for water at a well. We were attacked by a crowd of white folks and forced to get away from there in a hurry. One of the men in that crowd shot at us as we took off. That's what caused the cut on Louis' face. I got a good look at the man. Miss Amanda, it was Master Enoch. I couldn't mistake that face. Master Hiram and Andre were lying down in the bed of the wagon and I don't think Master Enoch saw them. Before we got far away Master Hiram roused for a spell and I told him what had happened. He wanted to know if Master Enoch saw him and Andre and I said I didn't think so. That's when he said we should head toward the army camps to throw him off our trail, because if he didn't know they were in the wagon he'd think I was going with Louis to the camp."

"Hiram's right then, Cassie. If Enoch follows you here you and those boys won't be safe. He's gone totally insane. Ever since his father sent him off to Ossabaw. I've never seen any one become so single-mindedly possessed as he is. I thought when you went away and he went to Ossabaw it would all be over, but it isn't.

"You do like Hiram says. Take your ma and those two boys and get out of here. Don't go back toward the Isle of Hope. If Enoch has figured out where you are he'll be coming that way. There's a small boat dock that Hiram built on a little creek that opens onto the Skidaway River, across from Modena Point. He and I slip away there from time to time when we want to be alone. The dock is hidden back in the marsh and nobody knows about it but a few of the servants. Cleophas usually goes with us to mind the horses. He can show you how to get there. Now go! We'll be all right here. I don't believe Enoch will harm us."

Tears were streaming down Amanda's face.

"Pray for Master Hiram, Cassie as I'll be praying for you. God bless you. Thank you for bringing him back to me."

****

Skidaway Road snaked through the primeval forests and the estuaries that were fed by the surrounding rivers and streams. Four miles south from its intersection with the Thunderbolt road the trail forked. The left fork skirted the Herb River and passed Wylly Island before it crossed over the Isle of Hope bridge.

"It's gettin too late in the day to go sashaying up to Roselawn," Enoch said. "There's an old abandoned turpentine still just across from the main house on this side of the river. I used to paddle over there when I couldn't take it any more at home. It'll do as a place to stay for the night. In the morning we'll be able to see across the river from there. There's a small store on the way. We can get some hardtack and beer there. Jim, you got any money left?"

"I got just a few pence left, Enoch. How 'bout you?"

"I got less than a pound of the money Hiram gave me, plus the few shillings the British paid us. We're gonna need to get some more money somewhere. Maybe there'll be some for the taking at Roselawn. I got it coming to me. Hiram never paid me near what I was worth for overseeing Ossabaw. And I never so much as saw a farthing from my pa's will."

The crimson of Enoch's face glowed even more vividly. The perceived injustice ate at him. His mood cast a gloomy pall over the group. The remaining distance was covered in silence.

It was nearing dark when they reached the still. All that remained of the old structure was the circular brick fire pit. The boiler supports had rotted away and fallen into the pit. There was a lean-to that Enoch had built to get out of the rain.

"Caleb, why don't you gather up some pine straw for us to sleep on. Jim and me'll make sure there ain't no critters in there. Don't want to go to bed with no rattlesnakes or moccasins, do we?"

While Caleb brought in several armloads of straw, the other two made sure the old still wasn't home to any of the vermin inhabiting the area. Satisfied that it was clear of snakes and rats, they gathered several old, rotting boards to form a sleeping platform. When finished they had fashioned a comfortable place for the night. The lean-to would prove useful. Heat lightning from the southwest lit up the sky and the roll of distant thunder heralded rain.

They huddled under the leaky shed eating the hardtack and beer they had bought. An occasional burst of wind whipped the rain underneath the shelter roof, forcing them to move further back into the recesses of the dank refuge. Darkness had fully descended when the rain finally slackened. When it stopped completely the dampened travelers rolled out their beds on the straw. They slept to a chorus of tree frogs, their raucous calls encouraged by the drenching rain.

****

Queen was adamant about not leaving.

"Miss Amanda, I cain't go off an' leave ya wif Master Hiram lak dis."

"Listen to me, Queen. We'll be all right. I'm sending someone over to Wormslow to get help. It won't take long for them to come. In the meantime, if Enoch shows up, we'll be able to handle him. You get some things together and go on with Cassie and the boys. When this all blows over, and I'm sure it will, I'll send someone over to St. Benedict's to get you. It won't be long I promise. Besides, none of the others know how to get down the river to Priest's Landing. You've been over there several times to see Cassie. You'll be their river pilot," she said with a laugh.

"Iffen ya says so Miss Amanda. But I sho don' lak leavin' ya wit dat man a skulkin round. I know he be fambly but dat man he be de debil hisself. He done caused mo grief fo dis house than anything I's ever seed. I jes got a bad feelin bout leavin ya. But I's gonna do it, cause ya says so."

Cleophas led the small group out the back of the barn and across the rice paddies spanning the low marsh behind. They walked gingerly across the dikes, careful not to slip into the muddy fields. Beyond the paddies, a seldom used path, now overgrown with weeds, led into the woods. From there it was about a half-mile to the small dock that was completely obscured from view by the drooping tendrils of several willows Hiram had planted there.

Two flat-bottomed jon boats, each nearly fifteen feet long, were turned upside down, resting on the bank of the slough. It was ebb tide and the receding water left the dock pilings standing in a sea of black ooze. Cleophas helped them turn the boats over. He reclaimed the oars that were leaning against one of the willow trunks.

"We can't wait on the tide to come back in," Louis said. "We'll have to drag the boats out to the deep water. Each of you ladies get into a boat."

Cassie and Queen placed their bags into the boats and hiked up their skirts. They stepped over the gunwales and settled precariously on the seats in the middle of the boats. Cleophas untied the ropes from the trees. The men pushed and dragged the boats through the mud until they floated in open water. Their shoes and breeches were covered with the black gumbo of the tidal creek. Andre and Louis clambered aboard and picked up the paddles.

"Goodbye, Cleophas," Cassie waved. "You take care of things here until we can get back. Look after everyone for us."

Queen wore a mournful expression. She had ventured away from Roselawn on very few occasions. She'd been to Skidaway a few times and over to Wormslow. Even a trip or two into Savannah with Miss Amanda. But this was a new experience and she didn't like it.

"I feels lak I's runnin out on Missy at da wust time." she said. "It jes don feel right. It ain't fitten tuh leave'er alone lak dat."

The two boats glided silently through the twists and turns of the tidal creek. Neither Andre nor Louis had much experience with rowboats but they adapted quickly to the rhythms of the oars and the currents of the stream. With each turn the water widened. The tiny tributary expanded into a sizable creek.

Cassie listened in silence to her mother's lamentations. When Queen's voice trailed off into resignation, Cassie answered her.

"Mama, Miss Amanda is just trying to take care of you, like you have taken care of her all these years. She loves you and she doesn't want you to be hurt by Master Enoch. He's brought enough pain into our lives. She doesn't want to see any more."

The pace of the ebb tide quickened and the two oarsmen no longer paddled but simply tried to hold the boats in the middle of the stream as they were carried along by the tide. They sped along through the wall of spartina on either side. They could no longer see where they had come from nor could they see where they were going. Their measure of apprehension rose with each bend in the tidal creek. Two wounded French soldiers, adrift in a strange land, separated from their army, their families, and their homeland. Two black slaves, mother and child, fleeing the resolute monster whose sickness has so profoundly altered the course of their lives. These four, for better or worse, bound together in their flight to Skidaway.

CHAPTER TWENTY-EIGHT

ENOCH AWAKENED AT FIRST light to a noisy screech owl just finishing its nocturnal rounds. He turned over to see Jim folding his bedroll.

"Where's Caleb?" Enoch asked, nodding toward the empty hollow beyond Jim.

Jim stretched his arms high above his head, trying to dispel sleep with a yawn.

"I don't rightly know. I just woke up. He's probably out there somewhere relieving himself."

"Caleb where are you?" Jim shouted.

A voice echoed back from beyond the trunk of a fallen tree.

"I'm just taking a shit. I been havin' the runs ever since I ate that mystery stew them niggers cooked up. I don't know what was in that pot but I shore don't want no more of it. I wish I had sumpin' other than this broom sedge to wipe my ass. It's already raw from the runs. I'll be through directly."

Enoch winced at the crudeness of the man.

"You know Jim, I'm liking that smelly bastard less and less with each passing day. He's starting to get on my nerves. If we didn't need him I'd run him off."

"Oh, come on Enoch. He's no worse than most of these ignorant peckerwoods. You just have to learn to ignore him. He's been working for me on and off for ten years. You get used to his profanity after awhile. If he wasn't such a hard worker I'd agree with you. Besides, you don't know what we may run into over there," Jim said, pointing across the river. "If Hiram is back that means his overseers may be there as well. Old Caleb's a good man to have around in a fight."

Caleb sauntered back into the brick shell of the still tugging at the rope belt holding up his trousers and muttering to himself.

"One of theses days I'm gonna have enough money to buy myself some good breeches and a fancy leather belt. I had one when I was living in the swamp. I was over to the Fargo settlement one night. Sold some skins to a trader there. Got drunk and found myself floatin' in the slough behind the tavern. Left my pants hanging out to dry and some son-of-a-bitch stole 'em. Never did catch the bastard who done it. If I didn't have the money for the skins hidden they'da stole that too. That's when I decided to give up the swamp life for good. Too easy to git yore head split open 'thout nobody knowin bout it. You just become gator food."

Enoch listened quietly to Caleb's rant.

"When I get back what's rightly mine there'll be plenty of money for your breeches and belt, and a whole new wardrobe if you want it. You just gotta' listen to me and do what I tell you. I don't need no loose cannon going off when we get down to serious business with Hiram."

"Enoch do you really believe you'll be able to sashay in there and demand that Hiram just turn over everything to you?" Jim asked. "He already ran us off once. What's to keep him from doing it again?"

Enoch reached behind him and picked up his musket which was leaning against the brick wall of the still.

"This," he said. "We didn't have much choice before, seeing as Hiram had the drop on us and all his niggers around to back him up. Well, we'll have three good friends with us this time. He knows there ain't three better shots in the territory than us. He'll be singing a little different tune this time."

"Caleb, see if you can scare up some grub. Maybe some berries or some game," Jim said to the still muttering man, "and be sure you wash your hands."

"All right, but I don't see why it's always me that's gotta get the food. Why don't you pull your weight some?"

"You're just better at it Caleb," Jim said, seeking to head off a quarrel between the two. "Maybe it's all those years living alone in the swamp."

"Yeah. You're right about that," Caleb said. "You boys git a fire goin' an' I'll be back directly with some vittles."

Caleb grabbed his musket and stalked off across the marsh in the general direction of Bethesda.

"I guess you're right, Jim. I can afford to put up with his wild yammering for a while longer. But, mark my words. When this is all over he has to go."

The report of a gun echoed from beyond the clump of trees into which Caleb had disappeared. It bounced off the curved walls of the still, appearing to come from all directions at once.

"That fool!" Enoch spat. "He'll wake up the devil himself."

"No need to worry about the folks on Roselawn, Enoch. As far as they're concerned it's just somebody out early looking to put food on the table." It wasn't unusual for hunters to be out at dawn when the animals were feeding.

"I guess you're right, Jim. I'm just a mite skittish. I don't mind telling you, I been waitin a long time for this day. I don't want nothing spoilin it for me."

Enoch walked outside and broke off a rotting limb from an old fallen pine tree near the still. The punk inside was dry, unaffected by the soaking rain. He took several handsful of straw from the platform and laid it over the dry tinder. He placed an armful of twigs and limbs across the pile then squatted and began beating the metal against the flintrock until the punk began to glow. Dropping to his knees, he blew on the ember until it burst into flame. Minutes later the brush began to crackle and the latent moisture in the wood popped as it turned to steam.

Caleb returned with a marsh rabbit the size of a small raccoon. It had been a good year for grasses along the edge of the marsh.

"Here," he said to Jim. "I killed it, you can skin it."

Jim eyed Enoch for his reaction. Enoch placidly ignored Caleb. He was lost in other thoughts of events yet to come.

"All right, Caleb. I'll skin and clean the varmint, but Enoch's gotta cook it. That way we all have a hand in the matter and no one has to get his nose out of joint."

Caleb smirked. His words had their intended effect.

The sun was clearing the tops of the tallest pines as Caleb drew the sleeve of his shirt across his mouth to wipe the last of the rabbit grease from his face. He grunted.

"That was mighty good rabbit, Enoch. Jim and you makes a pretty good cookin' team. I'll have to let you boys do that more often."

Enoch cringed, but maintained a cool exterior.

"You just do that, Caleb," he said, leering at the slovenly man.

****

The two boats emerged from their green prison walls to be greeted by the surging currents of the Skidaway, where it was born out of the Thunderbolt. They were just below the juncture. The powerful current pushed them southward.

"Thataway," Queen said, pointing across the water toward the northern tip of Modena Island. "We has tuh go 'round dat point tuh git inta da river dat goes tuh da landing. Once ya gits past dat point da current'll take ya dere."

Andre and Louis leaned into the oars, struggling to make headway against a tide that was running furiously toward the Skidaway narrows, around the Isle of Hope. It took almost half an hour to negotiate the half-mile of open water at this, the widest part of the river. Whitecaps whipped up by the strong northeasterly wind hurled brackish water over the squared prows. The air temperature was not yet sixty degrees and Cassie shivered with each spray of the autumn-chilled water. With sheer will, their muscles burning from the exertion, the two reluctant sailors forced the small craft around the point. Once they passed the invisible demarcation of the two rivers, the Thunderbolt took them into its embrace sweeping them toward Priest's Landing and the sanctuary of St. Benedict's.

Riding with the river current they covered the distance in less than an hour. The heavy rains had swollen the river, washing out several of the posts supporting the dock. They floated near the dock, lashed to it by the ropes that had tied them to the platform. They bobbed up and down in the water, crashing into the sagging structure as it tilted ominously.

"Louis, try to get your boat above the dock so that it wedges against it," Andre shouted above the wind. "I'll try to pull in right behind you."

Louis pulled mightily on his oar, forcing the boat toward the dock. He tried to fend off the flailing posts as they dipped up and down. There was a loud crunch as the boat spun around and banged into the platform. Queen scrambled up the incline and tied a rope around one of the remaining supports. She had barely finished when the second boat careened into the first, throwing Louis forward, striking his side against the edge of the dock. He screamed in pain and grabbed his ribs. Fresh blood oozed through his shirt. The blow had re-opened the old wound.

Andre was able to seize the side of Louis' boat and to throw a line across to Queen. Cassie leapt into the first boat then nimbly crossed to the dock. She helped her mother secure the line then returned to aid Louis. He had settled back onto the seat at the transom, shock evident in his eyes. His mind reeled at the thought that he had come all this way only to be done in by a boat crashing into a dock. He held his side and shook his head in disbelief.

Andre gathered up their few belongings and passed them up to Queen. He then helped Cassie maneuver Louis up onto the dock platform. Louis grabbed the edge and rolled his body over to a position against a support. His shirt was now covered in blood and the searing pain mounting with each movement and grimace.

"Stay here," Cassie said. "I'll go for help."

She charged up the small hill from the landing to the gates of the monastery and knocked loudly. She couldn't be sure she had been heard in the howling wind. She picked up a stone and banged more loudly. Moments later she heard the rasp of the metal deadbolt as it grated in its housing. She was overjoyed at the beaming face of young Brother Anthony peering out as he cracked open the gate.

" Cassie, where did you come from? We've all been worried sick because you were gone so long. We heard that the French and the colonists were defeated but there was no word about you. Sister Bernadette will be overjoyed. She has fretted herself sick. She has assumed all kinds of dire things befalling you. Come in! Come in! You'll catch your death in those wet clothes."

"I will Brother Anthony, but first there are others down at the landing. We need help. One of the men is injured. Can you come?"

"Of course I can. Let me tell the others of the great news and I'll be right down."

"Thank you," Cassie said. "I'm going back to help."

The monastery bell began to peal as Anthony and another young friar, Brother Mark, reached the dock. The entire population of St. Benedict's would soon know the joyous news.

The two brought a cart in which Louis was placed for transport to the infirmary. The two brown clad brothers, one on each side of the long tongue, pulled the cart up the incline with the bedraggled trio trailing along behind.

Sister Bernadette was at prayers when she heard the bell. Before anyone could respond a novice burst into the chapel with the news.

"Forgive me for disturbing the service Father, but I have great news. Sister Cassie has returned. She is at the dock."

The presiding friar crossed himself, uttered a brief amen, and dismissed the assembly. Cassie heard the shriek and saw the small figure in black robes dashing across the courtyard. Bernadette held her flowing skirts with both hands, preventing her from catching her wimple as it blew off. Burnished copper locks flowed wildly in the wind as she bounded ahead with total abandon. She crossed the remaining few yards in a flash and threw her arms around Cassie.

"Oh, Cassie" she cried. "I thought surely you were dead. Not one word since you left for Beaulieu. I have prayed for you constantly and now God has answered my prayers. I was sure that I had sent you off to your death. I couldn't forgive myself."

She held Cassie at arms length.

"Let me look at you. You've lost a little weight but otherwise you look wonderful. And Queen, it's been so long. I'm so glad you are here."

Bernadette was suddenly aware of the young soldier lying in the cart and the companion by his side.

"Cassie who are these young men?"

Not waiting for a reply she ran to the cart. She saw the bloody clothes on the soldier lying there.

"Come, let's get him to the infirmary right away. We must attend to that bleeding."

She led the party across the yard and into the infirmary behind the main building, retrieving her wimple along the way.

The brothers lifted Louis onto the examining table in the small room that served as the infirmary. Shelves lining the walls were filled with jars of colored liquids and vials of powdered roots and herbs. The room smelled of witch hazel and turpentine. Every cut and sprain, and there were many around the monastery, wound up here for treatment.

Sister Rosemarie was the resident physician for the inhabitants of St. Benedict's. She had no formal training in medicine but had worked for years as a nurse at Canterbury. She had much more medical experience than anyone else in the monastery and became its doctor by default. She came bustling into the little hospital, trailing behind Esther who had run to fetch her.

"Well, well," she said, "What have we here?"

She spied Cassie standing behind the table in the dim light.

"Cassie, is that really you? We had almost given up ever seeing you again. Thank God you're all right."

"Thank you," Sister Rosemarie. "It's good to be home again." For now she thought of St. Benedict's as home.

"This is Louis duFour. He is a French soldier from Saint-Domingue. He was wounded during the battle. The wound seemed to be healing nicely, but it broke open after he was slammed against the dock at Priest's Landing. We came here from Roselawn where one of the slaves, Mr. Thomas, was treating him with poultices and a salve."

The sister peeled back Louis' shirt to reveal the gaping wound. Blood was still flowing freely. She began to address the young soldier in his native tongue.

"The first thing we have to do is to get this bleeding stopped. She opened the drawer to a big chest and took out several cotton cloths. She took down a vial of clear liquid from a shelf. She told the brothers to hold Louis while she poured turpentine into the wound before bandaging it. Louis cried out, arching his back in an attempt to escape the fiery liquid. The brothers held him steady on the table.

"I'm sorry young man, but we need to keep the infection out if at all possible. Turpentine seems to work better than anything else I've used."

She pressed a large fold of cloth against the wound and held it for a few minutes. When she pulled it back the flow had diminished. She took a fresh pad and placed it on Louis' side, then wrapped several strips of cloth around his chest to hold it in place.

"There. That should hold you for a while. You should rest in bed until tomorrow. Try not to put any pressure on your side. I'll look in on you in the morning. Where is Mr. Dufour staying tonight, Brother Anthony?"

"I assume he and Mr. Dupre will stay in one of the empty cloister rooms," the brother said.

"Then I suggest you help him there and see that he stays in bed until tomorrow. Some good hot soup may be in order tonight. But don't let him go to the refectory. Have someone bring it to him."

With that the two robed friars helped Louis to his room while the women cleaned the infirmary.

"Cassie, I can't wait to hear what's happened to you since you left here," Bernadette said. "Obviously you've been on a much greater adventure than we envisioned." She put her hands to her face as if about to burst into tears. "I can't believe you're actually here." She hurried to put away the last pan then scrubbed the table.

"Come on, let's go to our cabin."

Two more acolytes had joined St. Benedict's since Cassie's departure. One of them, Ruth, was assigned to Sister Bernadette. The girl was only ten and her parents, who were freedmen, had died of the fever. She had no relatives in the small community on the Ogeechee where they lived. The itinerant preacher that brought her in, found her abandoned there. She was living in the wild on nuts and berries and scraps from the pig's troughs.

"Cassie. Queen. This is Ruth. She's the newest member of our family here at St. Benedict's. She's very shy. She's only been here a few days. Her parents died of the fever and there was no one to take her in. She and Esther can share a room and you two can have the other. Get your belongings from the cart and bring them in. I'll have everything ready when you return. Then you must tell me everything that has happened."

CHAPTER TWENTY-NINE

ENOCH, JIM, AND CALEB crossed the bridge onto the Isle of Hope early the following morning. They had encountered no one on the short stretch of road leading there.

"Keep alert now," Enoch warned. "We're not far from Wormslow. I don't want anyone from there to know that we're here. Don't need no interference from the high and mighty Jones clan. That Wimberley Jones is a dyed in the wool Whig, just like my brother Hiram. I'll betcha the two of them was on the other side of those trenches when the colonials fired on Savannah. With any luck, one of our boys could'a picked him off in the fighting. Maybe he's lying back there on the field rotting in the sun like those French dandies."

They reached the fork to Roselawn without seeing anyone. They were halfway to Grimball's Landing when they heard a commotion on the road ahead. Enoch put his finger to his lips and motioned the others to follow him into the woods. He knelt behind a tree and signaled to the others to get out of sight. The muffled voice became discernible as the rider drew near.

"Cleophas, ya ain't got no cause tuh be skeered. They ain't nothing out here on dis here road whut's gonna bother ya."

Enoch could not see the speaker from his position. He didn't recognize the voice, only knew that it was a slave. He recognized the name, Cleophas, as one of the groomsmen at Roselawn. When the horseman came into view he could see that it was a lone rider and that he was talking to himself. Enoch leaped onto the roadway and grabbed the horse's reins.

"Where do you think you're going nigger?" he shouted.

The horse reared in fright, throwing Cleophas to the roadbed. His eyes were wide with fright. He recognized the angry red face of Enoch Penrose.

"I's jest goin up da road tuh Wormslow, Massa Enoch. Miss Amanda, she tolt me tuh go dere fo help."

"What kind of help, Cleophas?"

"It's Massa Hiram. He done come back from Savannah and he got a bullet hole clear through him."

Enoch's eyes flashed surprise. "So, Hiram is back."

"How was he when you left Roselawn, Cleophas?"

"He pow'ful sick Massa. Miss Amanda an Miss Rebecca an Miss Sarah, dey's all acryin'."

"Is there anyone else there, besides the slaves?"

"No Massa, all da white folks, dey's still in town wit da army."

"Cleophas, do you remember Cassie, the girl who used to work in the kitchen?"

"Yassuh, I 'member her."

"Is she there?"

Cleophas hesitated. He knew he could say no and not be lying to Enoch, since she was gone. He was afraid of what Enoch might do to her.

"Nawsuh. She ain't dere."

Enoch pulled Caleb aside.

"Jim, you keep an eye on the nigger for a second."

"Caleb, I want you to take this boy off into the woods and get rid of of him. Throw him into the river. Anything to keep anyone at Roselawn from knowing he didn't make it to Wormslow until we do what we gotta do."

Enoch watched Caleb's eyes to see if his assessment of the man was accurate. When he saw his eyes flash and his face contort with a look of menace he knew he was right. The man had a blood lust. That could prove useful but it could also be dangerous. They rejoined Jim and Cleophas. Enoch took the reins of the horse. He walked into the woods and tethered the horse to a tree leaving enough rope for the animal to graze and reach water."

"Come on Jim," he said.

The two walked away toward Grimballs Landing. A few minutes later Caleb caught up to them. He was wiping his skinning knife with a dirty bandana.

"What did you do?" Jim asked Caleb, in horror.

"I just done what Enoch told me to do," he said.

"You killed that boy in cold blood. Why'd you have to do that? He wasn't going to hurt anybody."

"What would you have us do," Enoch said. "Leave him tied to a tree in the woods where the critters could get at him. Or turn him loose to blab to the high and mighty Joneses at Wormslow. No. It's better this way. We don't want no interference."

Jim's shoulders sagged in surrender to circumstance. The deed was done and nothing he could say or do would change that.

They crossed the causeway, careful to keep the high weeds and brush between them and the house. Once they were across the bridge Enoch led them down a path through the marsh to a small palm covered hammock directly behind the main house.

"We'll bed down here and get a little sleep. It'll start gettin' dark about seven-thirty. That's when we'll move in. I just hope they don't send nobody out to check on Cleophas before then."

It was almost sundown. Jim was on watch. Enoch and Caleb were sound asleep.

"Enoch, wake up."

He roused himself from the depths of a dream.

"What is it, Jim? You see something over there?"

"Yeah. It looks like several blacks have left the house and are moving toward the slave cabins. They probably finished cleaning up after supper and are going home. How many servants stay in the big house and the kitchen?"

Enoch rubbed his eyes, trying to dispel the sleep and focus on what Jim was saying.

"They useta have two in the house. A man and a woman. Plus two more who slept in the kitchen rooms. That was Queen and her ma,

Aba. I believe Aba died a while back. I don't know if anyone replaced her."

He rubbed his chin, the bristly whiskers reminding him he hadn't shaved in a while. "I'll take care of that soon," he thought.

"Let me think. There'll be the two women and three or four servants. Hiram and Amanda have a daughter, Sarah. She's probably at their house, down the lane beyond the slave quarters. That's maybe five or six people plus Hiram, and based on what the boy said I don't think we'll need to worry about him. We'll have to make sure no one comes in from the barns or the cabins."

"What do you plan to do Enoch?" Jim asked. "How do you expect to take Roselawn back with Hiram still alive?"

"Jimmy boy, what do you take me for, an idiot? I got it all figured out."

Enoch's eyes were ablaze again. They glowed with an intensity born of his maniacal focus on redemption. He would regain his rightful place in the world. There was no doubt in his disturbed mind that he was the rightful heir to Roselawn. Somehow he was convinced that Hiram had cheated him of his birthright. It was the old story of Jacob and Esau all over again. He knew that John Penrose, in his heart, had intended that all his estate should go to him. He was sure of it. Somehow Hiram had tricked his father or bribed the lawyers. He scanned the horizon from Grimball's bridge to the Thunderbolt. "All of this will be mine," he thought. "All the land, all the property and all the slaves --- and Cassie, when I find her."

"What do you mean, you've got it all figured out.?"

"You remember all those books I ordered when we were on Ossabaw?"

"Yeah," Jim answered. "What about 'em?"

"If you'da been paying attention you would've seen they were all law books. I've been studying up on the inheritance laws in Georgia and guess what?"

"I'll bite, what?"

"Georgia still follows the old British law of *primogeniture*."

"Primo what? What the hell are you talking about?"

"*Primogeniture*. That's Latin for firstborn. The law says that when a man dies all his estate goes to the oldest son unless the will specifically states otherwise. I reckon that Hiram bribed that bastard Sheftall to gin up a will making him the heir. Otherwise everything would have come to me as the firstborn. They figured I was stuck out on Ossabaw and nobody would question Hiram and his slick lawyer. Well I'm questioning him."

Caleb listened to their conversation in bewilderment.

"Wait a minute, you two," he jumped in. "What the hell does all that mumbo-jumbo mean and how the hell does it get me some new breeches and a decent belt?"

"Those law books say that when a man dies without a will, all his estate goes to the oldest son. If there is no son it goes to the oldest daughter, and," Enoch paused for emphasis. "If there's no daughter it goes to the oldest remaining brother."

"So," Caleb said, "what does that have to do with us? Hiram's already got everything."

"Yeah, but suppose Hiram dies. He has no sons. Sarah is his only child. So the only thing standing between me, as his brother, and the inheritance is --- Sarah. Do you get my drift?"

"Oh, come on, Enoch. Suppose Hiram *is* dead. You can't honestly be thinking about killing Sarah?" Jim shook his head in disbelief. "Killing a nigger slave is one thing but killing your own niece is something else entirely. Besides, no court's gonna award Roselawn to you if it knows you've murdered the rightful heir. All you'll get is the short end of a rope."

Enoch looked dumbstruck. The fire flickered from his eyes. His single-minded obsession had blinded him to the consequences of murder.

"You may be right, Jim. Especially if I wuz to wind up in some court with a Whig judge."

He sat for a while staring into the distance. He picked up a stick and began toying with the fiddler crabs sidling across the ground at his feet. After a while he looked up at the clearing night sky.

"I'm not giving up just yet. I've gotta think about this."

The crescent moon was halfway up the eastern sky. Jim and Caleb were asleep. Enoch was still holding the stick. He poked Jim.

"What's up?" Jim asked sleepily.

"I have the answer," Enoch said.

"Yeah. Well what's that?"

"We know that besides Hiram, who's no threat, only the women are in the main house, with maybe one or two servants. So, if we can distract the women long enough to make sure Hiram didn't make it, and take care of Sarah at the same time, without being seen, there'd be no way to tie me to anything."

"How in the world do you propose to do that?" Jim asked.

"Look, if Amanda is in the big house with Rebecca, and Sarah is in her house asleep, it's simple. We make sure Sarah stays asleep while we burn the house down. When the alarm sounds, the women and servants will run to the fire. That'll give me a chance to take care of Hiram. Then we'll all meet back here and leave the island. There'll be no way to connect us with anything. Then when I finish up with my other business I'll come back and take what's mine."

"Enoch we've already killed one man, but at least he was a nigger. I don't cotton to killing white folks, especially if it's your kin."

"Jim, they ain't no other way to do this. You either sign on or I'll cut you loose right here and now. You can scoot back to Savannah and those redcoat friends of yours. Me and Caleb can take care of this. On the other hand, if you stand by me you'll come out of this as the overseer of one of the largest plantations in Georgia. Now, what's it going to be?"

"There ain't no future for me back there. We both know that. And, I'm already an accomplice to one murder so it's not gonna make a big difference one way or the other. Just don't make me do it. I ain't got the stomach for it."

Jim looked nervously at Enoch, not knowing what to expect.

"You don't have to worry about that. I've got my man for doing murder."

Enoch prodded Caleb with his toe.

"Get up man, we got work to do."

****

Bernadette hung a cast iron kettle on a hook over the fire. The cabins built for the nuns by John Penrose were a vast improvement over the ramshackle huts they replaced. Each was built of logs and tabby with a main room and three small sleeping rooms. They had wood floors.

A stone fireplace almost filled one wall. It served to heat the cabin and to prepare meals when the women did not eat in the refectory or when someone was ill.

When the kettle began to steam she poured the boiling water into a teapot then served them tea in five earthenware mugs the girls had made. She popped the lid off a Dutch oven and handed a small scone to each. When she was finished she sat down and looked expectantly at Cassie.

"Well," she said. "I'm waiting. Tell me all about it."

Cassie took a bite of scone and a sip of tea.

"Sister, this is delicious. I haven't had a scone like this since I left here. It seems a lifetime, so much has happened." She took a deep breath before beginning.

"Andre and Louis, the two soldiers, were in the camp at Buley. They were assigned to drive the wagons when we went out looking for food and provisions."

She went on to relate the tales of the trips to the surrounding farms and of life at the camp as well as how she wound up with the French near Savannah.

"Louis was hurt early on after we got to the main camp. He was brought back to the hospital near where I was staying. I saw him there before he went back to his unit. He told me that Andre was all right but that the siege wasn't going as planned and they would probably have to attack Savannah.

"When the battle started the doctors and supply wagons were ordered to the front and since I had no other place to go I went along with them. I saw Andre and Louis as they went into battle. It was obvious the fight wasn't going well. I heard the bugles and drums beating retreat. And, I saw Louis return without Andre. The battle didn't last for more than an hour. There was such devastation that both sides agreed to a truce so they could look after the dead and wounded. I insisted that Louis take me to look for Andre and that's when we found him and Master Hiram. They were lying side by side in a ditch. Andre had a head wound and Master Hiram was shot through the shoulder. We couldn't get proper help for them so master Hiram said we should try to get back to Roselawn."

Cassie paused as she got to the part about the well. She was choked with emotion and hesitant to continue.

"It's all right Cassie. You're safe here. You don't need to worry," Bernadette reassured her. She sat down next to Cassie and put her arm around the trembling girl. Cassie resumed her story.

"We were at this well trying to get some water for Master Hiram and Andre when a mob came out of the woods and began attacking us. Louis was able to beat off the man that had grabbed me. We got back into the wagon and Louis got us out of there. When I looked back, one of the men was kneeling and aiming a rifle at us. I saw the flash just before the ball hit a board on the seat above my head. It splintered the board into a thousand pieces and one struck Louis in the face, but he was able to keep control of the horses and we escaped.

"It was then that I saw who shot at us. The man's hat came off and I could see that scarlet face. There was no mistaking that it was Master Enoch. He and two other men began to run down the road after us.

"Master Hiram told Louis to turn left at Montgomery Crossroads and head for the French camp, hoping to throw Master Enoch off our trail. We don't think he saw him and Andre lying in the wagon.

"After we passed the camps we turned down the road to Roselawn. We don't know if Master Enoch found out we'd passed the camps or not but Miss Amanda was scared that he would show up at Roselawn and cause trouble. She said we should get away from there to some safe place in case he did come. She made mama come with us. She was afraid of what he might do to her based on his past. Mama didn't want to leave but Miss Amanda insisted.

"Master Hiram was in a terrible state when we left. His wound had become infected and he was running a high fever. None of the other white men on the plantation have returned from Savannah, so only the women and slaves are there. I'm really worried about what will happen if Master Enoch returns. Miss Amanda was going to send Cleophas to Wormslow for help after we left. I sure hope someone came."

"I'm sure someone came," Bernadette assured her. "I just can't believe a man would harm his own family. From what I know of Enoch's parents they were faithful, God fearing people who raised their children properly. However, you do have to be concerned about what he did that got him sent away in the first place." Bernadette chose her words carefully. She didn't want to disclose Cassie's secrets to the girls. An agitated Queen could contain herself no longer.

"Miss Bernadette, dat man, he be pure evil. 'Sides what ya knows awready, I's heard dretful thangs from Ka'le an Kimba 'bout what went on ovuh dere. He 'lowed Kimba's boy Toby tuh die atter he done cut 'im wit a axe. He turnt dat white trash Caleb Hawkins loose on da slaves. More'n one wuz kilt by Master Enoch's dog, Nero. Some o dem stories done chilt my blood. They wuz 'fraid tuh tell Master Hiram cuz dey didn't know whut Master Enoch might do. It won't til Toby died dat Ka'le got da gumption tuh send Isaac back tuh Roselawn wit da story. I don put nuttin past dat man. He crazy nuf tuh do mos anything."

"Surely he won't come here with so many people in the monastery. That would be foolish," Bernadette replied.

"When ya's crazy lak dat, dey ain't no common sense. Iffen he wants tuh come, he'll come."

"We don't even know if he'll go back to Roselawn. I imagine he's still searching. He must believe that Cassie is with Louis somewhere in the camps around Thunderbolt. Since Roselawn is in the entirely opposite direction, there's no reason for him to think they went there." Bernadette sounded as if she was trying more to convince herself than Queen.

"Well, we're safe for a while," Cassie said, as she savored the last bite of her scone. "Mama, if you'll stay here with Esther and Ruth I want to spend a few minutes alone with the sister."

Cassie led Bernadette outside and down the shell-strewn path to the midden where she had received the devastating news that she couldn't be a nun.

"There's something I need to talk to you about," she said as they approached the site. She sat down on the familiar shelf of oyster shells and began to pour out her heart to her friend and confessor.

"Sister Bernadette, you are my dearest friend in the world. All I am or ever hope to be I owe to you. You have encouraged me, coaxed me, threatened me, until I achieved what you knew all along I could achieve. Even when I was denied my dream of becoming a nun like you, you didn't give up. You helped me to look beyond the disappointment for other ways to serve. You taught me to be patient and to wait on the Lord. Now I have come to a crossroads in my life and I need your advice."

"You know you can bring anything to me and I will not betray your trust," Bernadette said, flashing her beatific smile. "We are both dedicated to helping God's creatures find Him and to help set them on the path to a full and complete relationship with Him. That is why I felt you had the maturity and faith needed to go on the adventure that has been yours for the past few weeks. I knew that you would be a worthy representative of Him and would help others along the way. And, I knew this was a chance for you to discover that larger world outside the walls of St. Benedict's. You needed that chance to help you sort out where you would go with what you have learned and for the promise of freedom it could bring you to explore all your opportunities."

Cassie sat in open-mouthed astonishment.

"You could always read my mind even before I spoke a word," Cassie replied. "I have missed you so. There were times I didn't think I could go on in the midst of all the pain and horror. But, every time I wanted to give up I would think of you and ask myself what you would do. That always gave me the strength to carry on. However, there's one decision I made that is troubling to me. I need to know if I made it for selfish reasons or if it is truly in God's plan for me." Cassie gathered her courage and began to pour out her heart to Bernadette.

"During the first few days I was at Buley I spent much of my time on a wagon with Mr. Dupre. We talked for hours; of our childhoods, our families, our experiences. We got to know each other very well. Andre was especially nice to me and made every effort to see that I was comfortable and he tried to keep me out of danger. When we arrived at the camps near town it was obvious that he would be drawn into the conflict and I would be left behind. It was a very emotional time for both of us. We didn't know if we'd ever see each other again. The night before he was to leave he came to my tent. He told me he loved me and wanted to marry me. I was so shocked I didn't know what to say. I stammered about for a while and then told him I was committed to my journey to seek God's will in my life and to find his plan for me. He said there were other ways to serve God that didn't require separation from society. He told me of people back in Grenada where he was born who were missionaries from Europe. There were married couples among them and they were successful and happy in serving there. I was so confused. I told him to go back to his tent and return before dawn and I would give him an answer. He took me in his arms and kissed me. I've never been kissed before and I didn't know how to react. It was a wonderful feeling but I knew it was something I shouldn't be doing. I pushed him away and told him to leave. I laid there until dawn trying to sort out my feelings. Was it possible to be in love and to be doing God's work at the same time?"

Bernadette started to say something then realized there was more to Cassie's story. She kept her silence.

"Go ahead."

"Before the sun came up the next morning I stepped outside my tent. I couldn't sleep. We were in a field of corn that had been trampled by the army. Several doves were feeding on the corn. I saw a hawk dive into the midst of the birds and seize one of them. As he flew away a huge owl swooped down and snatched the hawk out of the air. The hawk screamed and dropped the dove as the owl carried the hawk away. The dove flew right at me and struck a limb over my head. One of its wing feathers fell and I caught it. I couldn't see it well in that light. I brushed it against my cheek and it felt wet. I touched my cheek and realized the wetness was blood from the dove.

"I never believed strongly in signs and omens although my grandma Aba was always talking about them, remembering when she was a girl in Africa. But, I felt that these things all happening at that time and in that place must have some meaning for me. I saw the freeing of the dove as God's way of telling me that I was free to choose a different way to serve Him and that I didn't have to become a nun to do so.

"When Andre came I told him about the birds and what had happened and I asked him if he thought it could be a sign for me. He told me of the many times he had seen men in the islands with mystical powers who interpreted signs for their followers. He said more times than not they foretold events in the people's lives. It was then that I realized I truly loved him and wanted to share the rest of my life with him. So my answer was yes. He was very happy. He said he would come back for me when he gained his freedom from the French. He asked me to come back here and continue to study and he would find me here no matter how long it may take.

"Did I do the right thing, Sister? I know that I love him. When I thought he was dead in that ditch I wanted to die with him. Do you think God can forgive me if I break my vows."

"Of course he can child. There are millions of people in the world but there are only a few priests and nuns who dedicate themselves totally to God. He needs believers in all walks of life. You can do as much or more for Him out there with Andre as you could here inside these walls. There are people like me, and Rosemarie and Mother Marie Michel, who made the decision to devote our lives to a monastic order like St. Benedict's. That is our choice and our way to serve. If we can teach and inspire people like you to take His word into the world, we have multiplied any talents we have a thousand times over. If you truly love Andre and he truly loves you then by all means you should marry him. You have my blessing and I'm sure the Reverend Mother will agree. Together, you can be true witnesses among your people."

"Oh, Sister you don't know how happy you have made me. You've lifted a huge load from my shoulders. I was so afraid you would be angry with me. I couldn't stand it if I felt I had disappointed you."

"You don't have to worry about disappointing me, Cassie. I know you too well. I know you would never do that."

Cassie rose to leave. Bernadette took her by the arm to stop her.

"Cassie, what about Louis and Andre, as far as the French army is concerned? Won't they be considered deserters?"

"There were so many men killed that day and buried in mass graves that I'm sure the army has no idea who lived and who died. They're probably getting ready to leave Savannah by now. For better or for worse Andre and Louis are here to stay."

She took a step up the bank.

"Can we go back to the monastery now? I'd like to see how they are doing. Louis was really in a lot of pain when we took him to his room"

Rain clouds were gathering over Skidaway Island as they made their way back toward the cabin. Early autumn storms continued to swell the rivers around Savannah.

CHAPTER THIRTY

Enoch waited until well after midnight. All the lamps had gone dark. Everyone should be asleep by now.

"Jim, you stand guard between the kitchen and the house," Enoch said. "Keep out of sight. If anyone goes or comes from the kitchen or house do that hoot owl impression of yours. Meantime I'm gonna sneak into the house and check on Hiram. When I'm done I'll come out the back to where you are.

"Caleb you go on down to Hiram's house. Check to see if any lights are on. If not you wait by the front porch for Jim and me. You got that clear, the both of you?"

Both men nodded in the affirmative.

It took only a few minutes to move through the paddies and yard to the house. Jim took up his post by the breezeway behind an oleander bush. Caleb slipped past the kitchen and moved stealthily down the lane toward Hiram's house. He stopped briefly when one of the slave's dogs barked. When the dog went silent he removed his shoes and continued on down the path.

When Enoch was certain that both lookouts were in place he stepped onto the veranda outside the room where Hiram was sleeping. He crossed to the door and listened for any sounds coming from the room. Hearing nothing he carefully opened the screen door and entered. He could barely make out the form of his brother lying on the bed. He looked around the rest of the room and saw no one else. With four short steps he was at Hiram's side. He knelt by the bed, listening. He couldn't hear his brother's breathing. He leaned closer and could smell the putrid stench of gangrene. Hiram stirred and emitted a raspy cough.

"So, you are alive," Enoch said "But with that gangrene you won't be for long."

Enoch sat on the edge of the bed, reflecting on his relationship with his brother. He recalled the happier days of their youth when they ran through the woods and went hunting and fishing together. But, all that changed on that fateful day.

"Too bad, Hiram. If you and Pa had just been a little more understanding things would have been different. Now you're lying hear at death's door and I'm gonna get it all. I don't see no need for you to suffer anymore."

Hiram's eyes fluttered open at the sound of Enoch's voice. There was a glimmer of recognition. He tried to speak. The words would not form. Enoch took a pillow and covered his brother's face. Hiram struggled briefly, but he was too weak to offer much resistance. After a few minutes Enoch took the pillow away and felt for a pulse. There was none. He replaced the pillow where he had found it and crossed back to the door.

"Goodbye, brother," he whispered. "I'm sorry it had to come to this but you gave me no choice." He quietly closed the door and walked around to the breezeway.

"Jim." he whispered. "You here?"

"Right behind you Enoch," Jim said, stepping from behind the oleander. "How's Hiram?"

"He's dead. Gangrene." He felt no need to elaborate further.

"Come on. Let's go down to Hiram's house. Quiet now. I heard one of the slave dogs earlier. Can't afford to have them settin' up a hullabaloo."

The two men traversed the quarter mile distance without further disturbance. Caleb was lurking behind a camellia next to the porch.

"Any sign of life around here?" Enoch asked.

"Nothing," Caleb said. "They was a dog barking but he shut up when I got past the quarters. I can't tell if they's anybody inside or not."

"All right. You go on inside. Keep your shoes off. Hiram's bedroom is at the top of the stairs on the right. Make sure Amanda is still up at the main house. Sarah's bedroom is right across the hall. She should be there. If she is you know what to do. We'll be here when you come back. Hiram always keeps oil for his lamps in the shed behind the house. Jim and me are gonna get some to help the fire along."

Caleb sneaked up the steps and across the porch. He carefully opened the screen door and stepped into the parlor. The staircase was just across the foyer. It was difficult to see in the dim light. He felt for the bottom tread with his toe and discovered that the stairs had a carpet runner. That would make things a little easier. He patiently placed one socked foot after the other making sure of his footing before proceeding. He took a full three minutes to scale the eighteen treads.

The door to Hiram's bedroom was open. He could hear no one inside. He walked slowly across the landing and peered into the darkened room. He entered so that the bed was between him and the windows. He could see that it was carefully made up and no one was sleeping there. He breathed a little sigh of relief. Now for the major task at hand.

Sarah's breathing was very quiet, but loud enough for Caleb to hear. He moved silently to the bed and took one of the pillows from a chair. He sprang onto the bed straddling the startled girl. He pinned her arms to her side and clamped the pillow over her face. He pressed down with all his strength. The girl struggled mightily but to no avail. Caleb's bulk was too much for her to move. He felt her body go limp. He pulled the pillow back and waited. There was no movement. His job was done. Enoch and Jim were waiting beside the front steps when Caleb returned from his grisly deed.

"How'd it go?" Enoch asked.

"No problem," Caleb said, as if he had just killed a fly. "She's done for."

"Good. Take this bottle of oil and splash it around on the back porch. Jim and me'll douse the front and side of the house."

When the three bottles were emptied Enoch took out his fire kit. He struck the flint three times before a spark ignited the soaked wood of the porch. In seconds flames streaked across the floor and up the walls. Caleb picked up a fallen limb from the yard and held it to the fire. It flared to life. He ran around the house and dropped it onto the back porch. The heart pine lumber used to construct the house burned like kindling. Within five minutes the entire external structure was engulfed in flames.

"Come on, let's get out of here," Enoch shouted over the roar of the fire.

He led them toward the barn behind Hiram's house and back to the hammock where they had plotted their crime. Crossing the clearing to the barn they were silhouetted against the fire. At that same moment Ka'le Akala was returning to his cabin from the outhouse. Something in the stew last night had given him diarrhea. He saw the flare-up as the fire ignited the back porch roof. The three men were no more than a hundred yards away and in the bright light there was no mistaking the face of Enoch Penrose.

"Fire! Fire!" he yelled as he ran toward the alarm bell in the quadrangle of the slave quarters. He pulled furiously on the rope until the clanging of the bell woke everyone on the plantation. Black men poured out of every door grabbing for the fire buckets on their porches as they went.

"Hurry! Hurry! Massa Hiram's house on fire," Kale screamed.

A large lagoon adjoined the property next to the house and within minutes the men had formed a fire brigade passing buckets of water down the line toward the fire. They made little headway in controlling the blaze because of the tinder-like qualities of the wood in the house.

Ka'le grabbed a horse blanket from the barn and soaked it with water. He draped the blanket over his head and dashed into the house and up the stairs. The flames licked at his legs and the heavy black smoke was suffocating. He knew that Miss Amanda was at the main house and that only Sarah was asleep upstairs. He burst through the door of her room. He lifted the limp form and threw her over his shoulder, covering her with the wet blanket. He stumbled down the stairs, nearly passing out from the smoke and fumes. The porch roof had caved in and Ka'le had to take Sarah through the parlor and out a side door. He ran across the yard and fell on the lawn, exhausted, retching, as others ran up to help. An agonizing scream pierced the night air.

"Sarah, oh my precious Sarah."

Amanda Penrose had come running at the first peal of the fire bell. She fell to the ground and lifted her daughter.

"Is she dead, Ka'le? Is she dead?"

"I don know fo sho Missy. She ain't breathin though."

Ka'le sat Sarah upright. He bent her torso over her legs. He pounded on her back with one open palm while pushing her up and down with the other hand.

"I's seed dis work on drownin folks befo. Don know iffen it'll wuk fo smoke," he said.

He continued the procedure for some time then laid the girl back down. Amanda bathed Sarah's face with a wet cloth. She felt her neck for a pulse. Suddenly, Sarah gulped and belched a small puff of smoke. Caleb had been careless and too sure of himself. He underestimated the strength and resilience of young Sarah Penrose. What Caleb had started the fire would have finished but for the heroic effort of Ka'le. Sarah continued to gasp for air.

Amanda cradled Sarah in her arms and cried. The horror of the last few days would have been magnified beyond comprehension had she lost Sarah. She was resigned to the fact that Hiram was not likely to recover from his terrible infection. Losing her daughter as well would have been more than she could stand.

The men on the fire brigade soon realized they could not put out the fire. It had become an inferno, so hot they could not get near enough even to throw water on it. Everyone backed off to where Ka'le, Amanda and Sarah sat on the lawn.

"How she?" one of the women asked, pointing toward Sarah.

"I think she'll make it," Amanda said, allowing the faintest smile to lighten her face.

"Thank you, Ka'le. Thank you for saving my daughter. I don't know if I could survive had I lost her. Please help me get her back up to the big house. There's nothing more we can do here. The house is a total loss. Do you have any idea how it started?"

"Missy, let's git Miss Sarah outta here fo we talks 'bout dat."

Ka'le evaded her question. They took Sarah to the master bedroom, upstairs. She was exhausted and semi-conscious from the ordeal. She fell asleep almost immediately. Ka'le went back downstairs with Amanda. Rebecca was coming out of Hiram's room. She too was crying.

"Hiram's gone, Mandy. He's gone."

She couldn't say any more than that. She crumpled to the floor, racked with sobs. Amanda entered the room. She stood by the bed, a portrait in stoicism. She fought back the urge to scream. She had known this moment was coming and she had steeled herself. She had to be strong for the others. She was in charge now. There was no time for hysteria. She sat down on the edge of the bed and stroked Hiram's face. It was still smooth from the shave Thomas gave him this morning. He looked so peaceful now. No more worldly cares. He was spared seeing his house destroyed and his daughter nearly killed. He had entered that eternal sleep that she herself had sometimes longed for the past few days. "No. I mustn't think like that . There's too much to do." She pulled the sheet over Hiram's face. When she looked up Ka'le was standing beside her, tears rolling down his cheeks.

"Massa Hiram wuz a good man, Missy. He never treated none of us bad. Him nor his pa."

Ka'le looked at the grieving woman with great sorrow in his eyes. You go on up and look atter Miss Sarah and Miss Rebecca. I'll see tuh things down here."

He didn't want to burden her with the news of Enoch just yet. Ka'le got some of the other men to help him move Hiram to the big table in the kitchen where he could be bathed and dressed for burial. He sent four men as lookouts around the property, in case Enoch returned. He walked back past the quarters to the smoldering ruins of the house. So much trouble and so much sorrow, all because of the private miseries of one evil man.

"Lord it ain't right," he mumbled.

He was up before dawn, waiting in the serving room for Amanda. He didn't have to wait long. She descended the stairs slowly, her face a mask of sorrow. The trials of the day before and the grief she felt now were mirrored in her reddened, deep-set eyes.

"Good morning, Ka'le. Have you seen to Mr. Penrose."

"Yassum. We took him tuh da kitchen. Da women done bathed an dressed him. I took his suit from da closet downstairs and dey dressed him in it. I hopes ya don mind."

"No Ka'le," she said forlornly. "I appreciate what you have done. I don't think I had the strength last night to do it myself. What about a casket for Mr. Penrose?" she asked, her voice cracking.

"I done had Seth make one up in da carpenter's shop. He wukked on it all da night. It made outen da best oak planks we gots. I reckons ya'll will lak it all right, Missy."

"I'm sure I will Ka'le. Thank Seth for me."

"Yas'm, I'll do dat. But fo I go I needs tuh tell ya whut I seed last night. I didn't wanna scare ya none den, so I kinda took care o' things myself."

He stopped to measure her ability to handle the news he was about to give her. He felt that she was in control.

"Las' night I wuz outside when I seed da fire. I seed three men arunning away from da house tuh da barn. In da light o da fire I could make out dere faces. Missy, dis hard fo' me tuh say, but one of em was Massa Enoch. The other two wuz dat overseer, Jim Pelham an dat no 'count fella, Caleb Hawkins. Dey ran cross da rice fields an I couldn't see dem no mo. I put some men out tuh watch so dey don't come back and s'prise us no mo.

"I reckons Massa Enoch and dem men dey set fire tuh yo house knowin' dat Miss Sarah wuz inside asleep. I don' know whut's wrong wit dat man dat he would try tuh kill his own kin. It jes' don' make no sense."

"No, it doesn't Ka'le. Enoch's mind has never worked like ours. He's always felt that the rest of the world was against him. I guess when Hiram sent him away he decided that he had been wronged and now he's seeking revenge. God help us if he comes back again. If he'd kill our Sarah there's no telling what he might do." Her face was terror-stricken.

"Ka'le, which way did you say Enoch was headed?"

"Back cross da paddies 'hind da main house, toward da bridge."

"My God," she exclaimed. "He thought he'd find Cassie and Queen here. When he didn't he went on a rampage. He knows if they're not here there's only one other place they can be. St. Benedict's. I just know that's where he's headed. What can we do, Ka'le?"

"I'll see iffen I kin head'em off. I believes I kin git tuh Skidaway fo dey do. If dey took da boat at Grimball's it'll take'em several hours tuh git dere. I kin cut cross Isle of Hope tuh da river an git one o da Wormslow boats. Dat'll git me cross an through da Runaway Creek landing head o dem. I'll leave word fo da folks at Wormslow tuh come ovuh here jes' in case Massa Enoch, he come back. I don' know whut happened tuh Cleophas. It ain't lak him tuh jus' run away lak dat."

"Yes, Ka'le. Please go to Skidaway. Father Titus must be warned. If those three show up there unannounced there's no telling what may happen. Wait here a minute. I have something for you to take with you."

She went to the desk in the parlor and took an envelope from the drawer and handed it to Ka'le.

"Ma'am I cain't read," he protested.

"I know. Show it to Father Titus and then give it to Queen. Now go. And God bless you."

****

Louis' breathing was labored. He didn't hear them enter the room. Bernadette lifted the sheet to look at the bandage. Blood had seeped through and soaked the sheet beneath him

"He's losing a lot of blood," she said in a whisper. "If this keeps up I don't think he can make it."

Andre stirred from his bed on the other side of the room.

"Is there anything we can do Sister?" he asked of Bernadette.

"I'm going for Sister Rosemarie. She knows more about this than anyone here. Cassie you and Andre stay here with Louis. I'll be right back."

In a few minutes Bernadette returned with Sister Rosemarie who began immediately to remove the bandages so she could examine the cut. She saw that it continued to seep blood.

"I hoped it would not come to this but it has. We must cauterize the wound. Cassie, you and Andre bring in a pile of kindling wood and start a fire. I'm going across to the blacksmith's shop."

When she returned flames were leaping up the chimney. The fat lighterwood was saturated with flammable resins. It burned furiously, creating an intense heat. Rosemarie had a strip of metal intended for the fashioning of horseshoes. She also brought tongs and heavy leather gloves. She donned the gloves, picked up the strip of metal with the tongs and placed it on the fire.

"Andre, you and Cassie will need to hold Louis firmly on the bed. The pain is going to be excruciating. If he's lucky he'll pass out. If he doesn't he's going to be hard to hold down."

When Rosemarie felt the metal sufficiently hot for the purpose she looked at the others. Andre stood on one side of the table with Cassie and Bernadette on the other.

"Are you ready?" she asked.

They all nodded. She snaked the white-hot strap from the flames with the tongs and brought it to the table.

"Holy Father forgive me for what I am about to do."

She pressed the flat strap against the gaping wound. The stench of burning flesh filled the room. Louis arched to escape the fiery iron, but was restrained. Brief seconds later Rosemarie removed the strap and took it back to the fire. She dropped the tongs and stripped off the gloves. Mercifully, Louis was now unconscious.

"There!" she exclaimed. "I think we did it. The flow seems to be stanched. We'll leave the bandages off for a while to see if the scarring holds. Cassie, you and Andre keep watch to make sure he doesn't rip it open again. I'll come back after vespers and put some salve on it and re-bandage him. He'll probably sleep for a while. The shock does that. It's nature's way of helping us to survive. Come on Bernadette, let's leave these two to look after Louis. They look like they have a lot to talk about." She gave Bernadette a knowing look and winked.

"Was it so obvious?" Cassie thought With the sisters gone, Cassie and Andre were alone for the first time since they fled Savannah. The silence was awkward. Both were so new at this. They were traveling a path that neither had been down before. There were no rules, no guidelines. Cassie raised her eyes to Andre's. He smiled back, reassuringly.

"I spoke to Sister Bernadette about us," she said. "I was afraid she would be angry and try to stop us. But she wasn't angry at all. She agrees with you. She thinks that together we can achieve as much or more than I could alone. Her concern was for what the French might do to you and Louis, as deserters. I told her there was so much confusion that no one knows whether either of you is alive or dead. There were dozens who deserted before we left Buley and nothing was done about them."

Louis stirred. He tried to move and Andre held him down.

"Careful. You'll rip open the wound and start the bleeding all over," he said

"What happened to me?" Louis asked. "I remember hitting the dock and being brought here. Everything after that is a blur. What happened to my side? It hurts like hell."

He realized Cassie was there and apologized for his language.

"I'm sorry Cassie, I didn't see you there."

"It's all right, Louis. Sister Rosemarie cauterized the cut in your side. I know it was very painful but she said it was the only way to stop the bleeding. She said you had lost so much blood already that you could die if we didn't get it stopped. She's gone to vespers now but she'll come back and check on you later and if everything looks all right she'll re-bandage you. Try to rest for now. We'll have some supper for you when you wake up."

"I am very tired," he said. "It's been a very hard few days. I just hope all the excitement is over."

Louis settled into the pillow and closed his eyes.

"Let's go over and sit under the window," Cassie said. "We won't disturb Louis there." She took Andre's hand and led him to the wooden bench. The evening light was fading. Rain beat against the windows and the wind moaned through the treetops.

"Andre, what do you think will happen to us now? If we get married I don't know if we'll be allowed to stay on at St. Benedict's. And what about Louis? He has no place to go either. We'll have to ask Sister Bernadette when she returns. She always knows what to do."

Andre lifted her chin and kissed her. That same feeling she had outside the tent returned. Her heartbeat quickened. It was reassuring to know that what she felt was not just momentary passion, but that she genuinely loved this man. His touch and his kiss aroused an age old instinct in her. It seemed to be an outcome that flowed naturally from their discovery of each other.

"Don't worry, Cassie. As long as we're together everything will work out. Having you here beside me is all that matters right now."

Louis stirred. Andre and Cassie rushed to his side as he began to thrash about. Andre held him down while Cassie felt his pulse. His heart rate was high and he had begun to sweat profusely. She prayed for Sister Rosemarie's quick return. The last strains of music from vespers drifted in through the door opening onto the quadrangle. Thank God. She would come soon. Minutes later Rosemarie and Bernadette came through the door. They took one look at Cassie as she stood beside Louis and knew something was terribly wrong.

"How long has he been agitated like this?" Rosemarie asked, as she pulled back the covers.

"Only fifteen or twenty minutes," Andre said. "He awoke and started trying to get up. Cassie and I had to hold him down. His fever is up and he's wet with sweat."

"This doesn't look good," she said. "The margins of the wound are very red and you can see the color moving into the surrounding area. The swelling is much more pronounced. The infection is spreading."

Rosemarie sighed and leaned against the table. She looked at Bernadette.

"Sister, get a pan of cold water and try to cool him off. The cauterization stopped the bleeding but it didn't burn out the infection. I'm going to apply a poultice to see if that will help to draw it out."

Bernadette and Cassie began applying cold towels to Louis' torso and head. Rosemarie hurried off to the refectory for cornmeal. When she returned she took down three of the jars of herbs from the shelf and ground them in a mortar. She combined the ground herbs with the cornmeal and placed them in a pan to warm over the fire. She wrapped the mixture in a large sheet of muslin and applied the poultice to his festering side. Louis shivered then fell back into unconciousness.

"There's nothing more I can do tonight. If the infection doesn't subside overnight I don't think Louis can live very long."

The other three stood in stunned silence. Just this afternoon he had been strong enough to row a boat for several miles. Now he was on the brink of death. It didn't make sense. Could a blood infection be so virulent?

"The three of you should take turns watching him 'til morning. Keep applying the towels and periodically reheat the poultice. Make sure it stays in contact with the cut. Don't let him get up. I'm going to get some rest but I'll be back after lauds."

Cassie kept the first watch while the others slept. Andre slept on the bench in the infirmary. Bernadette went to her cabin.

"Sister, will you please ask my mother to come. She's nursed many a sick child back to health at Roselawn. Her talents are sorely needed now."

"Certainly Cassie. Send someone to wake me after midnight. I'll come then to spell you and Queen."

When Queen arrived she set about warming and replacing the poultice. Cassie continued to apply cold towels in hopes of bringing down Louis' fever. He became delirious and spoke of people and events far away in Saint-Domingue. Cassie heard the muted chimes from the prior's office across the yard. She sent her mother to wake Bernadette.

"Mama, you rest until morning. I'm going to stay here and help the sister. When Andre takes over I'll sleep on the bench. I'll see you in the morning." She embraced her mother.

"Don't you worry, Mama, we'll get through this somehow. Just pray and keep the faith."

"I knows we will, chile. It's jes dat so much mis'ry done happened cause o' dat man. I prays tuh God dat he don' come here alookin' fo ya."

"I don't think he will but if he does Father Titus and the brothers will protect us. Even Massa Enoch must respect God's people. I know Miss Elizabeth taught him that."

When Andre took over at four, Louis' delirium had subsided, but the fever raged on, unabated. Andre was replacing the poultice for the sixth time when he heard the bell ring for lauds. The little community of St. Benedict's stirred to life. Robed figures carrying candles passed back and forth across the quadrangle. As dawn began to break across the marsh the first notes of a Bach chorale filled the morning air followed by the voices of the nuns and monks as they praised God for deliverance through another night. When the music ended the voice of Father Titus swelled in prayer and thanksgiving for God's mercies and protection. The last notes of the recessional were still echoing across the yard when Sister Rosemarie came into the infirmary.

"How is our patient doing?" she asked Andre "Did he have a restful night?"

"I'm afraid not, Sister. His fever still hasn't broken and he's been delirious, off and on.

She removed the poultice and examined the ever-widening circle of red around the gash in Louis' side. Fresh eruptions of pus seeped through the seared surface.

"It doesn't look good. There is one other treatment that I hesitate to try. I've used it on some of the animals with success, but I've never tried it on a human before. It is a radical procedure that I first saw at Canterbury. It was successful a few times there."

She paused, obviously wrestling with her decision..

"If we do nothing Louis will die."

Cassie awakened to the voices of Rosemarie and Andre.

"Sister Rosemarie, how is he?" she asked.

"Not good my dear. The fever hasn't broken and the infection is worse. I was just telling Andre that there's a radical treatment I've seen work a few times when I was at Canterbury. It's not very pleasant. One requires a strong stomach to see it through. Watch him. I'll be right back."

She returned carrying a small wooden box that she sat on the table near Louis. The box was covered with a square of cloth, tied around the rim. She removed the string to reveal a large glass jar inside. The jar too, was covered with a cloth and tied. Inside several bottleflies crawled about over a rancid piece of pork, their iridescent green and gold bodies shimmering in the morning light.

"I keep a colony of these in the storeroom of the barn for treating the animals. In the wild they feed and lay their eggs on carrion. They're scavengers. Part of nature's cleanup crew, along with buzzards, dung beetles and hundreds of God's other creatures. I take the maggots from the meat and place them into a wound. In a few minutes they begin to feed on the infection inside. If everything works right, they clean out the wound, it heals and the infection dies out. We'll have to pray that this infection is not so far developed that we can't stop it."

Rosemarie reached into the jar with forceps and removed the rancid pork. She carefully picked maggots from the surface and placed them into the cut in Louis' side. They began to wriggle and burrow into the layer of pus. Now everything was up to God --- and the maggots. Cassie and Bernadette turned away. The awful sight of worms burrowing into human flesh sickened them. They could only trust that Rosemarie knew what she was doing.

CHAPTER THIRTY-ONE

KA'LE APPROACHED THE BRIDGE over the Herb River with extreme caution. He didn't know whether Enoch was still on Roselawn or whether he had crossed over to Isle of Hope. He prayed that he and his two accomplices had stayed on the island for the remainder of the night and that he could get off ahead of them. He came up from the heavy growth along the road to survey the area. He saw no one. Carefully, he climbed the bank and crossed the bridge. In mid-span he looked down at the water. His blood ran cold.

"Good God," he uttered. "Ain't dere no limit tuh what dat man'll do? Now I knows why nobody done come from Wormslow."

There, floating face up in Grimball's Creek was Cleophas, his throat slit from ear to ear. Ka'le tried to push the image from his mind. There was nothing he could do for Cleophas now. But, he could prevent Enoch from further butchery if he could reach St. Benedict's before him. He looked down the creek towards Grimball's Landing and was relieved to see the boats still anchored there. At least Massa Enoch hadn't taken them yet.

"I hope dey's still on Roselawn an ain't gone tuh Wormslow Landing," he thought.

He took one last furtive look over his shoulder before breaking into a trot toward Wormslow. He covered the two miles in less than a half hour. He rapped on the back door. An elderly house slave answered.

Between breaths he said, "I's Ka'le from Roselawn. I needs tuh speak wit Massa Wimberley."

"Massa Wimberley, he ain't home. He still tuh Savannah."

"How 'bout da Missus? She be home?"

"Come up on da porch," he was directed by the servant. "I'll fetch her fo ya."

Ka'le sat on the bench used by visiting groomsmen. He fought to catch his breath. His heart slowly stopped racing and his breathing eased. He heard steps coming from around the corner of the veranda. A tall, patrician woman in a riding habit approached.

"Ka'le, I am Mrs. Jones. Amanda has spoken of you on her visits here. How can I help you?"

"Ma'am, awful bad things is happnin at Roselawn. Massa Enoch an two other men done come back an he done burnt down Massa Hiram's house. Nearly kilt Miss Sarah. An Massa Hiram, he wuz shot in da fightin at Savannah an he dead o da fever. Dey kilt one o da houseboys dat wuz comin tuh fetch help. Queen's girl Cassie and two black soldiers brought Massa home. Miss Amanda sent dem an Queen tuh Skidaway tuh git'em away from Massa Enoch. Now she thinks dat Massa Enoch be headin' fo Skidaway. I's tryin' tuh git dere fo dem but I stopped tuh ask fo yo help at Roselawn. Missy needs ya tuh come right away."

The words tumbled out of Ka'le's mouth faster than Sarah Jones could grasp the enormity of what he was saying. For a moment she was too stunned to speak.

"Ka'le, you go ahead and warn the folks on Skidaway. I'll send some men over to Roselawn right now and I'll go over as soon as possible. I'll also send for Mr. Jones and some help from town. As soon as they get here we'll send them to Skidaway."

"Da fastest way fo me tuh git dere is from yo landin' on da river. Do ya reckon it'll be awright fo me tuh take one o ya boats."

"By all means Kale. But hurry!"

Sarah Jones leaped into action even before Ka'le could cross the yard.

"Ernest, get two of the men to bring a carriage around for me. I'm going over to Roselawn. I want you to saddle up a horse and get on over there as fast as you can. There's been some trouble and I want you to look out for Miss Amanda. Be careful! Her brother-in-law Enoch may be there. He's the one stirring up the trouble."

"Yassum, Miss Sarah," Ernest said, as he ran toward the stables.

Ka'le was relieved to hear her quick response. He broke into a run again, down the oak lined lane and across the island to the river landing, still praying that Enoch was not there ahead of him. No one was out on the roads this early. He held his breath as he neared the bluff in the bend of the Skidaway. Thank goodness. Two boats were tied to the dock. He loosened the line on one of the boats and tied it to the stern of the other. No reason to leave such easy transportation available to someone else. He climbed down into the other boat and untied it. He picked up a paddle and pushed away from the dock, steering upriver. It took him a half-hour to round the tip of Burntpot Island. The mouth of Runaway Negro Creek lay just a quarter mile to the east. The whitewashed Parker mansion peered down at him from the bluff as he negotiated the turn against the current. He covered the distance in a few minutes and was quickly hidden from view by a winding corridor of sea grass. The creek meandered through the marsh for another quarter mile before ending in a small slough where there was a makeshift dock of logs, lashed together with wild grape vines. He tied the boats to a tree by the dock and ran down the overgrown path to St. Benedict's.

****

Enoch decided to remain on Roselawn for the rest of the night, unaware that Ka'le had spotted him fleeing the burning house. Secure in that belief, he felt safe in remaining to observe the reactions to Hiram and Sarah's death. He could hear the fire bell and the sounds of doors slamming as the slaves poured out onto the quadrangle. He stood behind the barn long enough to see that the fire was beyond control. By the time he reached the seclusion of the hammock the entire night sky was on fire. He sat with his back to a palm and watched the frenzied scene unfold. From this distance he could barely make out the slaves silhouetted against the fire, passing bucket after bucket of water up the line. He saw their effort begin to slacken. A self-satisfied smirk lit his face. He watched as the slaves recognized the futility of their efforts and backed away from the raging inferno. He saw several people rush down from the main house. They were gathered around someone on the ground. He couldn't tell who it was. Probably one of the slaves overcome by smoke and heat. He continued to watch until the weariness of the day overcame him and he dozed off. When he awoke the blaze had subsided. Heavy black smoke continued to rise from the blackened ruins. He went back to sleep, satisfied that he had accomplished his goal. Both Hiram and Sarah were gone. He could now reclaim his birthright.

Caleb was first to wake. Beyond the smoldering remains the early sunlight filtered through the smoke and haze creating a ghostly landscape. Figures were seen gathering around the burnt out hulk, poking at the charred timbers and digging through the ashes. He walked beyond the palms to the side of the marsh to relieve himself. He was sorry that he didn't have time to seek out the black girl he had tried to rape. The one old man Penrose had caught him with. Oh well. When we come back there'll be time for that. He buttoned his breeches and returned to the others. Jim Pelham had awakened and was pulling on his jacket against the early morning chill. Caleb walked over to the little copse where Enoch was sleeping and shook one of the palmettos.

"Time to get up sleepyhead. I believe we have some work to do today. I ain't forgettin' yore promise. I sure do need some new clothes. Not to mention a decent place to live."

Enoch moaned and groused at Caleb for the rude awakening. He rolled over and sat up to get a view of the slave quarters and the smoking ruins of his brother's house. In the hours between his last look and now, all semblance of the structure had disappeared. It was done. Now I can move on, he thought.

Hunger began to gnaw at them. They had not eaten for almost a day. They pulled the last of the hardtack and jerky from their packs and ate it for breakfast. They washed down the dry grub with the last of their water.

"We gotta get some food and water before we head to Skidaway," Enoch said. "It's too risky to go back to Roselawn. Somebody might see us. We'll have to get something on Isle of Hope."

With one last look back Enoch headed across the marsh and paddies toward the bridge. He kept to the shadows of the wild undergrowth. With the fire and the commotion there could be a lot of traffic back and forth to Wormslow. They must be careful. It took almost an hour of slogging through the muck to reach the bridge. Enoch edged himself over to the small bluff above Grimball's Landing to see if any boats remained. To his surprise one of Hiram's fishing skiffs was moored there. He signaled the others to follow and moved toward the dock. When he was sure there was no one about he emerged from the undergrowth and walked over. He undid the ropes and got into the skiff. The others followed. Enoch picked up one oar and handed it to Caleb. He took the other and knelt in the bow, pushing the craft away from the dock and out into the stream. He aligned himself with the tide and began to row toward the Skidaway River.

"Jim, keep a sharp eye out back toward the bridge. If you see anyone crossing let me know."

Jim sat on the third bench across the stern. He turned facing aft to get a clear view behind. Caleb sat on the middle bench, leaning forward as he pulled the oar through the water. With the aid of the current the boat moved swiftly down the creek. A mile into the journey Enoch stopped rowing. He motioned for Caleb to do the same. He eased the boat around a thick clump of reeds and into the mouth of a small slough that ran along the northern boundary of the Isle of Hope.

"The Dolan place is just ahead," Enoch said. "Their barns and outbuildings front on the creek. We should be able to get something to eat there."

In the lonely wanderings of his childhood, Enoch had traversed this waterway many times in his small bateau. He knew the Dolans as a "cracker" family that attended the same church. Their several children had joined the others in taunting him. He often saw them in the fields and yards as he passed, and always kept out of their sight.

"Steady now," he said. "Let's pull in and tie up at their dock. Jim, you stay with the boat. Whistle if you see anyone. Come on Caleb, you go with me."

The two scampered up the low bluff. They could see the outlines of the barn and the smokehouse, both partially obscured by a grove of elders. The limbs of these trees had provided the hollow bodies for the popguns used by the Dolan children to torment Enoch in the churchyard. He could still feel the painful welts left by the small, green, chinaberry projectiles. Dark memories of those episodes came flooding back and his latent hatred of Roscoe Dolan boiled up. He reached up to snap off a branch. He picked up a small stick with which to poke out the pithy center. He looked through the hollowed limb as if through a telescope, wishing he could use it for revenge on Roscoe.

Enoch motioned to Caleb to follow him as he crossed the yard to the smokehouse. He carefully pulled on the latchstring and pushed the door open. He stepped inside and waited for his eyes to adjust to the darkness. He could barely make out the row of hams hanging from the rafter. He lifted one from its hook and slung it over his shoulder.

"Grab one of those sides of bacon, Caleb. This ought to keep us going for a while."

They were retracing their steps past the barn and back toward the boat when Enoch stopped short. He put his hand on Caleb's arm and pointed toward the barn. He had heard something moving inside. He didn't know if it was livestock or a person. He motioned for Caleb to stay put as he crept toward the open door on the side of the barn. He raised himself enough to look through a knothole. Inside, doing the morning milking chores, was one of the Dolan granddaughters. She may have been Roscoe's girl. Roscoe was about Enoch's age so he could have a daughter in her teens. As he turned to leave his arm brushed against an old water bucket sitting atop a barrel, knocking it to the ground.

"Who's there?" a voice from the barn demanded. "Is that you Pa? I'm about finished. Just got one more cow. This first bucket's about full if you want to take it to the cold spring."

Enoch could hear her moving toward the door. He tensed to run but knew she would see them and sound an alarm. He waited until she stepped out into the bright sunlight. She was momentarily blinded. Enoch took that opportunity to grab her from behind, clamping his hand over her mouth. She dropped the milk pail and stared wild-eyed as Caleb came toward her. They drug her back into the barn.

"You scream girl and I'll slit your throat," Enoch warned. "Caleb, get a piece of that plow line and tie her hands behind her back. And give me that bandana."

Enoch stuffed the rag into her mouth as Caleb bound her hands.

"Are you a Dolan, girl?" he asked.

Her breath was coming in short gulps as she tried to breathe around the rag. She didn't respond. Enoch slapped her with the back of his hand.

"Answer me? Are you a Dolan?"

The terrified girl raised her head, red welts rising on the white skin of her cheek. Frozen with fear she nodded her head affirmatively.

"Are you Roscoe's girl?"

Again she nodded.

"I thought you might be. Do you know who I am?"

Her eyes lifted to his face, staring at the birthmark. She didn't respond.

"The girl knows me Caleb. What do you think we should do with her?"

"She'll be hollering to the top of her lungs that she seen you. Won't be no mistaking the man with the red face. She'll mess up everything you've already done."

"All right then, you know what to do."

The blood lust was shining in Caleb's eyes.

"Enoch, they ain't no use wasting such a pretty one like this. You mind if I have a little sport with her?" Caleb asked.

Enoch knew what was coming. He turned to leave, remembering his pain at her father's hands.

"Go ahead," he said.

Enoch stepped outside the door, making sure no one had heard the commotion. He could see Jim down by the water. No one was coming from the house. He stood in the doorway.

Caleb pushed the struggling girl back into the shadows of the corn shed. He grabbed her dress and ripped it down the front. Buttons cascaded across the floor. He ripped off her undergarments. She stood naked and shivering in the lone shaft of sunlight coming from a hole in the roof. He twisted her around and bent her over a feed trough as he loosened his pants and dropped them to the floor. A muffled scream escaped around the bandana as he entered her from behind. The resistance he felt told him she was a virgin, arousing him even more. He plunged himself into her, repeatedly. At climax he let out an animal bellow. Blood ran down the girl's legs as he withdrew from her. She moaned and struggled to breathe. Caleb nonchalantly pulled up his breeches, refastening the frayed belt. With the same nonchalance he pulled her head back and slashed her throat. He waited for her to stop thrashing before he removed the rag from her mouth. He cut her bonds, allowing her limp body to slide off the trough and onto the floor. Her lifeless eyes stared up at the roof.

"She ain't going nowhere," he said in explanation. "No use leavin her tied up."

He stared at the cloth in his hand.

"I reckon I'll have to wash this old rag. It's covered with blood and slobber."

He stuffed it back into his pocket.

Watching the rape had aroused Enoch. It brought back the dark episodes of his youth that his family never knew about. The slaves he had abused were too terrified of him to tell. He stood over the lifeless form of Roscoe Dolan's daughter, feeling a measure of revenge. He bent over and placed the elder tube between her bloody breasts.

"Caleb, grab what's left of that milk. I'll get the meat. Look around before you go outside. Don't want any more of the Dolans to see us."

Caleb peered around the doorsill. There was no one in sight. He picked up the half empty bucket and started for the boat. Enoch followed close behind with the ham and bacon. Jim saw them coming and untied the boat.

"What took you so long?" he asked. "I thought you mighta run into some of the Dolans."

Enoch looked at Caleb and mouthed the words, "Don't say anything."

There was no need in getting Jim all riled up. He was already squeamish about Sarah and Cleophas. Jim looked at Caleb as he stepped into the boat.

"Caleb, you've got blood on the front of your pants. What happened?"

"I snagged my hand on a nail in the smokehouse. Guess I musta wiped it on my pants," he said as he sat the pail of milk on a seat and started to push the boat away from the dock.

"This slough peters out up ahead," Enoch said. "We'll have to go back to the main channel to get out into the Skidaway. Caleb slice me off a piece of that ham. I'm starving to death."

Within minutes they re-entered the main channel and turned toward the Skidaway.

"Well boys, by tonight we'll catch up to them and then it will be complete," Enoch mused. "There's no way they'll know we're coming. We'll sneak up and surprise them. I don't want to get in a tussle with the priests if we don't have to."

Caleb swished the bloody bandana in the water.

CHAPTER THIRTY-TWO

KA'LE HAD NEVER BEEN to St.Benedict's, but knew from Enoch's description that there was a landing at the end of Runaway Negro Creek. He followed the weed-strewn path to the east across the northern tip of the island. The massive gate to the compound of St. Benedict's loomed ahead. He knocked loudly and waited breathlessly for an answer. A peep-hole slid open and the bright eyes of Brother Anthony peered out.

"Yes, can I help you?" he said to Ka'le.

"Yassuh! My name is Ka'le an I comes from da Roselawn Plantation. I's come tuh warn Miss Queen and Cassie. Massa Enoch, he comin 'dis way lookin' fo 'em. He done kilt some folks on da plantation and burnt down Massa Hiram's house. He nearly kilt his daughter Sarah. And Massa Hiram, he dead too from gittin' shot in Savannah."

Brother Anthony opened the gate enough for Ka'le to enter and led him to the prior's office.

"Father Titus, this man, Ka'le, has come from Roselawn Plantation with some bad news. There has been trouble there. It seems that Enoch Penrose has run amok and killed several people. He burned down his brother's house and is believed to be headed this way looking for Cassie and her mother."

Titus leaped to his feet and walked around the desk.

"When did you leave there, Kale?" the prior asked.

"Real early dis mawnin. I went tuh Wormslow fust an told dem whut wuz goin' on, den I took one of dere boats an came ovuh heah. It probly been 'bout two, maybe three hours since I left."

"Was Master Enoch alone?"

"Nawsuh. He had da ole overseer from Ossabaw wit' him. Massa Jim Pelham. An' he had dat no 'count, white trash Caleb Hawkins too. Dem's a bad bunch. Dey slit da throat of Cleophas an chunked him in da river. Dey tried tuh burn up Miss Sarah in her bed. We wuz lucky tuh git her outten da house. She won't breathin' fo da longest time. And Massa Hiram, he done died from da fever dat wuz caused by being shot in Savannah."

"Do you think those men were still there when you left?"

"Yassuh, cuz dey wuz a boat at Grimball's Landing. I reckon dey'll take dat boat tuh git ovuh heah. Probly, dey'll go out tuh da river an go down da Thunderbolt tuh git here. Dat be da shortest way," Ka'le added.

"If they left shortly after you did, how long do you think it will take them to get here?" the prior asked.

"I reckons 'bout five, six hours, dependin on dem coming directly heah. I spect dey gone need some food long da way, so maybe two, three mo hours."

"That means they should arrive here anywhere between three and six hours from now. Thank you, Ka'le. Your warning gives us some time to prepare and to decide what to do about Queen and Cassie," the prior concluded. "Brother Anthony, go and fetch them and the soldiers. Also ask Mother Marie and Sister Bernadette to join us."

When the young friar had vanished Ka'le remembered the letter in his pocket. He handed it to Father Titus.

"Miss Amanda say I oughta give dis letter tuh ya tuh read an den give it tuh Queen," he said.

The prior took the letter and moved to a window where the light was better. He broke the wax seal and withdrew four sheets of paper. He began to read. He smiled and looked briefly at the other sheets. Brother Anthony returned with Queen, Cassie and Andre. Bernadette and the Mother Superior soon joined them.

"Father, the other soldier, Louis Dufour is too ill to join us. Sister Rosemarie is with him in the infirmary."

"I see," Titus said. "Well, that can't be helped at the moment."

He made a complete circle of the room, his chin resting on his hand, groping for the best way to break the news.

"Ka'le here has come to us with sad news. His Master, Hiram Penrose has died from wounds he received during the battle in Savannah. This is a terrible loss to all of us. He was a great benefactor of St. Benedict's. If that were the end of it then the news would be bad enough."

Titus drew a deep breath and continued.

"It seems that Mr. Penrose's brother Enoch has returned. He showed up last night at Roselawn. He and the two men with him burned Hiram's house almost killing his daughter, Sarah. They also killed a houseboy, Cleophas."

Queen and Cassie cried out in disbelief. They burst into tears. The very calamity they hoped to spare Roselawn by fleeing had happened anyway.

"There's more," the prior continued. "Ka'le believes that Enoch Penrose is headed this way with two other men, Jim Pelham and Caleb Hawkins. They are obviously after Cassie. We all know the story of how Cassie came to us in the first place. What we have to decide now is how to deal with this situation. They'll arrive here in the next few hours. We're not trained to fight and we're taught that it's a mortal sin to take another's life. However, in a situation like this I believe the Lord will forgive us for taking up arms against these men. I pray that we can deter them without bloodshed. We have several hunting rifles here and we can probably hold them off until help arrives. We'll shut all the gates and man the barricades until help comes, and trust that no one will be hurt. Before we get to that though, Ka'le also brought us some good news." Titus picked up the papers from his desk and began to read the letter from Amanda.

Father Titus,

I am sending you this letter to carry out the wishes of my husband. His final request before dying was to ask me to prepare "writs of manumission" for Queen and Cassie Omoru. I have also included one for Ka'le Akala. I owe my daughter's life to him.

Please place your signature in witness to mine and give the writs to them. At the first opportunity I will have them recorded in the courts. God bless you and take care.

Respectfully,
Amanda Penrose

The prior handed the three letters to Queen, Cassie and Ka'le.

"What do dis mean, Cassie?" Queen asked. She too could not read. Cassie scanned the document. She began to cry anew.

"Ma, it means we are free. Miss Amanda has given you, me and Ka'le our freedom. We're not slaves anymore. These papers have set us free."

She first embraced her mother and then Ka'le, tears of joy flowing freely.

"Cassie that's wonderful news," said Bernadette. "Now, despite all the pain you've gone through, you have got your freedom. You are now free to move forward with God's plan for you."

Andre was glad as well, seeing his beloved Cassie so happy. But his happiness was tempered by the knowledge that even though she was now free, he was not. Furthermore, he was a fugitive from his country and a deserter from its army.

"Cassie I am so proud for you and your mother and Ka'le," Andre said. "But that doesn't change the fact that Louis and I are still fugitives and deserters, as well as slaves. If we are caught we'll be sent back to Saint-Domingue where we'll be tried and hanged."

"Andre, you are safe here at St. Benedict's," Cassie said. " Father Titus and the brothers will protect us. Besides the French don't even know you are alive."

"But, Cassie can't you see," he said "As long as we are here or anywhere in America, we'll never be safe from men like Enoch Penrose. We have to get to some place where he cannot reach us." Andre paused to steady his voice before continuing.

" Last night, when I was talking to Esther, she told me that she and her family were trying to get to Florida when they were capsized near here by a storm. They were told that the Spanish would take in all runaways from the north. The Spanish are bitter enemies of the British

They have promised sanctuary to anyone who can reach Florida. There is a fort just north of St. Augustine called Fort Mose. It is occupied by slaves who have made their way there after escaping.

"Esther said that she and her parents were clinging to a tree that had been uprooted along the riverbank and that just before her parents were swept away her father handed her an oilcloth pouch and told her to protect it with her life. She showed me that pouch last night. This is what was inside."

Andre unfolded a large square of sheepskin. It bore a map showing the route from Charlestown to Fort Mose along the inland waterways of the coastal islands. Each major island was inked in a different color and marked with safe havens along the route.. Slaves all along the way risked their lives to help those who attempted the journey. Cassie looked at the map. She ran her finger down its outline from Savannah to Florida.

"Are you suggesting that we should try to escape to Fort Mose?" Cassie asked.

"Yes," Andre said. "As long as Enoch draws breath he'll hunt us down. We can slip away while the monks here at St. Benedict's keep him at bay. By the time he discovers that we are gone we'll have such a head start that he'll never catch us. What do you say Cassie? Whatever we could do here we can do in Florida. God can use us wherever we are."

Bernadette listened with growing apprehension.

"Cassie, there are dangers you've never dreamed of in those waters," she said. "There are thieves and pirates and slave chasers. Stay here. You'll be safe. Father Titus and the monks can protect you."

Cassie was distraught at the thought of once again having to leave the place where she had found so much happiness. But she knew in her heart that Andre was right.

"Sister, Andre is right," Cassie said. "Master Enoch will never give up as long as he can reach me. In Florida, we will be beyond his reach. The Spanish will not see Andre as a slave. He too can be free."

"What about you, Queen?" Bernadette asked. "Will you go too?"

"I's been separated from my Cassie fo five years. Iffen she goes, I go. Maybe we can start a new life dere, witout ever havin tuh worry bout bein slaves agin, or hidin from men lak Massa Enoch."

"And you, Ka'le. Will you go?" the nun asked.

"Missy I's been a slave all my life. I wants a chance tuh live free. And I wants a chance fo my boy Isaac tuh live free. Dis look lak da only way fo' me tuh do dat. Massa Enoch, he ain't gone quit 'til he cotches up wit evuhbody he reckons done him wrong. He know dat I sent Isaac tuh fetch Massa Hiram when dey kilt Toby. Iffen he ain't stopped he'll hunt me an my boy down, free or not. Yessum, I's goin'."

"What about the other boy, Louis?" Father Titus asked. "He's in no condition to go."

"Wait a minute," Bernadette said and ran out. She returned with Sister Rosemarie in tow.

"Sister Rosemarie thinks Louis is not going to make it despite all her efforts. His fever is still raging and the infection seems to be spreading. He's unconscious. I told her of your plans to flee to Florida. She suggests that we move Louis to the little quarantine house she built down by Adam's Creek. It is well hidden and Enoch is unlikely to know about it. She and I will take turns with Louis until he recovers or, God forbid, he dies. That way when, and if, Enoch gets here, he'll have no way of knowing that any of you were ever here."

"I guess it's settled then," the Mother Superior said. "We must hurry and get you ready to travel. All of you come with me. With Father's permission we'll go to the refectory and pack food for your journey."

"By all means, Mother. Give them whatever they need. There are several waterproof sacks in the smokehouse. They'll need them in those waters, with the storms coming."

The small crowd of people filed out of the office and over to the storehouse by the refectory. Within a few minutes they had three large oilcloth bags stuffed with meat, vegetables, salt and spices. Ka'le asked if he could have one of the fire starter kits. Brother Anthony picked one up and stuffed it into one of the bags along with two skinning knives and a hatchet.

"There you go, Ka'le," he said. "You're gonna need these. It's pretty wild out there. You should be able to catch some fish and maybe trap some small game. It's a long way to Florida. God be with you."

The entire entourage gathered in the courtyard near the main gate. The somber nuns and monks watched as Ka'le and Andre hefted the heavily laden bags to their shoulders. Queen and Cassie picked up their pitiful belongings and stood by the men.

"God bless all of you," Father Titus said. "May He guide your paths and bring you His peace." He crossed himself and held out his hand to the men. Bernadette enveloped Cassie in her ample embrace and squeezed her heartily.

"Cassie, you take care of yourself. May God be with you. I expect to hear great things about you someday. God will provide and He will protect. I know that He has wonderful plans for you. Queen, Ka'le, Andre, God be with you. When you get to Fort Mose send back word that you are safe. We'll be anxiously waiting."

The October sun was at its zenith when Brother Anthony swung the gate open and the little band filed out. Ka'le led them down the path to Runaway Negro Creek landing. They piled the bags into the two boats. Ka'le led off with Queen. Cassie and Andre followed in the second boat. Cassie, Queen and Ka'le were turning their backs on the only life they had ever known, heading into an uncertain future, but a future full of hope, a future where they could all be free. Andre was seeking to escape his own past and to find his own freedom

CHAPTER THIRTY-THREE

THE SUN WAS DISAPPEARING behind the pines along the northern shores of Skidaway Island when the fishing skiff neared Priest's landing. The three men aboard were weary from the long row around the point of Modena Island and down the Thunderbolt.

"Let's pull in just north of the landing and tie up in the marsh," Enoch said. "I don't want anyone seeing us from the dock or the monastery walls. We'll hole up until after dark and then check the lay of the land."

There was a small creek feeding into the river about a quarter mile above the dock. It ran back under a grove of live oaks that afforded excellent shelter and shielded them from any prying eyes. Enoch steered the boat into a secluded anchorage and hopped out, sinking to his knees in the muck. Caleb threw the mooring rope to him and he tied it around the protruding knee of a bald cypress.

"Can't afford to start no fire," Enoch said. "We'll just have to slice off some of that smoked ham and finish off the milk before it curdles. It'll be dark in a couple of hours. I'm gonna get some shuteye until then. I suggest you do the same. We probably gone have a busy day tomorrow."

Caleb was chewing on a hunk of the ham. He washed it down with milk and produced a loud belch.

"You ought not to wolf down your food like that, Caleb," Jim said. "I've known folks to choke to death thatta way."

"Mind yore own business, Pelham," Caleb snarled. "I'll eat any way I want to. 'Sides. I ain't got many of my teeth left and it's hard to chew that stringy ham."

"Shut up the both of you," Enoch said. "Someone may be afoot in these woods. Keep your voices down."

The full moon cast long shadows on the forest floor as the sleeping men roused. Enoch looked at his watch. It was now past nine. He had slept longer than he intended.

"Come on," he said. "It's time to get started."

He led the way out of the grove of oaks and across the cart path that ran from the dock to the gate of the monastery. The barricade around the monastery, where the tabby walls did not extend, was constructed of large pine saplings set into the ground. They were stripped of their bark and sharpened to a point. The twelve-foot high logs were lashed together with ropes about two feet off the ground and again at eight feet, leaving a gap of roughly a half-inch between them. Enoch pushed against one of the logs. There was no give to it. He peered through a gap but could see no movement inside. He signaled for the others to follow and walked back to the edge of the woods, out of earshot.

"It looks as if the tabby walls run down the northern end of the compound and about half way along the sides. The rest of the fence is made of these logs. I'm going to circle around the entire monastery to see if there's any place we might be able to get in. You two stay here and wait for me."

Pelham and Hawkins moved further back into the tree line and sat, leaning against a fallen tree. Enoch set off on his search. Halfway between the end of the tabby wall and the southwest corner there was a tall gate set into the palisade. Enoch tried the gate but it was barred top and bottom from the inside. He continued his survey, rounding the corner and heading east along the southern perimiter. Another gate, identical to the first, was located in the middle of the southern wall. It too was securely barred. He could hear livestock noises through the fence. "The barns must be on this end", he thought. He made a mental note. This gate would lead to the fields and gardens. A few minutes later he was abreast of a third gate in the east wall, facing toward Romerly Marsh and Wassaw Island.

The northern wall was formed by the main structure of the abbey and the buildings housing the monks. There were watchtowers at both corners. He was careful to stay in the shadows in case lookouts were stationed. He had circled the entire monastery, soon arriving back where he left Jim and Caleb. Both were sound asleep.

"Fine sentries you'd make," he said, kicking them awake. "You're like the apostles. They couldn't stay awake long enough for Jesus to pray. I guess that's fitting since this is a monastery.

"Look, I found three gates besides the main one. One each in the east, south and west walls. They're all barred from the inside. I don't see any way to get in without someone seeing or hearing us. We'll go back to where we left the boat and bed down for the night. I've got to come up with a plan to get in there and find out where they're hiding Cassie and Queen."

They spent a fitful night under the trees near the boat. The mosquitoes coming off the fresh water lagoons were merciless. When they pulled the blankets over their heads to avoid the insects, the heat was stifling.. It was unusually warm for October. The bell announcing morning lauds woke Enoch. He prodded the other two awake.

"I laid awake most of the night," he said. "Those infernal mosquitoes were eating me alive. I don't think I've ever seen them this bad. At least it gave me some time to think.

"Here's what I want you to do. Caleb, you sneak around to the east gate. Make sure you stay out of sight. Keep track of anybody entering or leaving. Jim you do the same on the west. I'll camp out near the south gate. I want you to stay there all day so you'd better take some meat and water with you. Come back here when it gets near dark and we'll see what we've got."

"I don't know why we don't just go in there with our guns ablazin and drag them niggers outta there," Caleb groused. "Them monk folks probly ain't got no guns. Anyway, if they do they won't shoot nobody. It's agin their religion."

"We can't take that chance, Caleb," Enoch said harshly. "Now, get on over there and do what I said. And, don't you go falling to sleep. Your snoring will wake the dead. I'll see both of you back here tonight."

Caleb tramped off through the woods until he located a spot set back from the east gate. It was hidden from view yet allowed him to see anyone entering or leaving. Still muttering he leaned back against a tree, peering out through the dense underbrush toward the monastery.

The other two reached the west gate and Jim took up his watch. Enoch continued on, thrashing through the woods until he reached a spot near the south gate. He found a comfortable perch on an old stump and settled in. It was going to be a long and boring day.

It was nearing ten before any movement was noted. Enoch observed two monks leaving in a wagon pulled by mules. There were plows in the wagon. They were apparently headed to the fields south of the monastery. No one else came or went all day until the wagon returned at dusk.

"I hope the other two are having better luck," he said aloud.

When the gate was closed and locked behind the returning wagon, he retraced his steps to the camp. Jim was already there. Caleb was just arriving from the other direction.

"Did you see anything, Jim?" Enoch asked.

"Three or four of them monks came out and went down to the dock. They had a cart and I could hear them sawing and banging away. I reckon the dock got smashed when that storm blew through. They came back about three or four. One of em was totin a rifle. They may be better prepared than Caleb thought."

"How bout you, Caleb. Did you see anything?"

"It's kinda funny. Bout nine or ten o'clock this nun come outta the gate. She was totin a basket. She disappeared into the woods headin toward Romerly Mash. Twenty or thirty minutes later another nun came back up that same trail. She was totin that same basket. I reckoned the first one wuz goin out to pick some vegetables or sumpin. But, when the second one showed up with the same basket and nothin in it, it didn't make no sense. Well, I sat there puzzlin over that for a while. Bout one o'clock the second one comes out with that basket again and heads into the woods. Lo and behold, bout an hour later, the first one done come back."

A broad grin spread across Enoch's face.

"They've got somebody out there in the woods they're looking after. Must be another building out there, somewhere. But, it don't make no sense that they'd have Cassie outside the monastery. She'd be easier to protect inside. Tomorrow mornin we're gonna find out what those nuns are up to."

Before dawn the next morning Caleb led the others to his post near the east gate. They waited expectantly. Shortly following the bell announcing morning prayers, the gate opened. Sister Rosemarie appeared, a basket hanging from her arm. She passed within fifty feet of the hidden men. Enoch waited until she was well out of sight before speaking.

"If they follow the same pattern that Caleb saw yesterday the other one'll be along shortly. I'm gonna wait until she's back inside the gate before we see what's going on at the end of this trail."

True to Caleb's observation's of the day before, Bernadette walked back up the path, past the men, and rapped on the gate. Within minutes she had disappeared inside.

"Come on," Enoch barked. "Let's see what's goin' on out there."

The path looked as if it had not been much used until recently. Fresh machete cuts marked the wild muscadine vines that were pushed back from the pathway. The trampled weeds were still green. Whatever the nuns were doing out there, they hadn't been doing it very long.

"This trail ain't been used for a while," he said. "Those vines wuz just cut and the grass in the middle of the ruts is still green. I got a feelin that whatever we find has something to do with Cassie."

Enoch led the way. They had gone well over a mile before he held up his hand to stop them.

"There's a little shack up ahead. Can't be more'n twelve feet square. I can't figger why they'd build something this far out in the woods. You two stay here. I'm gonna sneak up there and see if I can get a peek inside."

Enoch moved off the path and circled around the small cabin. The woods closed to within a few feet of the place. He was able to approach it from behind. The back wall had no windows. He got down on all fours and crawled across the few feet to the building. About four feet up the wall there was a hole in the tabby. He rose to his knees and looked in. A black man lay on one of the two cots in the room. The black clad nun hovered over him. She lifted the covers. He could see the angry wound in his side. It was filled with a mass of wriggling white maggots. Enoch became violently ill. He managed to control his vomit reflex and scurried back into the woods. In one massive heave all the ham and milk from the previous day spewed onto the ground. He stood, bent over, hands on knees, as his stomach emptied itself. When he had nothing left to give he went back to the others.

"She's in there with the nigger soldier that was with Cassie on the wagon. Looks like I mighta winged him when I took that shot. He looks real bad. The hole in his side is full of maggots. I've seen them used before on cows to clean out pus, but never on a human being. Makes you sick to look at it.

"What I don't understand is why they've got him out here if Cassie and Queen are back at the monastery. But, I'm gonna find out. Jim you stay here off the trail. Whistle if you hear or see anyone. Caleb, you come with me."

Jim stepped off the trail and took up a position where he could look back toward the monastery. Enoch led Caleb up to the cabin door.

"You stay here outside by the door. If I need you I'll call. Don't let nobody else in."

Enoch braced himself and kicked the door open. He burst inside as Rosemarie was beginning to remove the teeming mass from Louis' side. She dropped the pan to the floor. The forceps clattered into it.

"Who are you? What are you doing here?" she demanded of Enoch.

"Oh, come on Sister. You know who I am. If you didn't before I'm sure Cassie told you about me. Told you I might come a'calling."

Rosemarie backed against the wall, fearful of what Enoch might do.

"What I want to know is why you and this nigger are out here in the woods? And I want to know where Cassie and Queen are?"

"This man has an infection. We don't know whether he is contagious or not, so we brought him out here to our quarantine house. As you can see he is very ill."

"All right, that answers my first question. Now answer the second."

Rosemarie did not want to lie but she also didn't want to betray her friends. She remained silent. Enoch crossed the room and stood with his face a few inches away from the frightened nun.

"I'll ask you once more. Are Cassie and Queen in the monastery?"

"No. They are not."

Enoch heard the hesitation in her voice. He was suspicious.

"Have they been inside the monastery?" he asked.

Rosemarie maintained her silence. She would not tell this man anything that would lead to harm for her friends.

"Caleb!" Enoch called. "Get in here!"

Caleb's large frame filled the door, plunging the small room into momentary darkness.

"Yeah, Enoch. Whaddaya want?"

"The sister here doesn't seem to want to cooperate with me. She keeps dodging my questions. We know this nigger was with Cassie last time we saw her. It stands to reason she came here with him, since she wasn't at Roselawn. The sister says she's not inside the monastery, but she won't answer me when I ask her if she's been here. She doesn't seem to be so afraid herself, but I kinda think she don't want nothing happening to her patient here.

"Now Sister, are you gonna tell me where they are or do we hafta get it outta this nigger?"

Her eyes darted from one man to the other.

"All right, have it your way," Enoch said. "Caleb, let's see if nigger blood is the same color as white folk's blood."

Before she could protest Caleb had unsheathed his skinning knife and drawn it across Louis' forearem. Blood spurted from the cut.

"Are you gonna answer me now or does my friend here have to see if the blood from his neck looks the same?"

"Stop it!" she shouted. "You barbarians have no qualms about killing people, do you? You've already killed that poor boy and tried to kill Sarah Penrose."

Enoch glared at Caleb. "You told me she was dead. Burned up in the house."

Rosemarie blanched, realizing that in her fury she had said too much. Enoch was quick to exploit her words.

"How do you know about Sarah Penrose?" he asked.

She said nothing.

"Cassie and Queen were not at Roselawn, so they couldn't'a known about anything that happened there. I'll ask you one more time, where are they and how did you find out about what went on?"

Rosemarie hesitated. Enoch nodded toward Caleb who placed his knife blade against Louis' throat.

"Wait! I'll tell you. I can't stand by and watch as you murder another innocent human being. It won't do you any good anyway.

"Day before yesterday Cassie and her mother showed up here with Louis here." She saw no reason to tell them about Andre if they didn't already know. "They said that Mrs. Penrose insisted that they come here for protection. She felt that if you didn't find them at Roselawn you might just go away and leave everyone alone. She was obviously wrong about that."

"That still don't explain how you found out about what went on," Enoch persisted.

He looked at Caleb again and Caleb pressed the blade tighter against Louis' throat. A trickle of blood ran down the side of his neck.

"Stop it," she shouted. " I said I would tell you. In the holy name of Jesus and Mary take that knife away."

Caleb eased back.

"Late that afternoon another man came. He said he was from Roselawn and was here to warn us that Enoch Penrose had burned down his brother's house and killed one of the slaves. He said you'd also nearly killed Sarah Penrose."

Enoch gave Caleb a withering look.

"You told me you had finished her and that the fire would cover our tracks. If what she says is true then all we did don't amount to a hill o' beans. If Sarah's alive she's still in line to inherit Roselawn, now that her pa is dead. Seems I can't depend on you to get anything right."

"Oh, come on Enoch," Caleb protested. "She's lying. Or, whoever told her that is lying. When I left that room she wasn't breathing and the fire was coming up the stairs. They ain't no way she coulda got outta there alive."

Enoch turned back to Rosemarie.

"Who told you that? What was the man's name?"

"He said his name was Ka'le and that he saw three men running away from the burning house. He said he recognized you in the glare of the fire. He said there was no mistaking your face."

"I'll kill that black son-of-a-bitch," Enoch said in a burst of rage. "This is not the first time he's caused me trouble. It was him who sent the boy Isaac over to fetch Hiram after Toby died. Now I've got even more reason to find Cassie. Where are they hiding Sister, if they ain't in the monastery?"

Rosemarie stared into Enoch's blazing eyes.

"I told you it won't do you any good. They left here that afternoon after Ka'le came. They're long gone."

"Where'd they go?" Enoch insisted.

Caleb menaced Louis again. She knew she had to tell Enoch what he wanted to know or he would kill Louis. And maybe her as well.

"They're going to some place called Fort Mose in Florida. It's a Spanish fort where they take in runaway slaves from the colonies. They promise them freedom if they swear allegiance to Spain and convert to Catholicism. Once they cross that border into Florida there's no way you can harm them. They'll be protected by the Spanish army."

Enoch plopped down on the other bed. His shoulders slumped in dejection. Everything he had tried to achieve was coming unraveled. He couldn't go back to Savannah. The English would try him for desertion. If the colonials caught him they would try him for murder. He had no choice but to keep going, to some place where no one knew him.

"God damn it!" he cursed. "There's no end to my bad luck. First God cursed me with this face. Then Pa cut me outta his will and gave everything to Hiram. All the niggers turned against me. Now, my one chance to do something to get back what's rightfully mine has failed. Well, I ain't gonna take it lying down. I came out here looking for that girl and since I can't stay here, I'm just gonna keep on lookin til I find her.

"Caleb, I'm gonna take the sister outside and tie her up. I can't bring myself to hurt her. My ma would turn over in her grave. But I can't let her go running off sounding the alarm either. The other nun will be coming back in a few hours to relieve her. We'll be long gone by then. You know what to do in here."

Enoch finished the last knot on the ropes around Rosemarie's wrists as Caleb emerged from the cabin. He was wiping the blade against his leg. He placed it back in its sheath.

"Come on," Enoch said. "Let's get Jim and get out of here."

Three hours passed before Bernadette returned to the quarantine cabin. She screamed when she saw Rosemarie bound and gagged. She quickly cut her bonds with the butcher knife from her basket. She ripped the gag from her mouth.

"Sister, what happened? Who did this?"

"It was Enoch Penrose and another man named Caleb. They threatened to kill Louis if I didn't tell them where Cassie was. I figured it didn't really matter since they've been gone almost two days. I'm afraid to go back inside. I fear they've killed Louis. The big, evil looking man was wiping blood off his knife."

"You stay here. I'll check on Louis."

Rosemarie heard a muffled scream and Bernadette reappeared.

"Your fears were justified, Sister. Louis is dead. His throat's been cut."

Rosemarie burst into tears.

"Bernadette, did I cost Louis his life? Is there something I could have done?"

"Don't blame yourself, Sister. They were not going to let Louis live no matter what you did. They just used his suffering to get you to tell them what they wanted to know. If you hadn't told they might have killed both of you. Louis didn't suffer. Death was quick. We both know that he wasn't going to live much longer anyway. He's just gone on to meet his Lord a bit sooner.

"Come. We must get back to the others. Mother Marie and Father Titus must be told. They'll send someone to bring Louis back for burial."

The forlorn duo walked dejectedly back to the monastery. Rosemarie was heartsick that Louis had died under her watch. Bernadette was frightened. Enoch was now moving through the waters off the Georgia coast, stalking her dearest friend.

CHAPTER THIRTY-FOUR

THE PASSAGE FROM THE dock on Runaway Negro Creek back to Wormslow Landing went smoothly. The river narrowed significantly south of that point. Long Island pinched in toward Skidaway quickening the current. The storm's deluge had sent the river well out of its banks. Andre and Ka'le struggled to keep the boats in the middle of the stream. Trees undermined along the riverbanks littered the river. They jostled for position in the narrow waterway. Cassie and Queen used their oars to fend them off lest they crash into the boats and capsize them. By mid-afternoon they were passing Green Island and making the turn toward the Vernon River. Burnside Island passed on their right. The river widened and the current returned to its slower pace.

"I know this place!" Andre exclaimed. "That's where we first hauled ashore from the ships. There's Buley Plantation, Cassie. That's where I first laid eyes on you."

Ka'le slowed to let Andre's boat slide alongside.

"Ya work dese waters long enuf," Ka'le said, "and ya gits tuh know all the nooks and crannies. I musta been past here a hunnert times gittin back and forth from Ossabaw to Roselawn. But I ain't spent much time below Ossabaw. Went down tuh Sunbury once wit Massa Hiram by boat. And down to Darien an Sapelo in a wagon. Had tuh pick up some mules Massa John done bought on Sapelo. We had a debil of a time gittin them mules back across da water on dat ferryboat.

Dey started acting up an near bout turnt da boat over. Took us near a week tuh git back home wit em. Never will fogit dat trip."

Cassie's anxiety began to subside now that they were miles from St. Benedict's. There were no other boats on the river as far back as she could see. She began to let herself believe that she might actually be free of Enoch. She allowed herself a little smile as she watched Andre's back muscles ripple under his shirt with each pull of the oar.

"Strange," she thought. "I've never paid much attention to the physical side of Andre. He was just there on the wagon and in the camp. Then, we were separated by the battle, so soon after he proposed. Everything that happened after that is a blur. He is taller than I remembered, and broader across the shoulders. His features are softer. It must be his mother's Spanish blood. His coloring is closer to Mama's than to mine but much lighter than Ka'le. Of course, both of Ka'le's parents were African."

"Andre," she said. "How are we to act? We are in this boat together and we'll be in these waters for days. You and I are engaged but not yet husband and wife."

Andre was surprised at the question. It wasn't something he'd given much thought to during their flight from Savannah.

"Well, with your mother along, I think we have to continue to treat each other as we did before, on the wagon. Good friends, but apart. I'll stay with Ka'le when we camp and you'll stay with your mother. Time will take care of all those details. We have our whole lives to get to know each other. Our main concern right now is to find our way through these waters to Florida and sanctuary. Then we'll see."

"Andre knows so much more of the world than I do," she thought. "He's certainly met many other girls before me. I wonder why he fell in love with me and not one of them? One day, when we know each other better, I'll ask him."

She let her thoughts run toward the future, imagining their life together. A booming voice shook her from her reverie.

"Better git set," Ka'le shouted. "We's headin inta Hell's Gate. Da water's pow'ful rough. Cassie, you and Queen hang on tight. Ya might oughta tie yoselves tuh the boat seat wif a rope case ya gits throwed out. Ya gits in dat water ya ain't coming back."

The unbroken swells rolling in from the Atlantic across Ossabaw sound created a maelstrom as they split around Racoon Key and rolled up the Ogeeche river on one side and toward Green Island and Skidaway on the other. It was one of he the roughest stretches they would hit. The boats pitched and rolled violently. Ka'le took the lead again, Andre following as closely as he could manage. At times he lost sight completely of Ka'le in the swells. He was frightened but fought to keep his fear from spreading to Cassie. He looked back and smiled as if this happened everyday and he had everything under complete control.

Cassie hung on for dear life. She felt her stomach churn. She became violently ill, vomiting over the side of the boat. The wind bathed her face in salt-laden spray. She had never felt so ill in her life. She succumbed to the violent lurching and slid down into the bottom of the boat and under the seat. She closed her eyes and prayed for the terrible pain to end. She laid her head on one of the oilcloth bags and closed eyes. Miraculously she drifted into a fitful sleep. When she woke the waters had calmed. When she sat up she saw an unending green expanse of land ahead. She had no idea how long she had slept. They were back alongside Ka'le's boat. She glanced over at Queen. Her mother's green tinged face said that she too had been sick

"Where are we, Ka'le?" she asked.

"Dats da north end o' Ossabaw," he said. "We's gotta backtrack up da Ogeechee fo a mile or two fo we finds da Florida passage down tuh the south end. Dat's where da plantation be. Dat's where Isaac be. It gone take us several hours tuh git dere. We gotta find us a little sand spit an hole up til mawnin. Can't go paddlin round dese waters in da dark. Ya git lost up one o dese side creeks an ya'll nevah git out."

They hauled the boats onto a narrow sandy beach where the Florida Passage became the Bear River. Sunset was thirty minutes past and the saffron light in the west was quickly dying.

"Ya better grab sumpin quick tuh eat den start digging yoself a hole in da sand," Ka'le said. "Fix it so's ya kin cover yoself wit da sand an put a cloth ovah yo face. The skeeters an' deer flies'll tote ya away iffen ya don't."

Cassie grabbed some biscuits and fried fatback and gave it to the others along with a cup of water each. They wolfed down the food and set to digging their beds in the sand as the insects began to swarm around them.

It was two months past the hatching season for alligators. The females sat atop their nests to guard against predators, anxious to snatch her hatchlings. The newborn alligators were less than two feet long. They made helpless and tempting targets. Even the bulls were known to cannibalize their offspring. Their bellows echoed across the marsh. Cassie had heard these sounds before but from the safe shelter of her home. Up close they were louder and more terrifying.

"Mama, you don't think the gators will bother us do you?" she asked.

"I don know chile, I ain't never been out amongst'em lak dis. Ka'le ya knows'em better'n me, what you think?'

"I ain't never heard uv'em botherin' no peoples befo. Cose I ain't spent lotsa time out here wit'em either."

Exhausted from the adventures of the day, they lost no time falling asleep. It was past midnight when Cassie first heard the noise. There was a thrashing in the water. She ripped the cloth from her face and sat bolt upright, scattering sand in all directions. In the pale light of a quarter moon she could see two large alligators rolling about in the surf. She gasped and reached over to poke Queen awake.

"Mama, wake up! There are two alligators fighting in the river. Come on we've got to get out of here."

The commotion woke Ka'le and Andre. They came running over.

"Ka'le we've got to get out of here," Cassie said. "If those gators come up here they'll kill us."

"Don't ya worry none, Missy. Dey's jest as skeert o you as you is o dem. Dey don lak da smell o humans. Dey won bother ya none long's ya don git twixt dem an da little'uns. Ya best git on back tuh sleep. Mawnin gone come on real fast."

Cassie rolled back into her hole in the sand and tried to go back to sleep. At every little sound she would look to see if it was one of the alligators. Finally, a few hours before dawn, she succumbed and drifted off to sleep. She woke to the far off sound of a rooster greeting the sunrise.

"Dat be da cock rooster ovah tuh Buckhead," Ka'le said. "He da biggest rooster I evah seed. He be nigh onto forty pound. He rule da roost ovah dere.

"Dey's fo plantations on Ossabaw. North End, Middle Place, South End and Buckhead. Massa John rented the South End from Massa Morel. He live in Buckhead. We be goin to South End.

"Da Indians what useta live here brewed a black drink from da berries on da holly bush dey called *asapo*. Dats how da name Ossabaw came about. We learnt to make a purgative outten dem berries."

The little island where they spent the night was at the mouth of Kilkenny Creek. South End was another three miles down the Bear River. The tide was receding as they resumed their voyage. Within an hour they could see smoke rising from the chimneys of the slave cabins. Ka'le guided them into a marsh creek that paralleled the row of cabins. He paddled up a narrow slough and beached the boat in a thicket of cattails. He was directly behind the third cabin. He motioned for Andre to pull alongside.

"Dat's Kimba's house," he said, pointing to the dwelling. "Isaac, he livin dere wit my brother. We's gotta be keerful. Don' want nobody tuh see us. Dey gots a new overseer. He a good man but he sho don want us runnin off wit his hands. Sides he don know we's free. Iffen he cotches us he'll take us back tuh Roselawn."

Ka'le told the others to stay put until he could check out the cabin. He looked both ways before scampering across the yard to the back door. He pushed the door open and entered. A few minutes later he called for them to come inside.

"Andre, dis my brother Kimba an my son Isaac," Ka'le said. "I done told dem bout what happened. I told dem we's goin tuh a place called Florida and dat I wants Isaac ta come wit us. Kimba say if Isaac be goin he be goin too."

"Ain't no reason fo me ta stay heah. My Lilla dead. They kilt Toby. You da only famly I gots left. Sides I wants to live free too."

"What ya think, Queen?" Ka'le asked.

"He yo brother, Ka'le. Ya wants him tuh come, it all right wit me. We gots room fo three in each o dem two boats."

"Cassie, you an Andre greeable tuh dat?"

"We can use the extra help with the boats, Ka'le," Andre said. "I think he should come with us."

Cassie nodded in agreement.

"It done settled den. Isaac. Kimba. Git yo things together. We needs tuh light out befo it field time an dey be missin' ya. Kimba, git yo castin net. An, Isaac go git yo gig. It be a long way tuh Florida and we gone need all the fishes and shrimps we can cotch. Grab whatevah food ya gots an throw it in a sack. And some water too."

CHAPTER THIRTY-FIVE

"**Come on, Caleb, put** your shoulder into it," Enoch pleaded. "We've got a lot of ground to make up. With three of us paddling we should close on em about four or five hours a day. I figure with all the twists and turns it's over a hundred miles to Florida. That'll take at least fifteen to twenty days for Ka'le. Queen and Cassie won't be much use to 'im, so they can't be goin too fast. They'll have to hang close to the shorelines. If they get caught they'll be sent back to Roselawn in chains. I reckon we can catch up to'em by St. Simons or Jekyll."

In the three hours that elapsed before Bernadette found Louis, the pursuers had rounded the tip of Modena Island and were riding the southerly currents of the Skidaway.

"That's the turn at Runaway Negro Creeek ahead," Enoch explained. "Once we clear that we have to be careful. There's several homes on the bluff at Isle of Hope and then we run by Wormslow Landing. There's usually a lot of activity there, so keep a sharp eye out. Hang close to the left bank so we can duck into the marsh if need be."

Wormslow Landing was empty when they passed by. The only person seen was a lone rider on the bluff between there and the Isle of Hope wharf. They were too far away to be identified so Enoch plowed ahead. He was obsessed with catching up to the runaways. The current quickened as they passed Long Island and shot out into the Skidaway

Narrows. They made the long turn past Burnside Island then looped back into the Vernon River.

"It's too late in the day to try to go through Hell's Gate. We get caught in there at dark and it'll be the end of us. There's a little beach on Green Island where we can hole up til morning. We'll get an early start and should get to South End by midafternoon, latest."

They pulled ashore and set about preparing a campsite.

"What's that grunting noise?" Jim Pelham asked.

"Sounds like a wild pig," Caleb said. "They root around looking for acorns this time o' year. You boys keep still. I want to see if I can still catch a pig by hand. Usta do it all the time down near Fargo. Ain't done it for a while. Start up a fire. We may have some roast pork tonight."

Feral hogs roamed unmolested across these islands. Their ancestors were brought here two hundred years ago by the Spanish, then abandoned when the missions closed. Some of the brutes grew to five hundred pounds with ten-inch tusks. Enoch and Jim sat quietly by the fire for an hour. There was no sign of Caleb.

"I think I'm gonna pull out some of that ham," Enoch said. "I've still got a couple of old biscuits left. We can eat that. Tomorrow when we get to Ossabaw we'll stock up. I know the new man Hiram sent down there. His name's Jacob Grisham. He knows Hiram sent me away, I'm sure. But, he ain't got no way of knowing what's happened since. He won't give me no hard time, me being his boss's brother and all. We'll find out if Cassie's been there and when they left. That'll tell me how long it's gonna take to catch em."

A piercing squeal filled the quiet night air. Minutes later Caleb broke through the brush dragging a hundred pound shoat. The pigs had worn a path to the waters edge where the oak trees were laden with acorns. Caleb had climbed onto a low hanging limb that spread across the area and waited. Half and hour later a small herd of pigs wandered into the clearing, rooting noisily through the underbrush in search of fallen fruit. One of the young shoats stopped directly beneath his perch. When the animal lowered its head to root for acorns, Caleb dropped from the tree, knife in hand, and stabbed it through the heart. The pig's squeal sent the rest of the herd stampeding through the woods to safety.

"I see you haven't lost it, Caleb," Jim said. "We didn't hear a thing until the pig squealed. How'd you sneak up on him?"

"Didn't. Just hung up in a tree til he came by. Easy as falling off a log."

Caleb's unintentional pun eluded both of them.

The three took turns rotating the makeshift spit. The pig dressed out at roughly sixty pounds minus the head and entrails. Three hours later they feasted on the fresh roast pork. The leftover hams and shoulders went into their bags, wrapped in burlap and oilskin.

The sun was peeking over Racoon Key when Enoch woke Jim and Caleb.

"You boys go down and wash up then grab a bite of that pork. We're shoving off in a few minutes. I want to get to South End before sundown."

The passage through Hell's Gate was uneventful. The tide was running in and the swells met with less resistance. It was at its calmest of the day. They reached North End and found the Florida Passage before ten. Queen Bess Island was behind them before noon and Kilkenny Creek fell astern by two. Enoch pointed the boat's bow toward South Beach and stepped ashore. He flipped open his watch. It was four o'clock, straight up.

"Good job, boys," he said. "We made it by four. Let's head up to the overseer's house and see what's going on."

Caleb tied the boat to the dock and the three strode across the little beach. There was no sign of life at the house. Enoch knocked. A little woman, her gray hair wound tightly in a bun, came to the door. She was wiping her hands on her apron.

"Howdy," she said, surprised at the sight of three visitors. "Ya'll come on in. My husband is out with the field hands but I expect him back directly. You fellas just passing through?"

"Thank you ma'am. I'm Enoch Penrose. You may have heard of me. I used to be the master of this plantation. I'm Hiram's brother. This here's Jim Pelham. He usta have your husband's job. This other fella is Caleb Hawkins. He usta work for me over here."

The frail looking woman blanched. Jacob had told her about Enoch and how Hiram had run him off. She didn't know what to make of his turning up unannounced. She hoped he wasn't returning to take her husband's job away. She recovered from the initial shock and asked her visitors into the parlor.

"If you gentlemen will have a seat I'll get you something to drink."

She bustled off to the kitchen, her heart and mind racing to know what these men wanted with her husband. When she returned with the tea and some cookies she had just baked, she heard the hoofbeats of Jacob Grisham's horse as he crossed the gravel path to the barn. She practically ran to the door. She wanted to alert him to their visitors. She met him halfway up the path. Jacob was fully informed by the time he entered his house.

"Gentlemen," he began. "Welcome to South End. I understand you're no strangers to our island, having lived and worked here before me. To what do we owe the pleasure of your visit."

"Mr. Grisham, I'll come right to the point. Some of our slaves at Roselawn have run away. Even though me and my brother Hiram ain't on the best of terms, he hired me and the boys here to track them down. We followed them to Skidaway Island, at the monastery there, and were told that they had set out for Florida a couple of days ago. I know that one of the niggers, a fellow called Ka'le, has a son and a brother still here on Ossabaw. Stands to reason he'd want to stop by and see'em before he sets out down the river. Have you seen any thing of em?"

"That explains a lot," Grisham said. "Day before yesterday when I came in from the fields, one of the hands told me that Kimba and Isaac didn't show up for work. We searched their cabin and didn't find anything wrong. We checked the docks and none of the boats were missing. The only way they could have got off this island was if someone else took them. I'm guessing they went with this Ka'le fellow. I sure hope you catch them. I don't want to have to explain to Mr. Hiram that I let two of his slaves escape."

"I thank you sir, for being honest and upright with me. When I return these runaways to my brother I'll be sure to put in a good word for you about your cooperation and all. Now if I could trouble you for some supplies we'll be on our way. We didn't have time to pick up much along the way. I'll see that you are fully compensated for anything you can spare."

"Certainly, Mr Penrose. You are welcome to anything we have. You're welcome to stay the night if you'd like. Beulah's a mighty good cook. She'll whip up a good supper for you."

"Thanks just the same Mr. Grisham, but every minute counts. If we expect to catch these niggers before they get to Florida we need to get back on that river tonight. They's a few hours of daylight left. We'll push on as far as we can before dark. By the way, is my old dog Nero still here?"

"Yes," Grisham said. "We keep him penned up down near the quarters. He's pretty vicious as I'm sure you know. We bring him out every once in a while to help run down some stray cows or to get rid of wild hogs. Isaac was the only one who could handle him. Strange, since I heard that Nero had attacked several of the blacks."

"Yeah, we used him a few times to chase down some runaway niggers. He's good at that. If you don't mind I'm gonna take him with me. He'll come in handy if we catch up with Kimba and Ka'le," Enoch said.

Enoch followed Grisham down to the slave quarters. Nero was in a ten-foot high barricaded pen. Enoch could hear him whimpering at the smell of his master.

"I'm going to let you go in first, Mr. Penrose. That dog almost took my hand off once when I got too close to him."

Enoch cracked the gate open and Nero's nose popped out immediately. He sniffed Enoch's hand and began wagging his stump of a tail wildly. He leaped up onto his old master and began licking his face.

"Down boy," Enoch said. "We'll have plenty of time to get reacquainted. We're going on a long trip. You're gonna get a chance at your favorite sport, nigger chasing."

Enoch removed Nero's collar from the gatepost and clamped it around the dog's thick, muscular neck.

"If you don't mind," he said to Grisham, "I'd like to get a couple of pieces of clothes from Kimba and Isaac. Might help old Nero here track 'em if we catch up to them on land."

Grisham had grave misgivings about what Enoch proposed, however, he did need to get his slaves back before Hiram Penrose found out they were gone. A few dog bites may be a small price to pay.

"That's all right with me," he said. "We'll stop at their cabin on the way back."

Caleb and Jim were loading the last bags of supplies into the boat when Enoch came down to the dock, leading Nero. He coaxed the dog into the boat and made a nest of old rags for him to curl up on. Jim and Caleb were wary of the animal. They had seen what he could do to human flesh. They were just as happy to have the dog curled up behind Enoch. Caleb picked up his oar and pushed the boat away from its mooring.

"Thanks for your help Mr. Grisham. We'll have those runaways back here in short order."

The relieved overseer was happy to see them go. Their presence made him anxious and uncomfortable, especially the dirty giant, Caleb. He'd heard tales from some of the slaves about the man's cruelty. "Good riddance", he thought.

"God damn it all to hell," Enoch cursed when they were well out into the sound. "With Isaac and Kimba they'll be able to go as fast as we can, maybe faster. We gotta change our plans. We'll put in at Sunbury and see if we can scare up some horses to take us down to Sapelo. We know they gotta go through there. We'll be able to spot em before they clear Doboy Sound. I know some of the folks down there. Pa usta deal with em, and he'd bring me along on occasion. They'll help us out. They don't like seeing runaways any more'n we do. Sets a bad example for their own niggers."

Enoch cleared the sound heading west into the glinting sun. The settlement at Halfmoon Landing on the Medway River was visible across the marsh. Colonel's Island, home to a large rookery of herons, egrets, storks and ibises, drifted by to port. Startled, multi-hued clouds spiraled into the sky.

Sunbury was three miles further inland, hiding behind the protective guns of Fort Morris. The fort had fallen to the British the year before. Enoch needed to move cautiously through the bustling town to avoid being identified as a deserter. He prayed that news of the battle had not filtered down to this neck of the woods. There was a token garrison in the fort since Major Cruger had taken the main force into Savannah. He hoped the main contingent had not returned since the battle. The soldiers weren't very popular with the majority Whig citizenry. They tended to keep a low profile, coming out only to quell civil disturbances.

"Jim, since you usta live in these parts why don't you go on into town and kinda nose around. See what's happening. Caleb and me are gonna lay low here by the river. We'll start up a fire over there in the woods. See if you can get some rice and flour in town. Maybe some vegetables too. I'm getting tired of this all meat diet we've been on."

Jim was back within an hour carrying a sack of groceries.

"There weren't too many people out and about," he reported. "Everyone's talking about the goings on up in Savannah. They're skittish about what the English might try to do now that they control the entire area. I heard one man say that there was going to be a meetin' at White's Tavern tonight. They're gonna talk about what to do if they send a full complement of troops back to garrison Fort Morris."

Enoch mulled over this bit of news from Pelham. He needed more information.

"Caleb, I want you to go to that meetin'," Enoch said. "I'd go but sure as I did somebody'd spot this face of mine and I'd have a devil of a time explaining why I'm down here. See if you can find out if anybody's heard of any runaway slave traffic through these parts. While you're at it, see if you can get us some whiskey. I'm getting powerful thirsty. And, don't you go getting into any scrapes with the locals. If you run into anyone you know just tell 'em you're on your way back to Fargo to work the swamp. Don't call no attention to yourself."

After a supper of roast pork, turnip greens and cornbread, Caleb headed into town. He looked forward to having a drink or two himself. He'd been in Sunbury a few times when he worked for Pelham in Darien. He'd whored around some but he didn't really know anyone here.

"Maybe I'll find out where the local whorehouse is and have myself a little fun," he mused to himself. He rattled the coins in his pocket before pulling them out. He looked at the sparse pickings. "Might have enough to pay for a two-bit whore."

Caleb staggered back into camp a little past eleven. He plopped down by Enoch, who was already asleep.

"Hey, Enoch, wake up. I brought you a bottle of hooch. Ran outta money and had to waylay a fella leaving the whorehouse. He musta been pretty important aound Sunbury. Had two bottles of bonded whiskey on him. None o that local rotgut. Here."

He handed the burlap poke to Enoch.

"Did anybody see you?" Enoch said. He was furious with Caleb's callous disregard of his orders. "I told you not to call attention to yourself. Last thing we need is a bunch of vigilantes coming out here with torches looking for you."

"Naw," Caleb said. "After I tapped this fella on the head and drug him around behind the livery stable, I tied him up and fixed it so he won't be hollering for help. We'll be long gone before anybody finds him."

"You'd better hope so. Last time you *fixed* something you sure messed up. *Fixed* it so I can't never go back to Savannah. What'd you find out?"

"They wuz talking about gittin the militia back together and taking the fort if the English didn't reinforce it. Trouble is they's still so many Tories in these parts that the Whigs can't keep no secrets. Ain't nothing likely to happen I figger."

"What about runaways?" Enoch asked.

"This one feller said they'd caught a few on the road over near Midway. Didn't sound like our bunch. Another man said the traffic along the rivers had picked up lately. He saw a few boats full of niggers floating past last time he went down to Halfmoon Landing. They were taking the inland cut past St. Catherine's. They were too far away to tell much about 'em. Coulda been ours, though."

Jim sat up, wakened by Caleb's slurred ramblings.

"Here, Pelham, have a swig," Enoch offered. "Caleb was able to snag a coupla bottles of Scotch whiskey. Musta come off one of the British ships. Some sailor probably swapped them for a roll in the hay at the whorehouse. Ya don't see much good stuff over here."

Half a bottle of whiskey was gone when the midnight curfew bell rang. Time for everyone to be in their homes and sobering up for Sunday church services.

"Better get some shuteye," Enoch said. "We hafta get on the road before sunup. I wanta be outta here long before they find that fella behind the stable. We'll head over toward Midway and see what we can find."

Nero grunted and moved closer to Enoch for warmth.

CHAPTER THIRTY-SIX

THE HEAVY SEAS CRASHING across the open waters of St. Catherine's sound buffeted the small boats on their reach from Ossabaw across to the leeward shelter of the island. The two- mile crossing took over two hours. The occupants were drenched and seasick. The men were arm weary and fatigued from fighting the choppy swells. Ka'le eased back on his oar and allowed the boat to drift for a few minutes. He smiled at Queen and Kimba.

The bluff at the northern head of St. Catherine's Island is the highest point along Georgia's coastal islands. The twenty-five foot promontory is visible from South End on Ossabaw. A hundred years before the Pilgrims landed at Plymouth Rock, the Spanish had established a mission there. Santa Catalina de Guale, named for the local tribe and their chief, was the northernmost outpost of the Roman Catholic Church in the new world.

"Dat wuz a rough ride," he said. "I sho do pray dat we ain't got much mo water lak dat tuh go through."

The other boat, with Andre, Cassie and Isaac caught up. The younger men, more resilient than their elders, chided them for slacking off.

"You old fellas look plumb tuckered out," Isaac said. "Me and Andre is good fo' another two-three hours."

Kimba glared at his nephew.

"Ya keeps smartin' off lak dat an' ya gone find yoself up one o' dese creeks witout no paddle."

Cassie laughed at the friendly banter. It was good to be among these people, her people, again. It was good to know they were heading into a new life together. Whatever hardships they may face along the way will be worth it, she thought. A rush of pride came over her as she looked at Andre. He seemed to carry himself taller since they left St. Benedict's, with more dignity, as if he sensed his days of bondage were over. He was not much older than she but he was mature well beyond his years. He had been shaped by a life lived in two different cultures, one free, one slave. He knew the joys of freedom and the trials of slavery. Now, together, they would teach each other to live free.

Ka'le pulled closer alongside the other boat. He asked Cassie to look at the map that Esther gave them.

"What do it show bout gittin round dis island?"

Cassie pulled the map from the bag where Andre had placed it. He had tied it to the boat to insure that it didn't get lost overboard. The map was critical to finding the correct passages through the labyrinthine coastal waters. She spread the map on her lap as Andre turned to help her.

"This point must be the South End on Ossabaw," he said. He ran his finger across the map of the sound.

"That hill over there is where they show the old Spanish mission, so we must be right here." He pointed to the large marsh island just ahead of them.

"There's a passage between that island and St. Catherine's that will get us out of this open water. It's called Dickinson Creek and it empties into the Newport River just before you get to the cut down the island. That will take us most of the way to the next big island, Sapelo. It shows a place in the crook of this creek where there is help from local slaves. I can't make out a place name but it looks like it's about two miles from here."

"Dat's da old Musgrove plantation. I don reckon I knows who owns it now. We kin git dat far befo da sun straight up." Ka'le said. "But, we's gotta be keerful. Stay close tuh da shore so's we kin duck inta da marsh iffen we sees anybody."

The boats made better time in the calmer waters of the island passage. The taller buildings of the plantation were now visible. The sun was not yet overhead. Ka'le hugged the shore and pulled into a small estuary north of the settlement.

"Isaac, ya come wit me. Da rest o ya'll stay here, outta sight. We's gonna see iffen we kin find da folks what's gone hep us. We ain't back in a hour, ya'll wait til dark an go on by. Ain't no need fo all of us tuh git cotched."

Queen rummaged through one of the sacks and took out some of the food from St. Benedict's. She parceled it out to the others. They sat in the boats and ate. Kimba kept glancing across the marsh where he saw Ka'le and Isaac disappear into the grass. As the minutes ticked by their anxiety grew. Surely their escape would not be cut short so soon. Could they trust the notes on the map? Maybe something had changed since it was drawn. Maybe a copy of the map fell into the wrong hands and someone was lying in wait. Fear mounted with each tick of the clock Finally, as the last vestige of hope was fading, the sea grass parted and three men appeared. It was Ka'le, Isaac and a tall, thin man with white hair and ebony skin.

"This be Micah," Ka'le said, in hushed tones. "He gone help us git past da settlement up ahead an find da way into da cut past da island. Queen, hand us some o dem vittles. We won't able tuh git none in the village. Too many strangers wandrin round.

"Micah been here nigh onta twenty year. He wuz on da same boat wit da African. He say soon's we kin gits tuh Sapelo, Bulallah'll hep us git on past all da trouble dere."

Bulallah, *The African,* was a living legend throughout the sea islands. He was an Arab, born in the Sudan and so universally respected by his white masters that he became the de facto overseer for the upper Sapelo plantation.

The three men finished their meal and prepared to leave. Micah took the oar in the first boat. Kimba and Queen sat in the middle and Ka'le paddled from the rear. Micah eased them back out into the main channel and crossed over to the western side. He guided the boat into a seemingly impenetrable barrier of marsh. Just as it appeared they would founder he turned the boat sharply left and they disappeared behind the green wall of grass, emerging into a narrow channel. The hidden passage cut directly across the corner of the marsh island, bypassing the triangular peninsula across from the plantation compound, before re-entering Dickinson Creek.

"Dis be a cutoff dat comes out on da uddah side o' da main house," Micah said. "Da buckrah don know bout it. Ussen done run probly fifteen or mo boats through here in da past few years." Buckrah was a word created in Geechee to differentiate white masters from black slaves.

It took over an hour to get through the narrow, overgrown passage. Micah stopped rowing as he approached the southern opening into the main channel. He stood up on the seat so that he could see above the grass. He quickly dropped back down.

"Dey's a boat out on da river. It be goin' north. Soon's it's clear we'll head out."

A few minutes later Micah repeated the exercise.

"Dey's gone round da bend. We kin move on now."

He led them out into the river and crossed back to the shore of St. Catherine's Island. He hugged the bank for another mile and a half until they reached the mouth of the North Newport River.

"Up ahead dey's a channel whut takes ya straight down the island. It gits narrow and shallow in places, but dese jon boats, dey'll gitcha through. Isaac an Andre may hafta git out and push evah once in a while, but ya kin make it all right. Not many o da buckrah takes dat cut cause dere boats draws too much water. It bout five mile as da crow fly to the South Newport. Dat's where it run into Sapelo Sound. But, it closer tuh ten wit all da crooks an turns. Ya mights wants tuh stop jest atter ya gits into da cut. Dey's a sandbar where ya kin spend da night. Ya gits out early tamorra ya kin make it fo dark. When ya gits ta where da big river runs inta da sound dey's anuddah good place to stop. Gittin cross dat stretch o water can be powerful hard. Ya'll start early an head southwest til ya gits tuh da top o Sapelo. Ya bes able ta see it when ya gits into da river. Den run down da marsh edge fo bout a mile an ya'll will come ta da settlement o Chucalate. Dat's where da Arab be. Dey normally ain't no buckrah dere but ya gots tuh be keerful. One o' ya go in fust an find da Arab. He'll tell ya what tuh do."

"What'll you do now, Micah?" Kimba asked.

"I'se gonna git off here an make my way back. Jes keep on headin' south til ya meets up wit da big river an' ya'll be jes'fine. Dey ain't no mo settlements on dis side o da island. It be all marshland, clear down tuh da south end. Take keer o yoselves. Tell da Arab I wuz askin bout im."

Ka'le maneuvered the boat close to the marsh where a small beach had formed and Micah jumped out. He waved goodbye and vanished into the grass.

****

Enoch woke to the distant sound of a bugle, announcing reveille. Fort Morris was stirring and he needed to be on the road. He had slept longer than he intended. He prodded Caleb and Jim.

"Get up fellas! We overslept. Get your gear together and let's get on the road."

Caleb sat up and yawned. He scratched his bearded chin and coughed to clear his throat.

"Ain't we got no time to eat?" he asked, peevishly.

"No. We've gotta be in Midway by ten o'clock. That's close to five miles, so get a move on."

Fifteen minutes later they were bustling down the road toward Midway. Nero trailed along behind, darting from one side to the other, exploring the smells left by other dogs.

Congregationalists seeking religious freedom founded Midway in the 1750's. Both Lyman Hall and Button Gwinnett were members of the community. Both signed the Declaration of Independence. Midway sat astride the major north-south artery connecting Savannah to Darien and Fort Frederica, the southernmost outpost of the British Empire in America. Midway became a thriving farming community

"Here's what we're gonna do," Enoch said as the steeple of Midway church appeared above the trees. "These folks will be in church til noontime." He flipped open his watch. "It's ten-fifteen now. We're gonna *borrow* one of them big carriages and light out for Darien. We'll have at least an hour and a half jump on em. They won't know who took it or where it's goin so I don't think we'll have to worry. We'll sell the rig in Darien and get some money. Caleb, you've spent some time on Sapelo. If we get over there, is there anyway they can get past without us seeing them?"

"Anybody coming down from the north by boat has to go through Doboy Sound. From the southern tip of Sapelo you can see clear across the sound. It's maybe a little over a half mile wide there."

A hearty rendition of *A Mighty Fortress is our God* drifted out the open windows of the church. Only a couple of groomsmen lazed about the church yard. Most of the rigs were parked behind the church in a stand of pines. The horses were either tethered or hobbled so they could forage for food.

"Jim, I want you to walk up to the front of the church and engage those boys in conversation. Tell'em you're just up from Sunbury and you're looking for a place to rest and get something to eat. Something like that. Just keep'em occupied for five or ten minutes til Caleb and me can hitch up a rig. We'll pull off through the trees and head down the road out of sight. When we are clear, I'll let out a sharp whistle. That'll be your signal to join us. Got that?"

"Sure, Enoch. I'll have a little fun with those boys. Maybe I can git'em to do a little dance for me. Offer em a tuppence. They love that hard candy at the grocery store. Do most anything for it. You boys go on. I'll take care of this."

Enoch waited until the boy's backs were turned before he and Caleb darted across the churchyard. He saw a marvelous rig with small wheels in front and larger ones in back. It was a phaeton with two leather covered seats. It also had an accordion top folded across the back. That'll come in handy if it rains, he thought. The two sorrels that pulled it were hobbled nearby.

"Caleb, you get the one under the tree and I'll get the other one," he said. "The harness is under the buggy."

Within a few minutes both horses were in the traces with their hames drawn tight. Enoch looped the chains over the hooks of the doubletrees and they were ready.

"Come on Caleb, let's get out of here before someone comes out back to use the privy." The wooden outhouse was only fifty feet away.

Jim heard the whistle and flipped a coin to the black that was dancing for him.

"Thank you kindly, boys. I'll be heading into town now. Hope that place you told me about has got some good fried chicken. I haven't had any good fried chicken since I left Charleston," he lied.

"How far is it to Darien, Jim," Enoch asked, when they were safely through town and headed south on the post road.

"Bout thirty-five or forty miles I reckon. Normally I'd say you could make it in a long day, day and a half, on horseback. With all the rains we've had lately I spec it'll take two maybe three in a buggy. The roads are gonna be in pretty bad shape."

"How long do you think it'll take those niggers to get to Doboy sound by boat, Caleb?"

"Lemme see," he said. "They left Ossabaw five days ago, on Tuesday. That puts 'em on the north side of Sapelo today or tomorrow. Another three days minimum, including rest, puts em in Doboy Sound on Wednesday, probably Thursday. I don't see how they can do it any faster than that."

"That gives us just two days to get to Darien and sell this rig. Then we have to find a boat and get over to Sapelo. We'll push on tonight until we can't see and get up at first light tomorrow. I want to be in Darien tomorrow night"

"That's a tall order, Enoch," Jim said. "You'll kill these horses if you do that"

Enoch's eyes blazed. He would not be deterred.

"The horses be damned, we're going to be in Darien tomorrow night."

****

Ka'le found the entrance to the north-south cut along St. Catherines's western shore with little problem. True to Micah's word there was the sand bar sitting in the middle of the creek. Beyond the bar he could see that the creek began to narrow considerably. That was good. The smaller the waterway the less likely it would be taken by others. The larger waterway just west of there, the Mollclark River, was the preferred route for commercial traffic and larger boats.

"All right now," Ka'le said. "Les move on down to da bottom end o' dat bar so's nobody kin see us from the big river. We gone put in fo dark so's Isaac kin cotch us some shrimps. I's sho nuff ready fo some."

The light was fading across the vast expanse of marsh to the west before the campsite was completed. Isaac grabbed his cast net and walked out into the water. He tied the pull rope to his left wrist and gathered up the ring of weights in his right hand. With a quick pivot of his torso he flung the net out over the water. The weights unfurled forming a perfect circle as the net dropped onto the surface of the water. It sank beneath the surface and Isaac pulled on the rope to close the ring entrapping whatever it had surrounded. He dragged the net back to the shore and inspected the contents.

"Whooee!" he exclaimed! "Dey mus' be two o mo pound o shrimps in here. An a few crabs too."

He dumped the contents onto the beach for Queen and Cassie to gather up and clean while he went back for another cast. When he was finished the party had an abundance of seafood for their supper.

"Isaac, you'n Andre git a fire goin," Ka'le said. "Build a canebrake behind it so ya caint see it from da river. Kimba an' me'll see things is tied down fo da night."

It was past nine. The dying embers from the cookfire cast a red glow across the group as they sat huddled on the sand. They were at once both satisfied and reflective.

"De Lawd, He been good tuh us," Queen said, breaking the silence. "He done brought us dis food an He done kep' us safe. He hepped us tuh find old Micah an He hepped us tuh git dis far. Yep. He mighty good tuh us."

"Amen," Kimba said. "We kinda one big fambly out here on dis little bar. It da fust time in my life I don gots nobody tellin me whut I gots tuh do. It sho feel good." He paused before adding. "But, it be a mite skeery." He sighed contentedly as they sat there for a while longer, each lost to his own thoughts.

Cassie rolled out her spread on the sand. She lay there covered with a heavy blanket against the autumn chill. A brisk wind blew in from the east bringing relief from the nighttime insects. The heavens were filled with stars. She could almost reach out and touch them. She turned to look for Cassieopeia. There she was, far to the north, spinning around the North Pole. Cassie was comforted just to see the familiar grouping of stars, to know that the heavens were still in order. She imagined Aba and Mose and the other departed saints up there, sitting with the Queen of Ethiopia, looking down and watching over her and her family. She drifted off to sleep, comforted and at peace.

Andre heard voices in the distance. He was running across the battlefield looking for Louis. He knew that he had left him here near this shattered gun carriage.

"Where is he?" The voices grew louder. He struggled up from the darkness. He sat up, realizing it was a dream. But the voices were real. They were coming from the north. Out on the river. He poked Ka'le.

"Ka'le, wake up," he whispered.

He put his finger to his lips and pointed north. Ka'le rolled over, instantly alert. He listened intently, cupping his ear to receive all the sound. They were over a hundred yards from the main channel of the River. The sand bar was four feet high between their campsite and the passing boat.

"Sounds lak a coast boat takin' stuff from down island tuh da nawth fields. One o dem folks be black. Da uddah one, he buckrah. I don figger dey kin see us down here. Long's we don make no fuss dey'll pass us rat on by."

The voices receded into the distance. Andre stood to see across the bar and up the river. He saw the stern of a small cargo boat as it disappeared behind the marsh. He gestured that they were gone before he nudged Kimba and Isaac. They crossed over the bar to wake the women. He stood for a moment to take in the beauty of Cassie's face as she slept. He reminded himself how lucky he was to have such a beautiful young woman. "As beautiful within as she is without," he thought. "She is the brightest, most intelligent person I have ever known."

" Cassie," he whispered. "I just want to stand here and look at you. When you are asleep like that you have the face of an angel. I'm so glad that you came with the Admiral to Buley. I can't imagine a life without you."

Cassie turned on her side, sensing someone's presence. She opened her eyes to see Andre squatting a few feet away, staring at her.

"What is it, Andre?" She sat up with a start. "Is something wrong?"

"No, Cassie, I just wanted to look at you. You are so peaceful and pretty in your sleep."

Queen began to stir. She had heard the tail end of Andre's soliloquy and despite not understanding the language she certainly understood the sentiment.

"Cass, I do reckon dis boy be love-struck. Soon's we gits to Florida ya'll kin git hitched up lak de buckrah do, seeings how ya'll both be free. I figgers dey'll be some preacher man in dis place we's goin' tuh an' he'll marry ya up."

Andre blushed. He hadn't intended for Queen to hear his comments. He was embarrassed. He had spent no time alone with Cassie's mother and wasn't at all sure how she felt about this stranger coming into their lives and stealing her daughter away.

"What did your mother say, Cassie, I'm still having trouble with English? You'll have to teach me."

"Well, first of all what my mother speaks isn't exactly English. It's Geechee, a language peculiar to these islands. What she said was that she looks forward to our getting married at Fort Mose by a priest just like the white folks do."

Andre's face creased into a huge smile.

"I wasn't quite sure how she felt about me taking you away from her. I'm relieved that she approves. Tell her that I love you and that I will take good care of you. I wish we were there already. I can't wait."

Cassie took her mother's hand.

"Thank you, Mama, for welcoming Andre into our life. He wants me to tell you that he loves me very much and that he will take care of me. I love him too, Mama. I never thought I could love anyone so much. And, we'll take care of you too, when we get to Fort Mose. I understand the Spanish allow the freedmen to run things at the fort. There should be opportunities for us in the big town nearby. It's called St. Augustine. Just imagine, a new life. Free."

Kimba took his gig into the shallows looking for the telltale signs of flounders settling into the sand. Within minutes he had speared three. Queen and Cassie prepared them for breakfast along with pan bread. They finished eating and stowed their belongings in the boats just as the orange fireball edged above the spartina.

"Let's git goin'," Ka'le said. "Micah say it gon take mos' da day tuh git tuh da bottom o da island. Ya kin see how narrow it gits downriver.

I jes hopes we don hasta git out an push da boats. Iffen we do I don know whedder we gon make it by dark.

"Cassie, read dat map. Tell me iffen dere's any other folks tween here an Sapelo whut might hep us."

"No sir," Cassie said, after studying the map for a few minutes. "It looks like there's nothing but marsh all the way."

"All right den. Boys we gots ta make dese oars sing today. Don wanna git stuck on dis creek tonight."

CHAPTER THIRTY-SEVEN

THE EXHAUSTED HORSES WERE bent over the log trough, inhaling great draughts of water. Their lathered sides heaved with each intake. Enoch had pushed them to the brink of their endurance. On Sunday night they rode until darkness forced them to stop. Enoch found a small waystation where they were able to buy some grain. The horses were fed and bedded down in the livery stable behind the tavern. The three slept in the hayloft above to conserve their dwindling reserves. They were back on the road before good light. The carriage pulled into Darien as dusk settled over the town.

"I'll tell you, I didn't think we could make it," Jim said. "I gotta give you credit, Enoch. When you set your mind to do something, you do it."

"Yeah, but now we gotta get these horses cooled down and rested before we try to find a buyer for the rig. You boys take care of that and I'll look around for a boat."

Darien was built on a bluff overlooking a large tributary of the Altamaha River. The Scots had called it New Inverness. Here, the river began to disperse itself across a wide sedimentary delta that extended for fifteen miles into the Atlantic. The main river emerged into Altamaha Sound, near the northern edge of St. Simons Island. The tributary, which bore the name of the town, flowed into Doboy Sound just south of Sapelo.

Enoch walked down the bluff to the docks where there were several coastal freighters moored. He also saw several smaller boats, belonging to planters on the numerous small islands of the delta. Some were unloading rice, indigo and naval stores while others were taking on supplies for the return trip.

"You fellas know the Spalding's on Sapelo?" he asked of two men who were loading sacks of flour into their boat.

"Yes sir," one of them responded. "We farm a spread up on Blackbeard Island. The owner leases it from Mr. Spalding."

"Hey, that's great," Enoch said. "My name's Enoch Penrose. My Pa sent me down from Savannah to see Mr. Spalding. We bought some mules from him a few years back and Pa was hoping he might have some more for sale now. He saw an advertisement in the paper last week and sent me down here to lay claim to six of em if he still has em."

"Pleased to meet you, Mr. Penrose. My name's Gordon Longfellow and this here's Luke Powell. You may be in luck. We got four mules from him a few days ago and there wuz eight or ten more in the pen."

Enoch was amused that his fabrications may have actually been rooted in fact.

"Do you fellas think you might give me and my two boys a ride over to Sapelo?" Enoch asked. "I'd sure appreciate it."

"Don't see why not," Longfellow replied tersely. "Sides, it'd be good to have some company. It's near twenty miles to Sapelo Landing. We get an early start in the morning. The tide'll be going out and we can get to Wolf Island by dark. They's kind of a river crossroads there with lots of traffic. Old man Joshua Elliot opened up a store there a coupla years back. He has a few rooms to let out. We'll stay there overnight and drop you at Sapelo the next day. Then we have to make the open water run up to Blackbeard. It'll cost you a shilling apiece at Elliot's for room and board."

"You're most kind, sir. I'll be happy to pay you for the transport. It's a mighty big favor to us."

"Naw, don't think nothing of it. It's the Christian thing to do. Always take the chance to help out your fellow man."

Enoch made his way back to the town. He found Jim and Caleb at the livery stable where they had washed and groomed the sorrels. They were contentedly munching on bags of oats.

"You boys won't believe what a stroke of luck I had. I found a boat that's going past Sapelo tomorrow. They agreed to give us a ride. We'll be there by Wednesday afternoon. We just have to hope and pray the niggers haven't got there before us. What do you think Caleb?"

"It'd be sumpin if they make it before Thursday or Friday. That's a mighty lotta water to cross and ya know they gotta stop for food and rest. If they don't think we're chasing em they ain't no reason for them to hurry. If we're there by Thursday, we'll catch 'em." He grinned at the thought, tobacco juice dribbling from the corners of his mouth.

Enoch and Jim entered the small office located at the front of the stable. The proprietor who had taken their payment for feed was hunched over a rolltop desk poring over his ledgers. The oil lamp hanging overhead provided little light. The wizened little man adjusted his spectacles and squinted at the murky page.

"Good evening, sir," Enoch said.

The little man looked at the intruder over the top of his rimless glasses.

"My name is Hiram Penrose. I am here on an errand for my father to buy some mules from Mr. Spalding out on Sapelo. We'll be buying a six team wagon and driving back up to Savannah. We won't be needin' these sorrels and that fine rig. I was wondering if you might make me a decent offer for them? We'll also be needing to buy that wagon and harness when we get back from Sapelo. So, if we can come to terms on the rig, I'll ask you to see if you can find one for us in our absence."

The man was quiet for a minute or two. He saw an opportunity to make a handsome profit on the two transactions. He already knew of a buyer in Ashintilly who was looking for just such a rig as a gift for his daughter's wedding. And he was certain he could find a suitable wagon for these men while they were gone. He didn't want to appear too eager. If he played this right he'd be able to buy that piece of property north of town. He'd had his eye on it for years. It would give him a place to raise horses and mules for his livery business.

"Well, I ain't got much call for such fancy rigs around here. If I take it off your hands it may sit around for months before I sell it. I can't afford to have my money tied up like that for long. Some notes I took in last month done lost half their value."

Enoch had dealt with his kind before when he ran Ossabaw. He'd play along until he knew what the old codger was up to.

"It's a mighty fine rig with good harness and two of the finest horses in the territory," Enoch said.

"Will you take payment in continental certificates or do you want specie?" the man asked.

"I prefer specie. Good solid coin holds its value."

"Aye, it does," the stable owner agreed. "But I'm a little short on hard money right now. I'll give you twenty-five pounds for the rig and horses, half in coin and half in certificates."

Enoch frowned.

"Sir, you insult me. They're worth at least seventy-five pounds in coin; six hundred in notes," Enoch said. "If that's your best offer we'll just drive them back to Savannah."

Sensing his dreams evaporating, the man quickly changed his tune.

"I tell you what. I'll give you twenty pounds in coin and three hundred in continentals. I think that's fair."

Enoch was in no mood to dicker. He needed to settle on a price and get ready for tomorrow.

"Very well, sir. You drive a hard bargain but I'm anxious to get on with my business here in your fair town. Now if you'll prepare the bill of sale we'll be on our way."

Enoch smiled cynically as he signed his dead brother's name and took the bag of coins. He folded the notes and stuffed them in his vest pocket.

"Thank you, sir. I look forward to seeing you again in a few days. I trust you can find a suitable wagon for me."

"I'm certain I can sir." He stood to shake hands. "It's been a pleasure doing business with you."

Visions of that horse farm filled his head. He could net fifty pounds or more on the two transactions. He had no thought for the sheriff's visit he would receive in a few days.

There was a bathhouse behind the tavern. Enoch treated the three to their first real bath since leaving Savannah. The tubs were old converted tobacco hogsheads found abandoned on the wharf and sawn in two. The men shaved then soaked for an hour. After a hearty dinner of steak and potatoes with ale they were off to their room upstairs. Clean bodies, clean sheets and full stomachs. Sleep came fast.

Enoch was up before dawn. He rousted the others and they stumbled down to a breakfast of flapjacks, molasses, sausage and hot coffee.

"Why don't we just stay here," Caleb said. "I could get used to this."

"Yeah, I just bet you could," Enoch said. "How long do you think that money'll last? And how long do you think it'll be before someone from Midway comes nosing around and finds that rig we stole? Naw, we gotta keep moving. And don't forget why we're here in the first place." The look returned. His eyes narrowed as if he was focusing his thoughts. "I'm gonna find that girl if it's the last thing I ever do."

****

The creek twisted and turned as it followed the contours of the island. Oxbows doubled back on themselves, sometimes requiring a mile on the water to achieve a hundred feet down stream. Andre looked at the map again but could not make out their position. There were no details or landmarks until they reached Sapelo Sound. They simply had to forge ahead and hope that they made the sound before sunset.

Cassie passed out hardtack and water to the men as they labored. Gulls and terns soared overhead, diving to snatch silvery fish from near the surface. Osprey nests dotted the marsh, perched high up in the stark skeletons of dead trees. An occasional manatee floated by, snuffling along the bottom in search of its favorite grasses.

"I reckon it be close on tuh three o'clock." Ka'le said "We gots maybe fo mo hours o daylight. We don see that big river fo then we's gotta pull in and find a place tuh bed down fo da night."

"There hasn't been any place to stop all day," Cassie said. "I just pray that we make it before dark."

Silence settled over the boats as they continued down the serpentine waterway. Isaac stood to shake the cramps from his legs.

"Whooee," he shouted. It had been less than two hours. "Look dere. Straight ahead. Dat mus' be da bar Micah wuz talkin bout. Da water gits wider beyond dere. Dat gots tuh be da Sapelo Sound."

Millenia of tidal crosscurrents sluicing through the cut had deposited sand to form the large bar where it met the river. The bar was a near twin to the one they camped on the night before.

"Hallelujah," Queen shouted. "Now we don gotta spend da night wit all dem bugs on da river. Isaac an Kimba, go cotch us some mo fish an shrimp?"

"Sho nuff, Miss Queen. Soon's we gits settled," Isaac said.

This time Ka'le beached his boat on the northern tip of the arrow shaped sandbar. It was wider, but not as tall as the one from the night before. They would need to be careful with their fire to shield it from boats passing on the sound. The women set about the task of building a fire while Kimba, Isaac and Andre prepared to fish. Andre asked Isaac to show him how to cast the net.

"Here, Andre," he said. "I'll show ya."

He slipped the draw rope over his wrist and coiled the line in his left hand. He continued by placing the ring and the weights in the same hand while picking up the opposite weights with his right hand. Then he pivoted and swung his right arm over his left while releasing the rope and ring. The net arced across the water landing with a loud plop before sinking. Isaac pulled in the net and dumped the contents. He then handed the net to Andre

"Here, Andre, you try it."

Andre copied the motions that Isaac had performed and flung the net around his body. His pivot was too fast and his release point too late. The net snapped back landing on Andre's head and draping over his body. The onlookers convulsed in laughter.

"I guess I'd better leave the fishing to Isaac," he said sheepishly. "If you depended on me we'd starve to death."

Cassie attempted to translate his words between spasms of laughter. She helped to extricate him from the net and handed it back to Isaac.

"You'd better hang on to this, Isaac," she said. "The only thing Andre can catch is Andre."

Queen scoured a scruffy patch of reeds for scraps of driftwood. She didn't see the thick black form lying under the washed up palm fronds. She reached to pull on a limb partially covered by the palms. She felt a sharp sting on her left hand. The water moccasin emptied its venom into her flesh before slithering into the water.

"Oh my God!" she screamed. "I been bit! I been bit!"

Cassie ran to her mother.

"Mama, mama. What was it?"

" I's fraid it wuz a cottonmouth. An a big un."

Ripples on the placid water followed the black head as it swam toward the opposite shore. The men came running. Queen stared at her hand in disbelief. It had already begun to swell.

"Lemme see dat," Ka'le said.

He pulled his knife and cut a cross between the two fang marks. Queen cried out. Ka'le put her hand to his mouth. He sucked on the wound. He spat out the mixture of blood and venom. He sucked again and again until nothing was left, then led the dazed Queen over to the camp and helped her to lie down.

"We's gotta git her tuh dat place on Sapelo. Dey's gotta have some medicines dere dat'll hep er. Come on. Les git back in da boats. Dey ain't much moon but we'll hafta do it."

Only a dim silhouette of the island was visible in the distance.

"Andre, ya be da sailorman here. Git a fix on dat point down dere an take da lead."

CHAPTER THIRTY-EIGHT

THE BOAT LEFT THE dock in Darien just as the sun rose over the delta. Hightower stood in the rear pushing and pulling on a long oar, like a Venetian gondola. The other man sat midship, facing aft with his oars fitted into swiveling oarlocks on the gunwales. He provided the bulk of the power while his partner kept them in midstream. The tide had begun its ebb an hour before and would be at its lowest in five hours.

"You fellas are welcome to pick up those extra oars and lend a hand. It'll get us to Mr. Elliott's camp earlier. He has some mighty fine home brew there."

That was all the incentive that Caleb needed. He grabbed one of the oars and began paddling furiously.

"Better slow down there, boy," said the helmsman. "You'll wear yourself plumb out in a mile or so. Slow and easy works best. Didn't yore mama ever tell you the story of the tortoise and the hare?"

Caleb answered the man with a blank stare, but heeded the advice. Jim Pelham took up the other oar and began a rhythmic stroke on the opposite side. The boat moved along at an accelerated pace, directly into the sun. Enoch sat in the front of the boat with Nero at his feet. He was sprawled out on several sacks of flour, his eyes closed, envisioning the culmination of a dream so long denied him. She was out there somewhere, on those waters

****

Queen's arm was three times its normal size. She lay in the bottom of the boat, unconscious, sweating profusely. Cassie repeatedly dipped a rag into the water to wipe her face. Kimba had applied a tourniquet above Queen's elbow in an attempt to slow the spread of the poison. They had been underway for over an hour.

"Better loosen that rope around her arm for a while," Andre said. "If you cut off circulation too long it'll cause blood poisoning."

Cassie released the rope. The color slowly returned to Queen's arm. But the red streaks radiating from the bite began to spread ominously.

"You see anything, Andre?" Cassie asked. There was desperation in her voice. "I don't know if Mama can make it much longer?"

"I can barely make out the shoreline. It's still a half-mile or so. We've passed the point we were aiming for. The settlement should be just ahead."

"Please hurry, I don't want my mama to die."

Andre and Isaac returned to their rowing with renewed dedication. They headed toward a small point of light to the southeast, Ka'le and Kimba struggling to keep up. That must be Chucalate.

Ka'le called across the gulf between the boats.

"Cassie, tell Andre tuh wait up when he git's close in. We's gotta be shore dey ain't no buckrah round. I gone go in fust an check thangs out."

The lead boat slipped silently through the wavy sea grass and slid onto the bank. Within seconds Ka'le's boat pulled along side. He threw his mooring line over to Isaac and stepped ashore.

"Ya'll stay here an be quiet. I gone be back soon's I kin."

He disappeared into the darkness.

Cassie stroked her mother's hair while she tried to cool her fever-ravaged body. Queen had brief spells of conciousness. The swelling seemed to have stopped but her arm took on an ugly purple-green hue. Cassie placed an ear to her chest.

"Her heartbeat is very faint, Andre," she said. "If Ka'le doesn't return soon it may be too late."

"Ka'le knows how sick Queen is. He'll come back as fast as he can.

Cassie, tell Isaac and Kimba to give me a hand and let's see if we can get Queen up on the bank."

Andre and Isaac stood knee deep on either side of the boat while Kimba kneeled beside Queen. He and Cassie raised her to a sitting position so that they could lift her over the side. They struggled, half-lifting, half-pulling until she lay on the grass. Cassie placed a rolled up blanket under Queen's head and covered her with another. And they waited.

Kimba saw it first. The sea of reeds parted to a parade of torches and lanterns.

"Look dere," he said. "Dey's a whole passel o' folks acomin'. I sho' pray dat be Ka'le an not da buckrah."

The majestic figure leading the group was well over six feet tall. He held his lantern high to survey the scene. He wore a brightly colored strip of cloth around his neck, orange and green and black. It draped over a shirt that came to his knees. On his head he wore a round cap of matching fabric. This could only be Bulallah, *The Arab.*

"Cassie, dis be Master Bulallah," Ka'le said. "He da overseer fo dis part o da island."

"Mr. Bulallah, please, can you help my mama. She's fading fast. I can hardly feel her pulse."

"Step aside child," the man said. "Let me have a look at her."

Everyone stepped back in the commanding presence of the Arab. He got down on his knees and touched Queen's neck. He felt her arm above the wrist. He pulled her eyelid up and peered into her eye.

"You men pick her up and follow me," he commanded.

The four men from the boats lifted Queen from the ground and followed Bulallah. The path emerged from the marsh and crossed an open field where remnants of a summer garden lay rotting and smelly. They passed between two rows of small cabins. At the end of the path stood a larger, whitewashed building. This was Bulallah's house.

"Bring her inside and take her to the kitchen," he said.

Two young girls ran ahead. When the party made its way through the house to the kitchen they found them waiting beside a table covered with quilts and a sheet.

"Put her on the table," the booming voice said.

"Simon, get my bag. Alice, bring me hot water. Everyone else stand back and give me room."

Bulallah took scissors and cut away Queen's dress, exposing her upper body. He examined the bite on her hand and the spreading red streaks.

"Hand me the bag."

He took out four small green bottles and emptied their contents into a pan. He mixed the powders and poured in a small amount of oil, making a paste. He applied the paste to her hand and wrapped it with a strip of clean cloth. He took a razor and made an incision in a vein on her arm. He applied more of the paste. He did the same where the veins ran to the heart, below the shoulder.

"Ka'le told me that it's been over two hours since the snake bit her. I don't know if I can draw out enough poison to save her. Cottonmouth venom is the strongest of any snake I know. If it was a big one, I may be too late. Y'all go on and eat. I'll watch her. I'll call you if anything changes."

Kimba led them out of the kitchen and into the dining room. Cassie hesitated. She couldn't bring herself to leave her mother. Bulallah sensed her distress.

"It's all right girl. You can stay if you want. I'll have Alice bring you a plate."

It was well past midnight when Cassie felt the hand on her shoulder. She had fallen asleep in the chair at Queen's feet, her head resting on the table. It was Bulallah. She knew from the look in his eyes what he was going to say.

"I'm sorry child. I was too late. Your mother's gone."

Cassie stared at him in disbelief. Queen couldn't be dead. She was too strong. She was indestructible. The realization that Queen was truly gone began to spread slowly across her features. She drooped in the chair and put her head in her hands. The initial tears transmuted themselves into racking sobs. Bulallah lifted her from the chair and held her until the heaving stopped. He pushed her to arms length. He looked down into her reddened eyes.

"No one knows the pain of losing a loved one any more than I do. From the time I was taken from Africa until now, I have seen two wives die and four children perish. It is never easy but Allah in his wisdom will help you through this. You must trust Him."

Cassie was confused. Who is this Allah he speaks of and what does he have to do with me. Bulallah saw the puzzled look on her face and smiled.

"I am a Muslim. I believe in the prophet Mohammed and the God, Allah. Allah is our name for the God Jehovah that you worship. Whatever name we give Him, He is our strength."

"Oh!" Cassie said. "I've heard my grandmother and some of the elders at Roselawn speak of Allah. I never really understood it. I've lived the past five years in a convent where I was studying to become a nun. But I know you are right. My God, your Allah, has seen me through some very difficult times. I pray he will see me through this as well."

She began to cry again.

"But it's so hard to lose your mother. With her passing, all my family is gone. Thank God for Ka'le and Kimba. They're like family. And Andre. I couldn't go on without him."

"Is he the young man who was with you?"

"Yes sir. He and I are to be married. It's a long story. He came to Savannah with the French army to fight the British. We were kind of thrown together through strange circumstances. After a while we fell in love. I don't know what Ka'le told you but I had to leave my home for the convent to escape a man who threatened me. Well that man showed up at the convent and we had no choice but to run."

"Ka'le told me a little of the story. Do you have reason to believe that this man is still after you?"

"Yes sir. I do. And, now with his father gone and his brother dead he seems even more determined to catch me. I don't understand why he's doing this. I asked my mother and her only explanation was that he is crazy and possessed by the devil. He has this terrible birthmark on his face and he speaks with a stutter. Since childhood he's been a loner and he was always getting into trouble with his family. He did something really bad many years ago. No one will say what. And then five years ago he tried to rape me. That's when I was sent away to St. Benedict's. Later he was sent to live on another island and I haven't seen him again until this all started. I thought it was all over with. But, like Mama said, 'with him it'll never be over with'."

"Come," said Bulallah, "we must tell the others and make preparations."

Cassie took a sheet that was lying on the bench beside her and spread it over her mother's body. She gently kissed her before covering her face. Her tears rained down on the white cloth.

The small cemetery occupied a field between the slave quarters and the barns. Most of the crude wooden crosses were gray, weathered by the salt air of the ocean. They passed a mound covered with freshly turned earth, its marker still bright. This was in a separate plot at the far end of the cemetery. A dozen graves occupied the area, each with a star and crescent carved into the upright. This was Bulallah's tribe. Most of the other slaves had converted to Christianity.

"That is my youngest son," he said matter-of-factly, pointing to the mound.

"He drowned in a storm last week while we were helping some others, like you, trying to get to Florida."

Bulallah had held fast to his faith and Mr. Spalding had allowed him to practice it. Five times a day he would spread his prayer rug and bow toward the east to recite his prayers. He read the Quran and kept diaries of his life on the plantation. It was a small concession by his owner in exchange for the faithful services of such a powerful man. Spalding never had problems on the north island.

Cassie, Alice and Alice's mother washed Queen's body and wrapped her in a flowing white sheet. Bulallah sent a man to get one of the pine coffins that he kept in the wood shop. Death always came unexpectedly on these islands. Kimba, Ka'le, Isaac and Andre raised the box to their shoulders and carried it across the yard to the freshly dug grave. It was just past sunrise. Their footprints traced a fresh path through the heavy dew.

"Oh God. Receive this thy servant into Your kingdom. Bless her spirit and bless those she leaves behind. Amen."

And it was over. Just that fast. All that remained of Queen Omoru was laid to rest in a little cemetery on an island she had never known.

"I'll see too it that she gets a proper marker," Bulallah said. "It'll just say Queen. I don't want anyone from the south asking questions.

Come on now. Let's have some breakfast and see what we can do to get you to Florida safely."

Bulallah paced back and forth between the table and the fireplace.

"Are you sure this man, Enoch Penrose, followed you when you left the monastery?"

"Well, no suh," Ka'le said. "We ain't seed him since I left Roselawn. But, knowin' what he done dere an' knowin' what he done befo', I ain't got no reason tuh think he ain't still a chasin us."

"Very well. Here's what I think we should do. I'm going to send Simon and another man down island to get some supplies from the storehouse on Mr. Spalding's place. While they're there they'll nose around to see if any red-faced stranger has shown up. If not we can take you down the main channel and set you on your way. If he's there we gotta go a different way.

"Simon, you and Cletus hitch up the wagon and head on down to Marsh Landing. Tell Mr. Spencer we need five sacks of flour and ten of cornmeal. While you're there ask around among the slaves if any strangers have shown up there in the last few days. You be careful and don't let on why you're asking. If anyone asks why just tell'em you saw some boats come by yesterday headin south and you're curious as to who it was. Soon's you find out get back here fast. You understand?"

"Yes, Papa. We'll be back before it's dark."

Bulallah went over the map with Andre, pointing out a few errors and adding other information. He walked the fields with Ka'le and Kimba. They shared their stories of Africa. They told him of Cassie and Queen and Aba. They explained what had happened in the battle and how Andre and Cassie were thrown together. And they talked of Roselawn and its secrets. When they reurned late in the afternoon Simon was unharnessing the team and loading the sacks into the storehouse.

"Well, son. What did you find out? Are there any strangers down island?" Bulallah asked, impatiently.

"Yes Pa, just as we feared, there are. Besides the red-faced man there are two others. They came over from Darien yesterday with Mr. Longfellow on the supply boat bound for Blackbeard Island."

"That changes things. When you and Cletus finish here come into the house."

"Yes, Pa"

The eight of them were gathered around the same table on which Queen had been laid out. There was a pot of coffee and some rice cakes on the table. Bulallah rose and began to pace anew.

"It would be a lot easier if you could just go down the Duplin River and straight across Doboy Sound to St. Simons. But that route takes you right by Marsh Island. We're going to have to double back a bit and get you into the waterway between Sapelo and Blackbeard. The problem with that is that you'll come out on the ocean side and have to cross open water for about five or six miles before you can cut into the creeks behind Wolf Island. I can draw you a map to get you through those waters. Simon and Cletus will get you down Blackbeard Creek to the ocean but you'll be on your own after that. When do you want to start?"

"We's been on da run fo a spell an we's mighty tired. Iffen ya don mind we'd like tuh rest up fo a day befo we sets out again."

"That's fine with me. That'll let me catch up on some more of the news from up north and give me a chance to get to know you better.

CHAPTER THIRTY-NINE

WITH JIM AND CALEB'S added muscle the boat reached Elliot's camp by noon. There was enough time left in the day to get to Sapelo before sundown.

"If you fellows are up to it I'd like to get on across the sound today," Longfellow said. "We've made good time this far and it won't be a problem getting there before sundown."

Caleb was first to speak. "Does that mean we ain't gonna stop at Elliot's. I shore was looking forward to some of that home brew."

"We'll have time to stop for a rest and to get something to eat. If it's all right with Mr. Penrose here you can have all the drink you want. Better go easy though. He makes a mighty powerful brew."

By two they had cast off from the dock on Wolf's Island. With full stomachs and light heads they rowed toward Sapelo. Enoch stood in the bow as they entered the open water of Doboy Sound. He could see the plantation house sitting on the high ground where the Duplin River met the sound. The water took on a decided chop as the swells broke across the many bars along the oceanfront. He had to take a seat to avoid being thrown out of the boat.

"It can get a little rough out here in the open water," Longfellow shouted over the wind. "If you ain't got your sea legs you better stay seated."

Aided by the offshore winds and the incoming tide, the row across the sound took little more than an hour. At six, the mooring lines were secured at Marsh Landing dock. A stately man dressed in riding clothes walked down from the house to greet them.

"Mr. Spalding, this is Mr. Enoch Penrose from up Savannah way. He says he's looking to buy some of the mules you advertised in the paper up there. Said he was down here a few years back with his Pa."

Spalding took in the birthmark.

"Why, yes. I do remember you Mr. Penrose. How'd those mules you bought work out?"

"Just great Mr. Spalding. That's why my Pa wanted to get some more. And those two jennies worked out great in the gardens."

"That's good to hear. I'll show you the stock we have left in the morning. Meanwhile you men come on up to the house and get cleaned up. We have a bunkhouse you can use. Longfellow, you and Luke gonna stay over tonight?"

"Why, yessir, Mr. Spalding, if it's all right with you. These fellows gave us a hand rowing so we made it over sooner than we expected. We'll get an early start in the morning so's we can get back to Blackbeard a day early. We got a lot of work to do before the weather turns. By the way, Mr Turner asked me to drop these tins of pipe tobacco off for you. He just got them in."

"Thank you. I've been expecting those. I've almost run out."

After dinner the men gathered on the veranda overlooking the river. Spalding passed out cigars and offered the men bourbon.

"We don't get many visitors out here after summer's gone," he said. "It's good to have you gentlemen here. I understand the British are still in control at Savannah and Sunbury. We've seen a few of their ships off the coast but none have come into the sound. The waters get a little shallow for those big boats."

"Yeah, that was quite a fight. The French and colonials had a lots more men than the Brits but they messed around too long. They let them bring in re-inforcements and build up the defenses before they attacked. By that time it was too late. I understand they killed almost a thousand men." Enoch was careful not to implicate himself with too much information. He didn't know Spalding's political leanings and certainly didn't want to alienate the man.

"Sir, we've had a long day and if you don't mind I think we'll turn in," Enoch said with an exaggerated yawn. "I'm looking forward to seeing those mules tomorrow."

"Quite right Mr. Penrose. Have a good night's rest and I'll see all of you for breakfast, before Mr. Longfellow gets underway."

Enoch hung back as they walked to the guesthouse. He motioned to Pelham and Hawkins to do the same.

"We gotta be careful," he said. "We can't talk much about what's going on in Savannah. Just gotta be kinda neutral. If he asks what we were doing just tell him we were over on Ossabaw and didn't get involved. When Longfellow leaves I'll talk to Spalding about why we're really down here."

The shrill call of a rooster, just outside his window, woke Enoch at dawn. He picked up a stone from the hearth and hurled it out the window at the offending bird. Between the sourmash brew at Elliot's and the bourbon after supper, he had one hell of a hangover. His mouth was dry and tasted of rotten barley. He got dressed and joined the others for breakfast. The Blackbeard Island boat left before seven. Spalding took his hat and coat from the peg by the door and led his visitors to the stables for a look at the mules.

"Mr. Spalding can I speak with you privately for a minute?" Enoch asked.

"Certainly, let's step over here in the sun. My old bones can't take the morning chill like they used to."

"I know what you mean. I've been waking up a trifle stiff myself lately," Enoch said.

"Mr. Spalding, I am interested in your mules but there's a more pressing reason that we're here."

The older man cocked his head with a quizzical look.

"We had a bunch of niggers to run away and we believe they're moving down this way on the water. I tracked them as far as St. Catherine's before I decided to go overland to try and head them off. I didn't want to get nobody else involved. Whoever catches them might just keep 'em. Lord knows so many disappear every year. I know you for an honest man and I know you'll help me if you can."

"Mr. Penrose, I don't know what I can do for you but I'm at your service. I too have been plagued with runaways. Seems the Spanish down in Florida are making it quite appealing for them. I've had several reports of their ships patrolling the waters as far up as Jekyll. How can I help you?"

"I want to post a twenty-four hour watch on the river. I know that if they're trying to get to Florida by water they have to come by here. I don't believe it's possible they've got this far already. Best I can reckon they should come through here in the next day or two. If you'll help me catch them I'm sure my family will make it worth your while."

"No need for that, son. Doing the right thing is its own reward."

The river was no more than two hundred feet wide at that point. No one could pass, day or night, without being seen or heard.

"Caleb, you take the first watch. Jim'll spell you in four hours and then I'll take over. Now, you keep alert, you hear. I don't want you goin to sleep and lettin them slip by."

"Don't you worry, Enoch. I wanta catch them niggers as bad as you do, all the trouble they caused."

****

Ka'le, Kimba and Isaac were asleep in the back room of Bulallah's house. The Arab sat on the front porch with Cassie and Andre.

"Andre, tell me about yourself. How did you wind up in the French army fighting in Savannah, Georgia?" Bulallah asked.

"It's a very long and complicated tale," Andre said.

He related the story of his childhood in Grenada, his sale to the sea captain and his subsequent sale into slavery on Saint-Domingue. He explained how the French needed more soldiers to aid the Americans and how he was pressed into service.

"And how did you and Cassie meet?"

Cassie picked up the story from there.

"I learned French at the monastery and the army needed someone to interpret for them in dealing with the locals. As part of the bargain I was to get my freedom. In the process I got involved in helping the wounded after the battle. Andre was wounded in the head and they wouldn't treat him so we took him back to the plantation for help. That's when we found out that Master Enoch was chasing us and we fled to the monastery on Skidaway Island. He followed us there and so, here we are."

"That's quite a story. When did you realize you loved Andre and decided you would marry him?"

"I had no intention of marrying him or anyone else. I had dedicated myself to God and to serving my people. I intended to return to St. Benedict's, hopefully to become a nun. As we traveled around looking for food we both talked a lot about what we wanted to do, what we wanted in life. I realized he wanted many of the things that I wanted. I came to know him as a kind and loving and gentle man. He was unlike any of the other men I had ever known. But it wasn't until I realized he was going away and I might never see him again that I knew I loved him. I didn't want to lose him. I was very confused and torn between my love of God and my love for Andre. He asked me to wait for him and said that he would come back when he was free, and marry me, no matter how long it took. Even then I was determined to go back and become a nun. Until something very strange happened."

She told Bulallah about that last night before she and Andre parted, before the battle. How he had asked her to marry him and that he would return before dawn for her answer. Then she told him of the dove, the hawk and the owl.

Bulallah was quiet for a long time after she finished her story. He stared off across the marshes toward the east. His thoughts stretched far beyond the reach of his eyes. He was back in Sudan with his family, ruling over his tribe. His medicine man was interpreting the signs and omens for him.

"Back in Africa, before I was taken, I was ruler over a great tribe. I ruled over many people and much land. I had wise men, elders, who interpreted signs and omens for me. Their wisdom helped me to make good decisions for my people. I believe what you witnessed in that field was a sign of Allah's love for you and for Andre. He was giving you His blessing and telling you it was all right to love Andre and to marry him, but that He still needed you to do His work. Sacrificial blood is always a sign of service. Never doubt the power of Allah, God, to speak to you."

Cassie was surprised to hear these same words from this wise man that she had heard from others who heard the story.

"Mr. Bulallah, you've lifted a great weight from me. Even though I had made the decision to go with Andre, there were still lingering doubts that I had done the right thing. I can tell that you are a wise and spiritual man. You obviously have the respect and trust of everyone here. I trust you. I believe you. Thank you."

"When will you be married?" he asked.

"I suppose when we get to Fort Mose," she said.

He looked into her eyes. He could see the eagerness there.

"Would you like to be married before you leave here?"

"Can we do that?" she asked.

"I've been marrying our people for years. Mr. Spalding allows me to do it and he recognizes the marriages as legitimate."

"That would be wonderful. When can we do it?"

"I imagine you will be leaving early tomorrow morning so we should do it today. You wake the men and I'll get everything ready."

Cassie and Andre ran to wake the others. Bulallah headed across the yard to a small building with what resembled a turret on top. It was in fact, the closest thing he could construct to a minaret. It was his mosque.

They were gathered in front of the table where the imam spoke to his people and read the Quran to them. In adition to Andre, Cassie, Ka'le, Kimba and Isaac, there were members of the chief's family and other adherents of Islam in Chucalate.

"Even before Muhammad came and gave us our rules for life," Bulallah began, "there was the wisdom of Abraham and the prophets."

He read from the Quran.

Recall that we took from the prophets their covenant, including Noah, Abraham, Moses, and Jesus, the son of Mary. We took from them a solemn pledge. I will give the scripture and wisdom. Afterwards a messenger willl come to confirm all existing scriptures. You should believe him and support him.

Then he addressed the kneeling couple.

"Do you agree with this, and pledge to fulfill this covenant?" Bulallah asked.

He waited as Cassie translated the words for Andre and then he asked again.

"Do you?"

Cassie and Andre nodded in unison and said,

"We agree."

"For me this is a covenant to carry out the teachings of Muhammad the Prophet. For you it is an agreement to carry out the teachings of Jesus. For all of us it is a pledge to honor those who came before us. May God be with you.

"Now there is one other tradition that we honor here. In my Africa, when a couple began a new family, it was customary to jump over a bundle of sticks to signify the building of a new home. Here we carry on that practice by having newlyweds jump over a stick broom." Bulallah signaled to his wife who produced a mulberry broom tied with colorful ribbons. He took the broom and laid it in front of the couple.

"Now, hold each other's hand and jump over the broom."

After they had complied he embraced them and said,

"I now pronounce you to be husband and wife."

An exultant shout went up from the assembled guests as everyone rushed to congratulate the beaming couple.

"Come," Bulallah said. "We shall prepare the wedding feast."

The big table in Bulallah's dining room was laden with the bounty of the plantation.

The wedding feast lasted until well into the evening. Finally the host rose and declared the party at an end. "I will be sorrowful when you leave but I will celebrate for you, for I know you can look forward to the most precious gift Allah can bestow upon us. Freedom.

"Andre, Cassie, I pray that God will be with you and that you will fulfill your dreams. I hope you have a long and happy life together and that God blesses you with many wonderful children. And to you, Ka'le, Kimba and Isaac, I pray that you live out your lives in peace and freedom. Now we must all get to bed. Tomorrow will be a very busy day.

"Andre, you and Cassie are invited to spend your first married night together in your own cabin. It's just behind the mosque. Good night. I'll see you all in the morning."

The small band stood on the Chucalate dock. Light was breaking in the east. Cletus and Simon were already in their boat. Kimba and Isaac were loading fresh provisions. Andre, Ka'le and Cassie were saying their goodbyes.

"Bulallah, why ya stays here?" Ka'le asked. "Wit all ya knows bout gittin tuh Florida why don you go too."

"Ka'le, if I can help just one of my people find his way to freedom I have done Allah's bidding. He has blessed me. But, who knows? Maybe someday I'll leave and go back to Africa."

He smiled at the thought and then put it from his mind. He shook Andre's hand. "You take good care of this girl, Andre. She'll make you proud. And Ka'le you get these folks to Fort Mose safe and sound." He embraced Cassie.

"Girl, you go on doing God's work. There are a lot of people in Fort Mose that need you. You take care of yourself now."

He was still standing on the dock as they rounded the bend leading to the mouth of Blackbeard Creek.

The creek meandered down the eastern edge of the marsh that divided Blackbeard Island from Sapelo. It would take eight hours to navigate the winding waterway before emerging into the Atlantic. The beaches across the marsh were rumored to contain the buried treasures of Captain Edward Teach, better known as the pirate, Blackbeard.

Cletus and Simon stood on the spit of land separating the creek from the ocean.

"When you get past that last point of land that you can see, there's a small island. Turn west past the island and you'll be in Wolf Creek. Keep going west for about a mile and the creek splits. Take the south fork for another mile or so and you'll be in the Altamaha. You gotta be careful in that part of the creek. There's a trading post about half way through. Try to pass there when it's dark. Usually it's just Mr. Elliot there. Sometimes coastal boats stop for the night. A mile south of there you enter Altamaha sound.

"Cross the sound and go west for a couple of miles, hugging the marsh. Then you turn south again down the broad waterway. From there you just follow the eastern shore and it'll take you right past St. Simons and Jekyll islands. Your map shows you where you can stop for help.

" When you get past Jekyll the next big island is Cumberland. Once you get there you're almost to Florida. The south end of Cumberland sits on the St. Mary's River, the border with Florida. Once across you'll be in Spanish waters and there will be help to get you to Fort Mose.

"Ya'll better stay here tonight and get an early start tomorrow. You don wanta git caught on the ocean at dark You can make it to Wolf Island tomorrow and then sneak past Eliotts early the next day. You'll be on St. Simons that night. From there you can be in Florida in four or five days."

The ocean swells were unusually benign for so late in the fall. They slid down the coast then crossed Doboy Sound as dusk began to settle. The forest along the southern shoreline of Sapelo hid them from Marsh Point. It was well past dark when they pulled ashore on the large hammock at the fork in Wolf Creek. They had been on the water for fifteen hours and were too tired to even eat. They made camp hurriedly and were asleep within minutes.

"All right, ya'll," Ka'le said. "It's time tuh git goin. Iffen Cletus wuz right, we's about an hour or so from the tradin post. I wants us tuh git past dere befo da sun comes up."

Rubbing sleep from their eyes the weary travelers climbed back into their boats for another long day. First light was breaking as they silenced their oars and glided past the marina. There were no lights visible. One boat was tied up at the dock. When they were well past the camp Ka'le exhaled.

"I sho is glad tuh be past dat place. We ain't too far from Darien an' I don want nobody runnin ovah dere wit tales about runaways." He failed to see the lone figure standing on the dock, urinating into the water.

CHAPTER FORTY

ENOCH HAD THE MORNING watch. In the distance a coastal freighter was crossing the sound toward Sapelo. He watched as the heavily laden craft made its tortuous way through the ebbing tide. There were four men at the oars.

"Morning, gentlemen," he called. "Throw me a line and I'll pull you in."

"Thanks, stranger," the man in the bow said.

"We're plum tuckered out from fightin that current. Been at it for bout four hours now. Ever since we left Elliots."

"We were just over there a couple of days ago," Enoch said. "We're down here to buy some mules from Mr. Spalding. Hail from up Savannah way. You fellas come outta Darien?"

"Yeah. We're taking a load up to St. Catherine's."

"We were just up there last week," Enoch said. "There was a big hulla-balloo going on. Seems some niggers ran away and stole a couple of their boats." Enoch waited to see if that news might elicit a response from the man. Instead a voice from the back of the boat answered.

"Funny you should mention that," it said. "I was out pissing off the dock just before light this morning. It was pretty dark but I could swear I saw a couple of boats go past. Couldn't make out who it was but they was four or five folks in em. Don't know if they wuz black or white. You could tell they was bein awful quiet. Thought it was mighty strange that somebody was out on them waters so early. I figgered whoever it was they was up to no good. Coulda been runaways."

Enoch cursed under his breath. " No! There's no way they got past here without us seein em," he muttered. "We've been watchin these waters for two full days now. If that bastard Caleb fell asleep I'll kill him." Gathering his emotions, he returned to the conversation.

"You fellas go on up to the house. I'm sure Mr. Spalding will feed you. If you see a big galoot with yellow hair up there, that'd be Caleb Hawkins. Tell im I'd like for him to come on down here."

"Sure thing, mister. Thanks for the hand."

Caleb came sauntering down the path about five minutes later, picking his teeth with a piece of straw.

"Them fellas said you wanted to see me, Enoch. It ain't my watch for another hour."

"Caleb I told you if you went to sleep and let those niggers get past us I'd kill you."

"What you talking bout, Enoch. They ain't no niggers got past me. I been awake on every watch. Even after midnight. Nosiree! Ain't nobody got past me."

The man's vehement denial led Enoch to believe him.

"Well how do you explain those two boat loads of runaways these fellas saw this morning goin past Elliots?"

Caleb looked flabbergasted.

"That ain't possible, Enoch. We been sittin here for two days. I ain't seen nobody. You ain't seen nobody. And I know old Jim ain't been asleep. He's so skeert o you he won't even pee without yore sayso. They must be some other explanation."

"We've been suckered," Enoch said. "Some way or other they got past us. I don't know how but they did. They musta had some help. There can't be another two boatloads of niggers coming through here. That'd be too much of a coincidence. Come on. Let's get Jim."

"Mr. Spalding, based on what those men told us those must be the runaways we're looking for. I hate to impose any more on your generous hospitality but I'd be mighty obliged if you would let us buy or borrow one of your boats. I assure you we'll bring it back to you just as soon as we catch those niggers. They can't be more'n six hours ahead of us now. With the three of us rowin we oughta catch up to em in a day or two. And we're still gonna need those mules when we get back. And, we'll have some more help to drive em home. That is if I haven't whipped em to death before then."

Spalding looked grim. He replied icily to Enoch's threat.

"I will lend you a boat, Mr. Penrose, on one condition. I do not believe in abusing slaves. One must deal with them firmly but that does not extend to physical abuse. If you catch them you must promise me that no harm will come to them."

Enoch recognized his misstep and was quick to recover.

"Oh, you don't gotta worry, Mr. Spalding. I was just lettin off a little steam. Pa don't allow us to beat the darkies either. I promise you they'll be in fine fettle when we get back here. If it's all right with you we'll get started right away. Don't want em to get too far ahead of us. And if it's not asking too much we'll need a few vittles to tide us over."

"Certainly. See Jonas in the kitchen and he'll fix you up. Good hunting Mr. Penrose. I'll see you back here in a few days."

****

Ka'le breathed a sigh of relief. They had cleared Wolf Island and crossed Altamaha Sound without seeing another soul. They were entering a no man's land of contested waters. Oglethorpe's early fortifications along St. Simons, Jekyl, and Cumberland had been deserted for many years. The occasional British or Spanish ship sailed up the inland waterway but couldn't get past the narrows around the abandoned Fort Frederica.

"Kimba, I reckon we be past the wust part," he said. "Bulallah say dey ain't no mo English folk down here."

"Dat may be so," Kimba said, "but dey's plenty mo thangs tuh worry bout. We gots lotsa mo open water tuh git through cordin tuh dat map. I reckon we gots nother fifty miles or so befo we gits tuh Florida. Den I don know how far it be tuh dat place we's lookin fo. Naw suh! Dey's plenty mo tuh go."

Ka'le nodded in agreement.

"You be right, brother. I spec we oughta start lookin fo a place tuh stop fo da night. Gone be gittin dark soon."

They had covered two thirds of the distance from the Altamaha to the open water between St. Simons and Jekyl. With continued good weather they could make St. Andrew's sound tomorrow. Then all that would lie between them and Florida would be Cumberland Island.

****

Twelve miles to their north, Enoch was checking his watch. He came to the same conclusion. After stopping at Elliot's to see if any other information on runaways had come to light, and finding none, they had resumed their journey.

"I figger they can't be more'n six or eight hours ahead of us now," Enoch said, as he threw more wood on the fire.

"If we can close the gap to three hours tomorrow, I reckon we oughta catch up to em the next day. I don't think they have any idea we're still chasing them." He rubbed his hands together gleefully. "Won't they be surprised? I want us outta here before day breaks tomorrow morning. If they're lazy and don't start early we'll be that much closer."

Jim Pelham sat by the fire turning a spit. The fat from three marsh rabbits sputtered as it dripped into the fire. Caleb's woodsman skills were still in good order.

****

For Cassie and Andre the days following Sapelo were a time for discovering each other. They slept apart from the men, and the men respected their privacy. They made love to the sounds of the marsh and the river. Their canopy was the moon and the stars. Slowly the sadness of Queen's death receded and the dread that hung over them began to dissolve. They talked about the future and looked forward to a life together, lived in peace and freedom. They all were adjusting to their new existence where no one was around to tell them what to do.

Heeding Cletus' admonition to hug the eastern limits of the marsh they moved into the winding Frederica River. They passed the burned out remains of the fort. To their west, as far as the eye could see, lay the golden marshes of Glynn, southernmost of the original eight counties created by the fledgling colonial government. Several other rivers and creeks emerged from the marshes to join the Frederica, flowing as one into St. Simons Sound. Across the open expanse of water they could see the northern tip of Jekyl Island. It was noon.

They faced a two-mile row across the mouth of the bay. They could see ten-foot waves crashing onto Jekyl's northern beaches. Easterly winds aided by a strong flood tide churned the waters. Kimba shaded his eyes and gazed skyward. He measured the arc of the sun. Drawing on his years in the fields he judged that they had seven hours of daylight remaining.

"I spect we can git cross in two hours," he offered. "It gone be mighty rough do. Dis water bout lak dat tween Ossabaw and St. Catherine's. We made dat in less'n two hours."

Ka'le trusted his brother's instincts.

"Cassie we's gonna head fo dat beach over dere on dat island. Kimba reckons we kin git dere in two hours. Ask Andre how far it be to da other end o da island. I'd sho lak tuh git dere today. Dem clouds a buildin' up tuh da south don look good. Dey's a storm acomin.'"

Andre studied the map. Based on the distance they had come that day he estimated the length of Jekyl to be six to eight miles.

"Ka'le," Cassie called. "Andre says the island is six to eight miles long."

"Dat means we gots bout eight tuh ten miles tuh go," he said.

"Les git far as we kin. Iffen we cain't make all o it we'll stop along da way."

The wide expanse of St. Andrew's sound loomed in the distance as the boats pulled into the mouth of a small creek for the night. There was a spit of beach and plenty of fuel for their fire. The sediment-laden flow of the Satilla and Little Satilla rivers pushed against the aqua waters of the Atlantic. Tomorrow's reach across the sound, tracing that demarcation, would be the longest stretch of open water thus far. And the most difficult. For with the building clouds came stronger winds.

****

Jim Pelham stepped ashore on the beach as the last arc of orange disappeared below the western marshes. His arms had never ached so. They had been on the water for nearly fifteen hours. Enoch drove them mercilessly, stopping only for a quick meal and to relieve themselves. His blood was up. He could smell them now.

"One more day," he whispered. "One more day."

****

The trip across St. Andrew's Sound was nightmarish. The waves and currents drove Ka'le and Andre toward the marshes. They struggled to keep moving southward while avoiding being driven into the shallows. They could see Cumberland in the distance. In another mile or two they would be in the lee of the island where the waves were not so violent. Cassie pulled her water soaked-blanket tighter. The chill wind cut to the marrow of her bones.

"Andre, are we going to make it?" she asked through chattering teeth.

Andre looked at Isaac whose gaze was fixed on the horizon, rhythmically raising and lowering his paddle, willing himself to keep moving toward that stretch of beach in the distance.

"Are you all right Isaac?" he asked.

Isaac hardly took notice. He continued to row. Finally, he turned to respond.

"I's all right, Andre. I jes has tuh hold a picture of freedom in my head. Long's I know it's out there, waitin fo me, I's all right." Isaac returned to his rowing.

"Yes, Cassie, we're going to make it. We've come too far to fail now."

The boat carrying Andre, Isaac and Cassie slid onto the beach of Little Cumberland Island. The other boat, still a quarter mile out, labored through the rough surf. The wind had steadily increased for the last few hours, and was approaching gale force.

"Andre, Ka'le and Kimba are struggling. Shouldn't we try to help them?" Cassie asked.

"Cassie, you build a fire. Isaac and I will go back for them."

The winds whipped the surf into a froth. The two young men pushed their boat back into the water and paddled out to the others. They pulled alongside. The boats groaned as their sides crashed against each other.

"Ka'le, get in my boat," Andre motioned. "Isaac will help Kimba."

The rains came. Vicious rains, driven sideways by the storm. The outer bands of a hurricane lashed the island.

The fire sputtered. Cassie studied the dunes above her and moved toward them. There was a washed out overhang beneath the roots of some trees. The trees teetered above the beach, threatening to topple forward. The winds from the leading edge of the hurricane had circled and were now blowing from the north, driving the boats toward the beach. She mounded up wood and straw in the shelter. She brought fire up from the beach then returned to watch the men come ashore.

"Get them up to the fire, Andre," Cassie said.

The four bedraggled men made their way up the dunes, dragging their few remaining provisions with them. They plopped down on the sand by the fire, thankful for the warmth and the shelter.

****

Enoch saw the smoke rising from their fire long before the island was visible. He knew they were close. Three hours ago they found the still smoldering fire on Jekyl. They would have missed it but for Nero's barking. Enoch removed his leash and the dog leaped overboard and swam ashore. When they caught up with him he was frenzied, chasing the smells left around the campsite. He dug furiously on the spot where Kimba had slept. It was the same smell from the cabin on Ossabaw.

"There they are," he shouted above the roar of the wind. "See that smoke over there. That's gotta be them." He stopped rowing and laid the paddle across his lap. "We don't want to land where they are," he said. "Let's go ashore above them and come at em from the woods. That way they'll be trapped on the beach."

CHAPTER FORTY-ONE

Enoch and Caleb approached from the dense forest above the beach. They held their rifles at the ready. Jim waited at the boat with Nero, lest his barking spook their prey.

"You come up from below, Caleb," Enoch whispered. "I'll come at em from above."

They were upon them before anyone could react.

"Well now, ain't this a cozy picture," Enoch said.

The men around the fire leaped to their feet. Cassie screamed.

"Don't you go doin' nothin' foolish boys. Me'n Caleb both have the drop on you, and neither of us can miss at this range." Enoch pulled the pistol from his waistband and fired into the air, signaling Jim to join them. Cassie screamed again.

"Don't be afraid, Cassie," Enoch purred. "I ain't here to hurt you. I've just come to claim what's mine. I guess old Ka'le there told you about the untimely death of my brother, Hiram. I thought we'd gotten rid of Sarah too. But I understand she was still alive when you hauled her outta that fire Ka'le. You're gonna regret that. If she'da died it would have all been mine. Roselawn, Ossabaw, you, Cassie, Kimba, Isaac." He looked at each of them in turn as he called their names. The fire was in his eyes. He moved closer to Isaac, putting the muzzle of his rifle under Isaac's chin.

"Good old Isaac. I found out it was you who went runnin to Hiram and told him all kinda tales on me."

"Please, Massa Enoch, don hurt da boy," Kale pleaded. "It wuz me whut sent im. He wuz jes doin what his pa tol im tuh do."

"You think I don't know that. It was all of you who sicked Hiram on me. You, Isaac and Kimba there." He glared at Ka'le with a malevolence born of the devil. "Don't you worry, boy. I'm gonna take care of all of you."

Enoch pulled the gun away from Isaac and trained it on Andre.

"And who pray tell is this nigger. I don't think I've ever seen him before. He ain't the one in the fancy soldier suit I shot at, is he? I thought we left him for dead back on Skidaway."

Cassie whimperd. Louis was dead. She stared at Enoch as she summoned up all her courage.

"No, Enoch," she said. "This is Andre. He is a French soldier. He is my husband."

Enoch looked at her blankly, stupefied.

"Your husband!" he screamed. "Who gave you the right to get married? You're still a slave. You belong to me. You don't have any rights. And where do you come off calling me Enoch. My name is Master Enoch to you."

Cassie swallowed hard. Her heart raced. Her palms were clammy.

"No, it's not," she said, softly. "Miss Amanda gave me my freedom when I left Roselawn. She also freed Ka'le. So you see I'm free to marry Andre, and I'm free to call you Enoch."

Enoch glared at her. "We'll see about that you little black bitch."

Nero's growl announced the arrival of Jim Pelham.

"Jim, you and Caleb tie the men up."

When they were all trussed and seated leaning against the dune wall, Enoch spoke to Caleb.

"Caleb, when we were coming through the woods back there I noticed some old turpentine cups nailed to the trees. Go back there and bring a couple down here."

As Caleb left the cave, Enoch took Nero's leash and tied it to a tree root protruding from the bank. The dog strained at the rope and lunged toward Kimba.

"You boys give me any trouble I'll turn ol Nero loose on ya. You've seen him bring down bulls, so I don't believe you'll want to mess with him."

The winds, which had subsided briefly as the eye passed, returned with renewed fury. Caleb returned with the pots

"Jim, the winds are getting stronger," Enoch said. "We better dig further back into the hill. It's gonna get worse before it blows over. Turn old Kimba and Ka'le loose and put em to digging. They ain't as likely to cause trouble as them young bucks."

Jim loosened the bonds on the two older men.

"Awright now, you boys heard Mr. Enoch. I wanna see the sand a flyin'," Caleb growled. "Now, git to it."

Enoch took the two pots of thick resin and sat them on the fire. Within minutes the contents had melted and flames licked over the sides, igniting them. The molten turpentine blazed up, casting strong shadows across the entire cave. Ka'le knew instantly what Enoch had in mind. In the blinding glare no one saw Ka'le pull the knife from his boot and drop it behind Andre. Andre moved so that he was sitting on the knife and could reach it.

"That's enough digging. Move them back and tie the other two up again," Enoch ordered.

Enoch's attention returned to Cassie. All eyes were on him. Andre was busily sawing through the ropes around his wrists and passing the knife to Isaac.

"All right now little lady, let's see if we can take up where we left off in the root cellar."

Cassie ran to the other side of the fire.

"Grab her, Caleb. It's gonna be fun doing her in the sand right in front of her husband," he sneered.

Caleb grabbed at her. Cassie jumped back and fell between Andre and Isaac. Caleb lunged for her and grabbed her arm, twisting it violently.

"You better do what he says, missy, or I'll jerk your arm right out of its socket."

Caleb never saw the knife. It buried to the hilt in his stomach, severing his aorta just below the sternum. He fell face down, screaming. Blood spurted from the severed artery.

"I been stuck, Enoch. I been stuck."

Enoch leaped across the fire toward Andre, his rifle coming up as he did. His foot came down on a limb supporting the pots. Molten, flaming turpentine catapulted into the air, enveloping him. He screamed as he fell back, flailing about in an effort to douse the flames. His clothes were saturated with the flammable liquid. Every time he stood they reignited. He ran toward the water hoping to quench the flames. To no avail. The intense heat would not allow it. He ceased his flailing and floated on the surf, small bursts of flame licking at him. All his hair was gone. The skin peeled back from his flesh. His lips were gone. His mouth was a skeletal grin. A small patch of red flesh floated on the surf.

Jim ran to Nero. He sliced the rope, freeing the animal. Nero made a beeline for Kimba, seizing him by the throat. Jim reached for his rifle. He aimed it at Andre. Before he could pull back the hammer, Isaac hurled his gig at him. It caught the man under the chin. The tines of the trident emerged from the back of Jim's skull. He pitched backward, the shaft of the gig pointing skyward, his hands locked around it in a death embrace. He stared up into the rain with lifeless eyes.

Andre and Isaac ran to pull Nero off Kimba. Andre drove the knife deep into the dog's side. Even that didn't loosen his death grip on Kimba's neck. Andre plunged the knife into the animal again and again until all life flowed out and its jaws relaxed. Cassie untied Kimba's hands. She held his head. His jugular was exposed and blood gushed out with every heartbeat. Ka'le worked free and came to his side.

"Ain't they nothin we kin do? We cain't jes let im die. Now dat he finally free da Lawd cain't jes let im die."

Kimba opened his eyes.

"Ka'le, I's been free evah since we lef da plantation. I's tasted whut it be like. Now I kin die in peace. I's goin tuh be wit my Lilla an my Toby agin. It ain't so bad."

Bubbles formed where the fangs had punctured his windpipe. One final gurgle and Kimba was gone.

****

The storm raged all night. The survivors huddled in their cave and prayed. Morning broke clear and fair. All the boats were gone. Swept away by the fury of the storm. Enoch's body was gone too. Taken by the winds and the water. They dug a shallow grave and buried Jim Pelham on the beach. Andre started back for Caleb's body. Ka'le placed a hand on his arm.

"Leave im dere," he said. His tone cautioned Andre to leave it be.

For Kimba they moved up into the trees and prepared a deeper grave. They covered it with heavy logs to keep predators away. Ka'le fashioned a cross of cedar limbs and muscadine vines. He placed it at the head of Kimba's grave. He knelt there for a long time, tears running down his face. Together, he and Kimba had survived capture in Africa, the middle passage and life in bondage. Now, it was hard to let him go.

"Cassie ya'll walk on up da beach. Me an' Isaac gots one mo job tuh take keer of. We'll be along direckly."

Someday, should someone stumble upon Kimba's grave, he will stare in wonder at the great oak growing at the foot. There, hanging by its ankles, high above the ground, they will find the eviscerated skeleton of a yellow-haired giant. On the tree next to him they will find the crucified remains of some great beast.

****

They were now marooned.

"What do you think we should do Ka'le?" Cassie asked.

"Well, we wuz headin south so I reckon we oughta keep on a headin south."

They began walking down the endless strand of Cumberland's ocean beach. They knew that some fifteen miles to the south lay Florida. Once they got that far, they would have to decide what to do. Cassie and Andre trailed along behind Ka'le and Isaac.

"Andre, I still don't understand why Enoch kept after me. It just doesn't make any sense. You know, there was once, when I was going away to St. Benedict's that I thought Mama was going to tell me. Then she became quiet and stopped."

"I have a feeling Ka'le knows," Andre said. "Why don't you ask him?"

Cassie ran to catch up.

"Ka'le. Why did Enoch do the things he did? Why was he chasing me?"

Ka'le stopped and gazed out across the Atlantic. His mind conjured up all the years of Enoch's evilness, all the pain he had brought. He looked into Cassie's eyes.

"I reckon now it don matter iffen ya know. Queen won't let us tell ya all dese years. She wuz protectin ya from da shame she felt. She didn't want ya to suffer whut she did. Ya see Cassie, ya ma told ya dat yore daddy died on another plantation befo ya wuz born. Truth be, ya wuz born rat dere on Roselawn, up tuh da big house. Ya ma wuz jes foteen year old. She wuz workin wit Aba in da kitchen. One day, when evahbody else wuz gone, Massa Enoch cotched her in her room and he took her. Nine months later you wuz born. Massa Enoch, he be yore daddy."

Cassie fell to her knees, dumbstruck. She looked up at Ka'le, choking on her words.

"Why, Ka'le? Why would he want to hurt his own daughter?"

"Well, atter Massa John found out bout him an Queen he near beat dat boy tuh death. He wuz awready mad at da world fo his mark an his talk. Now he wuz mad at you an Queen cuz da whole fambly done turned agin im and he blamed ya'll. I reckon he done gone plum crazy. Ain't no uddah way tuh splain it."

Andre helped her to her feet. He put his arms around her.

"It doesn't matter now Cassie. They're all gone. It's just the four of us. No one is chasing you anymore. We're almost home."

They walked arm in arm down the beach, she leaning against him, happy that she had someone in her life who loved her and would protect her.

They continued walking until they came to the ruins of the old Spanish mission, *San Pedro de Mocama*. Across the St. Mary's river they could see two ships lying at anchor off Amelia Island. The flags fluttering atop their masts were red and gold.

"Those are Spanish ships," Andre said. "That's the same flag I remember from Grenada."

"Do ya think dey'll be frenly tuh us, Andre?" Ka'le asked.

"I don't see why not. They're looking for people to come to Fort Mose, and that's where we're going."

The longboat came ashore at the base of the ruins. The Spanish were responding to the signal fire the castaways had built. The bonfire leaped over fifty feet into the air. It would be hard to miss.

One of the galleons was returning to St. Augustine in three days. The four survivors were on board. Cassie and Andre stood on the stern of the ship as it made its way down the coast. They were outside the captain's quarters. Night was falling. The captain saw them there as he returned from a tour of the ship.

"Good evening," he said. "I understand that this young man is of Spanish extraction."

Andre, summoning up his mother's language, responded in Spanish.

"Yes sir. I was born in Grenada when it was ruled by Spain. My mother was Spanish."

"Wonderful," the captain said. "Welcome aboard my ship. I trust you will enjoy our little cruise to St. Augustine. If there's anything I can do for you, let me know."

Cassie understood just enough of the captain's words to catch the last phrase.

"Andre, there's one thing I'd like to ask the captain. Ask him if we may use his telescope." Andre looked puzzled.

"Sir, my wife wants to know if we may use your telescope."

"That's an unusual request, but certainly you may."

He returned in a few minutes and handed an ornate, gold embossed, telescope to Cassie.

"May I ask what it is you wish to see, my dear?"

Cassie took the telescope and trained it on the northern sky. She handed it to the captain.

"See those five stars shaped like a 'w'. That's the constellation Cassiopeia." She pulled the collar of her dress down to expose the birthmark on her neck.

"Because of this mark I was named for the Ethiopian queen, Cassiopeia. She was banished by the gods to sit in that chair for eternity. I believe that all those who loved and protected me and died for me are gathered up there with her and they're smiling down and watching over me."

THE END